Nothing To Declare

Josef Kraus

Nothing To Declare

Wexford College Press

MENS SANA IN CORPORE SANO

Library of Congress Control Number: 2001089252

Published as a Wexford College Press paperback 2002
by arrangement with Watchmaker Publishing, Ltd.

ISBN 0-9709917-0-3

Wexford College Press
www.WexfordCollegePress.com
books@WexfordCollegePress.com

Printed and bound in the United States of America

1 2 3 4 5 6 7 8 9 0

À Belle

Me oh my, dear border sheriff,
I have little to say and less to tariff.
So grant my passage along with this swear:
That of this morn' truly, I have nothing to declare.

Lady of Mercia (1041)

Save for the copper and his mignons,
    The whole world loves a smuggler.

Johnny Teacher (1893)

.

DRESS REHEARSAL

From his vantage on the second floor, Thomas Breck saw little more than if his eyes were closed. A pounding rain clung to his window in sheets, concealing, though mostly blurring, everything beyond. He imagined seeing the airport bus in the distance, but it was only the asphalt drive playing tricks as it floated awkwardly in the glass, pushing itself one way then the next. The weather had been this way for days, an incessant deluge with reports of snow by nightfall. He was getting out just in time.

Christmas break had begun at St. Michael's Prep and on the floor below him, the other students waited. They jostled in the corridor, suitcases in tow, each enthusiastic at the pending departure. An airport bus was about to arrive, their first leg toward a home in which they didn't live. Any awaiting family might be a doting maid, or a mother or a father, or maybe all three if they were fortunate. Or unfortunate.

Tom Breck was somewhere in between. His parents were still together, living in the same house and sharing the same bed, although they never conversed, and hadn't for years. So he scarcely considered his family auspicious and, besides, there were more pressing issues to consider as his gaze drifted to the near line of beds. The one closest, the last in the row of twelve, had been assigned to him during the autumn term. It was farthest from the dormitory prefect, closest to the fire escape, and took some maneuvering to procure. The fire escape was necessary, not that flames might suddenly envelop the building, but rather it allowed him access to the outside world. With the prefect eleven beds away, and a legendary deep sleeper, Tom Breck could be off the school grounds, roaming the streets of Victoria on any given evening before midnight. Complete freedom was but a few metal steps away. There were no bed checks as the prefect was on guard, with his mouth wide open.

11

Tom's eyes narrowed thinking of the prefect, Ian Musters. A boy but four years older who pushed him around, detaining him on weekends and barring him from Saturday night television with false charges that were becoming more serious in nature. It had been the same for months, excepting the last fortnight when Musters abruptly ceased this behavior. Tom had bought him off, agreeing to supply the prefect liquor, without charge or questions, on demand. It was cheap, fortified Madeira, and in controlled doses it worked just fine—but not on the prefect. It seems Musters had a girl.

Kathy or Katie, or maybe Beth was her name. Tom didn't remember and didn't really care. He only knew she attended a Catholic boarding school on the opposite side of Vancouver Island. Cloistered on a dozen acres of shoreline were the one hundred girls and eighteen nuns of an ambiguous order in varying stages of anger—the ideal mix for a young man with a bottle of alcohol to get lucky. And Musters required this luck more than others.

A horn sounded in the distance, the airport bus announcing its arrival and, coincidentally, that of Ian Musters. He appeared at the doorway, moving quickly into the dorm and down the line of beds.

His tone impatient, Musters said, "Why aren't you downstairs, Breck?"

"You said you wished to inspect my suitcase, sir," Tom replied dutifully.

"Yes, but I meant downstairs, Breck. In line, with the others."

"Right... sorry. Well, here it is, sir."

Musters glanced at the open suitcase beside Tom, and repeated, "I meant downstairs, Breck. Like usual."

"I couldn't find my socks, sir."

"Don't give me that rubbish. It may work on the other prefects, but not with me." Musters lifted the suitcase from the bed, dumping its contents onto the hardwood floor. "You're clear to go, Breck," he said, grinning.

"Thank you, sir," said Tom. "Thank you very much."

The smirk dropped from Musters' face. "What are you up to?"

"Sir?"

"You know what I mean. There are things missing from the chapel."

"I'm sorry to hear about that. The vicar must be horribly upset."

"A dozen gold goblets have disappeared," advised Musters, separating the clothing on the floor with his foot. "You wouldn't know anything about this?"

"No, sir. First I've heard of it. Terrible, just terrible."

"The one caught with them will be expelled, you know."

"I know that, sir. Believe me, I know."

The horn from the bus sounded.

"Get your things packed, Breck. Is this your only grip?"

Tom threw his clothes back into the suitcase. "Yes, sir. The same old black bag with the green stripe. Same one. It belonged to my grandmother." He snapped it shut. "We were very close."

Musters grunted. "Get going, Breck."

Moving out of the dormitory and into the hall, Tom could hear the prefect directly behind him, the aged wood floor creaking beneath their feet.

"Fifteen days in the States," said Musters sardonically. "What do you and your uneducated American friends do, Breck? Watch baseball and steal cars?"

"Yes, sir. That's pretty much it." Tom picked up his pace, moving down the stairs.

Musters grunted again. "You know, you shouldn't be in the third form, Breck. You should be in the second or even the first. Or—how do you call it? Grade eight?"

"Eighth grade, sir. Just eighth grade."

"Right. Most Yanks are put back a year, instead you... you get pushed ahead."

"Headmaster made an error, I suppose." At the base of the stairs, Tom abruptly stopped in front of the locker room door.

"What are you doing, Breck?"

"I have to go to the loo, sir," he replied, thinking it best to use his prefect's vernacular.

"The loo?"

"Yes, sir."

"Good Lord, Breck... Right, but I'm coming with you."

"Very well, sir." Tom entered the locker room and quickly went inside the second toilet stall in the line of ten. Still gripping his suitcase, he shut the door, engaging the latch.

"Christ, Breck," complained the prefect. "You haven't got all day. The bus is waiting."

"Yes, sir. I know, sir. It must have been the kippers this morning. They were a bit off, don't you think?"

The bus driver sounded the horn, then sounded it again.

"Hurry, Breck."

Tom was complying with the command, although not in the

manner intended. Having placed his suitcase on the toilet seat, he pulled on a wood panel just above the reservoir. The panel ran the width of the stall and was connected to a series of concealed hinges allowing it to be lowered until its lip rested on the reservoir lid. Tom now stared into an ink-black crawl space connecting the locker room to the adjacent gymnasium. Reaching inside, he removed a large black suitcase—an identical black suitcase, with the same green stripe, as the one sitting before him. He carefully balanced the two on the toilet seat, then hurriedly placed the one shown Musters into the black hole. He slowly lifted the panel, hoping he had oiled the hinges sufficiently to ensure their silence, and quickly flushed the toilet. The panel clicked into place, its action unheard beneath the sound of the rushing water.

The bus driver blasted the horn.

"Move it, Breck!" said Musters. "Let's move it!"

Pulling the door open, Tom swung the suitcase forward. It was heavier than he remembered, much heavier than the one it replaced, and its weight pulled on his shoulder.

"You want the bus to leave without you, Breck?"

"No, sir," he replied, attempting to conceal the strain of the suitcase.

As they moved into the hallway, Musters whispered, "When you get back, my little American friend, you and I are going to have a very nice time together. Your free ride is over."

Tom stopped at the open door of the building and gazed at the idling bus before him, the rain drumming on its roof. "What's the matter, sir? Did your girlfriend dump you?"

"Why you little—"

Tom slowly faced his prefect. "Not to worry," he said softly, "it'll be my secret and besides, I believe our arrangement had run its course... don't you think?" and not waiting for a reply, ran into the rain.

Anger rushed through Musters, his body shaking as he took a step forward then stopped. Clearly aware of students watching him from the bus, he would have to wait.

The door slapped open and the driver appeared, taking Tom's suitcase. In the hammering torrent, words were briefly exchanged between him and his final passenger—a feeble attempt at a lecture for delaying their departure. The driver then followed Tom up the steps, the air brakes moaned and the belated journey to the airport began.

14

Sitting by the last window, Tom could see Musters in the doorway and sensed his rage through the shower. A price would be paid for such insolence were things as they seemed, but they weren't. Plans had been laid that would free Tom of any repercussions, real or imagined.

Ian Musters would never fully know what was to hit him.

* * *

Against the sweeping cold of the morning, Tatiana Gregòsh made her way down the frozen sidewalk. The taxi stand just ahead, she watched her feet to keep from slipping, ever mindful of the parcel clutched to her chest. She gripped it as a young mother might hold her child and to anyone observing, she would've been just that: a young woman with her child in the early Warsaw morning, were it not for her youth. She was but fourteen years old and too young to be wedded, but not by much. Childhood is for the wealthy, Tatiana remembered her uncle saying, like a fine home or automobile, it's just another spoil. There's no time for pretending, she must learn a skill before marriage or the Polish State chooses one for her. And it must be something unique, something required by those with means. After years of her uncle's guidance, this skill was about to be tested.

She found the stand empty. In both directions on the snow-covered street, there wasn't a taxi in sight except for a broken-down Wartburg parked against the opposite curb, its driver attempting repairs with a bit of rope. He slid on his back in the snow, pushing up on the dangling exhaust and Tatiana could hear his grunts followed by a few selected words of disapproval. Normally she would have smiled at such a sight, but since he was not going anywhere for the moment, neither was she.

Stomping her feet to fight off the cold, she thought to place her gloved hands in her pockets, but there was the package and she dare not set it down. She imagined the time to be just after nine o'clock and if a taxi didn't arrive soon, she'd be late. The rendezvous was set and couldn't be altered. Her uncle had no telephone in their two-room apartment and all her coins were needed for the upcoming fare. Tatiana was becoming anxious when she heard the Wartburg's engine turn over and catch.

Addressing the driver who had stepped back to admire his handiwork, she called, "Can you take me?"

His grease-covered hands on his hips, he turned and stared at her. "Where are you going?"

"The Inter-Continental Hotel."

"The one by the Flame?"

"Is there another?"

"No, it's just you don't look... never mind." He waved his arm. "Come on."

She moved cautiously across the icy road toward the taxi.

"Inter-Continental, right?" he asked, opening the rear door of the plastic car. The black of his hands stood out against the snow, as did a stripe of grease that ran down his cheek.

"Yes. Could you hurry?" she replied, and climbed into the back seat.

Getting behind the wheel, the driver slammed his door repeatedly until the latch caught.

"The heater might take a moment," he advised, jerking the car away from the curb.

Tatiana said nothing.

"Do you work at the Inter-Continental?" he asked into the rearview mirror.

"No," she said, glancing at his reflection.

"I didn't think so. You seem too young."

The car began to vibrate and quickly the driver downshifted.

"Is this as fast as you can go?" she asked.

"I'm afraid so."

Letting out a deep breath, she looked out her window.

"You know, I never get over to this part of Warsaw," said the driver, waiting for a response.

He didn't get one.

"The police had a checkpoint on Prusa Street." When she still said nothing, he continued, "I would probably get one-, maybe a two-thousand zloty fine for this car." Seemingly amused at such a penalty, he chuckled. "I can't afford that, young lady. So, anyway, I came through your neighborhood. First time, I think."

For the next few minutes it was silent inside the car except for the whining two-stroke engine and the sound of the tires crunching the frozen road.

"My name is Yuri," he said finally.

Tatiana glanced again at his reflection. "You have grease on your face," she advised him.

"What?"

16

"I said, you have grease on your face."

Looking in the mirror, he twisted his mouth to see the black line on his cheek and began to laugh, rubbing at it with the end of his coat sleeve.

"Thank you," he said, moving his eyes between the mirror and the windshield. "I'm always working on this car and getting dirty. I'd like to buy a new one but—" He shrugged.

Tatiana touched his shoulder with gloved fingers that gripped a faded blue handkerchief. "Here."

He took her gesture without a word and wiping at the mark on his face, glanced at the stained handkerchief. "I'm afraid it's ruined now," he apologized.

"That's all right. It was old."

"Do you have another?"

She shook her head.

"Thank you," he said. "That was very nice. My name is Yuri."

She grinned when their eyes met in the mirror. "My name is Tatiana."

"Tatiana," he repeated, as if he knew the name well. "That's Russian."

"Yes."

"So is Yuri, you know."

"Yes, I know."

He laughed. "Well, how do you like that? We Poles don't even use our own names anymore. The bastards have even given us their names."

"I don't mind," said Tatiana.

Yuri stopped laughing. "I don't either, really," he said, looking in the mirror. He laughed again.

Snow started to fall. Yuri turned on the windshield wipers but only the driver's side worked; the metal scraped against the glass, fighting its way up the pocked windshield like an aged metronome.

The unpleasant sound did not bother Tatiana. Such a trifling annoyance was unimportant, as so many things were—the standing in line for a loaf of bread, then another for measured butter, followed by another queue and another, hour after hour. Were these things important? Waiting in the cold for the fuel wagon, only to be told of an unannounced price hike, finally handing the hard-fought bread and butter to the kerosene covered man. Was this more important? Was anything?

She watched the pedestrians slip by her window, bundled in their winter clothes. They shuffled like their ankles were chained—shoulders hunched and heads down as if in search of some rumored trapdoor leading to a way out.

But there was a way out, a trapdoor to a better life, although the price for entry was everything the traveler possessed. Clutching the cloth-covered package ever tighter, Tatiana Gregòsh was about to learn this well.

* * *

Canada and the United States share an open border, never closed by peace or war or any other folly, something of a record in the history of mankind. But it was not open enough. On each side of the frontier, customs and immigration agents held their respective positions, patiently waiting, constantly observing. Although the Canadians, with their English-like etiquette, were more concerned in keeping pace with the visitor's bureau than any perceived naughtiness. Off to Whistler? Off to Banff? Have a good time.

And that was pretty much it.

Whereas the Americans had a different take on the situation. They wore side arms and concealed automatic weapons which could be easily retrieved. It was simple: Canada harbored the balance of malcontents that the Americans had not managed, as yet, to incarcerate. Or so it appeared.

To the American customs and immigration agent, even the most fundamental level of politeness was for sissies. And the boys in blue were not sissies.

Thomas Breck knew this. He watched them on his earlier trips through the border. They needed to hear certain things and liked their questions answered promptly within unwavering guidelines. Any variation on this would send the stumbling passenger to the back room for further consideration, sometimes for a few minutes and sometimes for years.

Tom had never seen the back room and planned on keeping it that way, pushing his black suitcase forward on the linoleum floor. Next in line to speak with customs, he was reviewing the potential dialogue when his eyes drifted to a photograph of Jack Kennedy on the near wall. Faded paint indicated the photograph had been recently moved to share space with the man who replaced him. Two black ribbons thumb-tacked to the cheap wood frame draped the sides of the handsome face, and that was all that remained of a young man's hero: a ten-cent photograph and a half-dollar frame. Just forty-five days earlier the world had made sense to Thomas Breck, but now it seemed adrift with everybody on their own.

He gradually resumed his vigil of the agent, still occupied with his current prey. An elderly Canadian couple displayed tickets indicating their destination, a visit to their daughter in Los Angeles or possibly Los Alamos. The man mumbled, speaking with a Cockney accent as if each word began with a vowel. The woman said nothing, though offered an occasional nod. It was going well, when abruptly the agent asked to look inside their suitcases. The man just before had had his possessions searched, though he was unkempt and unshaven—a traveler asking for trouble. But this crazed agent was searching everyone's baggage, regardless of appearance.

Tom could feel his palms sweating. Rubbing them together, he turned slightly. There was a young woman behind him, an American passport clutched tight in her hand. She smiled as he looked past her for additional travelers, but there were none, and the problem was clear: the customs man had nothing but time.

Tom glanced at his watch. It was three minutes to eleven. Nervously he began to wind the stem, looking out the darkened windows to the tarmac, hoping for another plane to touch down. One loaded with a few thousand passengers urgently in need of a connecting flight; but there was no plane, only the pounding rain that had followed him to Seattle and his apparent doom.

The man with the Cockney accent made a joke, though the customs man wasn't laughing as he inspected a price tag attached to a woman's blouse. He let the garment drop and began to feel the lining of the suitcase. Tom watched in amazement. He wanted to interrupt the proceedings and ask when such a policy had been implemented, or bolt for the door and never look back, but he only continued winding his watch.

Then all was well. The woman's baggage was left unopened and the couple sent on their way. The customs man now stood before Tom.

"Where do you live?" the man asked.

Powerless to immediately respond, Tom stared at the service revolver attached to the customs man's hip.

"I said, where do you live?" repeated the blue uniformed demon.

19

Tom stammered, "I—I live in San Francisco."

"How long have you been out of the country?"

"Uhm... I've been... I go to school in Victoria. Fall term."

"What?"

"Since September," said Tom, concentrating on the words. "August thirtieth is when I left."

"I see," said the customs man, eyeing the black suitcase on the floor. "Are you traveling alone?"

"Yes, sir."

"You're awfully young to be traveling alone. How old are you?"

"Fourteen, sir."

"What school do you attend?"

"St. Michael's."

"Are you continuing on to San Francisco?"

"Yes, sir," he replied, feeling his confidence returning. "I have a flight in two hours."

"From Boeing Field?"

"Yes, sir."

"All right, young man," said the customs man. "I was concerned we move you along if you had to be at Payne Field."

Tom's mouth opened slightly. He had plenty of time to catch his next flight or anything else for that matter, and so did the customs man.

"Why don't you put your suitcase up on the table?"

The words hung in the air.

"I beg your pardon?" said Tom.

The customs man squinted. "Your suitcase. On the table," he repeated.

Grabbing the handle Tom felt weak. The black suitcase was heavier than it had ever been and using both hands, he let it fall on the table.

"What do you say we look inside," said the customs man. It was not a question.

Tom could not speak. The box—his Pandora's box, which he'd spent months putting together—was about to be opened, unleashing more evil than he cared to imagine. Taking a deep breath, he touched the center latch and the end of it all.

A voice stopped him. Another agent was muttering in the ear of his inquisitor and Tom could make out some of the words. The man was apologizing for being late, saying something about heavy

20

traffic or an accident. Tom looked at his watch. It read eight minutes after eleven. Shift change was at eleven and the new man in blue was late and feeling bad. Tom did not feel bad.

The two men shook hands and the other half of the tag-team took his position.

The new customs man was fat and sweat covered his face. The brief run from the parking garage to his post had just about done him in. He began his own line of interrogation.

"Where are you coming from?" he asked.

"Victoria, sir."

Leaning forward, the customs man placed his hand on the black suitcase, then whispered, "Been to Chinatown?"

Tom wanted to scream. The fat beast knew; it was all a game. They had him cornered and were simply toying with him.

"I said, have you been to Chinatown?" repeated the customs man.

"No, sir." Tom shook his head vigorously. "Chinatown is out of bounds for the students."

"St. Michael's?"

"Yes, sir."

"I thought I recognized the crest on your blazer. Do you play hockey?"

"No, sir. Rugby, cricket, track and field."

"Soccer?"

"Yes, sir," said Tom. He lied. They didn't play soccer, but felt the man needed a positive response.

"So, you've never been to Chinatown?"

"No, sir," he replied. This time he was adamant, but needed to ask, "Why, sir?"

"Fireworks."

Fireworks? Thought Tom. Had the perspiring pig lost his mind? He must be joking. There's no money in fireworks.

"No, sir," he said. "My Mom won't let me have them. They're dangerous, you know."

"Not one or two M-80s inside here?" The customs man tapped on the suitcase with his middle finger.

Tom was at his end, uncertain if he could take any more of the mental high-wire act as the fat man grinned. They both patted at the perspiration on their faces. There was a heavy silence, then the stampeding sound of passengers down the far corridor. A plane had landed.

21

"Welcome back, young fellow," said the customs man, gazing at the advancing crowd, "and have a nice vacation."

Tom could not talk, but it didn't matter; the monster was no longer listening. Slowly dragging the suitcase from the counter, Tom slid it along the linoleum floor toward the door marked Exit. He hadn't the strength to lift it.

Thomas Breck stood at Arrival at San Francisco airport, studying the line of cars and more than occasionally his watch. It was three forty-five, just as he said it would be when he'd spoken with his mother: he would be standing at Arrival, between three-thirty and four. Please be there.

She was not there, nor would she be, and he knew it. But he would wait till four and maybe a bit after, just in case—she might remember the day and even the time, after all, she said she would.

A red Cadillac, just like hers, approached with its turn signal on. Taking a step forward, Tom raised his arm only to let it fall. An old man, barely able to see over the dash, was behind the wheel and not going to stop for anyone as he accelerated past a white limousine. The turn signal had probably been on for days.

Tom sat on the edge of his suitcase and looked again at his watch. Two minutes had passed. Exhaling deeply, he loosened his tie and resting his chin on his upturned palm, observed his fellow travelers. They chatted and laughed awkwardly with those that had come for them, as if they were being rescued from some desert isle. The women hugged and the men offered guarded pats on the back. Some bearded relative picked up a child in a starched white pinafore and she began to cry. She didn't understand, she had just been saved.

Sitting on his suitcase, Thomas Breck watched her. He watched them all.

* * *

Through the streaked glass of the parked taxi, Tatiana studiously observed the hotel doorman. His movements were like those of a dancer, opening the doors of the elegant cars, bowing with his arm extended and his braided hat doffed. The porters scurried, their carts moving toward the trunks of those arriving or departing; others for a breakfast and possible engagement with the powers-that-be. The Communist Party bosses preferring the elegant surroundings which a hotel like the Pinsk Inter-Continental could provide and, of course, the discretion.

That's what Tatiana's uncle had told her when he agreed to the meeting: it would be safe. The people interested in the package would be obliged to follow the rules of the capitalistic facility in the heart of Communist Warsaw. It was one of the few playgrounds for anyone with money and for this reason it was safe.

That's what he told her.

"Is there something wrong?" said Yuri, turning in his seat.

"No." She lied. An element had not been factored into the plans; Tatiana was scared.

Her view of the hotel doorman blurred, her reflection coming into focus—that of a young girl with a knitted wool beret, neatly tilted to the side, its light-green color accenting her black shoulder-length hair and the powder-white of her skin. The fear and the cold air pushed blush into her cheeks while deep blue eyes looked back from the frosted glass.

"What time were you to be here?" asked Yuri.

Faintly, she replied, "Nine forty-five."

"Then you best get going."

"Yes. I know."

"Maybe you could come another time?"

She looked again to the hotel entrance. A group of well-dressed travelers stood near the doorman, waiting for a taxi or chauffeured car. Their clothes, even from a distance, were something she only knew from store windows: the sable hats and fur trimmed coats of the women; the beautifully fitted topcoats the men wore so casually, their wealth so matter-of-fact as they chatted silently about things Tatiana could only imagine, their words forming small white clouds in the cold morning air.

"No," she said finally, reaching for the door handle. "This will be fine, thank you."

"Would you like me to wait?" he asked.

"No. I don't know how long I will be."

"Are you certain? I could—"

"Yes, yes thank you, Yuri," she said. "I am certain."

She climbed out and nervously stared at the hotel.

"Excuse me, Tatiana," he said through his open door.

Startled by the sound of her name, she replied, "What?"

"You owe me fifteen zlotys," he said, now standing beside her.

"Oh, I'm sorry. I—"

Watching her struggle with the package as she dug for the coins in her pocket, he asked, "Would you like me to hold that?"

"No, I have it."

But she didn't—it fell from her grip, the cloth cover falling open when it struck the ground. She grabbed at the flapping material and lifting the package from the wet asphalt, again pressed it to her chest.

"Here are eighteen zlotys," she said, holding out her gloved hand, "good-bye, Yuri," and after a brief hesitation, walked away.

Dropping the uncounted coins into his pocket, he whispered, "Good-bye."

The doorman of the hotel did not show her the same grace displayed for the other guests. He had become rigid, his hands clasped behind his back. Their eyes met as she stepped under the awning that protected him and his responsibilities.

"May I help you?" he asked firmly.

"I have something for someone… Someone staying here."

"Tell me the name."

She was reluctant to reveal such information, but saw no other choice. "Filipowicz," she said, looking up at the towering man. "Jaroslaw Filipowicz."

"Is that it?" he demanded, looking at the package.

"What?"

He reached for the guarded object. "I'll give it to him."

"No," she yelled, jerking her body away. "I am supposed to give it to him."

With his hands on his hips, the doorman stared at Tatiana. "Do you know the room number?"

"No." Her voice determined. "I don't."

"Very well," he said, lowering his hands. "Check with the desk. They will give you the number if this Mr. Filipowicz exists. But I don't want you wandering about. Do you understand?"

But she didn't understand, her uneasiness now replaced by anger. She said nothing more and walked into the foyer of the opulent Pinsk Inter-Continental. Moving quickly toward the gleaming counter, she positioned herself in front of the one hundred and more key boxes. A man placing an envelope in one of them turned to face her.

"Filipowicz," she said determinedly. "Jaroslaw Filipowicz."

Seeming to study her clothing, the man did not immediately respond. "And you are?" he asked finally.

"I am to meet him."

"Yes, but what is your name?"

"My name is Tatiana Gregòsh."

Flipping through a card file, he affirmed, "Yes, he is staying with us and it says he is expecting someone, but... It's a *Leszek* Gregòsh."

"That's my uncle," said Tatiana, glancing at one of the five clocks on the wall with the word 'Warsaw' written underneath.

"Well, I really should telephone—" A group gathering at reception interrupted him. "Room 111," he said quickly. "Just straight down the near corridor."

Tatiana hurried to the corridor. A brass plaque screwed into the wall with etched numbers read 101-121. She passed an open door; inside the room a maid, pushing a vacuum cleaner with one hand, adjusted a radio with the other. The contrasting sounds slowly faded as she continued down the corridor, passing the numbered doors. She ran her tongue across dry lips, looking to the next door and the one after, secretly hoping the room she was searching for had simply disappeared, but it hadn't. She stopped, looking at carefully aligned numbers that read 111.

She knocked twice and waited. Nothing. She knocked harder, and the door slowly opened as far as the engaged security chain allowed.

"Gregòsh, is that you?" came a voice.

"Yes," replied Tatiana.

The sliver of a man's face appeared in the opening between the door and the jamb. He squinted, studying her, and said, "Who are you?"

"I am Tatiana Gregòsh."

"Where is Leszek?"

"He is sick."

"Are you his daughter?"

"No, his niece."

"Do you have it?"

She nodded.

The man closed the door and she could hear muted voices inside the room. She again pushed her tongue across her lips to wet them but her mouth was too dry. She dabbed at the perspiration gathering on her forehead with the back of her hand, then quickly clutched the package.

The door opened.

"Come in," said the man. "Be quick about it."

Tatiana walked into a room only illuminated by a lamp near the bed. It took a moment for her eyes to adjust, then she noticed another person: a fat man seated at a table by the curtained windows. He stood when the door clicked shut.

"So your uncle is sick?" he asked.

"Yes," she replied, looking at one man, then the other.

"Why did he send you?"

"Because he is sick."

"I know that!" said the fat man. "Why did he send *you*?"

"Because... Because my uncle and I do this together," she said, her voice unsteady.

The two men glanced at one other as the man who had answered the door, asked, "What is your name again?"

"Tatiana."

"So, Tatiana, who is the artist? You, or your Uncle Leszek?"

She stared at the man now leaning against the door with his arms crossed and felt her fear spreading. "I am," she replied.

"Damn," said the fat man.

Tatiana did not understand, watching the man signal that the other approach. Slowly he crossed the room and the two men began whispering, their backs to her.

The fat man turned. "Is that it?" he asked, staring at the cloth-covered package.

Tatiana nodded once.

"Well then, let's see it," he said brusquely, pointing to the table.

Tatiana didn't move.

"Come on," said the fat man. Walking across the room, he turned on a floor lamp next to the table. "Put it here."

Glancing at the accomplice by the door, Tatiana did as she was ordered. The fat man began to carefully spread out the cloth covering.

"You have a typewriter?" he asked.

"No," she replied. "Typewriters are illegal."

"I know that!" He lifted a square of paper close to his eyes. "How did you get the information on the cards?"

"With pen and ink."

"My God," said the fat man, signaling with his hand. "Come and look at this."

The man at the door crossed the room and took one of the cards.

"It looks typed," said the fat man.

The other nodded.

"And the stamp," he continued. "Do you have a stamp?"

"No," answered Tatiana. "It's also pen and ink."

"Look at the letterhead," said the fat man more to himself than anyone listening. "Absolutely perfect... Whose thumbprint did you use?"

"No one's," she replied. "I drew that also."

"I see," he said, rubbing his large chin. "And the names on the identity cards. Where did you get them?"

"A soldier's graveyard by my apartment. Both of those men were from Gdansk."

"I see. Who else knows these names?"

"Only me."

"And your uncle?"

"Well certainly my uncle knows."

"Of course, young lady, of course. I was only wondering," he said, glancing at his accomplice.

The room fell silent save for the shuffle of the identity cards and documents being inspected, one by one.

"The letter *H*," said the fat man after some time, lifting a document closer to the light. "It jumps above the others in the sentence."

"All typewriters have one or two letters that do that," she explained. "It mustn't be perfect. That's why I spelled the word 'convenience' incorrectly. Because it usually is."

The fat man searched the document.

"It looks okay to me," he said, wrinkling his brow.

"See what I mean."

The fat man grinned at her, letting the document fall onto the table.

"So, your uncle... it's nothing serious I hope?" he asked.

"No."

"Not too much to drink, by chance?"

"No," she lied. "It's the flu or something."

"I see."

27

Tatiana was feeling claustrophobic. "May I have my money?" she asked.

The grin dropped from the fat man's face.

"Of course, young lady," he replied in monotone. "Of course."

The two men whispered again, the fat man watching her while seemingly giving direction to his associate.

"Your uncle is home?" he finally asked Tatiana.

"Yes, but I—"

"Do not worry," he said, nodding at the other man. "I'll give you the money. It's only that, in dealings like this, it's best to know where everyone is at any given moment. You understand—so it's all in the open, above board and all that."

Tatiana tried to understand the fat man as she watched his partner lift a leather satchel from the floor and drop it on the bed. Opening it with a key, he removed a bulging white envelope and threw it to the fat man who caught it with little effort. Working his pudgy fingers, he tore at the paper, revealing its contents.

Tatiana's eyes went wide. A small stack of American ten-dollar bills now sat on the table, glowing like precious stones under the near lamp.

"Here it is, young lady," he said. "Would you like to count it?"

Tatiana nodded. Her uncle told her to count the money, no matter what.

Taking the stack of bills, she immediately recognized something impossible to imitate: the smell that told her it was all very real. Then the non-drying ink the Americans used began darkening her fingertips to confirm it. The newness of the notes caused them to cling together. Separating each with her thumbnail, she did not notice the man by the bed moving quietly with his coat in hand.

The door opened. The accomplice left the room.

She looked at the fat man as the door clicked shut.

"My friend will be right back," he said. "Meanwhile, take your time. We must make certain it's all there, mustn't we?"

The money had temporarily calmed her, but the man's departure changed that. She was nervous, more than before. "It's all here," she said, pushing the bills together.

"But you haven't counted it."

She took a step back and said, "I trust you."

"But I would appreciate it if you would count it, young lady."

Tatiana glanced at the door, then back at the fat man—his large body and face, glistening from perspiration, were pushing closer.

Turning toward the door, she said, "I must be going. I have to be—"

The money exploded in her hands. The fat man was on her, his thick fingers at her throat and mouth. Unable to scream, she bit down, her teeth penetrating his flesh.

"Whore," he cried, lifting her from the floor by her buttoned coat. Her legs danced in the air as she screamed with all her strength. He threw her against the closet door and she bounced off like a child's ball, landing at his feet. The room began to blur, her attacker was everywhere and his hands were again on her body— her vision dimming, she watched the fat man's face recede even as he moved closer.

* * *

Sitting in the back of the racing yellow taxi, Tom Breck held tight to his suitcase. The driver had wanted to put it in the trunk, where luggage belongs, but Tom wouldn't let him. His prize had been too hard-won to lose sight of now.

The driver mumbled the address, determining the side of the street he should watch for as the engine began to groan up the steep grade. The apartment buildings had been replaced by the private homes of Pacific Heights. Semi-circular drives took the place of small carports and homes that looked like country estates were followed by others quartering more rooms than a small town hospital. The largest of all was a mansion at the top, before the road fell away to the ocean. It was here they stopped.

The taxi driver jumped from his seat as the wayward child in the back seat had suddenly become a man of means. The two-story brick home with the thick skin of ivy and the circular driveway that cut through the magazine-perfect lawn clearly impressed the veteran hack. He'd expect a gratuity in correlation to the surroundings and grabbing the handle of the black suitcase, moved toward the house.

Adjusting his leather bow tie, he looked about the imposing grounds. A rose garden sat in one corner and a collection of shaved trees in another. In the center of the lawn, blue and white perennials encircled a curious metal statue that stood over a story in height. Seeming to study it, he cocked his head as Tom opened the front door and asked, "How much do I owe you?"

"Twelve even with the luggage," replied the driver, his gaze fixed on the statue.

Handing him a twenty-dollar bill, Tom said, "Keep the difference."

Noting the denomination out the corner of his eye, the driver said, "Say, what is that... thing?"

Tom shoved the black suitcase into the foyer. "I don't know," he replied, stepping onto the polished black marble, "I've never asked," and pushed the door shut.

The house was dark. Standing motionless on the gleaming marble, Tom knew he was alone as lights were never left on in an unoccupied room, not even in the entry to aid the traveler. It was considered wasteful.

Tom's father drove a new Rolls Royce he'd purchased on the dealer's showroom floor for eighteen thousand dollars, not counting tax. His mother owned a bright red Cadillac with a white top and matching leather. Six thousand and change for that one-person land yacht, or, Tom had calculated, about three hundred dollars a foot. Pinching pennies on the electric bill clearly had its rewards.

Tom turned on the lights, all the lights. Even on the brightest day, with the sunlight drifting in, he would insist the chandeliers and floor lamps be illuminated. It helped, however briefly, to remove the silent melancholy he felt.

Noticing an overworked notepad on the entry table, he leaned forward to read the words. On it was written the odd chores his mother hoped to accomplish. The first task noted was a luncheon at Trader Vic's two days earlier and then dinner at L'Etoile just the evening before. Below that, Tom's name had been scratched in with the date and time of his arrival. They were both accurate and wondering what might have distracted her, Tom read the next line to see a bridge game jotted down. The time of his arrival and the gathering of the idle women of Pacific Heights had clashed. The cards, at a penny a point, had won.

Reading the remaining events, he kept his face expressionless. More luncheons and dinners, more games of cribbage and bridge were all duly noted, with those already attended cleanly ticked off. His mother was meticulous in carrying out her priorities.

All the actual work at the Breck household was left to the housemaid and the Spanish gardener. He must be of European stock, reasoned Tom's mother, as his coloring was light and he spoke English. The maid was from Iowa or Ohio or Idaho and

30

nondescript, dowdy and of reasonable temperament. A year earlier they'd had a pretty housemaid but it didn't work out, with Tom's father being less than discreet after the second cocktail, or the fourth. But the current domestic would dust the obvious parts of the furniture and pick up those things dropped, though more importantly, she made the perfect martini.

Though today there would be neither gin over ice, nor the sound of electric hedge clippers, as it was Wednesday. Both the hired hands had the day to themselves and that was fine thought Tom, reaching for the black suitcase. He could not have planned it better, wishing to avoid any trivial questions or prying eyes. He had things to do.

He walked down a carpeted hallway, stopping in front of the eighth door on the right as if he had come to an intersection, waiting for the light to change. This was his father's office, well secured by a dead bolt, but Tom pulled a key from his pocket and opened the door to the forbidden room. Switching on the chandelier, he went directly to the large desk by the window that neatly framed San Francisco Bay. For a few moments he studied the view, then gently placed the suitcase flat on the desk. The sound conjured a memory of the customs man that sent a shiver up his back. He quickly undid the center latch and lifted the lid.

Articles of clothing had been placed on the top: pressed shirts and sweaters, socks and underclothes. Tom removed these, then sat in the chair and ran his hand across the white plastic bags that filled the remainder of the suitcase. There were five across, three down and three deep. He checked to see none had been damaged, and none were.

The telephone on the desk rang and he waited until it fell silent. The call could have been from his mother or his father, but probably not. Regardless, now was not the time for a family chat.

Removing one of the plastic bags, he imagined its contents was worth three hundred dollars and possibly more, though certainly not less. This item had taken him weeks to acquire in such quantity, searching the back streets of Victoria's China District night after night. And it was prized, though not yet illegal in Canada where it was considered quaint, something to appease the Asian inhabitants. Tom had before him an ancient remedy for male impotence, forty-five horns from the Malayan white rhinoceros. And they were going to make him rich.

But first things first.

Unzipping a pouch on the inside of the suitcase lid, he removed a chalice whose yellow coloring could be seen through a layer of thin paper. He unwrapped this protective sheet, placing the gold artifact on the desk to study its workmanship. The multiple layers of pounded and twisted metal depicted a scene of some note from the King James' Bible. Although he was uncertain which scene that might be as he turned the chalice slightly on its base.

A student at St. Michael's could lie to a master on any given subject. He could cheat on his fortnightly or possibly during matriculation in his quest for the greatest of Universities. Even being found drunk or off the school grounds, which usually went together, would not necessarily demand the harshest of punishments: the student's expulsion. But the theft of a sacred object, on the level Tom had before him, would require such measures to be taken. He was studying a goblet that had been stolen from the chapel one day before Christmas break. A dozen in all were removed from a vitrine the vicar meticulously designed under the pulpit. It was a shrine to his religious good taste and it had been desecrated by a student who, when captured, would certainly be expelled. The vicar was too distraught and the crime too great for any possible forgiveness.

Well aware of this, Tom spun his chair to face the electric typewriter, placing a blank sheet of paper in the carriage. The machine began to purr as the metal arms snapped to order. The words had already been written in his head. The correspondence would be short and to the point, a note of guilt and contrition.

The letter was intentionally dated incorrectly and addressed to the Headmaster of St. Michael's Academy, Victoria, British Columbia. The author then wrote of his remorse in being part of such a contemptible deed—that he had purchased a gold goblet from one Ian Musters, on the day following the crime against the Church. The transaction took place in the sports locker room on the ground floor of Bolton House. Tom added the sum of five dollars had been paid for the goblet, feeling such a low price would further infuriate the reader, and that in the box accompanying the letter, the headmaster could find the article in question. He kept the majority of the words to one syllable and intentionally misspelled the odd one, wishing to distance himself from the message. Again he wrote the negotiation took place in the sports locker room, should the reader miss it the first time, and misspelled the word 'anonymous' at the bottom of the page.

Rereading the words, he thought back through his plan to be certain nothing would be left to chance.

He'd stolen the dozen goblets around midnight the day before Christmas break. Tom got into the chapel by way of the bell tower after jumping from the roof of the science building onto a breezeway that connected the two buildings. He easily jimmied the lock on the vitrine and carried away the prize in an empty laundry bag.

The idea of stealing the goblets came to him after watching the vicar hold one aloft during one of his more painful sermons. The value of the item to the clergyman was obvious and the ramification of their theft, guaranteed.

He thought to the next step of his design. He'd placed the remaining eleven goblets in the sports locker belonging to Ian Musters with a five-dollar bill rolled inside one to give the letter additional credibility. The goblets were hidden beneath the unwashed sweat clothes of the grubby prefect and could be easily found with a poke of the headmaster's cane. And they surely would be. Ian Musters would be expelled, with any dreams of attending Oxford, Cambridge or even McGill all but dashed. The black spot, as it was called, would follow him through school and, in ways, throughout his life.

Tom planned to mail both the letter and the packaged goblet the following day. To avoid the postmark of San Francisco, he would take the ferry to Sausalito and post them from there. The headmaster could read Old Greek and Latin but a fundamental road map would be too ambitious. Excessive education ate at one's common sense, reasoned Tom, and besides there were four other students from California at St. Michael's, two in the junior school and two in the senior. Enough possibilities to thwart the thought of his involvement and after all, the writer was surrendering.

Quickly addressing an envelope, he folded the letter inside. He'd prepare the goblet for mailing later, as it was getting late. Tom glanced at his watch. It was one minute past seven. He had waited too long for his mother to appear at the airport and now needed to make a phone call. Plans of an even more pressing issue than the destruction of Ian Musters were at hand.

He removed a square of paper from his wallet. Seven numbers were written on it, with the last two deliberately transposed. Lifting the telephone receiver, he dialed the numbers in their proper order. The line engaged and a telephone on the other side of town began to ring. He would limit the number of rings to seven, he decided, not wishing to appear overly eager. But he needed the phone to be answered; he needed to know if the deal was on.

The line went silent. Someone had answered but was not speaking. There was only the hum of the connection.

Tom said, "Hello, Mr. Wu?"

"Yes. Who this?"

"This is Tom Breck."

"Oh, *Bleck*, how you?"

"I fine," replied Tom, then amended, "I *am* fine, Mr. Wu."

"That good. That good."

"Right." Tom scooted his chair closer to the desk. "Uhm, you remember what we spoke about in your store last summer?"

"Uh, I not sure."

Tom hoped the man was just being cautious. He tried a different approach.

"It was last August, Mr. Wu—"

The man cut him off. "You back from England?"

"Canada," said Tom quickly. "I'm back from Canada, Mr. Wu."

"Ah, yes... you have nice *tlip*?"

"Yes, a very good trip, Mr. Wu."

"That good, so... How I help you?"

The man was playing a game with him. Their last conversation had been too specific, too precise for Mr. Wu to forget, or else it was over. The white plastic bags sitting before Tom were suddenly useless and of no value. Without a market, he might as well have brought back sawdust.

But he had no choice. He had spent days in Chinatown searching for someone who would be interested in buying the contraband. The other merchants refused to even discuss the issue; whether it was Tom's race or age that made them nervous, or just possibly they were honest, it didn't matter. Mr. Wu was his only hope. Tom decided it was a game; it had to be.

"I guess you can't really, Mr. Wu," he replied, sounding indifferent. "It's just your name was the first on my list of people to call when I returned. But I can see you're not interested, so—"

"Bleck," said Mr. Wu.

"Yes?"

"Where you?"

"I'm at . . . I'm in San Francisco, Mr. Wu."

"Okay, so maybe you come by store?"

Tom smiled. They were now circling, with foils drawn.

"Well, I'll try," he said. "If I can find the time. Maybe tomorrow."

"What time?"

"Noon, okay?"

"Noon okay."

"Fine, Mr. Wu, I'll see you—"

There was a click, then the annoying gasps of a telephone disengaged. Tom slowly replaced the receiver. He was bothered by the abrupt end to the conversation and then imagined that Mr. Wu was taken aback. He *was* interested in the white plastic bags sitting on the desk and now Tom knew it. That must be it he rationalized, leaning back in the chair, because what could be simpler than two people exchanging items of equal value? Each had something the other wanted. Nothing could be simpler.

* * *

Tatiana could smell him. The stench of sour sweat dripped from his face onto hers as his hands gripped her neck. She gasped, feeling the weight on her chest, trying to strike at the fat man with her arms, but it was no use. He outweighed her by three times and more, and was going to kill her. She let out a wail, but it was not her voice that filled the room. It had come from the fat man and he screamed again, a battle cry of sorts she imagined. She fought to breathe, waiting for the inevitable blow.

Then it was silent, followed by voices, sounds of simple conversation full of meaningless words. Air rushed into her lungs and she began to cough. Her throat was free of the manic grip and the weight on her body was gone. She felt she was dying and the pain was being mercifully removed. Then she again heard a voice. A hand slid under her head and another behind her shoulders.

There was the voice: *Tatiana… Tatiana.*

Her name. Say it again, she thought; she wanted to hear it again.

Tatiana… Tatiana.

She began to sob, throwing out her arms toward the words.

"Are you all right?" came the voice. "Try and stand. Can you stand?"

35

She nodded, her throat aching as she tried to speak, "Yes." She felt herself being lifted. Holding on to the arms that raised her, she searched for footing on the floor.

"We must go," said the voice. "Lean on me."

Pushing at her tears, she looked up as her vision cleared. It was Yuri, his black-stained hands clutching her like a fragile doll.

He softly repeated, "We must go."

"I—" She did not finish.

On the floor lay the fat man. His back propped against the end of the bed and his face bloodied. The table lamp lay next to him with the shade missing, but the bulb still burned, illuminating the beaten man in the dark of the room like a spotlight on a fractured statue. His face had caught the full force of the lamp's base when Yuri used it as his weapon.

There was a sudden scream from the doorway. A housemaid had stumbled on the scene. She glanced at the young girl and the man who held her, then to the fat man with his crushed face aglow. A sight so horrible demanded another cry, its sound rushed into the room.

"Let's go!" said Yuri.

Tatiana's senses were returning. "The documents," she said. "I must have the documents." Quickly moving to the table, she gathered them, then looked to the bed. "Grab the attaché case, Yuri."

"But—"

"Hurry!"

Yuri did as he was asked and moved out the door, into the hallway with Tatiana following. The chambermaid cowered against the wall, her hands up in defense. She appeared about to scream a third time when she seemingly noticed the ten-dollar bills scattered about the floor. Looking both ways down the corridor, she entered the room and pushed the door shut. Just a few minutes of tidying up would be necessary before notifying management of the terrible scene in room 111.

And that was all the time needed for Tatiana and Yuri to move through the hotel and outside. They walked quickly by the occupied doorman to the Wartburg and climbed in. The engine let out a loud backfire and the car jerked onto Krolewska Street, moving away from the elegant Inter-Continental Hotel. Turning one corner, then another, the taxi entered Old Warsaw, clattering along the cobblestone street before slowing behind a horse-drawn carriage in their path.

Rolling her window down a turn, Tatiana touched the top of her head. "It's gone," she said, her voice desperate.

"What's gone?"

"My beret."

"Is it back in the room?"

"Yes… Yes, I'm sure."

"Was your name in it?"

"No."

"Then you can get another."

"But—"

"You're alive," he said. "Don't worry about a hat."

Tatiana looked out her window. "Is he dead?" she asked.

Yuri pulled the car to the side of the street and stopped. "He was going to kill you," he said. "Why?"

She wiped the corners of her eyes but said nothing.

"Why, Tatiana?" he repeated. "Why did he want to kill you?"

"Is he dead?" she asked again. She wanted him to say no. It would all be okay if he said no.

"He was a pig."

"Is he dead?" she demanded.

Yuri nodded. "Yes."

"The papers," she said faintly. "It was for the identity papers."

"I saw them when you dropped the package in the parking lot," Yuri said as if to himself. "That's why I followed and hid in a broom closet at the end of the hallway. Then I heard you cry out…"

Looking at Yuri, she touched his hand.

"But why?" he continued, maintaining his gaze out the windshield. "There was the money on the floor—the American dollars. I have never seen so much money."

"I don't know."

"What were the identity papers for?"

"I don't know," she repeated, her voice louder. "I don't know."

"How did this man find you?"

"What?" she said, sounding confused.

"The man in the room. How did he know to contact you?"

"My Uncle Leszek. He met them in Krakow."

"Them?"

"There were two men."

"Two men? But there was only one. Where was the other?"

"He left," said Tatiana, her eyes welling with tears. "When we were talking, he just left."

"Did he—" Yuri stopped, then said, "Where is your uncle now?"

"Home," she replied. "He's at our apartment."

Pulling away from the curb, Yuri shifted up and the taxi began to shake, but he maintained the speed, then pushed it faster. Moving through Old Warsaw, he cut off a carriage, causing the horse to arch in an attempt to bolt.

"What are you doing?" she said, taking hold of the door handle.

"Where do you live?" he asked, ignoring her question. "How far from the taxi stand where I picked you up?"

"Slow down."

Yuri yelled, "Where do you live?"

"One block south," she replied. "One block south of the stand."

The taxi shot through an alley, then onto Krawkowskie Street toward a ring of connecting roads. A lone white-gloved policeman stood in the center, watching the advancing Wartburg, its driver moving it faster than tolerated. The white gloves began dancing in the air, signaling the taxi to pull over.

Yuri did not pull over, nor did he slow the speeding taxi. Cutting through the ring, the Wartburg passed the policeman now blowing his whistle.

"You should have stopped," said Tatiana.

"He has no car and no radio. He was alone."

"But he now has your plate number," she advised him, loosening her grip on the handle. "He'll get you later."

"Later?" said Yuri, shaking his head. "Don't you understand? There is no later. Everything we are now doing is for the last time."

"But…" She did not finish the sentence. She didn't need to. A man was dead and they were responsible. There would be no claim of self-defense because there was no such thing in the act of committing a crime. Tatiana and Yuri were on the run.

A queue waited at the taxi stand where they'd met. Each hopeful rider waved. Yuri accelerated.

"Which is yours?" he demanded, nodding at the upcoming apartment blocks.

"Number 48," she replied, lifting her arm. "With the green stoop… there." She was pointing at nothing. Each building looked the same with their layers of city pollution and decay, except possibly one—it had a stairway that at one time, many years earlier, might have been painted green.

"Number 48?"

"Yes."

Yuri braked and the wheels stopped, but the car didn't. The bald tires, unable to grip the asphalt through the slush, slammed into the curb. Tatiana was thrown forward, stopping a collision against the windshield with her arm.

"What is your apartment number," he demanded.

Tatiana collected herself, pressing her palms against the dashboard.

"What is your apartment number?" he repeated, pushing his door open.

"Two," she answered. "Apartment two."

"You wait here," he said.

Tatiana watched him quickly make his way up the stairs, disappearing into the doorway of the gray building. Faded numbers above a useless electric bell read 48.

Sitting back in her seat, she felt tired, thinking again to the morning: the simple walk to the taxi stand and the plodding drive to the hotel; the door of the room when she knocked and the strange men and the stranger questions as the documents were carefully examined. She touched her bruised neck, then put her hand over her eyes, trying to block out the thoughts. She could still smell him. It was still there: the foul odor of the fat man, the memory of his battered face in the dark room.

And the money left behind. The ten-dollar notes that could lift her from the life she had been tossed into, scattered across the hotel room floor like autumn leaves. She turned in her seat, using both hands to lift the black leather case. Opening the latch, she found the case full of innocuous white envelopes. She opened one and stared at the contents before rapidly opening another, then another still. Her breathing became hurried.

The black case was full of French and American currency; fifty and one hundred-dollar bills in one envelope, five hundred and one thousand franc notes in the next. There was a fortune on her lap.

The worth of the identity papers suddenly became clear. They were not needed for some future offense, because the crime had already been committed. The papers were needed for the two men to get away, out of Poland. Out of the Communist bloc.

As she snapped the black case shut, her thoughts moved again to the hotel room; to the men and their petty questions. Their concerns that were so simply answered. *Where did the names come from? How were the fingerprints created? Did she own a typewriter? Who else knows the names? Who else?* Her eyes widened. Throwing open the door, she lifted the black bag as if it were suddenly empty and jumped out of the car. She ran along the sidewalk and up the stairs into the dirt-gray building. Moisture clung to the interior walls and filled the depressions in the uneven floor to reflect a sliver of light at her feet. It came out of a partially open door with a wooden number 2 glued just above the glass eyehole. She stopped in the entry, panic rushing through her. She cautiously took a step forward into the broken shadows, retracing the footprints she had made a thousand times before. She moved toward the light, its static glimmer pushing across her feet like a warning. There was movement inside the apartment, blocking the open door and darkening the entry. She stood still, waiting in the hallway dusk with the black bag and documents gripped tight.

Suddenly light shot into her eyes. Reaching out with her fist, she pushed the wooden knob. The weight of the door pulled against the worn hinges as the apartment interior slowly came into view. Standing with his back to her was Yuri, who slowly turned, his hands together under his chin.

"I'm sorry," he said softly.

Tatiana knew why he was sorry and she wanted to let out a scream to let him know she was sorry too. Sorry about everything. But she only pressed her lips together while her eyes moved across the small room to a tattered couch in the corner. On it lay the only family she had ever known. He looked back at her with his eyes wide open and arms outstretched as if to welcome her home. Blood from his twisted mouth had already dried to a blue-black stain along his jaw line. A dark line encircling his neck emphasized the white pallor of his face.

The black bag and documents fell from her grasp, landing at her feet.

Moving quickly, Yuri caught Tatiana as she was about to collapse and gently lowered her into a chair. He pushed the front door shut. "You mustn't stay here."

She said nothing.

"He knows you," he continued. "The man who did this knows you and you can identify him."

Tatiana was still silent. A tear broke from her eye and ran down her cheek. Yuri removed something from his breast pocket and dabbed it gently against her cheek. It was the faded blue handkerchief.

"Do you understand, Tatiana?" he asked.

She nodded.

"I can get you to the frontier with Czechoslovakia. But... Do you have any money?"

"What?" she asked, as if the question were irrelevant.

"I have a little, myself," he said, his eyes narrowing. "The Czechs will demand some proof of... What do you call it?" Shaking his head, he then blurted, "Money. You need money, Tatiana."

She stared at him. What he was saying had nothing to do with her. Everything had been torn away: her family, her home, her everything. She watched Yuri speak but could not understand the words.

He pushed back her tears with the handkerchief, but was incapable of stopping the way she felt.

"*Tatiana...Tatiana.*"

He was doing his best, she thought. Just an hour earlier he had brought her back from the precipice, but this time she felt herself falling. Too much hit her and she was not prepared. Who could be prepared? Who could be?

"*Can you hear me? Can you hear me?*"

He reached out his hand.

"Yes, Yuri," she said softly, taking his hand. "I can hear you."

"Do you have any savings?" he asked.

"Savings?" she repeated. She had never used the word. How could someone have savings? Would someone with savings live in an apartment like this? She knew of no one with savings.

"I mean—"

"Yes," she said, glancing at the black bag. "I have some savings."

"Good," he said. "Grab those things you need. We must be off."

"There is nothing I wish to take." She stared straight ahead and repeated, "Nothing."

Yuri pulled gently on her hand.

"My uncle," she whispered. "I must—"

"You must leave him," he said. "The state will take care of him."

41

"I cannot—" Tatiana stopped. She did not have the strength to continue. She would listen to Yuri.

Military trucks clattered outside the window. Yuri quickly moved to the window and looked through the torn shades.

"It's okay," he said.

Tatiana began collecting the fallen documents. "Will you take the black bag, Yuri?"

"I have it," he replied. "There's nothing you want to take? You won't be coming back, you know."

"I know."

Opening the apartment door, Yuri glanced each direction in the dark hallway before signaling all was clear. Tatiana followed him to the top of the stairs and then stopped, looking back over her shoulder before leaving the gray building that had been her home.

They got into the taxi and, without another word, drove through the clouded day and endless towns, making their way to Krakow before nightfall. It was there Tatiana told Yuri the truth about the black bag and the fortune it contained. She'd decided to trust him, to always trust him, this man who had saved her.

They continued on to the town of Lod, where Czechoslovakia lay just a kilometer ahead. Tatiana spent that evening in a small hotel room amending the documents they carried. Yuri became her father as she aged him slightly with her pen and ink, a necessary combination for the Czech border guards and less paperwork for the Poles.

The ailing Wartburg was left on a busy street with the keys in the ignition. Within twenty-four hours its location would be forever lost, as car parts were more valuable than the car. Yuri bought an old diesel Mercedes. Tatiana purchased them new clothing.

The dealings with the Polish border police were routine as a small number of zlotys changed hands. They were accepted into Czechoslovakia on forty-eight hour visas, time enough to reach the Austrian frontier.

She asked Yuri to stop the car as they drove onto Czechoslovakian soil that early morning. It was a clear day, warmer than it had been, only she did not get out. But as she had done at her apartment door and would do for the remainder of her life, Tatiana Gregòsh turned her head, and looked back over her shoulder.

* * *

42

Flowing through the waterfront streets of Sausalito, the heavy fog was like an overdone cosmetic, clinging to the storefronts, attempting to hide the imperfections. Nothing broke through it, save for the occasional cry of a seagull or headlamps of a slow moving car. The town was running at three-quarter speed, the weather saw to that.

Tom Breck squinted into the mist, unable to see any movement on the water's edge, when he heard a bell. He began to run down the wharf. The ferry to San Francisco was pushing off with its one and only call for foot passengers. The steep grade of the dock fell into the fog, almost straight down, causing him to grab for the handrail before jumping onto the boat's foredeck. The chain bulwark rattled into place, then the gangplank immediately lifted clear by way of an overhead pulley. The lines were disengaged and the deck hands signaled to the wheelhouse that all was secure. A whistle sounded—one short, two long—and the SS Tiburon departed, her diesel engines advancing to all ahead full.

Tom collapsed in one of the plastic chairs screwed into the deck. Trying to catch his breath, he glanced toward the center of the bay and the island of Alcatraz. Over a dozen pulsating lights pushed through the mist to let any vessel know of an even darker passage ahead. A century-old warning to the locals and possibly to a young smuggler who quickly looked away, thinking of the customs man only the day before. Though he knew they would not lock up a fourteen-year-old boy in a place like Alcatraz, they would lock him up nonetheless. They might be amused with his level of high jinx, but they would find a place for him; something with the word 'detention' in the title, or 'home for boys' mentioned. Tom didn't mind being close to trouble, as long as he wasn't in it.

Yawning, then shaking his head in an attempt to push away the fatigue, he thought to the evening before. His mother had come into his room sometime during the night, well after midnight he was certain. He had known it was her without looking or hearing her voice. There was a scent that wrapped around the way she lived, the smell of gin and cigarette smoke which seemed to herald her presence.

And the words, always the same words: "*Tommy? Are you awake Tommy?*" And he was, but would never say, lying with his back to the intruder. "*I'm sorry I missed you today at the airport...I really am.*" Kneeling next to his bed, she'd sighed, her declaration sufficient and the guilt retired. "*Did you have a nice trip? How is school? I saw Flicka Uppinghouse the other day...you know, Sally's mother? You two would make such a nice couple. Why don't you call her while you're here? We could have her over...Yes; we could have her to the house. Oh, and Tommy...Tommy?"*

The same pledge, like an erratic tape recording, and then the fatigue would set in. The weight from her daily responsibilities becoming too much, she sat on the carpet, her back to the wall and her eyes closed, giggling at some unknown thought, uttering a word or two before falling asleep. Alone at last with her son.

Her son, left alone, stared through the curtainless window at the blue-black sky. The first breath of fog crept across the face of the moon while he listened to the sound of his mother and her separate life.

The boat's foghorn sounded just above Tom's head. Taken from his thoughts, he rubbed his eyes while struggling with another yawn. He had left the house early, before the maid and the gardener arrived, and before his mother and father awoke. Just as the sun started to light the day, he arrived in Sausalito with the packaged goblet and the letter incriminating Ian Musters. But standing by the mailbox above the docks, he had hesitated. The package suddenly felt more like a high explosive than a solution to any problem. Its potential was too ominous, too permanent.

It was his father's way, he had seen it: the complete destruction of any adversary who made the mistake of crossing him. One such man had appeared at their front door some years before. Tom remembered him well and the Panama hat he gripped while pleading for what was left of his livelihood, only to be turned away by the tormentor, without a second thought.

But Tom Breck had second thoughts. His plan was perfect and any chances of its failure were remote, but suddenly none of it mattered. There was another consideration, a human consideration.

After walking the streets of Sausalito that morning, he had found himself in front of a five and dime. The package and the letter were at his feet, the bomb and its triggering device still separated as he waited for the shop to open. At ten o'clock he entered, and choosing a get-well card from the display, wrote a brief note to his prefect, some words of concern for Ian Musters.

The simple paragraph stated the writer had reason to believe a plot had been concocted to discredit the ambitious prefect: a plot of dire consequences. Musters would find one of the dozen goblets stolen from the chapel in a following package. The remaining eleven were hidden, for reasons only the thief could explain, in the prefect's sports locker. Tom then added that Musters might wish to return the purloined objects to the vicar personally and by this, receive full credit for their recovery.

Also Tom wrote any needless pursuit of the actual villain on the part of the prefect might possibly cause another plot to be contrived, one even more sinister than that before him, which would obviously benefit no one.

He did not sign the note and printed the words in a style foreign to his own. If Musters were able to construe the actual author, it was unimportant. A salvo of sufficient strength had been fired to make the prefect reconsider any possible retaliation and an unspoken truce would reluctantly take shape. The plan was perfect.

Or so Tom imagined, letting the package and note drop into the mailbox after throwing the original letter away. But Ian Musters would be unavailable to receive the thirty-cent card with its desperate warning. The headmaster, having been sufficiently distraught, had already begun his own search of the school grounds, eventually finding his way to the sport's locker room without any prompting from an outside caller.

As Musters remained at the school during the Christmas break, he had already been summoned into the headmaster's office and questions put to him for which he had no answer. The headmaster wished to know the location of the twelfth goblet; if it would only be returned, then a plea bargain might be arranged. Where was it? Had the five dollars found in one of the goblets been the price paid for the missing item? Why had he taken them? What did he hope to gain? The questions were asked again and again; questions for which the prefect had no response other than his own lament.

Ian Musters was unceremoniously expelled before noon that same day. St. Michael's was not a democracy and there was no hearing; the headmaster had no choice, as the vicar insisted. The collection of goblets was returned, but incomplete.

Tom's card of warning would arrive the day after Musters left school, to be forwarded on to his family's home in Lyme Regis, England, where he returned in shame. However the card would never make it to England with the postage deemed insufficient, and having no return address, it'd be thrown onto a pile of other such forgotten things. And the package would go no further than the office of the bursar, who, upon opening it, would run with a certain glee toward the chapel. The goblet returned to the vitrine like a final stone being set, though it was too late for Ian Musters. The damage had been done.

Tom watched docks of San Francisco rise up through the fog, thinking about his decision to spare the prefect. He had made a conscious choice to separate himself from the Breck family legacy. He would not be like his father.

Tom moved ahead of the other passengers as the boat docked. The crossing took longer than usual and there wasn't much time.

Dodging the speeding cars along the waterfront, he headed into the financial district. A street clock read five minutes before twelve as he crossed the intersection, moving away from the economic center of the city. He ran underneath the archway signaling the entrance of Chinatown and moved down the one-lane road. The buildings were small and the street signs, marked in Chinese characters, suggested a foreign place. Shopkeepers displayed their wares on the sidewalk; the same items found at the more elegant stores, but half the cost, with no guarantees given. All sales were final in Chinatown.

He searched for the storefront in the mist, finally spotting the small sign above the recessed doorway. Its words were in Mandarin save for the bottom line that read, *Ling Wu, Pharmacist.*

No lights were on in the small shop, only the floating glow of the outside fog illuminated the cabinets and shelves. It was as he remembered: the endless collection of bottles and jars, and curious things hanging from the overhead beams; uprooted plants drying and others being kept moist; twigs in one glass container and leaves in the next with their identity marked in unknown symbols. It was all there. One or more of the mysterious ingredients that sat row after row on the stacked shelves could reverse any malady the clientele suffered. Ling Wu cured anything, even the most desperate of requests, and this is why Tom had searched him out. To offer him an ingredient more rare and dear, than all the others he possessed.

The hours of operation were painted on the window and it should have been open for business, but the door was locked. Tom was late but not by much, just a few minutes. He wondered if Ling Wu had changed his mind, thinking better of the risks, and hoped Tom would just go away. Maybe the deal was off.

Adjusting the knapsack on his shoulder, Tom again searched for any activity inside the dark pharmacy when a voice called: "Bleck?"

Tom tried to make out the small man walking toward him. "Yes."

"You late."

"I know, Mr. Wu," he admitted, but thought better of explaining. "I lost track of the time."

The small man grunted. "You by self?"

Tom nodded; then realizing Ling Wu could not see the gesture in the meager light between them, replied, "Yes."

Ling Wu stepped forward, now but an arm's length away. They were the same height, the fourteen-year-old boy and the middle-aged man. Ling Wu wore a heavy coat, scarf and a knitted cap, as if he were in freezing temperatures rather than the mild San Francisco winter.

"You come in," he said, working the key in the lock.

They moved inside, Tom's eyes adjusting to the darkness as he followed the Chinaman through the labyrinth of tables, counters, and boxes piled up from the floor. They walked behind a screen that hid the entrance to a back room. It was filled with open crates and excelsior scattered on the brick floor, their feet crunching the wood shavings as they walked.

Ling Wu switched on a table lamp and abruptly turned. "You show me," he said, pointing at a near rolltop desk.

"I—"

"You not have?"

"Yes, only—"

"You show me," he repeated, tapping the desk top with his forefinger.

Tom removed a plastic bag from his knapsack, placing it on the desk.

"This," he said, "is the horn of a white rhinoceros."

"How you know?" demanded Ling Wu.

"How do I know what?"

"This can be horn of cow . . . or goat."

"Yes, it could be, but it isn't."

Ling Wu touched the white plastic. "How much?" he asked, staring at the bag.

Tom smiled. "Well, I thought you might wish to make me an offer."

"No," said Ling Wu loudly. "How much here? How much weigh?"

"Six hundred grams, I believe. The scale was old."

Ling Wu sat down in the chair and taking a knife from a drawer, cut the tape sealing the bag. He slowly rolled the plastic open as though it were a jeweler's swatch of loose diamonds that might easily spill, though only a chalk-white bone appeared, a seemingly worthless item a dog might bury rather than something Ling Wu would be touching delicately as he was. He ran the tips of his fingers along the blanched spine.

"You have more?' he asked.

"Yes."

"How much?"

"Approximately fifteen kilos."

"How much?"

"I said about fifteen—"

"No!" said Ling Wu. "How much you want?"

Tom was beside himself. The deal was on. Putting his hand to his mouth, he said, "Nine thousand dollars," through his spread fingers.

Ling Wu shook his head.

"No," he said, rolling up the plastic bag. "Too much."

Watching Ling Wu close the bag, Tom waited for the counter-offer. But there was none, not one word of compromise as the white plastic was rolled tight.

"But that's what you said you'd be willing to pay," he reminded the Chinaman, trying to stay calm.

Ling Wu stood. "You go now."

Tom was dumbfounded. It was all there: the buyer, the seller, the goods so obviously coveted, but the deal was over as quickly as it had begun.

Ling Wu turned off the lamp. "You go now," he repeated in the darkness.

Tom lowered his hand to the desk, but could only feel the greasy wood top. The bag was gone.

"I keep it," said Ling Wu.

"What?" exclaimed Tom, reaching for his knapsack.

Ling Wu took a step forward. "You leave this too."

"No—"

Tom stopped. He could feel the knife used to open the bag now at his throat.

"So what you do?" asked Ling Wu, holding the blade tight against the skin. "You call cops?"

Tom was terrified. Visions of the Oriental man and martial arts rushed through his thoughts. Ling Wu might master any one of those methods of combat.

The knife began to cut. Panicking, Tom threw up his arm, hitting Ling Wu's hand with enough strength to push it away and grabbed his knapsack. Like an orchestrated move, the thirty pounds of animal horn collided with Ling Wu's chin, snapping his head back as if he had been hit by a controlled upper cut. And that was all that was needed, for this Oriental man had a penchant for liquor and long naps, and had never once studied the martial arts. He dropped to the floor, now motionless.

Tom stepped backward, searching for some justification. He had killed the Chinaman in self-defense, but it didn't matter. He had killed a man. The police would ask what he had been doing in the back room of the pharmacy. They'd find out; they always found out.

He moved for the door of the small room, then stopped. There was the other plastic bag and he must have it back. Tom turned on the desk lamp. Unable to see it, he began searching the desk; first one drawer then the next. Each was empty of the bag, but the last held a metal box with a pistol on top. He pushed the gun off the box with his forefinger and it fell to the side with a thump. Opening the metal box, his eyes went wide. It was full of cash and the sight of it made him angry. The Chinaman could have bought his goods outright, but instead chose to steal them. This was inexcusable.

There was a strange sound. Turning off the lamp, he listened in the darkness. There it was again. Ling Wu was coming round. He was not dead, but had been knocked unconscious. Tom again turned on the lamp, watching the Chinaman roll onto his side, his hand to his jaw.

Counting the money, Tom jerked his gaze between it and the awakening man. The Chinaman attempted to sit up, gradually opening his eyes.

"Our agreement," said Tom, "was to have been three hundred dollars per half-kilogram, Mr. Wu."

The bewildered Chinaman stared at Tom. "What you talk about, Bleck?"

"These were your numbers, Mr. Wu," said Tom loudly. "Not mine."

"You steal my money!"

"No, Mr. Wu. I am taking the eight thousand dollars I would have agreed to if you had bothered to negotiate. So really, you're getting a deal."

Attempting to stand, the Chinaman slipped on the wood shavings as Tom placed the money into the back pocket of his jeans and moved toward the door of the small office.

"You come back." screamed Ling Wu. "I get you, Bleck."

Angrily, Tom turned to look at the struggling man. "What are you going to do, Mr. Wu?" he demanded. "Call the cops?"

The Chinaman found his footing and jumped for the drawer containing the pistol. At the sight of the man's speed, Tom quickly turned, knocking over the door screen as he fell forward into the shop. Struggling to stand, he could hear the sound of the gun being cocked. That singular noise seemed as loud as the pistol firing, the bullet hitting the wooden showcase next to Tom's head with a slap. Ling Wu was not going to be bothered with telephoning anyone. Crawling on his belly, Tom managed to get in front of the case when the next bullet hit. It blew through the glass cover just over his head, spraying shards across his back. The Chinaman was coming after him.

Tom got onto all fours and made for the front door of the shop, racing through the maze of boxes.

Standing at the door of the back room, Ling Wu appeared to be listening. Tom's hand slipped on the filthy floor and he fell forward, letting out a groan. The Chinaman didn't hesitate. Aiming for the sound, he fired. The bullet shot through a row of glass canisters, blowing out their treasured contents like floating ash, intensifying the room's darkness.

His prey cornered, Ling Wu moved forward.

Tom crawled to the door only to find a steel tongue running from the keyhole into the jamb. He now understood the reason for the Chinaman's deliberate advance. The only way out was gone.

The hammer of the gun snapped into position and another bullet was fired. It whistled by Tom's head, slapping into the wall next to his ear. Glancing back, he could see the Chinaman's knitted cap bobbing behind the stacked boxes. Then it disappeared.

Tom trembled as perspiration gathered on his face. He wiped at his eyes, listening to the advancing footsteps. Then there was silence, broken by a rattle followed by the curious sound of coins being fumbled. Tom realized what was happening; it was not coins, but bullets. The Chinaman was reloading.

A shadow shot across the room. It came from the storefront window. Someone had walked by, trailing their silhouette through the glow of the outside fog. Tom dropped to his hands and knees, moving quietly toward the window. The jingling stopped and so did he, holding his breath, listening for the advance of the Chinaman. Immediately a sound came from behind the far counter: the shuffle of feet and then the snap of the gun's action falling into place.

Tom had no choice. The window was the only way out. He looked about the floor for something heavy enough to throw at the large pane. There was nothing but excelsior and thin pieces of wood from the shipping boxes. He picked up one, then let it fall; it was useless, and the canisters and jars were out of reach. He looked over his body—his belt, the jacket, his shoes—and considered everything. Nothing was of sufficient weight to break through the glass.

The footsteps continued. The top of the Ling Wu's knitted cap appeared again just above the near stack of boxes. In a moment the Chinaman would be in view. Tom glanced at his hand. It was shaking. Making a fist in an attempt to control the fear rushing through him, he knew he would have to strike the window with his hand. Looking at the towering glass, it suddenly appeared impenetrable. It would break into razor-like shards and cut him in two; his hand would be severed as the guillotine of glass dropped straight down from the impact. Uncertain if he should strike the corner or the center of the window, he removed his windbreaker, wrapping it around his hand, looking again at the window that appeared like a looming skyscraper. Taking a deep breath, he drew back his arm, but he hadn't moved quickly enough. Ling Wu was now behind him. Tom heard the click of the gun's hammer and instinctively fell on his stomach as it discharged. He didn't hear the bullet going into the wall or the soft thump of flesh being penetrated. The bullet's target was the neatly painted hours of operation in the corner of the storefront window. The hole was simple and appeared ineffective. But it wasn't.

The window Ling Wu used to display his wares had survived numerous earthquakes and tremors from the fault below. But a lead bullet, even the small caliber used by the Chinaman, was too much for the ancient plate glass. A small fractured line appeared and then another. A crack suddenly shot diagonally to the opposite corner and the glass began to spider web. The window made a groaning sound then exploded, its shards spraying into the store. Ling Wu threw up his arms as protection and that was all the time Tom needed. Diving through the opening, he quickly got to his feet and ran straight into the curtain of fog which lingered as if patiently waiting.

Swallowed up in the mist, everything around him was a blur: the doorways and building façades, the intersections where impatient drivers objected to his presence by sounding their horns. The street signs came rushing up, one after the other, and he continued to run, no longer knowing where he was; up one hill and down another the fog would thin, then eat him up as quickly. His throat, bleeding slightly from the knife wound, stung when he touched it. He was beginning to tire. His legs hurt and his lungs pounded as they grabbed for air, but he dare not stop.

CHAPTER ONE

Twenty-one years later

Looking in the bathroom mirror, Thomas Breck shook some drops of henna onto his hair, gradually rubbing it in. His natural light brown color began darkening, till it was almost black, and greasy in appearance. Intentionally leaving it uncombed, he removed a stained blue jumpsuit from the near hook and slipped it on. Again he glanced in the mirror. He had not shaved for three days and the thick stubble made him look older. The dirty hair made him look vapid.

It was coming together.

He put on a pair of scuffed work boots, letting the frayed cuffs of the jumpsuit stay inside one boot but not the other—a man on the go all day might let his appearance slip, he reasoned. Removing a black beret from the counter, he placed it on his head, pulling one side down to touch his ear. This was the style of a contemporary laborer, a provincial cap with a rakish tilt. An ascot could be added, something old and grubby, but he thought better of it. He would only be there twenty minutes if all went according to plan, somewhat longer if not.

In the mirror's center, he observed the name *Jean-Paul* stitched on his breast pocket, and that is who Thomas Breck had become: Jean-Paul Van der Elst, delivery driver for World Express Transport, freight carriers and customs brokers, centered in Brussels, Belgium, with offices worldwide. Or that was what the documents would say—and government documents, sufficiently stamped, initialed and sealed with all taxes paid, never lie.

He looked at his watch. It read five minutes after seven, and time was standing still. The sun had set and the dark of winter had more than enough time to settle over the city of Brussels. He wanted to be done with it, but he couldn't be early. He needed to arrive exactly at eight o'clock.

With a final glance at his reflection, he determined he was ready and moved to the door leading to the entry hall, but reaching for the porcelain handle he stopped.

The front door of the house was opening. He looked again at his watch, as if he had misread it, but he hadn't. It was six minutes past the hour.

Slowly turning the handle, he eased the bathroom door open, and said, "Michelle?"

There was the sound of rustling, then the front door slammed closed.

"*Non, Monsieur Breck,*" came a voice. "*C'est moi.*"

"Chantal?" he said.

"Yes, Monsieur Breck."

It was the maid. He didn't understand. She always left by five and never returned until the following morning. But there she was, fumbling about in the entry.

"Did you forget something?" he asked.

"No, Monsieur Breck." She sounded as if she were now in the kitchen. "I do not believe so."

"So what are you doing here at this hour?"

"The party, Monsieur Breck," she answered. The refrigerator door opened, then closed. "I am preparing for the party."

His brow wrinkled. "Somebody is having a party?" he asked, looking again at his watch. Time was no longer standing still. It was taking off and beginning to fly.

"Yes, Monsieur Breck." Chantal moved from the kitchen toward the dining room. "You are."

Tom began to chew on his lower lip. He could have a comfortable conversation with Chantal from behind the bathroom door, and it could continue throughout the night, but Jean-Paul Van der Elst needed to be on his way. He wanted to open the bathroom door, walk to the entry where he would remove his oilskin jacket from the hall tree, move out the front door and across the gravel drive to the garage where he would get in his vehicle and be on his way. That is what Jean-Paul Van der Elst needed to do, but a maid preparing a soirée had him blocked.

"What time does this party begin?" he asked, hoping to send her on some trumped-up errand.

"Seven-thirty, monsieur." Her voice was loud. She was standing just outside the bathroom door, rummaging through the linen cabinet.

"Seven-thirty?" he whispered.

"Yes, monsieur." She had heard him. "Madame Breck told me seven-thirty. I am quite certain."

"Yes, yes. Of course, Chantal." Again he consulted his watch. The guests would be arriving at any moment.

She moved noisily back toward the dining room as Tom glanced into the hallway. The jacket he needed hung in the entry, still in her path. Quietly shutting the door, he moved into the bedroom and opening the wardrobe, began searching for a replacement. There was nothing. Only suit coats and a blazer with a crest on the pocket, but Jean-Paul Van der Elst would not likely be the member of any yachting club. He removed a topcoat and went to the window. Flipping the latch, he pushed on the frame, but it would not budge. Since his wife had acclimatized the house two years before, there was no reason for it to open; a working window was unnecessary with an interior temperature that never varied more than one-half degree.

The doorbell sounded. The first of his wife's guests were arriving.

Tom hit the top of the window frame with the butt of his hand. The glass cracked in the corner. The damage was unimportant as he was prepared to remove the pane if necessary. Then the window began moving up. Hurriedly sitting on the ledge, he swung his legs through the opening and dropped onto the white gravel below.

Headlights came to life, shooting their beam around the property like a search lamp. He pressed himself to the wall of the house. The lights and motor shut down. A car door opened and closed. There were footsteps on the gravel and the doorbell rang again. The maid greeted the latest intruder and the front door shut.

Pulling the window closed, Tom moved across the gravel drive, stopping in front of the garage door to listen in the darkness. It was quiet. Any guests already inside the house would be circling the liquor cart, with the maid shuffling into the kitchen for ice and mixer. No one would be listening as the springs of the large door retracted.

The Renault cargo van was as he'd left it. The newly painted sign on the side could barely be seen in the darkness and he wondered why he'd bothered. But someone might be watching when he arrived at his destination, and it was done, like any of the small precautions, just in case. The dome light illuminated a briefcase between the front seats as he climbed into the van and turned the key in the ignition. He decided against engaging the headlamps as he pulled away; the white glow of the gravel drive would guide him to the road.

The clock on the dash read seven twenty-five. He needed thirty minutes. He should arrive just in time.

* * *

It had started to rain and Tom tapped the wiper switch briefly, clearing the windshield of the parked van as he observed the far warehouse. All appeared normal, with nothing unusual. One of the half dozen metal doors of the building was lowered shut.

He placed the briefcase on his lap, carefully lifting it open. Sitting on top was the document he needed, though it was incomplete—there was no tax stamp. He knew to wait until the last minute before attaching it. The cheap glue caused the stamp to wrinkle almost immediately. He had made that error before; he remembered the agent flicking the upturned corners with his finger. Tom had explained that water had been spilt on it, or white wine, he could not remember, but the lie had worked. The customs agent bought the story; another might not.

As he attached the counterfeit stamp, he glanced at the clock on the dash. It was four minutes to eight. Flipping the wipers, he again checked the activity inside the depot. Another metal door came down, then another. He shoved the document into his breast pocket and hurriedly removed his topcoat.

The fifth metal door came down with a crash. Taking a deep breath, he put the transmission in reverse and pushed the gas pedal to the floor. The van shot backward, accelerating through the empty parking lot. He swung the front end around until the back windows aligned with the last open bay door. Pushing the Renault faster toward the warehouse, he braked only a car length away from the concrete ledge and coasted up to the large rubber guards until the van's rear bumper tapped gently against them. Quickly moving to the back of the van, he threw open the two rear doors and strolled casually inside the customs depot as the chain was being pulled on the last metal door.

The man gripping the greased chain turned to look at the wall clock above him. It was exactly eight o'clock.

"What do you want?' he asked.

Tom smiled. "I am here to pick up some cargo," he replied in *Bruxelloise*, a French dialect that would be accepted by those at Zaventem Airport, where Flemish was spoken. A man speaking pure French would most certainly be shown the door.

The man grunted.

"Here are the papers," he continued, removing them from his breast pocket.

Dropping his grip of the chain, the man jerked the documents from Tom's hand. "Wait here," he said, moving toward the plywood office that sat in the center of the depot. He looked again at the clock on the wall.

"Thank you," said Tom, preserving his smile.

Another man cut across the open warehouse on an electric Hyster. He swung the rear wheels at an angle, backing it up against the wall to park it for the night. Glaring at Tom, he jumped from the seat and walked toward the office.

It was perfect. The customs warehouse was closing down and each man was ready to go home, having little time to waste on an after hours pick-up. Tom was not there to make new friends, or spend time leaning against freight containers, involved in idle chatter. Too much time could be dangerous.

A uniformed customs agent emerged from the plywood office and approached the open bay door, squinting at the document as he walked. He had a cigarette hanging from his mouth and an automatic weapon from his shoulder.

Tom's mouth fell to a straight line. He had never seen a weapon at customs and the mood darkened with each click of the agent's metal-tipped heels.

"There is no record," said the agent, still reading the paper, "of this cargo being ready for pick-up. We have had no time to inspect it."

That's it. Now you've got it. That's the whole idea.

"I don't know anything about that," said Tom. "My boss just told me to come and pick it up."

The agent's cigarette danced up and down as he mumbled, "World Express." He looked at Tom. "Have you ever been here before?"

Yes, last year. Don't you remember? My hair was blond and I had a mustache. I told you that I was Finnish and had just gotten the job and you felt sorry for me and gave me the cargo. Don't you remember? Don't you remember?

"No," said Tom, eyeing the automatic weapon. "I haven't."

"Well, we close the depot at eight."

I know that. Any fool would know that. Good Lord, it says that on the door just outside.

"Really? At eight?" Tom rubbed his stubbled chin. "I got lost and I have to deliver the cargo tonight."

The agent stared at him through the drifting cigarette smoke, then glanced at the open rear doors of the van. He frowned and turned toward the office.

"Hans," he yelled, holding up the document. "Grab this cargo."

Tom said nothing more.

A man ran from the office, jumped onto the forklift, and drove toward them. He did not slow down. Snatching one copy of the document from the agent as he passed at full speed, he turned the forklift's wheels toward a row of loaded pallets stacked to the ceiling.

Tom no longer had to force his smile; cargo was being rescued.

Again the customs agent looked at the document as he removed the exhausted cigarette from his mouth. "Turn around," he said, and dropping the butt, crushed it with the sole of his boot.

"What?"

"I said turn around," he repeated brusquely.

Facing the open door of the depot, Tom felt a hand press against his shoulders, then heard the click of a pen. The customs agent was using his back to initial the document.

"Here," he said, dangling the freshly inked paper over Tom's shoulder. "Give this to the driver when he brings your cargo round. Okay?"

"Okay."

His duties complete, the agent walked away, the automatic weapon slapping against his waist with each step.

Just a few more minutes...Just a few more minutes.

Then it happened. A voice rumbled through the warehouse, its sound bouncing off the walls and ceiling, off everything in its path. Only two words were spoken, two simple words.

"*Bon soir*," repeated the voice.

Slowly, Tom turned. Standing but an arm's length away from him was an unshaven young man in a French-blue work suit. A beret sat atop his head and the look was completed with an ascot carefully knotted about the neck. Tom could have been staring into a mirror except the image opposite wore a grin. Tom had no grin.

The words still tolled in his head; the two ordinary words. It was not their presence that troubled him, but the accent. It was French. A Walloon had been hired to work at the Flemish-dominated Zaventem Airport and whether he was someone's brother-in-law or distant cousin, it didn't matter. He was there, speaking in *Bruxelloise*, and he wanted to chat with a soul mate, the kindred person of Jean-Paul Van der Elst.

"My name is Serge," said the young man, putting out his hand. "I heard you speaking with Günter."

You heard me speaking? What did you think, Serge? Did I sound okay?

"Oh? My name is Jean-Paul," said Tom, gripping his hand.

"I just started here," Serge advised, continuing to shake Tom's hand. "Today's my first day."

Your first day? How fortunate. But you really should have called in sick, Serge. You really should have.

"That's wonderful," said Tom.

"Oh, I don't know," he whispered, glancing about the warehouse. "I don't speak the language… If you know what I mean?"

Tom forced a smile.

"Where do you live?" asked Serge. "What commune?"

Where do I live? What commune? Is that what you said, Serge? All right listen: I live in Wolowe St. Pierre and have a maison de maitre *on two hectares with five bedrooms and four baths. There is a full-time gardener and maid. The wine cellar contains over three thousand bottles and there is a twenty-year vertical collection of Chateaux Palmer and Lafitte. I have a four-car garage that contains a Mercedes C convertible, a Jensen Interceptor, and a twelve-cylinder BMW coupe. How about you, Serge? How about you?*

"I have an apartment in Ixelles," said Tom. "A studio."

"Oh, Ixelles is nice… Are you married?"

Married? Now you want to know if I'm married? Yes, Serge I'm married. Michelle is her name. She's French and she's beautiful. I met her at a fundraising for the Opera House two years ago. You

59

know, there I was strolling about when I saw her across the opulent foyer. I was wearing my new tuxedo and she was in a one-of-a-kind Yves-St. Laurent gown. She was the most attractive woman I had ever seen. She seduced me that very night, Serge. You should have been there. You really should have been there.

"No," said Tom. "I'm single."

"Yeah, me too. What school did you go to?"

I'm not feeling well, Serge... School is it? Okay, I went to the University of London and received a degree in Economics. Then to the University of Sorbonne at Brussels where I majored in French Literature and would have graduated, but decided on a career somewhat more lucrative. Remember the house and the cars and the wine and the beautiful Michelle I just mentioned? Things like that don't come cheap, Serge.

"State school," said Tom. "Until I was sixteen."

Serge laughed. "Yes, but which one?" He wanted to know; it was only small talk, but he needed to know.

Which one? Which one?

Tom could feel his hold on the situation slipping. He knew of no public school he could easily name off like the days of the week or the letters of the alphabet. He had never planned on such an obscure question and Serge was waiting for a response. Tom looked back into the warehouse while he delayed for time; time to think. He had driven by the public schools many times, watching the children cut across the street after class, kicking their footballs and dragging their books. But he never noticed the names. There had been no reason to notice their names.

His mouth grew dry; he could feel the neatly groomed accent slipping away. His hold of the dialect was leaving him and he was afraid to open his mouth again. Afraid of what might come out.

Tom wondered why he'd chosen to become such a person. He could have been Finnish again, but he might have been recognized, then possibly Spanish, or Portuguese. Yes, Portuguese.

Who speaks Portuguese?

He wiped his forehead with the back of his hand, still trying to think of a public school.

A public school.

The customs agent, the automatic weapon still hanging from his shoulder, appeared at the door of the office. He glanced at his watch, then looked at the forklift dancing with a large overhead box. He said something to the operator and began walking toward Tom.

Until the cargo was down on the concrete floor and heading toward the bay door, everyone had plenty of time—time to hang around and chat. The one thing Tom wanted to avoid was happening.

The agent fired up another cigarette as he came closer, the smoke swirling above his head. The employees at customs could be with their wives or girlfriends, or any other distraction if not for the driver from World Express Transport.

Tom looked at Serge. The grin was gone, replaced by the squinting of the young man's simple eyes. The click of the customs agent's boots came closer and Serge was waiting.

Time was up.

"St. Sulpice," said Tom in a matter of fact way. The name had come to him. "I went to St. Sulpice."

Then all became silent. The boots against the concrete floor and the electric forklift jamming its pronged fingers against the wood crates fell mute. All sound shut off in the warehouse. Serge was not responding. Maybe the inquisitor had gone to St. Sulpice also and didn't remember a Jean-Paul Van der Elst. Maybe St. Sulpice did not exist? But it did. Tom remembered the name.

"That's not funny," said Serge.

Funny? I didn't want it to be funny. I've had all the laughs I can take for one evening, Serge.

"What do you—" Tom stopped. He did not need to finish the question. He knew where he'd heard the name of St. Sulpice. It was a state school and it did exist at one time, but not anymore. The Germans bombed it during their invasion in the last war, killing half the students and teachers inside. St. Sulpice was now a memorial; a bomb crater left intact with a plaque listing the names of those lost in the carnage. It was a place of reverence never to be spoken of lightly. Until now.

"I—" Tom thought to attempt an apology. A way out of what he had said, but it was too late.

Serge took a step backward. It was an unconscious move to let Jean-Paul Van der Elst know that he was now alone. His ally was retreating and making tracks for the enemy camp. A glimmer of suspicion was forming about someone attempting to retrieve uninspected cargo at customs.

The sounds of the cold building slowly returned: the metal taps of the agent's boots and then the whine of the forklift's motor. The cargo box, removed from its perch, was on its way toward the waiting van.

Tom glanced at Serge, then at the customs agent. There was nothing he could do. Only act as if all was normal as he walked away from the two men who were now sharing a word. Serge had something on his mind and was making it known to the armed agent.

Moving alongside Tom, the forklift operator took the document from his grip. Tom picked up his pace. He could only imagine the conversation between the two men behind him.

The metal prongs dropped to the concrete floor and began pushing the wooden box toward the open doors of the van. It was almost there. Just a couple nudges further and the cargo would be out of the warehouse, safely inside the escape vehicle.

Then the agent spoke, and he yelled the words again to be certain there was no doubt: "Stop where you are!" He threw his cigarette aside. "Go no further!" He was speaking to both the driver and the dubious Jean-Paul Van der Elst.

There was no uncertainty; the cargo box was to be opened.

The driver shut down the forklift as the agent removed the initialed document from his chest pocket and studied its information, noting the weight, the point of origin—the contents.

"Open it," he said.

Eager to oblige, Serge retrieved a crowbar from its holster on the side of the forklift and began twisting the metal band that wrapped the wooden box. The band snapped off cleanly, falling to the concrete floor with a clatter. Serge pried up the lid. The nails whined, ripping out of the wood one by one.

Just outside, the rain fell harder. It danced along the roof of the cargo van, making a chaotic drumming sound that rolled out of the rear doors. Tom's eyes wandered as he listened. He said nothing, holding his place by the bay door. The crowbar moved to the next set of nails. It was now out of his control.

The wooden lid fell to the side of the box and Serge grabbed at the thick paper covering.

"Wait," commanded the agent, reading the document.

Serge stopped, his hands poised, waiting for the command to continue.

"*Des tableaux*," said the agent, noting the description of the contents. "Paintings is it?"

Tom faced his prosecutors. "I don't know," he replied calmly. "I'm just the driver."

Grunting, the agent nodded at Serge and the onslaught continued. The paper covering was torn into shreds as the attack gained momentum. Hands flew wildly, with no concern for the word stenciled on the plywood box that read *Fragile*.

Serge pulled up a large flat square, also covered in thick shipping paper. Without waiting for consent, he tore at it, gradually revealing the soft colors it hid.

The agent put his hand on Serge's shoulder. "Stop," he said.

Reluctantly, Serge obeyed.

Letting his hand drop, the agent pulled down on the remaining paper to reveal an unframed oil painting. The colors were brilliant, depicting an innocent scene of the seashore: a beach in the summertime with angled parasols shooting up from the sand; people in the water and people out; the yellow-white sun shining in the cloudless sky.

Serge grabbed a second square from the wooden crate and frantically stripped away the paper, only to find another painting. This one was a still life, a vase with autumn flowers.

The customs agent touched the canvass, running his forefinger to the name of the artist in the corner. "Jan Karski," he said softly. Then, looking at the document clutched in his hand, he read the point of origin: "Budapest."

Serge grabbed for another square in the box but the agent stopped him.

"That's enough," he said, putting his hand on the paper covering. "Put them back."

"But—"

"I said put them back," he repeated, seemingly annoyed with the half-witted Walloon and his groundless suspicions.

The forklift operator restarted the engine.

Lowering the paintings into the box, Serge's eyes returned to their simple appearance.

"Be here on time in the future," said the agent over the sound of the cargo box being pushed along the concrete floor.

Tom said nothing.

The box dropped off the edge of the landing into the backend of the cargo van. The forklift driver tapped it in further. Then the agent nodded at Serge, who closed the doors of the Renault. As they clicked into place, the agent turned, his gun slapping at his side. He walked back to the office and slammed the door shut. Its sound echoed off the interior walls.

Serge stood motionless, the crowbar in his hand, waiting for Jean-Paul Van der Elst to be on his way.

Tom walked to the landing, about to jump to the asphalt, but felt unable, instead taking the half-dozen steps that were off to the side. Through the pounding rain, he heard the last metal door of the warehouse come crashing down. The parking area became dark— only a distant street lamp fluttered its tired yellow glow.

As he opened the driver's door, Tom looked at the side of the van. The recently painted *World Express Transport* was being removed in streaks by the heavy rainfall. In another few minutes the fictitious company, like its driver, would be gone.

* * *

The rain had stopped. Stars were attempting to break out and the temperature was dropping—Tom could feel it through the partially open window as he drove into his garage. Shutting off the van, he stared at nothing in the darkness, listening to the tick of the cooling engine.

He had been lucky. He'd made plans and taken precautions, but he had been lucky. And you cannot be lucky forever. Sitting in the black void of the garage, he recalled the hand of the customs agent moving across the canvass, touching the artist's name in the corner. He remembered what his partner had said:

Even if they see it, they won't see it.

He thought that would be too much to assume. To hold something of such value and not know what it was.

Running his hand along the dash, he opened the glove box. A small light came on, illuminating the neatly arranged contents. He removed each item one at a time, placing them on the passenger seat. There was an insurance certificate with the gray card showing ownership of the vehicle, a screwdriver, a cotton rag, a box of matches, and a silver hip flask from which he took a drink. The cognac inside was almost gone, the balance having been consumed earlier as he sat in the van outside a downtown bar. He'd driven there to wait for his wife's party to die out and her friends to disappear. Tom cared for none of them, but he loved his wife desperately and so he said nothing, or almost nothing.

He'd waited outside because he had been refused entrance into *Les Quatre Saisons Hotel-Bar*; a tie was required, the doorman had said. So he parked on the street opposite, drinking the rare cognac from the hip flask, waiting for the hours to pass and the party to end. Waiting for the rain to stop.

He lit a match and holding the flame under the insurance document, watched it run up the thick paper. Dropping the remains into the ashtray, he did the same with the gray card, as both were forgeries, manufactured for that evening's work.

The minute hand on the dash clock jumped up one number: it was twelve minutes to midnight. Grabbing the cotton rag, he moved to the back of the van, pushing away the box lid before carefully removing a painting.

Like the customs agent, he placed his finger in the lower right corner, touching the name of the artist. He then emptied the last of the cognac on the rag and rubbed it gently over the signature.

Tom squinted in the scant light. The painted letters began lifting off the canvass to reveal others. The first and second letters were clear: an R and then an E. He turned the rag again, pushing gently. An N and an O appeared. He took a deep breath, keeping his stroke delicate. The letter I came to life and finally an R. The year would be just below. He began to rub again. The date, 1862, became just as clear as the name. And like he had been told, even in the clouded light of the cargo van, a painting by Pierre-Auguste Renoir was a thing of beauty.

* * *

As if reading a note from a jilted mistress, Stuart Endfield stared at the folded squares of paper. They contained words from someone he wished he had never met, who refused to go away. Opening one of the squares, he studied the writing, looking for any errors, but there were none. The figures and the signatures were unfortunately accurate on each, and he possessed a number of them: eighteen in all.

Stuart Endfield was in trouble. The papers were duplicates of gambling markers with a local casino to the amount of over three and one-half million Belgian Francs or, in a figure that he could more easily understand, fifty-one thousand British Pounds. In either currency the numbers were overwhelming, almost suffocating, and time was running out. He had to make the bits of paper good.

Letting the marker fall to the desk, he looked out his second floor window of the British Embassy to Teverun Avenue below. The traffic was intense as always, with headlamps flashing and brake lights glaring, horns sounding and drivers gesturing. There were no pedestrians to be seen, save a woman pulling her handcart. Giving up on the crosswalk, she made a dash through traffic at the corner and was almost hit. Watching her possessions scatter on the sidewalk, Stuart Endfield gave a crooked grin—he expected nothing less.

To him the Belgians were little more than barbarians in such things. Their refusal to queue, and the lack of refuse bins along the street, put them but one step away from living in the jungle. His stay in Belgium was becoming hardship duty, needing to be supplemented. He mentioned this to the embassy paymaster, who would certainly look into it. That was six months ago, he'd heard nothing back.

Though even a major adjustment in his salary would not approach the money needed for the gambling markers in front of him. And if he did not pay soon, the gambler would contact his superiors at the embassy and tell all. Stuart Endfield had been threatened with this. It would be his doom. He would lose his position as secretary and be thrown out of the diplomatic service. The weight of this possibility crushed him. He could not sleep and could barely do his work. Two evenings before, he had considered suicide and pondered the options: a bullet to the head, carbon monoxide, or possibly poison. But he owned no gun, drove no automobile and had no idea which toxin should or could be purchased. He felt incapable of escaping his problems by any means. He felt he was drowning.

Then an offer was presented. Not through normal channels such as a letter in the post, a telephone call, or a planned meeting, but by way of a chance conversation at a cocktail bar. A word or two spoken in jest, but he knew the speaker, a man named Mégot, was serious. A large amount of money was mentioned for little effort on his part, but nothing more was said. Just to think about it. After days and weeks of living with his oppressive debts, he decided to bite the attractive hook.

In the last four hours, Stuart Endfield, the perfect Englishman, had made the conscious decision to become a crook.

The task was simple: he would remove a dossier of a man on file at the embassy, a man he had never heard of, and present it to Mégot; it would be studied for a few minutes and then returned. That was all. For this, Stuart Endfield would be paid three hundred thousand Belgian Francs or, as he quickly calculated, almost five thousand British Pounds.

It was not what he owed. But it would buy him some time. Some time to breathe, and so he did it.

Four hours earlier, before anyone arrived on the second floor and while the janitor was pushing his sweeper down the hall, he went into the file room and removed the dossier from the cabinet. He'd been given a key to the room some weeks before so he might use the photocopier inside after his broke. It was about that time Mégot had presented the hypothetical plot, so he kept the key. Sometimes he'd place it on his dining table, staring at it while he ate. It seemed to emit a certain power, a wonderful power. It was a way out.

The stolen file now lay on the table before him, next to the gambling markers and a contrast to the horror they represented. Anxiously, he looked at the clock on the far wall. It was five minutes before ten. The telephone call would come at any minute, the call from Mégot to see if he had been successful.

Stuart Endfield tapped the dossier's brown folder with his forefinger as he waited. He had not looked inside, unable to imagine what made it worth so much money. The traffic outside caused the window to vibrate slightly as the clock's minute hand jumped one tick. The telephone on his desk sat silent. He tapped his finger harder against the file, then flipped it open, keeping it at arm's length while his eyes moved along the words.

They read:
Name: Thomas Allan Breck
Nationality: American
Date of birth: April 22, 1948
Place of birth: San Francisco, California
Married: 1982 to French National, Michelle Rita de La Grave.

Background: Attended: St. Michael's Academy, Victoria, British Columbia, Canada—graduated 1968; attended: University of London, London, England—graduated 1972; attended: La Sorbonne de Bruxelles.

Listed Occupation: Art dealer

Actual Occupation: Contrabandist; Suspected smuggler of untaxed tobacco, liquor and wines from Netherlands into Britain; 1969-1972. Never arrested, never charged. Suspected smuggler of stolen artifacts from Eastern Bloc to the Benelux, 1973 to present. Never arrested, never charged. Currently living in Brussels, Rue Père Damien 26, Wolowe St. Pierre.

Pulling the file closer, Stuart Endfield let out a deep breath. The dossier was of no great importance. This man was not a friend of England, but an enemy, and he would not be betraying any trust by letting Mégot have a glimpse of it. He continued to read the single page file. It had been updated in the last six months, though nothing new had been added other than a list of accomplices who were also only suspects and never charged. Closing the file, he smiled. The money could be taken with no guilt. Stuart Endfield was doing nothing wrong.

The telephone rang. It was exactly ten o'clock. He placed the receiver to his ear, but said nothing.

"Monsieur Endfield?" came a voice. It was Mégot.

"Yes, speaking."

"Would you like to take a coffee?"

"I suppose… Yes, I would."

"That's good," said Mégot, his tone pleasant. "Do you know the hotel La Legende by La Grand´ Place?"

"No, I… Yes. Yes, I do know it."

"Good. That's good. Let us say in thirty minutes?"

"Very well. In thirty minutes."

"Please do not be late, Monsieur Endfield."

"I won't—I—"

The line went dead.

Letting the receiver drop into the cradle, Stuart Endfield stared straight ahead. The deal was on.

* * *

La Legende was an economical hotel, quite small and, as yet, non-rated by the government board. That is to say it had no stars by its name and afforded the guest few luxuries save its central location. There was no room-service waiter, bellman, concierge, or information director, and only by law did it serve food. This was done in the lobby, which, at this hour of the day, was known as the breakfast-room. Guests checking out mingled with others drinking coffee, and each seemed to be smoking a cigar, a cigarette, or pipe.

Through the haze, Stuart Endfield recognized the man he sought, sitting in the far corner, his lower face hidden by a French newspaper. Taking the chair opposite him, Endfield placed the briefcase at his feet and, folding his hands on the table, glanced at his watch. It was half-past ten.

"Good morning, Monsieur Endfield," said Mégot, peering over the newspaper. "Do you have it?"

"Yes."

Mégot folded paper, laying it between them. "Let me see it."

"In here?"

"Yes, monsieur. In here."

Sensing a need to show caution, Stuart Endfield glanced round the lobby. Satisfied everyone was harmless, he lifted the briefcase from the floor and removed the dossier, hurriedly slipping it under the newspaper.

Mégot took his time lighting a cigarette, then brushing the newspaper to the side, opened the file.

"Do you want some coffee, monsieur?" he asked.

"No... No, thank you."

"Did you have any difficulty getting this?"

"No, I didn't."

"That's good," said Mégot. "So, I may keep this, monsieur?"

Stuart Endfield's eyes widened. "No!" he said. "I must return it."

"You didn't make a copy?"

"No. That kind of paper—it's impossible to copy."

"How clever," said Mégot, retrieving a pen from his jacket. "The British are always so clever."

"Could you hurry, please?"

Mégot began to write on the corner of the newspaper. He took a long drag on his cigarette, then casually picked a piece of tobacco off the tip of his tongue.

"I say," repeated Stuart Endfield. "Could you hurry?"

Mégot said nothing.

Stuart Endfield grew more anxious. "Why do you want to know about this man?"

"Pardon me?" he said as if he had only just heard Stuart Endfield speaking.

"This man," he repeated, glancing at the front door of the lobby. "Why do you want to know about him?"

"Because he is interesting, monsieur."

"Interesting?"

"Yes, monsieur. He is interesting."

"But, why do you want him?"

"Did I say I want him, Monsieur Endfield?" Mégot responded curtly.

"No, only why—" Stuart Endfield thought better about continuing. Giving a thin smile, he pointed at the package of cigarettes on the table. "May I?"

Mégot nodded.

Awkwardly, Stuart Endfield lighted one, squeezing the filter effeminately between the tips of his fingers. He rarely smoked and it showed.

Mégot laid his pen on the table. "There, you can have the file," he said, exhaling deeply

Stuart Endfield quickly returned it to his briefcase. "May I have my money now?" he asked.

"Of course, monsieur," he replied, removing something from his jacket pocket.

Terror overcame Stuart Endfield and the cigarette fell from his grip. Mégot did not place any money on the table. No five or ten thousand Belgian Franc notes slid toward him, but a square of black paper which he recognized all too well. It was a gambling marker—an original that would certainly match one of the duplicates he possessed.

Calmly picking up Stuart Endfield's fallen cigarette, Mégot placed it in the ashtray. "The marker is for three hundred thousand francs, monsieur," he said, leaning back in his chair. "As per our agreement."

"Where did you—"

"I bought them, monsieur. I now own them," Mégot said indifferently. "I now own you."

Stuart Endfield was in shock. Placing his elbows on the table, he lowered his face into his upturned palms. He could feel his life spiraling down.

"There is something I would like you to do for me, monsieur," said Mégot, seemingly oblivious to Endfield's torment. "This man in the file you gave me. I would like you to talk with him. You did notice his name? You did look at the file?"

Stuart Endfield was silent, his face still pressed into his hands.

"Of course you did," continued Mégot, crushing his used cigarette in the ashtray before picking up the one discarded by

Endfield. "Anyway, monsieur, I would like you to speak with him. Be my... I don't know. My emissary, I suppose."

"No. I can't," blurted Endfield through his fingers. "I won't."

Mégot signaled to the waiter for more coffee. "But you will, monsieur, and I will tell you why." He spoke firmly, as if giving orders to a disruptive child. "I am asking you to do something very simple and for this I will return an additional marker. If you do not, then I will be obliged to notify your superiors at the embassy of the situation."

Endfield slowly lifted his head. "But you do not understand," he said, his voice pleading. "I would be kicked out of the diplomatic service. The humiliation. You do not understand."

"But I do understand," said Mégot loudly, his tone angry. "I understand such things completely. Now we will discuss it no further, monsieur. You will speak with this man as I ask."

The waiter appeared. He placed a dented tin pot on the table and then left.

"Coffee?" said Mégot, lifting the pot.

"When?"

"Monsieur?"

"When do I speak with this man?"

"I will let you know."

"And what am I to say?"

"That, I will also let you know." Mégot dropped a cube of sugar into his cup. There was an uncomfortable silence, broken only by the clinking sound of the spoon against the cup. "It is curious, monsieur," he continued. "You have not asked me why. Why should I want *you* to do this? Why do I not simply speak to this man myself?"

Endfield stared at Mégot through the floating cigarette smoke. "Would you tell me?" he asked.

Mégot laughed. "No, I would not. It is just curious, that's all." Taking the gambling marker from the table, he shoved it in Endfield's breast pocket. "You will hear from me, monsieur."

Without another word Endfield stood. He wanted to turn and walk away, but felt unable to move. He stared at a faded poster on the wall, thinking the blackmailer would ask for something else, something more he needed to know for which there would be no answer. But he only heard the sound of breakfast dishes being thrown into a sink and whispers in languages he did not understand.

* * *

After adjusting the napkin on her lap for the second time, Michelle Breck placed her elbows on the table, pressing her hands together as if she were about to pray. She stared down the long table at her husband while he poured a cup of coffee.

"Well it's nice to see you finally shaved," she said caustically.

Tom Breck smiled, but said nothing.

"Where were you last evening?" she asked.

Stirring cream into his cup, he looked at his wife. The dining room was now silent, except for the faint sound of the maid in the near kitchen and the rustle of his wife adjusting her napkin once again. Her beauty broke through the sour look she forced upon her face as she waited for a reply. Even with her lips pursed and brows frowning their disapproval, she was the most beautiful woman he had ever known—the only woman he had ever loved.

"I had a meeting," he said, gently resting the spoon on the saucer. "About a painting."

"Until two in the morning?" she asked.

"I'm sorry about the party, Michelle."

"No, you're not."

Tom did not respond. He knew there was no point. Her side of the conversation had been prepared during the night; each question and each response already contrived.

"Antoine Débuchere waited until midnight to speak with you," she said, straightening the salt and pepper shakers on the table. "It was something important."

"I thought he was here. I noticed most of the fifty-year-old cognac was gone."

"Guests are supposed to enjoy themselves," she blurted.

"Not that much, they're not."

She appeared angry and about to speak when the maid entered the dining room, carrying a large silver tray.

"Good morning, Chantal," said Tom, relieved by her appearance.

"Monsieur," she responded, appearing indifferent to the tension in the room. Lowering the tray slightly, she moved toward the far end of the table, displaying the toast and two omelets it held.

"Nothing for me, Chantal," said Michelle, waving her off. "I'm not hungry."

"Well, I am," said Tom, removing his coffee cup from the plate before him. "What kind of omelets do we have this morning?"

"Plain omelets, monsieur," replied the maid. "Madame mentioned we should start watching our diet."

Tom stared at the two yellow wedges. "I see," he said softly. "Do we have any fruit?"

"I did not have time to shop this morning, monsieur," she apologized.

"But what time did you leave last evening, Chantal?" he asked.

"When everyone had gone," Michelle replied, sounding irritated.

"Busses run past midnight?" he asked.

"Antoine gave her a ride," said Michelle, again answering for the maid.

"Chantal," he said, and looking at his wife, added, "Why don't you take the remainder of the day off."

The maid appeared startled. "Monsieur?"

"You've worked enough in the last twenty-four hours," he informed her, lighting a cigarette. "You need a day off."

"But—"

"We'll see you tomorrow, Chantal."

"Very good, monsieur," she concurred, averting her eyes from her mistress as she turned, tray in hand, and hurriedly left the room.

Tom waited for the firestorm that was certain to come from the other end of the table. But nothing came. Michelle, his beautiful wife, remained silent.

He wondered why he had done it, as he looked at her through the white smoke of his cigarette. Why he had chosen to embarrass his wife in front of the maid. Why he had not asked her opinion and included her in the decision. Michelle lived with him and shared his bed, but not his life. She knew nothing of his affairs or where the money came from that allowed them such a comfortable life. Half-truths concealed the source, distancing her further from who he was. He felt her slipping away, hiding behind her own secrets.

I love you, beauty. Do you know how much I love you? Do you know?

He knew she did not.

The maid stood in the hallway with her coat buttoned, adjusting her scarf for the long wait at the bus stop, when the telephone rang. Tom looked through the glass doors, watching her perform the final duty of the day.

She spoke into the receiver, tugging at the scarf with her free hand. She nodded and letting her arm fall, opened the French doors slightly.

"It's for you, monsieur."

"Who is it?" he asked, unwilling to leave the table before an armistice could be arranged.

"I do not know," she replied. "He has an accent, monsieur. It sounds distant."

"I really don't wish to speak with anyone."

"He said it is important, monsieur."

"Very well." He moved toward the waiting telephone. He would finish the conversation as quickly as possible, then return to his wife.

Taking the receiver, he heard static racing through the line.

"Yes," he said.

"It's me."

Tom recognized the speaker. "You are not to telephone here," he said softly.

"I know that," said the voice. "It is about Tatiana."

Tom's eyes narrowed. "Yes—yes, what is it?"

"She has been arrested."

The static grew so loud that Tom moved the receiver slightly. "Did you say arrested, Yuri?" he asked, using the caller's name. If the police were now involved, their secret was out and there was no need for further discretion.

"Yes, this morning." Yuri's voice now sounded frantic. "It was the State Police, out of uniform. They came to the house."

"What were the charges?"

"There were none. No charges, not a word except she was under arrest," he shouted over the hissing line. "Did you have trouble yesterday?"

"No, nothing. It all went well."

"Then I don't understand," Yuri said, his voice breaking. "What can we do?"

The front door of the house clicked shut, startling Tom. Turning quickly, he saw the maid had gone. "The charges," he said, trying to think of an answer. "You must find out the charges and then we can arrange to get her out on bail."

"There is no bail in Hungary," said Yuri. "But—"

"What? What is it?"

"I'm not sure," he replied so faintly Tom could barely hear. "I'll call you when I find out."

74

"Right away. You call me right away."

The line went dead. Yuri was gone.

Slowly replacing the receiver onto the cradle, Tom turned to look through the glass of the French doors into the dining room. But he saw nothing, other than memories that hit him like a jolt—the memories of a decade earlier, when it all changed. He had been able, until that very moment, to keep it all hidden, nicely tucked away from his day-to-day thoughts.

It had been this same month, ten years before—maybe it was even the same day, but he didn't allow himself to remember if it was. He did remember the rain outside his apartment window in London, and taking the telephone call from the attorney in San Francisco while he stared into the bleak morning light. He remembered the words spoken by the man, each one economical— as if there were a tariff on them—while he informed Tom that his parents were dead.

An automobile accident on the Pacific Coast Highway, single car, the attorney had said, hinting it was somehow less serious with no other parties were involved, and no potential litigation. Tom's father had been drunk, possibly more than usual, with his business problems as they were. He had been unable to negotiate a bend in the road and his car had dropped two hundred feet down into the surf. And of course, there were the rocks.

The attorney had asked Tom what he should do, in words still spoken so sparingly, insinuating there was an option to the terrible news. That if he answered quickly enough, none of it need be true.

Could you bring them back? Tom wanted to ask. There are some things I would like to say; there are some things I forgot to say. Could you bring them back? But he didn't respond to the attorney's question, other than state he would catch the next plane out.

He tried to remember the flight, and the taxi ride into San Francisco, but he couldn't. Only the ceiling of gray-black clouds above the cemetery was clear in his memory. Stacked one on top of the other, they floated across the sky in uneven measure. Those closest to the ground seemed to move quickest, as if to avoid the priest's futile words. Chapter and verse, Tom remembered thinking, so the man in the black robe wouldn't

75

have to think on his feet or say something more kind than was due. And it was kept brief. Then one casket was lowered, followed by the other. Just a few steps apart, they disappeared into the ground and were covered, and it was over.

The half-dozen mourners then departed, save for the attorney who gripped a ledger Tom needed to read. He placed it on the hood of the waiting limousine, explaining, with the painful nature of this business, it was best done quickly and besides, there was so little to go over. Flipping to a page marked by a clip, he stated in the same manner he'd used on the telephone two days earlier that there was nothing left; the Breck family money was gone. Then, before Tom could speak, he interpreted the rows of numbers, that the brackets indicated a negative figure. There were many brackets, touching everything beyond the remnants of the family business to include the house and its furnishings, all mortgaged to the hilt.

"To the hilt," Tom had whispered, uncertain what it meant, as if it were some legal slang to include the attorney in the list of creditors.

There was a cashier's check attached to the final page of the ledger; it was for the sum of thirteen thousand dollars and if Tom would only sign his name he could have it, then be on his way.

Tom had hesitated, not because there was an alternative to barter for a better deal, but because he was staring at the end of a family fortune once rumored to be one of the greatest in San Francisco—a family fortune reduced to the value of a used car by way of neglect and drunkenness. In only thirty years, Tom's father had wiped out four generations of family toil.

Or that is what the attorney alluded to while his manicured finger jabbed at the dotted line with Tom's name underneath. "Sign here," he had said repeatedly. "Sign here and we can close the books on this sordid business." It all came out like a threat, insinuating the secret would be safe, if Tom would only sign.

Taking the gold-plated pen offered him, he recalled the bank of clouds, a somber backdrop to the attorney's clothing: the light green tailored suit, cream-colored shirt and magenta tie. It all seemed so inappropriate, the man attired like a circus clown at his parent's funeral. Tom remembered his anger at the lack of respect while he signed his name before slapping the ledger to the ground.

He'd then caught the first available flight back to Europe—to Amsterdam, but he didn't care. He only wanted to be away. Sometimes he glanced at the cashier's check before shoving it back into his breast pocket, knowing his life would never be the same; knowing that he was alone for the first time, and what he must do.

In Holland he had boarded the first train south to Rotterdam and after less than two hours exploring the city, took a room in a small hotel overlooking the harbor. It was cramped and uncomfortable, but it allowed an unhindered view of the inland port.

He could see the cargo moving between the trucks and train cars and ships. It was all very methodical and would have moved at a greater speed were it not for the customs house. Each truck was obliged to stop there and present a declaration of goods. This is what he studied, hour after hour, from his third floor window.

He tried to discover how the customs officers chose which trucks to search, and those to leave alone. The truck's size did not seem to be a determining factor, nor did one transport company receive preference over another. Using binoculars, he could make out the shipper's name printed on the cab doors and covering canopies, but there appeared to be no pattern to the searches. Whether the truck was new or old, clean or dirty; whether the license plates were Dutch or French; whether the driver was light or dark skinned; whether the goods were exposed to the weather or not, being tobacco products or clothing or automobile parts—he saw no discernible guide by which the customs officers operated. It appeared purely random.

By the fourth day Tom had calculated that one in sixteen trucks was searched, though the busier hours seemed to give the greatest single advantage. And it was the same for the train cars, save for one difference: the flatbeds that held a single container were searched approximately one out of every thirty times—much greater odds, though he had no way of knowing what they contained, leaving a variable which could take weeks to determine. This was a luxury he did not have.

After five days in the small hotel, he had returned to London and giving notice on his apartment, moved his possessions to the coastal city of Dover where he rented a two-story summer home that was available till May. This gave him time. After purchasing a high power telescope, he began his study of the near harbor—specifically the trucks arriving from the continent by boat. Like Rotterdam, it was all perfectly mechanical, though that is where the similarities ended.

The British customs officer was much more vigilant, almost tyrannical. One in three trucks was searched, not one in sixteen, and though the single container trucks were inspected less frequently, inspections were nearly as ruthless. After two days of watching the activity on the docks, Tom remembered thinking his odds were no better than those offered by the flip of a coin. This would not do.

He had briefly considered choosing a different country in which to carry out his scheme, but the outrageous British taxation on luxury goods was too tempting to resist.

At the end of the third day he had returned to London, where he cashed the check for the thirteen thousand dollars, then directly caught a flight for Budapest. He recalled this being the easiest part of his plan, as, within two days of his arrival in the Communist country, he had managed to exchange the thirteen thousand dollars on the black market for the equivalent of twenty-five thousand dollars in Hungarian forints.

With this money he called upon the Marlboro cigarette factory, a factory duly licensed by Phillip-Morris, and made a proposal to the manager: Tom would purchase five hundred cases of the cigarettes on the condition the red and white packages be slightly altered. All Hungarian writing was to be replaced with English— English identical to packages of Marlboros found in London or Glasgow or any British city. The manager at first refused, claiming the request was highly irregular and possibly illegal. However, after Tom handed him the equivalent of one year's salary in cash, the retooling of the printing machines began.

Having one week before the completion of this step, Tom began visiting art galleries in Budapest, informing the directors he sought an artist particularly adept with pen and ink, for a commission of work depicting Hungarian rural life. Each director was accommodating and at the end of the first day, Tom had the names of thirty artists, all masters with pen and ink.

He started at the top of the list and needing to show great caution, arranged an appointment with the artist. He kept it casual, before letting their conversation drift to politics. If the artist appeared content with his life, or possibly pro-Communist, Tom excused himself and moved to the next name. He always went to the artist's studio, where he could observe their lifestyle, evaluating the quality of material items like the carpeting, the glassware and the furniture, noting if there were a radio or a television or record player. The more expense shown in such things, the more likely the artist would be to accept Tom's commission, a commission that could bring wealth.

After two days of searching, he had found no one acceptable and was at the end of his list, save for one. The final artist was different, not because she was French, nor because she lived in one of the more upscale neighborhoods of the city—her flat was furnished as well as any home in the West—but because she seemingly had a bodyguard. A man some ten years her senior who had a noticeable Slavic accent, much different from Hungarian or Czech, and Tom imagined it Russian, upon hearing his name was Yuri.

Occasionally when the artist spoke, she had the same accent, lingering just above the French words she used. Something so subtle would probably go unnoticed to the average listener, but Tom heard it and he knew a part of what he needed in an artist was present: she had a secret, and it was well guarded in her French persona.

The meeting went one hour, then two, but Tom did not bother having her sketch a pastoral scene of the Hungarian countryside. Instead, he immediately presented a small crest, no larger than the head of a tack, which he wished her to mimic. In less than five minutes, after retrieving her pens and inks, she had. He remembered it being identical, perfect in colors and size, but something had put him back. She'd calmly asked, how many he would like? One thousand? Ten thousand? Fifty thousand?

Informing her he would need enough for every package inside five hundred cases of cigarettes, she had simply nodded before saying the crests would be placed at appropriate intervals on strips of clear tape; a simple machine could be fabricated for such a process, she added. The color blue would be on one side, with the color green on the other, any white being unnecessary as the package bottom was itself that color. The tape would be pressed tight, then cut by razor, bonding unnoticed to the clear plastic wrapper. That final part of the work, she had further explained, being the most laborious, could be accomplished by a handful of elderly women she knew in a small village not far away; the price being a few forints per carton. It should take less than one week.

Was that acceptable? he remembered her saying before referring to the crests as tax stamps, which they were.

And is there anything further? she had asked, and he recalled that he did not immediately reply, but handed her a series of documents, mostly boilerplate—import-export forms and purchase orders with receipts—which he wanted duplicated.

Again she had nodded at the simplicity of his request, informing him that paper of such quality would be difficult to obtain, though not impossible; could he give her two days?

He had agreed to that, and to all the rest over a bottle of wine that Yuri obediently served them in the dining room. The timing, the method, the quality, was all perfect, leaving Tom one final negotiation: what was her price for such work?

And with this question she did not hesitate, as if she had determined her response hours earlier. She immediately needed enough money to complete the job at hand—less than one hundred dollars, she had calculated, though for her work she wanted something greater: she wanted to be his partner, requesting twenty percent of the profits when the job was complete.

She then again asked, was this acceptable?

Tom recalled those words and that moment as clearly as anything in his life. The woman with the shoulder-length black hair and the clear blue eyes, unblinking while she waited for his response, was willing to do her work for something different. She was betting on Tom, placing her faith in his ability to succeed, seeming to know he would. And initially taken back by such a declaration, he had found himself warning that he might not be successful; that it might take months, and he had no way of knowing what her share would actually be. But she had only raised her hand as if to say she understood. She was willing to take such a risk.

They made a toast to seal the bargain and the following morning, the work began. The documents were ready within two days and the tax stamps within five, as were the cigarettes, which were picked up by truck with no difficulties. The elderly women—all widowed and on meager pensions—proved to be industrious in attaching the tax stamps, completing the job inside of forty-eight hours.

Tom then booked the five hundred cases on a Hungarian Malev cargo flight of which he was also a passenger. From his window, as the plane taxied from the gate, he saw his partner standing in a field just beyond the terminal, the man Yuri at her side. They both raised their arms to say good-bye, like relatives wishing he travel safely. He remembered it well, and the weight of their faith in him added to the upcoming gamble.

When the Malev flight landed in Paris, Tom took a connection on to Scotland with his cargo. He contacted a local shipping company in Glasgow, informing them that an error had been made with a shipment of cigarettes, and would they please forward the five hundred cases on to Amsterdam?

This was not normal procedure, though not uncommon. The purchasers of his goods could have changed their minds or, in this case, as Tom had explained, they'd had insufficient funds. By this method the cigarettes were not inspected by British customs but merely picked up by the shipping company and moved on to the Netherlands, where this time Tom explained that he personally had made a great error: the cigarettes were in fact destined for England and would the shipping company truck them there by way of Dover?

Tom remembered the shipping agent laughing at his foolishness and offering Tom a slight discount, which he accepted. However, Tom had not been foolish, nor was he the bumbling cigarette salesman he pretended to be. It was all part of the plan. Now the shipping company had a single bill of lading that indicated the cargo of cigarettes originated in Scotland, with no mention of Budapest or Paris, and this is what the driver of the truck would present to British customs.

Or this is what Tom imagined as he paced across the second floor bedroom of his house in Dover. He recalled being unable to eat while he waited for the cargo to arrive on one of the incoming ferries. His eye pressed to the telescope, he studied each truck, looking for the shipping company's name; looking for anything irregular. He had also begun to drink as the stress seemed to mount with each passing hour, and an empty cognac bottle sat at his feet, beside another freshly opened.

Did the shipping company suspect something? Had they voiced their suspicions to customs upon arrival? The cigarettes might even be stolen in transit. Though he had purchased insurance, it was merely for show; any investigation would reveal he used a fake name, making it impossible to collect. The chances of failure had mounted in his thoughts before the cargo truck finally rolled off the ferry at Dover.

The driver's innocence of anything unusual was possibly the greatest single advantage as he handed the bill of lading to the customs man. Looking through the telescope, Tom saw few words exchanged before one case of cigarettes was removed from the truck, then another, until twelve cases sat on the asphalt, each being carefully inspected.

Tom recalled the perspiration that sometimes clouded his view in the telescope. He again watched the customs man's demeanor while holding the clipboard with the bill of lading attached. Then, it was over. The customs man issued a series of papers to the driver and the cases were returned to the truck.

It had worked: the American cigarettes, obviously having originated in Scotland and possessing all British tax stamps, had returned to England, and were free to go.

After watching the truck move up the hill to catch the A-26 to London, Tom had collapsed onto the floor. The weight of the stress and the liquor had caught up with him. But he didn't care.

The next day he paid off the shipping company, asking them to store the cargo until a buyer could be found, which was accomplished within twenty-four hours. The owner of a grocery store chain purchased all five hundred cases at a discount of eight percent below wholesale and, with no argument, paid in cash.

The Breck family fortune, so callously lost, was slowly returning. Tom remembered the stacks of twenty-pound notes that filled his safety deposit box, but he felt a joy almost as great upon returning to Budapest. He and his partner shared a bottle of wine after Tom gave her the twenty-percent as promised, sharing his good fortune with someone who had trusted him, unconditionally.

It was then she had taken his hand and told him she was not French, asking that he excuse her slight deception. She then told him to call her Tatiana: "My name is Tatiana Gregòsh."

It was all so long ago, but Tom remembered it well.

And he knew that he must move quickly if he were to now save her, before the police started pounding on *his* door. He needed to get rid of the painting hidden in the garage; only then could he safely help Tatiana.

Lost in his concern, he pushed the French doors open, noticing that Michelle's chair was empty. He had been looking into the room, but did not see her leave.

About to call out her name, he heard a car engine turn over. Pulling back the window curtain, he saw her Mercedes coupe race along the white gravel drive toward the street. The brake lights flashed briefly, then she was gone.

He instinctively looked at the dining table. Balanced against her plate was a note. He read the words:

Tom,
I am going home for a time. I will telephone later.
Michelle

Home, he thought. That meant her father's house south of Paris. The house she grew up in, the house she spoke of often; a place where she could still be a little girl and no one would mind.

Her father told him that all of her life she had been protected, possibly too much, and it was too late to change. Was Tom prepared to protect her? Protect her from everything? Did he love her enough? If he could, if he would, there might be a chance. If not, he'd best be on his way.

He had been warned.

But Tom did love her enough; she was the only woman he had ever loved.

The telephone sounded. He ran back into the hallway and lifted the receiver, but there was only the drone of a waiting line.

* * *

Inspector Jules Beauviér had thought better of it and hung up the telephone. There was more to the telex that sat before him than a simple inquiry. Much more, and he could feel it.

An oil painting had been found in the safe of an art dealer who had died the evening before of a heart attack. The fact that an art dealer possessed a painting was not unusual, but this was the only painting he owned and was by Claude Monet. Everything else in the gallery was a print or a copy and of little value. A second-rate art dealer possessed a painting worth millions of francs, whose author was long since dead and its whereabouts unknown for the last forty years. This demanded more than a simple telephone call.

Taking the telex from the desk, he reread it, to be certain of each word. It had been sent by the prefect of police in Namur, where the art dealer was found slumped in the archway of his front door. The telex read that the dead man was eighty-three years old and there was no sign of anything irregular. It had been a fatal heart attack and a routine inspection by the coroner. The painting was discovered in a safe that had been found closed, though not locked. Its singular position in the steel vault caused the inspecting officer to take note of the artist.

And there was something else. Written on the back of the painting's frame was a seven-digit number followed by a series of letters. None of it made sense at first, but the prefect of police often traveled to Brussels and drove through the commune of Wolowe St. Pierre, the most direct route to the Hotel Ste. Claire police station. The letters etched into the wooden frame were *WStP,* as if to remind the writer where he was calling, as the numbers more than likely belonged to a local telephone. The age of the art dealer could possibly be the reason for such a fundamental reminder or perhaps it was simply an act of habit.

From this the seven numbers could be placed in proper order. The first three digits were 387, but there was no such prefix in Wolowe St. Pierre—only 785, 784 and 783. Assuming the last four digits to be constant, the prefect of police consulted a reverse telephone directory. If need be, the last four digits could be moved about until all possibilities were exhausted.

However, there seemed no need. The first name to arise from the puzzle belonged to a registered foreigner living in Wolowe St. Pierre. An American by the name of Thomas Allan Breck who listed his occupation as an art dealer—a self-employed art dealer with no place of business, but who nevertheless maintained a two-hectare estate in the most exclusive commune in Brussels.

The Namur prefect of police felt an inquiry should be made and so did Inspector Jules Beauviér of the Belgian Gendarmerie. But not too hastily.

The painting was now in a police van on its way to the University of Ghent, where a noted professor of art history would determine its authenticity; if it were a fake then nothing more than fraud could be charged, if that, with no obvious victim. If it turned out to be authentic, then... The crimes began mounting in Beauviér's head. For starters, he'd present charges of theft, smuggling and tax evasion to the Tribunal at the appropriate time. And only then. Inspector Beauviér was a patient man, and not usually excited.

Until August of 1984, Jules Beauviér had been recently retired and living in the town of Brugges by the coast. He had a cottage one kilometer from the beach with a small garden incapable of growing anything but sand. A lifelong bachelor, he reluctantly purchased a dog for companionship, but it had run away almost immediately, leaving him again to his boredom, his garden and, after just six months, retirement was killing him.

Then the call arrived from the minister of justice; the man near panic. His country needed Jules Beauviér and he was being reinstated by order of King Bedouin, or so he was told, a request impossible to refuse.

The minister of justice described a dire situation: a gang of four thieves known as *Les Maudits* was attacking the large supermarchés throughout Belgium in an extremely violent manner. Entering a supermarché in the late afternoon, they fired off a burst from an automatic weapon before robbing the customers, rifling the registers and finally the safe. An additional burst of automatic weapon-fire signaled their escape, which they always made in a recently stolen Volkswagen GTI. Then, within one kilometer or less, they transferred to a Mercedes four-liter sedan or greater. It was always the same, they were still on the loose, and something must be done.

Beauviér knew the situation and the method of operation. He also knew the minister of justice was as concerned with keeping his own job as finding the violent thieves, but politics didn't interest Beauviér. He was a policeman, nothing more. The minister of justice could blather on, justifying the initial failure of the Gendarmerie, as long as he wished. The facts were simple: Beauviér was back on the force and away from his garden of sand.

It had taken him but three months and eight days to end the terror of *Les Maudits*. They struck once more before he could convince the minister of his simple plan by first, announcing the hopelessness of the situation to the press: the police could be present at most supermarchés in the country, though not all, as there were not that many men available. And there were not. However secondly, and unannounced to the press, he conscripted the army, a dormant service since the end of colonial hold on the Congo—an adequately trained military which did little but dress for parade, would immediately begin moonlighting.

The profile of the police was high, almost extreme, as they stood guard in the parking areas and within the supermarchés forcing *Les Maudits* to take the path of least resistance—to attack those supermarchés clearly left unguarded. But they were not. Soldiers out of uniform sat in their personal cars just outside the remaining supermarchés or walked their aisles, and waited. The most expensive police operation in Belgian history was underway.

Two months and twelve days later the thieves struck. The soldiers, having had no enemy to fight in over twenty years, were keen for a skirmish and not in the mood for prisoners. And they took none. The

85

Volkswagen GTI, trying to exit the parking area at high speed, was caught in a crossfire. It was a slaughter. The make of the car and its occupants became unrecognizable when the fuel tank exploded in the one-sided firefight. Allowing the fire to burn itself out in a victory pyre, the soldiers radioed to their commander, who in turn informed Beauviér that the terror of *Les Maudits* was over.

And so was Beauviér's job on the force. After a small celebration and the awards ceremony where he received medals from both the Gendarmerie and the military, Beauviér was told he would be allowed to stay in his office for the month of December if he wished. After that it was back to Brugges, the high winds of the North Sea, and the garden.

Until now.

He looked at a small calendar on his desk. It was Thursday, December 2, 1984. He had twenty-nine days left at his post as an Inspector of the Belgian Gendarmerie, with all its powers. Twenty-nine days in which to find out everything he could about a mysterious painting of remarkable value and its one link, an American art dealer with no known place of business.

Pushing the intercom button on his telephone, Beauviér lifted the receiver.

A voice came on the line. "Yes, Inspector."

"I need a car and driver, Sergeant," he said, his eyes still fixed on the small calendar.

"Of course, Inspector," said the officer. "Where shall I say you'll be going?"

"I'll be going nowhere, Sergeant," said Beauviér. "I need someone followed."

"I see, Inspector."

"Is there a problem?"

"No, monsieur," he replied. "It's just that you will need someone very capable for such an assignment and—" The line went dead.

Abruptly, there was a knock on Beauviér's door.

"Enter," he said, still holding the receiver.

The door opened and in walked the sergeant he had been speaking with. "Pardon me, Inspector," said the young officer, breathing rapidly. "But I would be the man you want for such an assignment."

"It will be twenty-four hours a day, Sergeant. Not eight to five like you have at this time. It could be very boring. I do not even know what I'm looking for—"

"Yes, monsieur," the sergeant interrupted. "I understand completely. I will follow this man everywhere he goes, only sleep when he sleeps and take note of everything he does, twenty-four hours a day. Is there anything else?"

"Yes, Sergeant," said Beauviér softly. "Have you ever followed someone before?"

There was a pause. "No, monsieur."

"But you've trained for it?"

"Yes, like all cadets, monsieur."

Beauviér shook his head. "I do not want a police vehicle used. Do you have a car?"

"Yes, monsieur."

"Do you have a gun?"

"No, monsieur."

Placing his elbows on the desk, Beauviér folded his hands together. "You have always been a desk officer?"

"Yes, monsieur."

"Why do you want to do this?"

"I want to be a policeman," said the sergeant, clearly not apologizing for his position.

Beauviér stood, slowly turning to look out his window at the police parking area. The motorcycle officers in from the winter weather had lined their machines in perfect order, one after the other against the far brick wall. They were Harley-Davidson motorcycles from America and Beauviér thought them absurd. They were too big and too loud for the small roads they patrolled. The officers could drive state-of-the-art BMW motorcycles designed for the confining cobblestone streets of Brussels, or even the newer Japanese bikes that could run circles around their American counterparts. But the thundering machines won over the motorcycle police and the bureaucrats agreed. Both groups, thought Beauviér, had seen too many movies.

"So you want to be a policeman," he whispered.

"I beg your pardon, monsieur."

Beauviér quickly turned and said in a firm voice, "Go get a gun. A sidearm, anything you're comfortable with… and a two-way radio. We must be in touch with one another at all times, understood?"

"Yes, monsieur."

"Find someone to immediately replace you at your desk. You—What is your name, Sergeant?"

"Martin," replied the young man. "Sergeant Henri Martin."

"Very well, Sergeant Martin." Beauviér took the telex from his desk. "Read this on the way to requisition. We don't have much time."

"Yes, monsieur."

Watching the young policeman move out the door and down the hall, Beauviér whispered, "We have twenty-nine days, Sergeant Martin. Twenty-nine days."

CHAPTER TWO

In 1872 the city of Buda, situated on the right bank of the Danube River, and the city of Pest, on the opposite shore, decided for commercial reasons to become one. For the next three-quarters of a century, Budapest stumbled in and out of prosperity and wars along with the rest of Europe, until its takeover in 1948 by communists. Almost overnight, the Hungarian economy fell into third world status, along with her capital city. Desperate for Western currencies from any source, the communist bureaucracy began turning its eye to otherwise, questionable immigrants. Deutsche marks, French francs and the like, bought any fugitive from the West a comfortable lifestyle and protection, as Hungary maintained no extradition treaties, save for Moscow. Like in the American Wild West, many of Budapest's wealthier inhabitants were dubbed, 'The Hole in the Wall Gang,' because they were untouchable as long as their money held out, unless of course, they were outbid.

* * *

She had changed her name. For over twenty years she was Alice Malinaud, artist and French citizen living abroad. She used the name as a cover, hoping everyone would continue past and let her be. And up to now, they had.

The two policemen, dressed in suits and topcoats, arrived at her home on the Pest side of the Danube River in the early morning. The words one of them spoke at the front door—that she was under arrest; bring nothing but one suitcase—didn't frighten her. In a strange way, she had been prepared for those words. But after twenty years as Alice Malinaud, being identified by a name she knew as a child did frighten her. The policeman opening the rear door of the car called her Tatiana Gregòsh.

89

Neither man spoke when they drove past the police station. The black sedan raced by the well-known jail, continuing on the two-lane road that bordered the Danube, and Tatiana just assumed there was a more suitable place for such a wanted criminal. Something more secured.

She had not been handcuffed and was offered a cigarette that she refused, again without a word spoken. Rolling her window down a half-turn, with no objection from the men in the front seat, she let the winter wind push against her hair. Her initial fear at hearing her given name spoken had temporarily subsided, though now she was concerned for Yuri.

He had seen the two policemen coming up the walk and intended to confront them, but Tatiana said he should hide. If they were after her, then she would need his help. If they were after him, then he would need hers. Either way, a showdown with two members of the State Police would aid no one.

For only the second time in twenty years, Tatiana and Yuri were separated.

The black sedan continued on at a leisurely pace, the ashen sky of the December morning hugging their route. They journeyed over thirty kilometers in as many minutes before the driver pulled onto the gravel drive of a small hotel situated on a protruding bank of the Danube. The hotel's walls, and even the roof, had been painted an uneven gray, seeming to match the winter shade of the river.

Parking the car by the hotel entrance, the driver went inside as the second policeman opened Tatiana's door. He held it in place like a hired chauffeur, indicating that she follow the driver. She pulled the lapels of her topcoat tight about her neck, listening to the uneven sound of their feet on the gravel. They moved into the lobby, its interior cold and musty. There was the clatter of a furnace engaging as dust blew from a near floor vent.

A back door on the riverside of the hotel slammed shut. The driver appeared and walking to the reception desk, briefly studied a series of room keys held to the wall by hooks—there were eight in all. He removed one and signaling to Tatiana, she followed him up the near stairs. The other policeman remained behind, leaning against the front door as he lit a Russian cigarette.

Tatiana brushed against the staircase wallpaper. It was riddled with holes, as was the carpeting that continued down the hall of the second floor. She stared at the four doors ahead of her, each one closed, save for the one farthest from the stairs, the one that faced the river. The policeman pointed to it and she obliged, slowly walking inside the room.

Turning quickly, she cried, "Why am I here?"

For the second time that morning the policeman spoke. "Why is anyone, anywhere?" he asked in turn. "For the money, Tatiana Gregòsh. For the money."

The door shut and the lock clicked over when, somewhere on the Danube, a ship's horn bellowed.

* * *

Tom had heard nothing further from Yuri and felt time working against him. He needed to clean up any lose-ends, anything that could be used as evidence against him or Tatiana. And there was one such bit of evidence in the city of Namur, eighty kilometers southeast of Brussels.

He ran from his house to the garage and climbed into a car parked at the far end. Turning the ignition of the Jensen Interceptor, he watched the needle of the tachometer dance about as the engine, rocking on its mounts, attempted to idle. The outsized cam, turning over like a square Ferris wheel, forced a lumbering roar out the exhaust that reverberated off the garage walls. The English-made coupe with the American engine was preposterous, and he knew it. It consumed more fuel in the space of one kilometer than a fully laden transport, and occasional electrical problems would sometimes shut down the entire vehicle. So he rarely drove it, instead keeping it in the garage and under cover ready to be used for one purpose. Only a handful of cars in Belgium could keep pace with the Jensen, and the local police or Gendarmerie operated none. With the arrest of Tatiana and fear of his world unraveling, that purpose was invoked.

He had no intention of being followed.

Backing the rumbling Jensen onto the gravel drive, he looked to the house, its storm shutters lowered. With the temperature continuing to fall, the maid had closed them, arguing that it would save on electricity. His wife would have disapproved. She never concerned herself with saving money; there were other things more important, and Tom found it easier to say nothing.

He had not heard from Michelle, though she should be at her father's house by now. It was just south of Paris in the village of Milly-La-Forêt, though not a word, not even from her father to say she was well. Tom wanted to go after her, to bring her home if she would agree, but it was impossible now. Tatiana had been arrested and the painting must be disposed of. He needed to rid himself of the evidence and he needed the money. The cost of his latest enterprise was staggering. Cash was falling through his fingers.

Responding to a bare touch on the accelerator, the rear tires spit the white gravel back, pushing the car along the drive and out to the street. He turned toward the autoroute heading east toward Luxembourg. Once on it he would meet no serious police presence as the speed limit, marked at 130 kilometers per hour, was rarely enforced. Tom did not bother looking into his rearview mirror for anything irregular. In a few minutes he would be pushing the Jensen to over 200 kilometers an hour and nothing could follow. So he did not bother to check the mirror. This was another mistake.

* * *

Sergeant Henri Martin stared at the white steam hissing from the radiator cap as the whistling sound began to soften and a clattering noise took its place. He looked closer at the overworked engine, trying to determine the source, before realizing it came from the two-way radio attached to his belt. He hurriedly lifted it to his mouth.

"Yes, Inspector," he said.

"Where are you, Martin?" asked Beauviér, his voice clear.

"The autoroute to Luxembourg, monsieur."

"Very good, Sergeant. When did he leave his house?"

Flipping open a small notebook, Martin glanced at his watch. "Thirty-one minutes ago, monsieur. At two-fifteen."

"Are you keeping a safe distance?"

Martin stared down the long stretch of highway. "You could say that, monsieur," he replied.

"What is it, Sergeant? Is there something wrong?"

"It's his car, Inspector," he answered reluctantly. "I've never seen anything like it."

"What are you talking about?"

"I was approximately two hundred meters behind when suddenly, it took off, like I was standing still, monsieur. I accelerated to 190 but he kept gaining and then my car overheated and... Well... Here I am."

"Are you broken down, Sergeant?" yelled Beauviér.

"Yes, Inspector."

"Good Lord," he said, and then there was silence.

"Monsieur," said Martin timidly.

"Yes?"

"I am certain he is going to Namur."

"Why, Sergeant?" Beauviér's voice was curt.

"The art dealer, and the painting... The Monet, Inspector."

"It may be a fake. We still don't know," said Beauviér. "And he may go right by Namur, Sergeant, straight to Luxembourg. Maybe he banks there and is simply going to draw out his money and leave the country forever."

"Yes, monsieur. Maybe. But I don't think so. The Monet, it's too valuable. If it were my painting, I wouldn't leave it behind."

"The art dealer is dead, Martin."

"Yes, monsieur, but he does not know that."

"If he goes to Namur, he will."

"Not necessarily, Inspector. The press was not notified and the gallery is locked. He might wait for the return of the art dealer."

"Yes—possibly," said Beauviér. "How long until you can get going again?"

The radiator had ceased spitting steam and, checking the interior temperature gauge, Martin said, "Fifteen, maybe twenty minutes, Inspector."

"All right, Sergeant. Keep me posted. If he is there, if you find him, let me know immediately."

"Yes, I will—Monsieur?"

"What is it, Martin?"

"I am not making excuses, Inspector, but there is *no* car that could have kept up with him."

There was no further response from Beauviér.

Returning the radio to his belt, Henri Martin sensed the clumsiness of his initial efforts, though unknowingly, he was right about one thing. Thomas Breck was on his way to Namur to check on the disposition of the painting and would be there when the sergeant eventually arrived. But he was wrong about all cars being incapable of keeping up with the Jensen. A limited production 450 SEL Mercedes-Benz, with a seven-liter engine could easily keep pace, and as Sergeant Martin waited on the side of the road, the driver of this car had Thomas Breck in view.

* * *

93

Stuart Endfield ordered another Pimm's Cup. This was his third and he had been in the tavern less than forty-five minutes. The consumption of alcohol in the early afternoon was unlike him, though he could not help himself, the liquor seeming to ease his worries.

He opened a day-old Financial Times on the table and stared at the words. They meant nothing to him and unable to focus on their purpose, took a mouthful of his drink. Then desiring a cigarette, he ordered some. The waiter returned with a package of unfiltered Gaulloise, the only brand the bar carried, and Endfield tore at the cellophane, hurriedly removing one of the stubby cigarettes. He struggled with a match until the black tobacco finally caught, pushing the hot smoke down his throat. Immediately he began to cough and his eyes watered. The tears were as much from the strong tobacco as the sense of helplessness he felt; Stuart Endfield was becoming physically ill from the mounting stress of the last twenty-four hours.

The key to the file room, having dropped from his hand when he paid the waiter, now sat on the corner of the table. As a means to retrieve one of the gambling markers, it had become useless, its earlier power gone. They had changed the lock to the file room. Within hours after he removed the dossier on Thomas Breck, someone had decided too many unaccountable keys were floating about and reworked the lock. Though he was not under suspicion, as this was a common practice, Stuart Endfield still felt he was going to be sick.

Wiping at his eyes with a cocktail napkin, he then attempted another drag of the cigarette. It was easier this time as he let the smoke roll out from his lips. He grew more adept in his use of stimulants with each puff of the tobacco and every gulp of his cocktail. And, although muddled, he was feeling better.

Tucked between the last two pages of the Financial Times was the stolen file on Thomas Breck. In a panic, he had almost thrown it away, but then reconsidered. The file had been updated some six months back, and might be due for periodic review at any time. They would find it missing, triggering a search for the misplaced keys to the file room and their borrowers, and they would start searching for him. He must get back into the locked room; he must replace the file. With that done, he would deal with Mégot man-to-man, convincing him that he could be of no further assistance.

He nodded at the idea, then swallowing the last bit of his red cocktail, raised the cigarette to his lips.

* * *

Thomas Breck parked the Jensen under a street sign indicating the Fortress of Namur lay straight ahead. The fortress had an adjacent children's park that, like the fortress itself, had been abandoned, was under decay, and rarely visited. But a coin-operated ride for children remained: a large plastic rabbit with a plastic saddle that did little but shake like a car on a washboard road.

He knew it well.

He and Michelle had found themselves at the fortress on their first trip out of Brussels. They had known each other only two weeks when she spoke of a village near the French border and asked if he would like to join her. He was falling in love and now they would be alone, on a trip together, for the first time. Within thirty minutes of her request they were on the road, the car packed with all they might need.

It was two years earlier, on the sixteenth of May. He didn't know why he remembered the date, but he did. They had driven for some time when she noticed a tourist sign referring to the Fortress of Namur. And out of curiosity, they took the winding road up the side of the hill to discover the children's park with the mechanical rabbit. Climbing aboard the blue and white machine, Michelle took hold of the plastic saddle while Tom dropped coins into the box. The rarely used motor began to whir, finally jumping to life, and she laughed like a young girl, clutching the back of the twenty-franc machine. She had asked for one more ride, then another. They never made it to the town on the French border, but found a near hotel and stayed there for three days.

Tom remembered it well.

A passing delivery van brought him from his thoughts and exiting the Jensen, stepped onto the cold street, the cloth-covered Renoir under his arm. He gripped it tight, deciding to walk the half-kilometer to the art dealer's gallery. It was safer.

The narrow sidewalk hugged the storefronts he passed, the road falling away with the slope of the hill. The trees were free of their leaves save a few that twisted in the cold afternoon wind. He glanced in the bars and restaurants along the steep road, all with their fireplaces ablaze. In the bars, men gathered round the spout of their preferred beer. The restaurants, closed after lunch service, would not reopen until seven or later—a time of retreating commerce in the town of Namur, but not for Tom Breck. He needed to know the results on the sale of the Monet. He needed the money.

The gallery storefront under the most brilliant light was nondescript, but in the evening shadows it appeared nothing more than a black box, the entrance and single display window all but concealed. It was beside this window that Tom now stood, though it displayed nothing more than his own reflection. The gallery was blacked out, and he tried to make sense of the closed business. The aged dealer, a Monsieur Buchon, had agreed never to leave. The Monet was too valuable to risk being found by anyone and, like a kidnap victim, it was to be guarded at all times, but Buchon had apparently broken the rule.

Tom sounded the bell, then tapped on the glass display window with a coin. There was no response, and he felt his stomach turn in knots. He owned two paintings: the Monet left in the care of Buchon and the Renoir he carried. Both were acquired at an extremely high price in the eastern bloc and were all he possessed. Could Buchon have sold the Monet, taken the money, and fled? He had never before. The earlier smuggled paintings had been sold as planned and the money divided. Possibly the value of this Monet was too great to resist? A Monet, Tom thought, was too tempting. Who could resist so much money?

He searched his key ring for the duplicate to the gallery door. As he turned to place it in the lock, he saw the proprietor of the adjacent bistro advancing.

There was no greeting, no shaking of hands. The words of the bistro owner cut through the cold air. "Buchon is dead," he advised, his white apron dancing against his stomach.

Seeming to misunderstand, Tom squinted as if he no longer spoke the language. "Pardon me?" he said, cupping the key in his hand.

"You're here to see Buchon, aren't you?"

"Yes—"

"Well, he's dead."

That's impossible. He can't be dead...He can't be.

Tom said nothing. He kept his face expressionless.

"He was old," continued the man. "They said he was eighty-two."

"They?" said Tom. "What do you mean *they*?"

"The police."

"The police?"

"He was dead, monsieur. I called them."

"Of course... How? How did he die?"

"A cardiac." He pointed at the gallery, said, "There, in the doorway," and appearing cold in his thin shirt, turned and moved back inside the bistro, ending their conversation.

Tom again faced the glass display window, staring into the darkness. He and the man Buchon worked together, but were not close. It was a relationship of convenience, nothing more. For the old man it meant a large amount of money and a sense of excitement, searching out buyers for the smuggled paintings. It had begun some five years earlier in Brussels, after Buchon attempted to sell Tom a forged Chagall. The painting was passable; though the artist's name had been spelled with only one L. Tom then knew he had a man he could work with. Later, thinking Namur to be less conspicuous, he rented this storefront. It worked perfectly. The first smuggled painting was by a lesser-known artist and Buchon moved it quickly, finding a buyer from Marseilles—a French mobster who did not care where it came from.

The paintings became more and more valuable with each sale, each dash across the border—reaching a crescendo with the Monet that was only surpassed by the Renoir. And now Buchon was dead and the police had been called.

Tom studied the gallery's interior. The large steel safe stood in the shadows and the Monet should be inside, or, if it had been sold, the cash would be in its place. Those were the rules.

Though the police might return at any time, the Monet could not be left behind. The sudden arrest of Tatiana, and now the shock of Buchon's death, however, caused him to be careless. As he turned the key in the lock and moved inside, he failed to notice a silver Mercedes just down the street, its driver motionless behind the wheel.

Quietly closing the door, he waited for his eyes to adjust, then cautiously stepped forward. Suddenly a drumming noise filled the room, startling him. The wall radiator was releasing pressure, knocking loudly for a few seconds before it stopped. He stepped toward the safe, its metal door with the black tumbler and white numbers now clear.

Kneeling, he applied the combination, repeating each number to be certain, and slowly opened the heavy door. Staring into the black hole, he knew. The Monet was gone. He searched for any money left, any sign of the painting. There was nothing. He felt unwell and perspiration ran down his face, conjured by the dry heat of the room. The wall radiator again adjusted its temperature, but the sound was more shallow and stopped after two knocks. It was not the heating unit he heard, but the gallery door opening. Then it closed.

He looked toward the gallery window as it darkened, as though by a curtain hurriedly drawn. A faint outline took shape. Then Tom felt a sharp pain in his stomach and another at the base of his neck. Gasping for air, he fell to the floor and raised his hands, but they were knocked away by a blow that cut at his face. He could taste his own blood as the broken light of the room blurred and fell dark.

* * *

Stuart Endfield entered the Embassy without looking or speaking to anyone. Making his way to the second floor, he leaned against the corridor wall to keep from falling. He thought the near wallpaper smelled of toner and cheap cologne, wiping at his nose with a crumbling cocktail napkin, listening for any movement, anyone approaching. His ears began ringing—it was a high-pitched hum, seeming to get louder, and then it vanished. He'd had six drinks, one after the other, at the tavern round the corner. At the time they made him feel better, but now they made him feel nauseous. He wanted to be home, back in England. He wanted to go fishing and stay in some country inn with a girl he once knew, though her face was unclear in his memory. Everything was unclear, and in this wobbly state he was about to spy on a fellow worker, trying to be discreet as he watched a woman inside the near office.

Molly Pembrooke had a level of authority on the second floor. It allowed her the reading of all letters and documents, except those classified, before they were sent out. If she found a mistake in grammar or a typographical error or just general sloppiness, she would circle the offense in red ink and send it back to the party responsible. She was the marm of the clerical staff and had access to each room on the second floor. Molly Pembrooke was the keeper of the keys.

Stuart Endfield gazed at his watch. It was three minutes to five, although he had to check twice to be certain. His head was spinning.

The bitter liquor and cigarettes seemed to have made his breathing heavier. His back pressed to the wall, he looked again into the small office where Molly Pembrooke was finishing her duties. She was placing numerous papers into a large purse before arranging some odds and ends in a desk drawer. Endfield saw how meticulously she moved, each movement building up to the reason for his presence. Finally, she reached for a small ring of keys by the desk lamp and spun them about her finger, occasionally glancing at the clock on the wall. As the minute hand advanced to twelve, she dropped the keys into the center drawer and slid it closed.

Endfield hurriedly walked toward his office. He would wait there, until the right moment.

* * *

Stuart Endfield had fallen asleep at his desk, the liquor having caught up with him. He had thought to lay his head down for a moment, but instead passed out. The vibration of traffic outside his window brought him round and running his hands down his face, he blinked his eyes in the darkness. A hangover pushed against his temples as he lifted his wristwatch to catch the light from an outside street lamp. It was almost seven, he hadn't much time—the embassy guards would soon begin patrolling the halls.

Keeping the lights out, he made his way into the hallway and stopping at the last door before the stairs, pulled it open. The yellow-white glow from the streetlights shone into the dark room, coating the walls of Molly Pembrooke's office. Entering, he moved to her desk and grabbed for the center drawer. It wouldn't budge, so he pulled harder, hoping it might be jammed, but it wasn't. It was locked.

He heard a sound in the hallway—a guard was coming. Glancing at the doorway, Endfield considered making a dash, but hadn't time. Falling to all fours, he crawled into the leg opening of the desk, pulling his knees tight to his chest. The ceiling lights in the office came on and a guard stood at the door. He had heard something, thought Endfield, and would enter to find him cowering under the desk. The dossier on the American was in his coat pocket and they would find it. He pulled his knees closer.

The guard's boots brushed against the carpeting with each step, then stopped as a telephone rang. It sounded distant, possibly on the floor below. The guard mumbled something and there was a click.

The room again went dark.

Endfield let his knees fall from his chest. He could barely move, his legs having cramped. Struggling to scoot forward, he struck the desk with his head and the drawer slid open. He had inadvertently triggered the catch. Grabbing Molly Pembrooke's keys, he rushed to the file room and moving inside, pulled a cabinet drawer open. His head pounded. Everything was blurred and he could barely see, but he dared not turn on a light. Running his forefinger along the file cards, he at last found the letter B, smoothing out the dossier before dropping it into the folder. He then rushed back to Molly Pembrooke's desk, replaced the keys, made certain the drawer was again locked, and returned to his office.

Stuart Endfield laid his head on his desk, trying to catch his breath. He felt no sense of relief with his mission accomplished, only a terrible fatigue. But that was fine. He was safe and, for the moment, could rest.

But he couldn't. The telephone by his head rang, startling him. He answered it.

"Yes," he whispered.

"Monsieur Endfield." It was Mégot.

Possibly from the hangover, possibly from fear, he shivered briefly. "Yes," he repeated.

"I want you to speak to the American now."

"How did you—"

Mégot cut him off. "You were not at home, monsieur. And since you have no interests other than gambling and your job at the Embassy, it was not hard to deduce where you would be."

Endfield said nothing.

"Did you hear me, monsieur?" demanded Mégot.

"Yes. I heard you." Endfield ran his free hand across his forehead, trying to think of a way out, some reason that would make the man disappear. "What am I to say?"

"You will tell him that you can help with the woman."

"Woman? What woman?" Endfield stopped. The ceiling lights in his office were now ablaze and a uniformed guard stood at the door, his gun drawn.

The two men stared at each other.

"Oh, it's you, Mr. Endfield," said the guard loudly, returning his side arm to its holster. "Your name was not on the check-in sheet. The second floor was supposed to be empty."

"I suppose I forgot to sign in," Endfield apologized.

"That doesn't sound like you, sir," complained the guard, stepping into the office. "It's something that I should report, you know, Mr. Endfield."

"I know," he said, rummaging through his hangover to think of the guard's name. "I've just had so much on my mind lately. I simply forgot. It won't happen again."

The guard appeared satisfied with the response from Stuart Endfield, the perfect Englishman, and more than likely didn't want any unnecessary paperwork regardless. "Very well, sir. Please see it doesn't. I'll be downstairs if you need me." He turned and left the office.

"Thank you," whispered Endfield, watching the guard disappear from view.

The lights were still on, but the guard had not asked why Stuart Endfield sat in the dark like a thief. Looking at his hand still gripping the receiver, he slowly returned it to his mouth. "You said there was a woman..." His voice trailed off.

"Yes, you will tell the American that you can help him with the woman in Budapest," said Mégot. "You will call him and tell him. Do you understand?"

"Yes... I mean, no. How can I help him with this woman?"

"Listen, monsieur." Mégot sounded impatient. "He'll want to see you when you tell him this. Make a rendezvous, but not at his home—somewhere public. Make it for tomorrow evening at eight o'clock. He'll agree. I will meet you at the hotel where we met before, at six, with the details. Remember, someplace public."

The line went dead.

Endfield chewed on his upper lip. He wasn't certain if he could continue. The stress was too much—the haunting gambling markers, the stealing of the file, and now the meeting with the American smuggler about some woman in Budapest. He didn't think it possible, but it was getting worse.

His head throbbed as his eyes wandered around his office, touching on the personal items that reminded him of home. A black and white photograph of a cricket team he'd played with hung smartly on the wall. He was a bad athlete and won the position by default, with no one else available in his form. He knew this but bragged about his years on the team, hinting that he was the captain and that it was a First Eleven. In truth, he had been kicked off the following year, though he'd told no one and packed his kit every day before leaving the house. His mother wishing him well, hoping to see him play one day. The lies about who Stuart Endfield was, began early.

Just above the photograph, he noticed a chip in the paint, as if someone had hit it with a hammer. He had not seen it before and squinting, moved his gaze up the wall to a thick black wire, twice the size of a telephone line, that ran the width of the office. It was new, he was certain.

Slowly standing—his eyes fixed on the black wire—he walked across the room. It entered his office from the one next door, where the wall and ceiling came together, then exited into the file room. There appeared only one purpose to the thing.

Abruptly, he ran to Molly Pembrooke's office and straight to her desk. Quickly finding the release, he opened the drawer and removed the keys. He did not care about the guard or anything else as he made his way to the file room and threw the door open. Hitting the light switch, he looked to the ceiling. Screwed to the corner, about the size of a shoebox, was a black camera with a small, pulsating red light.

Casually turning off the lights, he closed the door and returned to Molly Pembrooke's office. Dropping the keys into the drawer, he checked, as he had before, that it was secure. His face slack, he walked mechanically back to his office and shut the door. He glanced at his hands. They were pale, as if no blood remained in his body, and he felt his knees going soft. The room started to darken and he took one step before collapsing, almost silently, onto the carpeted floor.

* * *

After Sergeant Martin's car overheated, it took longer than expected to get back on the road. Three hours longer. He had to summon a roadside assistance truck and after endless tinkering under the hood, he was again headed toward Namur, to find the American. His first effort in tailing someone was not going well and he had not reported back to Inspector Beauviér, deciding to wait until there was some good news.

It was early evening before he arrived in Namur, but finding Tom Breck's coupe proved to be no problem, with it being twice the size of most cars. It sat parked about a half kilometer from Buchon's gallery, just below the Fortress of Namur, and appeared to have been there for some time—the hood was cool to the touch and covered by a dusting of snow, which had fallen some two hours earlier.

Originally confident of the American's early return, Martin had hidden himself across the street from the Jensen in the shadow of a bank's doorway. Though now he was uncertain, imagining that Breck might have an apartment nearby, or possibly contact with an additional gallery, with additional paintings.

The street was quiet, as it had been for some time; the town, all but closed up. He could hear faint voices through the large window of a nearby bar, the sound of a woman laughing and the slamming down of an empty glass. Then a door, somewhere down the street, slammed shut. Time was pushing ahead, and no Thomas Breck. Martin decided to check Buchon's gallery. Stepping out from his hiding place, he moved quickly down the street, sometimes at a run, and it took him less than five minutes to cover the half-kilometer. Avoiding the lights of an adjacent bistro, he kept in the darkness, making his way to the front of the gallery. Standing at the window, he lifted his hand to block out the glare. Only the nearby street lamp allowed him to see anything at all.

The safe where the Monet had been found was well hidden in the shadows leaving only a tipped over floor lamp in view, its cord jerked from the wall. The gallery appeared void of life, and still no Thomas Breck.

Out of the corner of his eye, Martin saw a dark silhouette moving toward him. A man from the bistro stepped closer, taking a drag on a cigarette.

"Looking for someone?" he asked, smoke rolling from his mouth.

"No," replied Martin. "I'm not."

"Well, it doesn't matter. He's dead, you know."

"Dead?"

"Buchon, the old man who owned the gallery. He's dead. A cardiac, right there in the doorway."

"Oh, yes... I heard something about it."

"So, then, who are you looking for?"

"I said I wasn't looking for anyone."

The man took another drag. "You with the police?" he asked.

"Why would you think—"

"You just look like a cop," the man interrupted. "That's all."

Martin began walking away.

103

"That's what I told the guy earlier," the man continued. "How Buchon had died and all about the cops. The cop part bothered him, I thought."

Martin stopped, his gaze straight ahead. "Someone was here before?"

"Yes."

"What did he say?"

"Nothing, really. He was just looking through the window, like you."

Moving next to the man, Martin said, "What did he look like?"

"Hah. You are a cop. I knew it."

"Yes, I am, and if you don't answer my question we will go down to the local jail until you do," he promised the man. "Now what did he look like?"

"Okay, okay. I was just having fun. He was your age, maybe a bit older, and had light brown hair, almost blond, but taller than you. My height, I'd say."

"Did he have an accent?"

"You know that's the funny part." He dropped the cigarette onto the sidewalk and crushed it out with his foot. "When we first started talking I thought he was a Frenchman—Epernay or Reims, somewhere in Champagne. I' m pretty good with accents, you know." The man stopped talking and looked thoughtful.

Martin said, "Well?"

"That's just it, I'm not sure. When I mentioned the cops, the accent changed. It started going all over the place. Like he was Belgian, from Brussels maybe, and then back to being a Frenchman and then…" The man shrugged. "I don't know. It was kind of curious."

"He didn't sound American?"

"My goodness, no. I know an American when I hear one."

"And what time was this?"

"About four."

"I see, and when he left, which way did he go?"

"Didn't see him leave."

"What do you mean?" asked Martin. "Did he just stand on the sidewalk?"

"No. He went inside the gallery. I'd seen him before. He knew Buchon." The man shivered briefly. "Look, that's all I know, and it's cold." Turning, he went back into the bistro.

As the door closed, Martin moved again to the gallery window, so close his nose touched the glass. Glancing at the lamp on the floor, he noticed something else, something he had not seen before. He tried the door handle. Finding it locked, he threw his shoulder against the edge of the door, but it held. He then kicked at the lock just above the handle. The door pulled away from the jamb; another kick loosened the lock slightly. A final kick splintered the frame and sent the door flying open.

Moving into the gallery, he tripped on the threshold and stumbled to the floor, the wind knocked out of him. He blinked his eyes in the darkness and, trying to catch his breath, turned his head to see the bloodstained face of Thomas Breck just beside him. He sat up and took hold of the American's wrist.

The man from the bistro appeared at the open door. "What are you doing?" he yelled. "You shouldn't be destroying people's property, cop or no—" The man stopped his tirade, staring at the lifeless body.

Martin faced the door. "Call an ambulance," he said.

His mouth agape, the man did not move.

Martin exploded. "I said, call an ambulance!"

As the man ran toward the bistro, car headlights briefly illuminated his distraught face. They came from a silver Mercedes, its driver slowly pulling away from the curb.

* * *

Traffic was light on the Danube. Less than a half dozen vessels appeared on the river, peacefully pushing their plumes of smoke into the still air. Just beyond the line of trees on the far shore, a train rushed along, moving in and out of sight. Its locomotive blew a whistle, and standing at the river's edge, Tatiana thought it strange, listening to the sound fade. There were no crossings, no roads and no life to be seen. There were only the boats, now motionless, as if on parade. She glanced at the policeman by the hotel entrance, his expression indifferent as he watched her. She had only a few minutes to be outside, probably the length of his Russian cigarette.

It was a cold morning, colder than it had been, but she did not care. She was glad to be out of the musty room with its confining walls—the single window darkened by a painter's brush and the door locked tight. She felt she must get away, and it must be soon.

As far as she could see, there were no houses or other structures; if she made a run for it, she would not get far. They would bring her back and chain her to the bed. The policeman had told her the consequences of an attempted escape, and once more about the money. She did not understand. If they wanted money, she had told them, she would gladly pay. But like earlier, there was no response, other than the creaking floor as the policeman walked away.

She thought of Yuri, wondering how he was. They had been through so much, escaping across Czechoslovakia to Austria all those years ago, then on to France where their money bought them peace. There she had become Alice Malinaud and Yuri, unable to lose his heavy accent, became her business partner to anyone asking; the business partner constantly at her side.

On Tatiana's twentieth birthday, he'd asked her to marry him and it caused a scene. She accused him of betraying her trust, saying they were together only out of convenience, nothing more. She recalled the look on Yuri's face as he left their house and disappeared into the French countryside, and how the words she'd spoken made her ill, wishing she might take them back.

She hired a private investigator who found Yuri three weeks later in Provence, in the village of St. Paul, where he'd tried to find work. Having no papers, he had been arrested and though about to be deported, was too proud to telephone Tatiana for any documents that might save him. She smiled, remembering his return to their house and the days that followed. They'd spent hours together walking in the countryside, where they spoke new words. Two people will never be as close as we are, Tatiana professed one afternoon. She remembered Yuri lowering his head to conceal his emotions.

A shrill whistle brought Tatiana from her thoughts. She turned to see the policeman waving his arm.

"Just another minute," she called. "Please, just another minute."

The policeman shrugged and removing a new cigarette from its package, turned his back to light it against the breeze.

A barge came into view. It was being pushed by a flat-nosed tug that churned the water up and away as it advanced. Such a slow pace, with everything moving in a new time designed for prisoners. Tatiana watched the two vessels creep toward her, wondering about Yuri, then about Tom; wondering if she would get out alive, when abruptly a whistle rang out. The cigarette was finished.

106

CHAPTER THREE

The white-jacketed doctor fiddled with the cloth strips, wrapping them one way, then another, his eyes following the curve of his fingers like a tailor applying the final touch.

"A minor concussion, and you needed four stitches on your head," he said finally, in response to an earlier question. "The cut on your face needed nothing. Just keep it clean. It could have been worse."

"Oh," said Tom, flinching briefly from the hands on his wound.

"You're lucky," said the doctor. "You know who did this?"

Tom avoided the subject. "So, I can leave?"

"As far as I'm concerned. But there's someone in the hall who wants to see you first."

Tom sat up in the bed. "Who?"

"A cop. A gendarme."

"Is he the one who found me?"

"Yes, incredible luck. He was walking by the gallery and noticed you on the floor." The doctor stepped back to admire his work, then turned, moving toward the door. "I'll send him in."

Tom's eyes narrowed. "Pardon me, Doctor."

The doctor stopped. "What is it?"

"Do you know if there is a Gendarmerie in Namur?"

Shaking his head, he said, "No, not that I know of... But I suppose there must be," and pulled the door open. "Take care of yourself, Monsieur Breck."

Tom watched the white-jacketed man leave the room and thought about the gendarme just outside. A gendarme who found him by incredible luck. Leaning against the headboard, a pillow at the small of his back, he waited.

The door at last opened and a man near Tom's age entered. He wore no uniform, but street clothes: a checkered shirt and blue jeans, black tennis shoes, and he carried a bright yellow ski jacket. But he still looked like a cop, thought Tom as he noticed a two-way radio slung beside a holstered side arm.

Taking a chair from the corner, the gendarme sat down, laying the yellow jacket on his lap. He gave a wry smile and said, "How are you, Monsieur Breck?"

Tom briefly touched the bandage on his face, then the one on his head. "Just great," he replied.

"That's good, Monsieur Breck. That's good." The policeman appeared uncomfortable, crossing, then uncrossing his legs. "My name is Sergeant Henri Martin. I am with the Gendarmerie," he said proudly. "I found you."

Tom nodded. "That's what I heard. Thank you."

Martin hung the ski jacket on the back of his chair as if he were going to stay for some time. "I would like to ask you a few questions, if I may?"

"Of course," said Tom, casually folding his hands on his lap. He was not uneasy with the sergeant's presence. The police were something that never concerned him. He took them as something to protect his home from burglary, or to avoid when driving too fast, nothing more. They were too removed from his line of work. Tom's crimes were victimless—no money missing, no car stolen, no assault or murder. For when a painting was delivered and the money exchanged, that was it, and no one was the wiser. Especially the police.

The gendarme cleared his throat. "What were you doing inside the gallery of Monsieur Buchon?" he asked meekly.

Tom smiled. "Do you have a cigarette?" He wanted a moment to think. To determine how much truth should be in his answer.

"No," said Martin. "I don't smoke."

"Oh—okay."

Martin's brow wrinkled. "Well, Monsieur Breck?"

Tom adjusted the pillow at his back and, not looking at the policeman, said, "I am an art dealer and Buchon had a gallery."

"So you knew him?"

Tom paused, refolding his hands on his stomach, then said, "Yes, vaguely."

"But, you know that he is dead?"

"Yes, I know."

"So he sold some of your paintings?"

"Occasionally."

"Did he possess any of your paintings at the time of his death?" Tom's jaw tightened. "No," he replied.

"I see," said Martin. Removing a square of paper from his shirt pocket, he laid it on the bedcover next to Tom's folded hands.

"What's this?" he asked, glancing at the paper.

"It's the front page of last night's *Le Soir*. I thought you might find it interesting."

"Is that right?"

"Would you look at it, Monsieur Breck?" Martin leaned back in his chair, appearing more at ease.

Tom slowly unfolded the clipping. He was no longer complacent, no longer at ease; his hands shook lightly from his injuries and then from the headline he saw. It was in large type, usually reserved for national tragedies like a declaration of war or the death of the king. Though this tragedy was not national, it was for Thomas Breck alone. The headline read: 'Missing Monet Discovered in Namur.' A three-column story followed, but he was unable to read one word. The news was worse than he'd imagined. He let the clipping fall from his hand.

The policeman's eyes narrowed. "You did not read the article, Monsieur Breck." Taking it from the bed, he read aloud, " 'The masterpiece was found in the unassuming gallery of a Monsieur Yves Buchon, age 82, who was found dead of a heart attack, the evening of Wednesday, December first.' Don't you find that interesting, monsieur?"

Tom said nothing, keeping his gaze straight ahead. The sergeant continued, " 'The Monet was discovered by the local police in a safe at the back of Buchon's gallery. It was immediately taken to the University of Ghent for authentication and verified by the renowned expert, Pierre de Vries. The oil painting is by the French impressionist, Claude Monet, titled *The Haystacks*. It had been missing since the onset of the Second World War, stolen by the Nazis from the collection of Ambroise Vollard in Paris in 1941 and then rumored to have fallen into the hands of the Russian army in 1945. Its whereabouts since had been a mystery, until this week when it was discovered during a routine inspection following the death of Monsieur Buchon.' "

Returning the article to his pocket, Martin repeated, "Don't you find that interesting, monsieur?"

The shaking in Tom's hands was spreading through his body. With his financial world continuing to disintegrate, he felt himself unable to respond. Finally, he replied, "Yes, I suppose."

"You suppose, Monsieur Breck?" said Martin firmly. "An obscure gallery owner who is in possession of a painting worth millions of francs. A man you dealt with who is discovered to have only one item in his shop worth more than a few francs. And it turns out to be a Monet, and you *suppose* this is interesting?"

Tom glared at the sergeant. He was certain the policeman knew more than he was saying. The lecture was too contrived; too thought out. He also felt his being found in the gallery was no accident and the headline in *Le Soir* was no surprise to the policeman. Martin was playing with him and it made him angry.

"What do you want from me?" he said.

"I—"

Tom cut him off. "What do you want, monsieur!" he cried. Then suddenly, he grabbed his temples with both hands and groaned.

Martin lightly touched Tom's shoulder with his hand. "Are you all right, Monsieur Breck? Should I call for the doctor?" he asked, his voice sympathetic.

Tom gently shook his head, still holding it with his hands. "No, I'll be okay."

Neither man spoke while Tom slowly lowered his arms, laying his back against the metal headboard with his eyes closed.

Martin watched Tom, seeming to study the bandaged head and small plaster across the left cheek. "Someone tried to kill you, Monsieur Breck," he said. "Do you know who that might have been?"

Tom opened one eye and then the other, returning the sergeant's stare. "I have no idea," he answered curtly.

Standing, Martin walked to the frosted window. "The heat was off in the gallery, monsieur."

"What?" said Tom. "What are you talking about?"

"The temperature dropped below zero last evening. Had you spent the entire night in the gallery, you might have died."

"Well, thank you again," he said, his tone insincere.

"You don't understand, Monsieur Breck. Someone intentionally turned off the heat and left you there to freeze—to death."

Tom remembered the sound of the wall radiator clicking to life in the gallery. He recalled the knocking sound just before he was attacked. "Thank you," he said in a softer tone.

There was clattering on the other side of the door and a gurney wheel squeaked in hallway. Both men looked awkward, their eyes slowly moving to stare at the frosted glass of the window as if it were a roaring fire or an inspiring view, but there was nothing to be seen in the milky glass save the silhouette of a near tree limb dancing in the winter breeze.

The annoying sounds ceased and with the room again silent, Martin said, "I tried to telephone your wife."

Tom looked at the policeman. "You what?" he said angrily.

"Your wife, monsieur. I tried to telephone and let her know what had happened. But there was no response."

"She's out of town. At her father's."

"In France?" asked Martin, immediately looking down at the floor, seeming to know his mistake.

Tom said nothing. His eyes narrowed to dark slits, observing the policeman.

"I know your wife is French, Monsieur Breck," said Martin timidly. "It's in your record."

"Record? What record?" Tom asked, his voice unsteady.

"With the commune of Wolowe St. Pierre, monsieur. When you registered, your wife Michelle was listed as a dependent."

Tom pulled the bed covers up tight to his chest. "Yes," he said. "Of course."

"I know you are tired, Monsieur Breck. But I must ask you a few more questions."

Tom let out a deep breath. "Very well."

Martin removed another square of paper from his pocket. "Was anything taken from you in last night's attack? I have here a list of the things you had on you . . ."

Closing his eyes, Tom ignored the policeman's words. He had tried to avoid thinking about it, but the Renoir was gone. The last thing he owned of any value was now missing, along with the Monet. He was systematically being stripped of any wealth he possessed. He thought of his bank accounts and how much money remained. He must help Tatiana and that would take all of it. The policeman's voice made Tom irritable. He thought of Michelle and how he missed her. She had gone to her father's—or maybe not. Now he was certain of nothing, other than he had little cash.

Slowly, he opened his eyes. The words of the policeman were again clear: "...a gold and steel Rolex, a Du Pont lighter, also gold, and 14,223 francs." Martin looked up, returning the paper to his pocket. "These were the items found on you after the attack... So it was not robbery, Monsieur Breck."

"Really," said Tom caustically.

Martin squinted. "Did you have something else with you last evening when you went to see Buchon?"

"No, of course not." He tried to smile, but was unable. "Like you, I was just passing by."

Martin faced the window, and said, "Your French is very good, monsieur."

Tom mumbled, "Thanks."

"Where did you learn it so well?"

"My wife is French. I had no choice."

"But your accent."

"What about it?"

"You have none," said Martin, still with his back to Tom. "I mean, you could have been born down the street from me."

Tom grinned. "Are you saying we might be related?"

Martin turned. His face was angry. "Don't mock me, monsieur. That's what you are doing, isn't it?" He spit the words. "When I came into the room you spoke differently. Your accent was French, not Belgian. But now you have heard my speech and you mimic it; like a parrot. The nuances. The way you end each sentence with your voice pitching up. That is the way I speak and I know it. You are making light of me, Monsieur Breck. And *you* know it."

Expressionless, Tom watched Martin lift his ski jacket from the chair, then stare at the floor as if he had forgotten what he was doing.

"I'm sorry, Sergeant, if I somehow hurt your feelings," said Tom, his accent unchanged.

"This is a serious affair, Monsieur Breck," he advised, taking a step toward the bed. "And I do not mean the assault." Putting on his jacket, he continued, "I mean the painting, the Monet. It was stolen in 1941 by a bunch of German thugs in uniform. We don't look at it as a casualty of war but as a theft, nothing more. So anyone possessing the Monet is part of this crime. Unlike the United States, monsieur, there is no statute of limitations in Belgium. Seven years can pass or seven hundred, it does not matter. The person who has this painting hidden or hung on the wall of his home, or who tries to sell it for a profit, is as guilty as the Nazis who originally stole it. And the penalty for this is prison. Do you understand?"

Tom's head pounded, his stomach screwing into knots as he listened to the sermon. There was a sour taste in his mouth from something the doctor gave him. He wanted to spit it out and scream at the policeman to let him be. He turned away from Martin, again adjusting the pillow behind him, and said casually, "I really wouldn't know what you're talking about, Sergeant."

Tom faced the policeman. The two men's eyes met and neither blinked. Almost a minute passed before Martin moved next to Tom, placing a white card by his folded hands.

"That is my number, should you need anything, Monsieur Breck," he said, his voice calm. "You can reach me at any hour." Turning, he walked toward the door.

Tom did not move, his gaze straight ahead. "How long have you been following me, Sergeant?"

Martin stopped at the door. "Pardon me?"

"You said my wife was French and that you got the information from the records at the commune. But since I was assaulted on Friday night and today is Saturday, that would be impossible. That office is closed and won't open until Monday morning." He calmly picked up the policeman's card. "And the city-code on this card, Sergeant, is zero-two. That is for Brussels, not Namur. So I'll ask you: how long have you been following me?"

Martin turned slightly, casually repeating what Tom had said moments before, "I really wouldn't know what you're talking about, monsieur."

Tom did not watch the gendarme leave the room, as his gaze had drifted to the wall basin, its polished steel reflecting the outside light. Uneven stripes clung to the walls, crisscrossing over the near window and his unblinking eyes.

* * *

For no reason, the police had towed the Jensen. It had been parked properly and there was no meter to pay, but they towed it nonetheless. After paying a small fine for its release, Tom immediately noticed something wrong. The hood was slightly ajar; someone had opened it. A car being towed does not need its

113

engine checked and the interior had been vacuumed. There were usually cigarette ashes about the shift column, though now it was clean; like the day he bought it.

They had searched the car from front to rear, looking for something, but there was nothing to find. Tom never left a paper trail. He burned anything which might be incriminating, but now that seemed irrelevant. They were on to him and he felt certain Sergeant Henri Martin of the Gendarmerie was leading the chase.

Driving from Namur on the autoroute toward Brussels, he stayed in the right lane, taking his time while checking the road behind. And though there was ample fuel in the car, he pulled into a gas station, driving slowly by the pumps to the convenience store where he backed into a parking space. Lowering the window, he lit a cigarette. He felt no one had followed him, though he continued to watch the station entrance. A transport came in, rolling up to the pumps reserved for large trucks. After five minutes a ragged BMW 1502 with Italian plates creaked up to the air dispenser, an elderly man behind the wheel. Another five minutes passed and no other vehicle entered the station.

Tom pulled his topcoat about his neck, glancing at the shoulder torn in the assault of the evening before. He pinched the two pieces together, only to watch them separate again when he let go. Two buttons had also been ripped off and the material flapped in the winter wind as he walked into the store.

A young boy and girl were studying the candy in a display rack by the cashier. The little girl turned, whispering to the boy, who then looked at Tom. They both giggled and then started laughing, almost hysterically. Tom glanced at his reflection in the glass door of a cooler. He then moved to a large barrel that was filled with caps, grabbed one, and went quickly into the lavatory.

He looked at himself in the mirror. The white bandages on his head made him appear foolish, as if he were wearing a small turban. He removed them, grimacing as they tugged at his hair, then placed the cap on his head to hide the unsightly wound. It helped little. The plaster on the side of his face had turned gray, and he hadn't shaved. He looked and felt terrible.

Walking back through the store, he dropped a thousand francs by the cashier, then moved outside and climbed into his car. He pushed the Jensen through the station, the gas pedal to the floor as he reached the entrance to the autoroute. The tires spun briefly on the asphalt and the transmission jumped one gear, then another. He looked straight ahead, moving the car to the passing lane, flashing the headlamps to clear the way. The quivering needle of the speedometer read 180 and was climbing.

He wanted to be home.

* * *

Inspector Jules Beauviér stared at the parking area from the ground floor window of his office. A mechanic was working on one of the police motorcycles, parts spread around him like an unsolvable jigsaw puzzle. Three toolboxes were close at hand—one for metric, one for British Imperial, and one with a large hammer, Beauviér imagined, should the first two options fail.

Smiling, he turned to face Sergeant Martin, who stood in the center of the room.

"So, you spoke with the American," he commented, his expression suddenly serious. "Do you think that was wise? Now he knows you."

"Well, he knew someone found him, and certainly someone would let it slip that it was a gendarme," replied Martin. "It would have been stranger had I not paid him a visit."

"I suppose you're right… So he is involved with the Monet?"

"Yes, monsieur, he is."

"That's good, that's good," said Beauviér, rubbing his hands together. "And you feel someone tried to kill him last night?"

"No, I do not."

"But the attack, and the heat being shut off."

"I don't really think he would have frozen to death, monsieur. I just said that to scare him."

"And did you?"

"I'm not sure. Something bothered him."

Beauviér squinted. "Then why the attack?"

"There are two reasons, I believe," said Martin, removing his jacket.

Motioning at a near chair, Beauviér said, "Please, Sergeant."

Taking a seat, Martin said, "He was robbed."

"What? But the Cartier watch."

"Rolex, monsieur."

"Right, and the gold lighter and all the cash and…" His voice trailed off, waiting for an answer.

"That is not what they were looking for."

"Well? What were they looking for? What did they steal?"

Martin cleared his throat. "I do not know, monsieur."

"What do you think, Sergeant?" Beauviér sounded annoyed. "He had another Monet in his back pocket?"

"I don't know, monsieur. He may have."

"Do you have any idea what that painting is worth?"

Martin quickly replied, "No, Inspector,"

Beauviér moved from behind his desk. "Here," he said, handing a newspaper to Martin. "Bottom corner of the front page."

It was the weekend edition of the International Herald Tribune. Martin's eyes went straight to a small article, just a few lines at the bottom of the page that read: 'Discovered Monet Valued by Auction House.'

Beauviér opened the window a crack. "Well? What does it say?" he asked impatiently.

Martin read the article aloud: " 'The London auction house of Sotheby's has stated that if the recently discovered Monet titled *The Haystacks* were to come up for bid, it would bring between two and three million dollars, according to Harris Ashford, company spokesman.' " He lowered the paper, looking straight ahead. "I had no idea, monsieur."

"So, you see," said Beauviér, proud of a point well made, "it's not likely he had another painting of such value. And why, if he had an additional Monet, would he take it to Buchon's gallery?"

"But why not, monsieur?" Martin asked, not looking at Beauviér but straight ahead. "First, he did not know that Buchon was dead. They probably did not communicate by telephone. As we know, Buchon's telephone records showed he never called the American, from the gallery anyway. So, Breck would simply come by the gallery periodically to pick up any money from a sale or to bring by an additional painting. Not necessarily another Monet, but possibly something of like value. A Rodin, for example... or a Vermeer... or, I don't know, monsieur. There are many masterpieces still missing from the wars, both the First and Second, let alone conventional theft."

He looked at Beauviér, then continued, "Breck had a key to the gallery on him. I checked it early this morning to see if it worked the lock, and it did. Then I returned it to the envelope with his possessions, but said nothing. I didn't want him to think we had anything but speculation. The American obviously went inside the gallery last evening to check on the Monet or retrieve cash from the corner safe. It was wide open when I found him, even though it had been accidentally locked by one of the officers on the day of the discovery." Martin took a deep breath. "Breck had a key and knew the combination to the safe. This is not a one-time affair. It may have been going on for years."

Beauviér placed the palms of his hands flat on the desk as the pink in his face softened. He watched Martin for some time, then said, "Where is the American now?"

Martin glanced at his watch. It read twenty minutes before one. "I suspect he's on his way home. I had his car impounded and searched. They finished just before noon and gave it back to him shortly thereafter. I asked Bernard Rappaport—he's a corporal with the city police—to watch his house in Wolowe St. Pierre. There was no point in my trying to chase after him, and it seemed imprudent regardless. He is certainly looking for any sign of being followed. I thought it best to back off for the moment."

Relaxing his stance, Beauviér pulled out a handkerchief, refolding it before dabbing at his face. The air coming in the open window did not seem to help, while the sergeant's words troubled him. "What does this Corporal Rappaport know?" he asked.

"He knows to telephone when the American returns home, nothing more," Martin said confidently. "He's an old friend."

"I see—and the police in Namur? What reason did you give them for wanting his car searched?"

Martin grinned. "They didn't need one, monsieur. They love to search private property and besides, it was a slow Saturday in Namur."

"That's good, Sergeant—very good. You have not searched his home in Wolowe?"

"No, monsieur. He has a maid. She left at noon, but then it was too late and I didn't want Rappaport to be caught. That might jeopardize everything."

Beauviér nodded and placing his hands flat on the desk again, appeared to study his fingernails. "The attack on the American."

"Monsieur?"

"You said there were two reasons for the attack on the American: the robbery and something else. What?"

Martin scooted forward in his chair. "Someone is trying to break him," he said softly, as if it were a secret.

"What are you talking about, Sergeant?"

The light from the window caused Martin's intelligent eyes to shine a brilliant blue as they locked on Beauviér. "When I walked into the gallery last evening," he recounted, his tone deliberate, "there was this feeling I had when I looked at Breck on the floor. If you could have seen it you would understand. I know it doesn't make any sense, if what I am saying about the theft of an additional painting is true. The way he was attacked. The blow to the face and the shutting down of the heat as if... As if to make the American suffer."

Beauviér frowned. "That's nonsense, Sergeant."

Martin looked at the floor. "Yes, monsieur."

The telephone rang. Beauviér took his time answering.

"It's for you," he said, handing the receiver to Martin.

Only a few words were spoken before Martin hung up and hurriedly reached for his jacket. "The American is home. I will keep you informed, Inspector."

Watching Martin head toward the door, Beauviér said, "Don't lose him again, Sergeant. He'll be moving quickly and without warning, now that he knows you're on to him."

"No, I will not," Martin promised. "But, he is clever, monsieur."

"Really? Clever, is he? Well, this clever American will soon be in prison, Sergeant."

"Yes, monsieur," he said, and left the office.

Grabbing his topcoat from the stand, Beauviér followed the young sergeant out the door, keeping just out of his sight.

* * *

Entering the foyer of his home, Tom Breck called his wife's name, followed by the maid's. He waited for a response, received none, and went into the kitchen.

Next to the sink sat a stack of mail and a notepad the maid used to keep track of callers. The page was full, though it was the same person on each line. A man had called every hour since eight that morning, insisting he speak with Tom only. The maid had written after the second call that the man had an accent.

Tom felt certain it was Yuri. Looking at the clock on the wall, he knew he would shortly have information about Tatiana.

Thumbing through the mail, he pushed aside the bills, then

opened an envelope from his bank. Normally he didn't care what the monthly statement said, but now things were different.

The single page noted a deposit in the middle of November for seven hundred thousand francs—his last seven hundred thousand francs. And then the final figure on the page gave him the news: there were but twenty-eight thousand francs remaining in the account.

The paper fell from his hand. "Twenty-eight thousand," he whispered.

It was not enough to pay the mortgage on the house, and the maid, and the gardener, and the year-end land taxes are due, and—the list was endless.

He looked again at the statement to see that one week earlier, there was a withdrawal of five hundred and fifty thousand. It was a transfer to a bank in Barbizon, France, a town only three kilometers from Milly-La-Forêt, where Michelle's father lived.

She had all but emptied the account.

A sharp pain cut across his forehead. He opened the freezer compartment of the refrigerator and removing a bottle of Russian vodka, drank straight from it. His eyes began to water as a small amount of the vodka ran from the corner of his mouth. The pain was not gone.

He again lifted the bottle when the wall telephone rang. He looked at the clock. It was two minutes past one.

Hurriedly answering, he said, "Yes."

"Mr. Breck?"

It was a man, and he had an accent, but it was not Yuri. The accent was English.

"Speaking," he said impatiently.

"You don't know me but—"

"I'm really not interested right now," Tom said, thinking it to be some fundraising on behalf of the British community or an upcoming sporting event to display the Union Jack. Because of his last name, he was sometimes mistaken as one of their own and had fallen onto a list of benefactors. "Maybe next month, okay?"

"Mr. Breck, please listen," said the voice loudly.

Tom was about to hang up when he heard, "It's about Tatiana Gregòsh." He swallowed, and said, "Yes, I'm listening."

"If we might get together this evening, Mr. Breck. Say about eight o'clock."

119

"Why not now?" he asked. "Come to my home. I can give you the address."

"No, tonight would be best, and someplace public."

"Look. You can tell me now, over the phone. What do you want?" His voice trembled slightly and he knew it. But he also noticed the man on the other end sounded uneasy.

"I'll tell you tonight, Mr. Breck."

"Okay, fine. You're the boss." He tried to stay calm, not wanting to antagonize the caller. The vodka he'd ingested was clouding his thoughts. He had to think. He wanted somewhere safe. "There is a bar in La Grand' Place," he said abruptly. "The southeast corner next to Maxim's café. The name of the bar is Le Cerf. Do you know it?"

"No, I do not. I was thinking we could meet—"

"Well, it's public. You said you wanted someplace public, didn't you?"

"Yes, yes… that will be fine." There was a pause. "What is it called?"

Tom spelled out the name, then said, "At eight o'clock, right?"

"At eight, Mr. Breck."

"Please, tell me your—"

The line went dead.

He looked again at the wall clock. There were less than seven hours before the meeting and no doubt the man would want money. The few thousand francs remaining in the bank would not help and Tom would have to explain that he needed time. But that might not work. If they had the daring to kidnap Tatiana, then killing her would be no problem. He hurriedly dialed a number from memory, waiting for someone to pick up.

There was a click. A man answered, said, "Benton Motors."

"Charles?"

"Yes."

"This is Tom Breck."

"Ah, Thomas. How are you? Wait… More importantly, how is that beautiful wife you keep hidden away?"

Tom nodded as if to convince himself. "She's fine Charles. Just fine."

"Wonderful. So, what are you in the market for today? Or did you just call to say hello?"

"I'm not buying today, Charles. I'm selling."

"I see. What are you selling?"

"The Mercedes, the convertible. You said you could get six hundred and fifty thousand for it. That you had buyers for such a car."

"Yes, that's true. But I told you that in June, Thomas. This is December. The demand for a convertible is not there. In a few months we can get your price."

"I need to sell it now, Charles."

There was a pause. "I understand, but you're not going to like what I can give you."

"How much?"

"Three hundred thousand."

"I'll take it."

"All right, if you are—"

"And the BMW. How much?"

"The twelve-cylinder?"

"Yes."

"Now, there is never a good time of the year for a car like that. The road tax alone costs more—"

"I don't need a history lesson," Tom complained. "How much?"

There was no reply. Then he asked, "Are you okay, Thomas?"

"I'm fine. How much?"

"I'll also give you three hundred for the BMW, okay?"

"Thanks. Now listen, I'll come by your garage in about an hour with the gray cards and the keys. Someone will have to pick the cars up at my house. So if you'll have the money ready, I'd appreciate it."

"It's Saturday, Thomas."

"Okay, a check then."

"Sure. What about the Jensen? You still have it?"

"Yes, but I need it for the moment."

"I can give you a good price on—"

"I'll see you in an hour, Charles," he said, and hung up.

Tom rubbed his hands together. He now had some cash; not much, but it was a start. Moving quickly to the bathroom, he threw off his clothes. The blue work suit hung on the hook of the door where he left it. He hadn't imagined wearing it again. The end of any further smuggling had been so close, the money so near. He angrily zipped up the front and glanced at himself in the mirror. He removed the cap from his head, replacing it with the beret. He had not shaved for twenty-four hours and the plaster on the side of his face made him look different: exactly like Jean-Paul Van der Elst, after a bar fight.

Slipping on the black work boots, he moved into the hallway. The oilskin coat was in a drawer by the front door. The maid had wanted to throw it out, complaining it was dirty and smelled of kerosene. She didn't understand its value. Putting it on, he went to the dining room window and opened the curtain slightly. The strange car was still there, parked on the other side of the front wall with the hood now up. A young man appeared to be tinkering with the engine, though there was something not right. Tom sensed he was being watched.

In the Renault cargo van, dressed as Jean-Paul Van der Elst, he might get by the young man, but he couldn't risk it.

He turned on the overhead chandelier, feeling that sufficient, and moved back into the kitchen, opening the refrigerator door. Rifling the contents, he found a package of beef filets and shoving them in his coat pocket, climbed upon the kitchen counter. He unlatched the window, then lowered himself through the opening into the back garden. Cutting across the flowerbed, he grabbed a wooden box sitting against the garden wall and climbing on top, squinted into the neighbor's estate.

Situated on almost a hectare, the small chateau had an Olympic pool, filled and heated year-round. The owner was a corrupt electrical contractor who was sometimes in politics, and sometimes in jail. He was very old and very wealthy and extremely paranoid.

Tom cleared his throat loudly and that was all it took. Two black Labradors raced around the corner, their teeth showing.

Removing the package from his pocket, he threw the meat at the swimming pool. One piece landed in the center of the water and the other near the edge. Both dogs immediately moved to the bait, leaning forward as they tried to avoid the water. It didn't work. One dog went in and the other began to howl, running back and forth along the edge of the pool.

"Come on, boy," he said softly. "You can do it."

As the dog in the pool devoured the meat the other went wild, finally leaping into the pool. When the second dog hit the water Tom was off the wall and running, the heavy work boots pulling down on his legs.

Glancing out the corner of his eye, he saw the dogs paddling across the pool to the steps. They had finished the meat and were coming after him. The wall was just ahead; he slid into it on the wet

122

grass. Raising his hands to lift himself, he cried out. There were bits of broken glass mixed in with the mortar that ran along the top of the wall. Droplets of blood formed on his palms. He turned. The dogs were halfway across the lawn.

Taking off the oilskin, he laid it over the broken glass and jumped up, letting his upper body fall forward to the street below. Lying on the ground, he reached up for the dangling arm of his jacket and pulled, but it wouldn't budge. The dogs had the other arm and weren't letting go. He felt the material tear and releasing his grip, watched the jacket disappear over the stonewall.

He stood and looked at his hands. The cuts were superficial. Folding his arms across his chest to keep warm, he moved hurriedly toward the near tram stop, although there was no need. He was certain he had not been followed.

* * *

Stuart Endfield fidgeted with a tin ashtray on the table, spinning it one way then the next. The scraping sound appeared to irritate Mégot, who moved his hand across the table, firmly placing his forefinger on the ashtray's edge. Endfield quickly pulled his hands back, folding them together on his lap as he glanced at his watch. It was twenty-five minutes before eight. The two men had been together for over an hour and a half, and most of it in silence.

Removing a cigarette from a package on the table, Mégot began tapping the filter against the nail of his thumb.

"So you know what to say, monsieur?" he said calmly. "Would you like to go over it again?"

Not looking at him, Endfield shook his head. "No, I know what to say."

"We do not want any mistakes, you know."

"I know," he said, still shaking his head.

With the tobacco sufficiently compacted, Mégot placed the filter between his clenched teeth. The cigarette danced up and down as he inquired, "You returned the file on the American without any trouble, I imagine."

Stuart Endfield twitched. The sight of the camera screwed into the wall was still clear in his memory, as was his waking up on the floor after collapsing in his office, followed by the nausea he felt all night, unable to sleep. He had considered fleeing, although he did not know where; he had considered catching a train to anywhere before he was discovered on the attesting film—the cat burglar in the dim light of the file room, rifling his country's secrets.

And he would have fled, but for the talkative guard at the embassy. Endfield asked him about the new cameras in the embassy—now they were everywhere, it seemed—mentioning how pleased he was that security was at last being tightened. But the guard was not comfortable with their performance. There were sometimes gaps in the recording—whiteouts, he called them—that might last a minute or more, and that was not the worst of it. After seventy-two hours the tape would run out and not be replaced, only flipping itself to begin recording over the previous seventy-two hours. The guard thought this very unfortunate. Stuart Endfield, of course, could barely control his joy. It meant that if there were no obvious reason to view the film in the next three days, the account of his crime would soon be erased.

He had been elated at the news, though still cautious as he said, "No, no problem at all."

"That's good, monsieur," said Mégot. "It would be a pity to have something trivial get in the way."

Endfield said nothing, staring at his folded hands.

Mégot lighted his cigarette. The rising smoke draped between the two men like a screen. "Do you want another coffee?" he asked.

"No… No, thank you."

A waiter cleared their empty cups from the table, then lifted the bill, searching for any money underneath. Finding none, he turned and left.

With the waiter out of earshot, Mégot said, "Why did you choose to meet at Le Cerf?"

"Pardon me? Oh, I didn't. He did."

Mégot's brow wrinkled. "Listen to me, Monsieur Endfield," he said, his voice stern. "You are in charge of this meeting. Not the American. Do you understand?"

"Yes, yes. I understand. Only—"

"Only what?"

"Only… What you're asking. Why would he accept my demand?"

"He will accept. He has no choice."

Endfield's voice became excited. "Then what's to keep him from calling the police? You have kidnapped a woman and are holding her for—"

Mégot cut him off. "Keep your voice down." He drew closer, resting his elbows on the table. "Trust me. There will be no police, okay?"

Endfield nodded.

Mégot glanced at the clock on the wall. "It's only a fifteen minute walk to Le Cerf, but you might as well get going."

Endfield scooted his chair back.

"There is one more thing, monsieur," said Mégot, removing something from his jacket pocket. "Here."

Mégot tossed a gambling marker into the center of the table. Endfield quickly grabbed it, then stood motionless, his shoulders slumped like an old man.

Grinning, Mégot crushed out his cigarette in the ashtray. "At this rate, we will be dead-even before you know it, *mon cher* Endfield." He then glared at the Englishman. "I will call you at your apartment in three hours. Please be there."

Taking his umbrella and bowler hat from the near chair, Endfield walked to the door of the hotel. Now it was more than the blackmailing that made his stomach twist and his palms sweat. Dark scenarios jumped across his mind as he moved into the black winter night. The police could be lurking at every corner, he thought anxiously, but that seemed less important than the unknown reaction of the man he was about to meet.

Lifting his umbrella against the light evening mist, he walked slowly along the cobblestone street with the crushing fear that tonight he might die.

* * *

The bright lights of La Grand' Place could not penetrate the stained glass windows dotting the south wall of Le Cerf. Small votive candles flickered on the tables, adding little to the lighted fireplace in the corner, leaving the bar's interior quite dark. It was also quiet. There were few clients, though this was a typical Saturday night, who were no louder than the occasional snapping log.

Sitting at a table, a newly purchased oilskin jacket on his lap, Tom Breck glanced at his watch, then the front door. No one had entered since he arrived. There was a couple by the fireplace drinking overpriced Irish coffees and an old man hunched over a candle, attempting to read a copy of last week's *Le Figaro*. And that was it, a normal weekend crowd at Le Cerf. The prices, being the highest in the city, kept out the riffraff, and everyone else for that matter.

The owner, an Irishman named John Clark, had purchased the bar in 1946 after serving with the Royal Parachute Corps. He once stated that he jumped into Belgium in 1938 and never left. With the war having begun in 1939, Tom wondered how much truth there was to his history, but never said a word. John Clark never questioned him about his source of income, so they got along well, and over the years, had become friends. Tom was counting on this friendship as he waited.

The appointment with the Englishman was at eight and Tom had been sitting, unacknowledged by the barman, for forty-five minutes. He did not mind. Not being recognized in his laborer's clothing was what he wanted. But now he wanted a drink. He grew uneasy, with the meeting drawing closer. He raised his hand, but the barman didn't look up, keeping at his chore of straightening a small glass of toothpicks. Tom knew the problem: the bar was elitist and he was not welcome as Jean-Pierre Van der Elst, working stiff.

He moved to the bar, placing himself opposite the barman. "I want a pastis, extra ice."

Not looking up, the barman advised, "A pastis is seven hundred francs. You still want it?"

"No, I don't."

The barman smiled.

Tom leaned forward, his nose almost touching the barman. "Make it a double, and I'd like you to bring it to me. I'm sitting there," he said, jerking his thumb over his shoulder. "And if you spill any, then you and I are going to have a problem. Do you understand?"

The barman slowly looked up. He studied Tom, the unshaven man with the dirty clothing and tattered beret. He stared longest at the plaster across his cheek, then looking surprised, said, "Excuse me, Monsieur Breck, it's you… I mean… I didn't… Any particular label, monsieur?"

"Ricard," he replied, then returned to his table.

Pouring the drink quickly, the barman hurried from behind the bar, carefully watching the clouded liquid so none might spill. He placed three white cloth doilies on the table: one for the glass, one for the pitcher of water and one for a dish of almonds. Tom watched the meticulous display of hospitality.

126

The barman said, "Anything more, monsieur?" as he seemingly forced a smile.

Tapping on the edge of the table, Tom felt there was more he would like to say, but simply shook his head.

Abruptly, he heard clapping.

John Clark, standing in the shadows of the staircase, began walking down the steps. "Well done, my boy," he said, still applauding. "For a minute there I thought we might be having an old-fashioned bar fight. You had me going, but then I saw your hands, Thomas. A man who works bent over a shovel all day very rarely has his hands so manicured, and so lily white. It might play well with Dubliners, but in Limerick they'd see right through the make-up. You should really wear gloves before you take your act onto the road."

"I guess I forgot them."

John Clark let out a belly laugh. "How are you?" he asked, taking Tom's hand. "It's been some time."

"Fine," he replied, and for the next few minutes the two men shared pleasantries, and a joke or two. Then Tom's tone grew somber. "It's not true, John."

The Irishman squinted. "What's not true?"

"That everything's fine. I need to talk with you."

"Well, here I am lad."

Tom glanced at his watch. It was seven minutes to eight.

"I'm in trouble."

"I'm listening," he said, scooting his chair closer.

"In a few minutes a man is going to walk in here. I'm not sure what it's all about, but it's not good."

"How might I help, Thomas?"

He whispered, "Keep an eye on me, in case things get… I don't know… out of hand."

"Consider it done, lad."

"Don't you want to know what my beef is with this guy?"

"What, and spoil the surprise?" said John, standing. "Consider your back covered, Thomas, and I must say I'm proud of you. You always seemed so carefree. I hated you for it."

The front door opened and a cold wind shot into the small bar as John Clark moved toward the fireplace. Tom stared at the entry, but the wooden door still hid the person entering.

Finally, the door closed and a middle-aged man appeared, shaking rain from his umbrella. He wore a dark pinstriped suit, a blue and white striped shirt and clashing polka-dot tie. Then there was the bowler hat. The discordant clothing was of conservative taste, and Tom knew this was his man—the Englishman promising news of Tatiana.

The barman waved him forward, pointing to an empty stool, but the man ignored him. Slowly removing his bowler, while looking about the room, he glanced at Tom in the weak light, then the old man with the newspaper. Taking a step forward, he studied the couple by the fireplace, before slowly moving his gaze to John Clark, who was now smoking a cigar. The room fell quiet.

Tom said to the man, "I think you're looking for me."

Stuart Endfield dropped his umbrella; it clattered on the wood floor.

"I am Thomas Breck. Are you here to see me?"

Squatting, Endfield grabbed the umbrella, briefly steadying himself before standing. "Yes, I am."

It was the same voice, the same accent, thought Tom, pointing to the seat opposite. Endfield moved to it, his gaze lowered as he cautiously sat down. Laying the umbrella and bowler hat on his lap before folding his hands on the table, he finally looked up, but said nothing.

"Do you want a drink?" asked Tom.

"Yes," he replied. "Very much."

The barman did not need to be called, rushing from behind the bar, he placed a cloth doily in front of Stuart Endfield's hands, now clasped together like something was hidden behind them.

Endfield said, "One of those," and nodded at Tom's pastis.

The barman hurried away. With the sound of jostling glassware, a sense of normalcy returned to the bar. The couple in the corner began talking as the old man loudly snapped a page of his newspaper into place, meanwhile John Clark, leaning against the back bar, calmly puffed on his cigar. Tom became still, watching Endfield fold, then unfold his hands on the table.

The barman returned and placed the drinks on the table. He glanced at each man. Neither Tom nor Endfield looked up. The barman left.

Endfield took a large drink of the pastis.

"Who are you?" asked Tom.

Endfield did not answer the question, but said, "I am here on behalf of someone."

"Who?"

"A man named Mégot," he replied, and finished his pastis in one swallow.

Tom's brow wrinkled. He thought it a strange name. "Yes. I'm listening."

"He would like you to do something for him."

"Why? Why should I do anything for this man?"

"For the woman."

Tom felt the anger returning and no longer felt any sympathy toward the bumbling man across the table. "Tatiana?" he asked, his voice hard.

"Yes," said Endfield.

Tom reached for his drink, his free hand squeezed into a fist. "So if I do what this man wants, this Mégot, then she will be set free?"

Tipping his glass forward, Endfield gazed into it as if to confirm it was empty. Tom motioned to the barman for two more.

The old man coughed loudly, flipping another page of the paper as the couple in the corner began embracing. The barman appeared and set down two glasses, leaving the empty one that Endfield still studied.

"If you agree to help Mégot, then she will be set free," Endfield explained, to the empty glass.

"And that's it, no strings attached?"

"There is one string attached, you could say."

"Yes?"

His eyes lifted, moving to the plaster across Tom's cheek. "Mégot would like one million francs."

Tom slammed his fist on the table. "I don't have one million francs," he cried.

The outburst, besides making Endfield jump, also upset the quiet of the bar. The couple, pulling away from their embrace, whispered to one another as they watched John Clark, who took a step forward, then another. The old man continued reading, oblivious to any disturbance.

"He said you would say that," cried Endfield defensively.

"Who said?"

"Mégot."

Tom leaned forward. "So everything being said here is this… this Mégot?"

Endfield nodded. "Yes."

"So who are you?"

"His messenger."

"Then what do you get out of this?"

"Nothing, I promise you. Nothing."

"I don't believe you!"

Endfield pushed the empty glass aside, lifting the full one to his lips. His hand was unsteady.

Quietly, Tom asked, "What does Mégot want me to do?"

"So you agree?" said Endfield, a look of relief in his eyes.

"I agree to nothing. I want Tatiana set free."

Picking up an almond from the dish, Endfield stared at it. The candlelight pushed the long shadows of his fingers across the table. "There is a machine here in Belgium that Mégot would like moved."

"Moved where? What kind of machine?"

"I don't know where and I don't know what it is. He said he would tell you after he receives the one million francs."

Putting his hand to his face, Tom began kneading his mouth with his fingers. The wound under the plaster twinged. He stared at Endfield. "Why me?" he asked. "What did he tell you to say for that question?"

Letting the almond fall back into the dish, Endfield said, "I am to say: because you are the best smuggler he knows."

There was a pause, then Tom said, "If a man has the power to have Tatiana arrested, he can certainly move some machine." He took a deep breath. 'Where is it to go?"

"The machine is to leave Belgium. This much I know. And, contrary to belief, not all policemen can be bought."

"Did Mégot say that also?"

"Yes."

"How much time do I have before... before you need your answer?"

"As much time as you want, but—"

"But, what?"

"But, everyday the price for the release of the woman goes up one million francs until the amount becomes so large you would never be able to pay it."

"And then?"

Endfield grew agitated. Lifting his glass, he spilled some pastis down the front of his tie. "She will be killed," he whispered.

Hearing the words, Tom grabbed the lapel of Endfield's suit coat and began slapping him. First one glass, then the other, fell to the floor and shattered. Blood ran from Endfield's mouth. Putting up his arms in a feeble defense, he attempted to stand, tipping the table over. Tom, his eyes wild, kept slapping him. Then, screaming a profanity, he threw him back into his chair.

A hush fell over the room as John Clark moved from behind the bar, speaking briefly with the couple at the fireplace. He then moved to the old man and whispered in his ear. The old man grunted and putting on his coat, headed out the door. The couple hastily followed.

Pushing the door closed, John Clark turned the key and faced the two men. "I couldn't help but be noticing your dissension, Thomas. However, I believe you're being a bit too diplomatic. So, what do you say I beat him to a jelly?" he suggested calmly, removing his jacket. "After all, no one's to be the wiser and... It'll be on the house."

* * *

Pressing the binoculars to his eyes, Sergeant Henri Martin panned the American's house through the windshield of his parked car. He searched from one end of the property to the other, only to find nothing had changed—there was but one light on, no discernible movement, and no one had come or gone for seven straight hours.

He began adjusting the focus on the glasses when the two-way radio let out a squawk.

Raising it to his mouth, he said sleepily, "Yes?"

"He's at La Grand' Place," Beauviér said.

"What? Who's at La Grand' Place?"

"The American, of course."

Martin sat up straight. "But that's—"

"I'm outside La Maison du Cygne, by the relief. Get down here now, Sergeant."

"Yes, I—"

The radio went dead, and Henri Martin felt like a fool.

In the time it took to drive the four kilometers from Wolowe St. Pierre to La Grand' Place, it had started to rain, and with the temperature just above freezing, snow could replace the deluge at any moment. It was a sour night, though Martin was able to park near La Grand' Place, a short distance to where Inspector Beauviér waited.

131

A metal canopy protected the entrance of La Maison du Cygne and a half-dozen pedestrians mingled underneath, shielding themselves from the downpour. Near a brass relief in the stonewall stood a lone figure in a topcoat. He wore no hat, his thinning hair flat to his head from the rain, and the corners of his mouth were turned down. Beauviér did not look pleased.

Running under the canopy, Sergeant Martin swallowed to catch his breath, and said, "I'm sorry—"

Beauviér cut him off. "He's in Le Cerf."

"Where?" he asked, pushing the hood of the ski jacket from his head.

"The bar, Le Cerf. Straight across, on the corner."

Martin peered into the curtain of rain. There were two well-known taverns, four and five stories high respectively, with their roofs hidden in the bleak weather. He knew of them, but the small building at the corner, he did not. "How long has he been inside?" he asked, trying to make out the bar's entrance.

"Since seven."

"I don't understand. How?"

"He went out the rear door of his house."

"That's not possible," Martin countered. "Rappaport and I both checked the back door. There were two dogs that almost took our heads off on the grounds of the adjoining house."

"I thought he might notice he was being watched," said Beauviér. "So I covered the back door. After all, it was you that told me he was clever, Sergeant."

Martin looked at Beauviér. "What time was this?" he asked.

"Just after one."

"What? This afternoon?" He was no longer apologetic. He was upset. Beauviér knew the American had left hours before, yet left him sitting outside in the cold, like a clown.

"I almost missed him myself," said Beauviér, his voice soft. "It was the plaster on the side of his face."

"But you have a photo of him."

"Yes, as he normally is."

"I don't understand."

"He's dressed as a laborer. He is wearing French blue worker's clothes, even a beret."

Martin's brow wrinkled. "Really?"

"Yes, and an oilskin."

Looking again at Le Cerf, Martin said, "Why, do you suppose?"

"I don't know," he replied. "To escape us, I imagine. Maybe something else."

"Who is he with?"

"I don't know that, either. Other than the American, only one person has gone in since seven. Then about thirty minutes ago three people left."

"You did not go in?"

"No, I have a feeling he would spot me for a cop, and I don't want to be seen. Not yet anyway."

Martin stepped toward the square. "There are windows on the south side of the bar."

"Yes, I tried that. It's warped antique glass and I couldn't see a thing. It's like a kaleidoscope; one person looked like twenty."

Martin flipped up the hood of his jacket. "That old glass always has cracks in it. I'm going to take a look," he said as much to himself as Beauviér. "I'll be back in a minute."

Not waiting for approval, Martin hunkered his body and ran into the square. Jumping the odd puddle, he cut across the cobblestones, keeping one eye on the front door of Le Cerf. The wind was picking up, pushing the rain into his eyes and soaking his jeans. His tennis shoes felt like sponges. He moved past the facade of Le Cerf, to the side of the building. Blinking the rain from his eyes, he stood on his toes, attempting to look through the windows, but the leaded glass was stained, blocking any view. He went to the next window and the next, each seemingly darker than the one before. The last window, before the entrance of a connecting shop, had a glimmer of light breaking out; no thicker than a pencil, it came through an opening where the lead had collapsed and only time seemed to hold a small triangle of glass in place. Martin pushed it gently with his forefinger, enough that he could now see into the darkened bar.

It was all but empty of customers, with no one behind the bar. A fireplace illuminated the far corner and the three men before it. One sat in a large chair, its back to him; another leaned against the mantle smoking a cigar as the third paced between them. And it was that man he knew. He had seen the plaster across the left side of his face before, at the hospital in Namur; the man pacing was the American.

Guarding his breathing, Martin turned his head in an attempt to hear the conversation, but the rain slapping around him turned the words into gibberish. He could make out the inflections, nothing more. He looked again to the three men. The one smoking the cigar leaned forward, flicking an ash into the fire. Martin didn't recognize him, and the man in the chair he couldn't see completely, save the side of his face. But Martin could clearly see the American. He was dressed in the laborer's clothing that Beauviér described: the black beret and boots of a man who might live in an Algerian commune. It was not the clothing of someone with two hectares and a *maison de maitre* in Wolowe St. Pierre.

Martin shook briefly from the cold. Raindrops ran off the end of his nose and the damp was pushing through the skin of his ski jacket. Brushing the moisture from his eyes, he abruptly turned. Brilliant lights were illuminating him from a car moving slowly through the square, its driver searching for a way out. Martin dropped down, but felt it was too late. The car's headlights certainly created a silhouette in the leaded glass. Slowly lifting himself, he again looked through the small hole. The man smoking the cigar was now moving across the bar toward him, the American watching.

Martin stooped, moving back along the wall to the front door of the bar where he gently tried the handle. He then made a dash across the square.

Running underneath the metal canopy, he leaned forward, placing his hands on his knees. Beauviér stood close to the building, his upper body in the shadows.

"Could you see anything?" he asked.

"There are two others with the American," answered Martin, trying to catch his breath. "And the front door is locked."

"Did you recognize the others?"

He shook his head.

"Could you hear anything?"

Standing upright, he said, "No, nothing."

Suddenly, thunder clapped and a rain cloud exploded. The square turned black in the deluge. Beauviér glanced at the sky. "Bring up your car, Sergeant. I want to know who we have here," he said, over the sound of the drumming rain.

"Yes, monsieur." Running from under the metal canopy, Martin kept his gaze down and did not notice a man in a silver Mercedes who was studying his every move.

* * *

134

As John Clark stood at the stained-glass window, a bell in La Grand' Place struck nine times. In the silence that followed a burning log snapped, spitting a piece of ember onto the wooden floor. Kicking it back into the fireplace, Tom Breck said, "What is it?"

John Clark gently touched a small opening in the leaded glass with his thumb. "I don't know. Thought I saw something. I guess not." Returning to the fireplace, he took a drag on his cigar. "Christ, it's really pissing out," he said, addressing Stuart Endfield, who sat in a near overstuffed chair. The Englishman's eyes cautiously moved toward him, then jerked away.

The telephone behind the bar rang. No one spoke until its cry finally died out in mid-ring.

Tom said, "Tell me about the markers again," and began pacing in front of the fireplace.

Endfield took a deep breath, letting it out slowly. "There were eighteen in all," he said, his tone remorseful. "They totaled fifty-one thousand pounds."

"British or Irish?" said John Clark, smirking.

Endfield said nothing.

"Right," said Tom. "And how many are left?"

"Sixteen remain with Mégot."

"Well, you're not making very good progress, are you, Stuart?" said John Clark.

Tom glanced at the Irishman. "So Mégot threatens to turn these over to your boss at the embassy, right?" he asked.

Endfield nodded.

Tom stopped pacing, his back to the fire. "Then you will be dishonorably discharged and forced to return in disgrace to... Where are you from?"

"Luton—in Bedfordshire."

"Christ, man, I can't blame you for that," said John Clark, cigar smoke rolling out his mouth. "Who the hell would want to live in bleeding Luton?"

Tom glared at John before looking at Endfield. "So you stole my file from the embassy and showed it to Mégot?"

"Yes," he replied uncomfortably. "I had no choice."

Tom picked up a glass of whiskey from the mantle and took a drink. Returning it to the mantle, he asked, "What did the file say, Stuart?"

Hesitating, Endfield ran his tongue across his lips, then said, "It mentioned your wife and education and where you currently live and—" He grabbed his glass from the table next to him, clutching it with both hands.

"And?"

Endfield blurted, "And that you were a suspected smuggler and you had a partner in Budapest by the name of Alice something—it was a French name, I'm not good with French—but her real name was Tatiana. I don't remember the last name. And where she lived, and that she had a bodyguard named Yuri and... and that's everything. I give you my word." Seemingly finished with the confessional, he consumed the remaining whiskey in his glass, then asked, "Are you still going to beat me up?"

"No," said Tom.

John Clark said, "Pity," and flicked an ash from his cigar into the fire.

Tom asked, "Did the file say what I smuggled?"

"Yes," Endfield replied, adjusting himself to the chair. "It mentioned cigarettes and liquor when you lived in London."

"That's it?"

"Yes."

Tom stared at the Englishman. He did not understand. Someone knew about the paintings and he'd hoped it would be the man called Mégot. Now he was not sure.

He said to Endfield, "When do you speak with him again?"

"Mégot?"

"Oh, Christ," said John Clark, rolling his eyes.

"Yes," said Tom. "Mégot."

"Eleven o'clock tonight, at my apartment."

"He's meeting you there?"

"Oh, no. He'll telephone."

"And what if you're not there?"

Endfield's upper body swayed as he shook his head. "I wouldn't want to think about that."

"Okay, then what? After you check in, what happens?"

"I don't know. I suppose he'll expect me to have the money and ask how everything went, like before."

"How will you get him the money?"

"We meet at the hotel, La Legende, in the lobby."

"What a dump," mumbled John Clark.

Tom wrinkled his brow. He looked at the Irishman and asked, "How much money do you have here?"

John Clark grinned. "I have one million if that's what you mean."

Tom walked over to him, said softly, "Thanks, John," then turned to face Stuart Endfield.

"Right, then. You'll have your money," he went on, his tone optimistic. "When Mégot calls tonight, you tell him everything went swimmingly, or however you speak with him. But don't say more than necessary and don't change your mood with him. It's important that you stay the same. If he made you nervous before, well, stay nervous. Don't start getting comfortable."

Gazing into the fire, Endfield said, "I don't think that will be a problem."

"Good, then tell him you want to meet at La Legende like usual; say that... Say you don't like having that much money around your apartment and—"

"What are you going to do to him?" asked Endfield, still staring unblinking at the fire.

"Let me worry about that."

"I'd like to, but I really can't. Don't misunderstand me, but what about the markers? I can't allow them to be revealed, not after all of this."

"You'll do whatever Thomas tells you to do, man," yelled John Clark. "If he says dance naked in front of the Queen herself, you'll do it. Do you understand?"

Tom put his hand up, waiting for John Clark to stop before saying, "Listen Stuart, this Mégot has something we both want. Your bit, the gambling markers, will be a piece of cake. Mine I'm not so sure about. But I don't want you to worry. This time tomorrow, all of your problems will be over." He took a deep breath. "You have my word. Okay?"

"I suppose I don't have a choice," Endfield complained, staring at his folded hands.

"But you do, Stuart. Just make sure it's not the wrong one," said Tom firmly. "You play straight with me and I'll do the same."

Endfield put his hands on the arms of the chair. "Very well, then... May I go?" he asked.

His eyes, in the sharp light of the fire, were emotionless, like those of a man heading to trial, the verdict already in. Tom wanted to ask if he was all right, if he could make it, but thought better of it. He was uncertain of the answer himself as he said, "Yes, you may go."

John Clark walked behind the bar and began fiddling with something on the floor. After a few minutes he returned, handing Tom a large envelope. "There's one million," he said as though he were giving directions or a simple greeting, not an envelope containing a great amount of money.

"Thanks, John. I can get this back to—"

"I know, Thomas."

Nodding, Tom looked at Endfield. "Stand up."

The Englishman quickly stood.

"Where do you live?" asked Tom.

"The Sablon."

"Okay," he said, handing him the envelope. "Now it sounds like the rain has slowed, but take a taxi. Don't walk. No point in getting mugged."

Endfield held the envelope in one hand, then the other, appearing uncertain what to do with it.

"Where's your overcoat?" asked Tom.

"I don't have one."

"All right, turn around." Taking the envelope, Tom lifted the bottom of Endfield's suit jacket and pulled at his belt. "Loosen it." As Endfield complied, he tucked the envelope lengthwise on the inside of the waistband. "Okay, cinch it up," he said, letting the tail of the jacket fall.

Endfield turned. There were bloodstains on the collar of his shirt and his pinstriped suit was rumpled. His lower lip, cut where Tom had struck him, was beginning to swell. His dapper appearance was gone.

Walking to the table, still upturned from the fight, Tom gathered the bowler hat and umbrella from the floor and held them out as Endfield moved toward him. "I'll call you at eleven-thirty," he said, watching Endfield carefully place the bowler on his head. "What's your number?"

"Four-two, three-eight, three-nine."

"And your address?" he asked, moving to the front door.

"Number twelve, *rue des Minimes*… Apartment number thirty-six."

Unlocking the door, Tom let it swing open as Endfield moved past him onto cobblestones, shimmering from their coat of rain.

Endfield turned as if he were about to speak, but only continued across the square.

Watching the Englishman disappear into the darkness, Tom whispered, "Eleven-thirty, then," and pushed the door closed.

Letting out a deep breath, he looked across the room at John Clark, who said, "Do you trust him?"

"No, not really."

"That's wonderful," he said, lowering himself into the chair before the fire. "So what's your plan with this Mégot?"

Tom shook his head. "I was hoping you might have an idea."

Laughing, the Irishman coughed on a mouthful of cigar smoke.

* * *

Henri Martin looked down the shadowed street, unable to see the end of it over a slight rise. He knew it ended in a cul-de-sac, with no connecting side streets; he knew there was but one way in and out.

Once connecting the Palais de Justice, the small carriage route had been used for the transport of prisoners—weaving up the side of the hill, it allowed a certain discretion. And so the name *rue des Minimes* came to pass, a street considered as trivial as the people who used it. But the road became too small for modern vehicles and was eventually sealed off with a brick wall now covered in decades-old ivy. The neighborhood had changed. Expensive apartment buildings were built beside shops featuring Chippendale and Louis XIII, each business catering to the now wealthy inhabitants, and the prisoners no longer passed by.

Henri Martin knew the story. His father told him one summer day when they walked in and about the Sablon with its Michelin-rated restaurants and chauffeur-driven cars. A neighborhood reserved for cafe society and, more recently, the foreign nationals imported to work in the bureaucratic labyrinth of the European Union; modern cars and modern ways against the backdrop of a tired street, winding its way from nowhere.

The man Henri Martin was following lived on this street. He rented an apartment in one of the newer buildings that towered above the sidewalk. It had a well-lighted entrance with an aged doorman dressed up like an officer of some forgotten army. But he only carried the odd package and answered the occasional bell. A few minutes earlier, this same doorman had given a shallow bow to a man sporting a bowler hat and an abrasion on his lower lip. It was Stuart Endfield, the perfect Englishman, who then immediately disappeared into a waiting elevator.

Concealed in the dark gap between street lamps, Sergeant Martin saw the doorman's courtesy from the vantage of his parked car. Then, after a minute or less, ceiling lights illuminated in a third floor apartment and Endfield appeared in the window, quickly pulling the curtains closed.

Martin, now certain where the Englishman lived, thought he might be in for the night when a car approached from the closed end of the street, its headlights off. He could see it advancing, studying its reflection in his side mirror. It was an older Mercedes—beige or silver, or possibly gray. The creeping hum of the car's engine was suddenly interrupted by the sound of laughter. A couple on the opposite sidewalk had stopped to embrace. The Mercedes also came to a stop, its driver watching. The couple, unaware of the onlooker, stood at the entrance of Endfield's apartment building. The man began searching his pockets as the woman giggled, trying to help. They struggled playfully, when abruptly keys fell to the sidewalk with a metallic clatter.

Their sound triggered something in the driver of the Mercedes who, throwing open his door, jumped out. The interior light flew to life, but he moved too quickly for Martin to see his face. The driver pushed past the couple in the now open doorway and into the foyer, quickly disappearing up the staircase.

Squinting at the unusual scene, Martin's eyes drifted up to the third floor apartment and then back to the idling Mercedes. He gradually recalled seeing this same car in Namur—he was certain, it was the same car and the same lone driver.

Martin shoved his door open and in his haste, caught his foot on the rocker panel, falling hands first onto the wet cobblestone street. He scrambled to stand, then raced toward the building. The couple was gone, the door again closed.

"Police," he cried out, pounding on the glass with his fist.

Finally the doorman, sleep in his eyes, appeared from behind the concierge desk.

Martin pressed his identification card to the glass, and again yelled, "Police."

The old man removed a pair of half-glasses from his pocket and placing them on his nose, stepped forward. Squinting his puffy eyes, comparing the card's photograph to the bearer, he finally nodded, releasing the catch.

Moving into the foyer, Martin waved off the mumbling doorman, noticing the light above the elevator was climbing—third floor, fourth floor. A bell rang and a telephone sounded as he leapt the first few steps up the staircase. The identification card dropped from his hand, but he let it be, grabbing instead for the handrail. He reached the first landing, then the second. His breathing was labored, not from the physical demands on his body, but from a strange fear rushing through him.

He moved up to the next landing, and the next. His pace slowed; the third floor was just ahead. Unzipping his parka, he removed his gun from the holster, pulling back the hammer as he stepped onto the landing. It was dark except for a stream of light cutting across his feet. His back against the wall, he gripped the gun with both hands and swung out into the open hallway. The stream of light suddenly poured into his eyes, yellows and reds, and it blinded him. Something else filled his vision—brilliant and glaring colors, blues and even brighter reds and then it fell dark, leaving but a silhouette in the near doorway.

Dropping to one knee, he searched for something, anything in the darkness. He heard a loud cry as the black silhouette advanced.

Martin shouted, "Police. Halt," then felt a sharp pain in his throat.

Again he was blinded by the colors—the yellows and reds surrounded him, and sensed his strength slipping away. He slumped to his side, and taking aim at the retreating shadow, pulled the trigger.

CHAPTER FOUR

Christmas fell over Brussels like an enormous patchwork quilt. Almost overnight, the streets took on the appearance of a different city. Thousands of lights now illuminated the gray winter pall, all shaped into wreaths and stars and sugared canes that hung from every street lamp and government building. Nativity scenes were bountiful and lavish, but none surpassed the creation that stood center stage in La Grand' Place.

Each character was alive, save the child in the manger. University students, mostly drunken, took on the responsibility of Mary, Joseph and the three wise men, who were invariably out cold before the final tourist passed. The neglected mule would then kick loose the fencing, allowing a lamb or two its freedom, only to become *côtelette d'agneau* by morning.

The spirit of the season was abundant. The time for sharing had arrived.

* * *

Inspector Jules Beauviér took his hand away from the dead man and stood. He looked again at the wound inflicted across the stomach. A knife of some size had been used, one large enough to cut a loaf of bread or summer melon with a single stroke. The face of the dead man revealed no clue, save a spot of dried blood on the swollen lip from an earlier altercation. And were it not for the dead white pallor, the man on the carpet might as well be sleeping.

As he walked into the open kitchen of the small apartment, Beauviér noticed a calendar attached to the icebox. Studying the days of the week printed in English, he squinted at the word *Wednesday*, thinking it to be misspelled. He then looked to the attached photograph; it depicted a snow-coated tavern dressed up

143

for the holidays and a man, suited like St. Nicholas, standing at the open door. The words *Seasons Greetings from Marks and Spencer* were printed on a banner that draped the roof, partially eclipsing a half-dozen plastic deer tethered to an orange sleigh.

Below that was the date. It read Tuesday, December 7, 1984, and Beauviér had but twenty-two days remaining in his post as Inspector. On January 1, he would be obliged to pack his bags and return to Brugges on the North Atlantic coast, to his home and garden and dormant existence. Only twenty-two days remained.

Slowly turning, his gloved hands folded behind his back, he asked, "How is he, Doctor?" as he watched a policeman cross the room.

The white-jacketed man squatting on the carpet looked up. "He is not stiff. No rigor mortis as of yet, Inspector," he advised, nodding at the blanched face of the Englishman.

Beauviér blurted, "Not him. I mean, Sergeant Martin. How is Henri Martin?"

"He'll be fine," replied the doctor and, noticeably embarrassed, faced the firemen attending the near gurney. "Just fine, Inspector."

"Are you sure he can't talk?"

The doctor shook his head. "In time, but not now."

"Is he lucid?"

"He's coherent, if that's what you mean."

"Then he can write?"

"If he could before, then he can now."

The two firemen lifted the gurney as Beauviér moved across the room to stand beside the prostrate Martin. He studied the sergeant's wounded throat, wrapped in layers of white bandage, and the blackened eyes fluttering against the bright lights. Martin attempted to smile, but only grimaced before letting his mouth fall to a straight line.

Touching his shoulder to stop him from any further movement, Beauviér took a deep breath and said, "We are at number twelve, *rue des Minimes*, apartment number thirty-six, Sergeant." He paused briefly. "There is a dead man by the front door. An Englishman. His name is Stuart Endfield and he works—worked— for the British Embassy."

A police radio squawked and Beauviér signaled that the officer, standing guard in the corner, should shut it down. He then glanced at his watch. "He was killed by a sharp instrument some forty minutes earlier, according to the doctor—that is to say, he was

144

stabbed with a knife, and simply bled to death. The stomach wound was serious; had we arrived earlier..."

The doctor, closing his medical bag, said, "It would have made no difference. The Englishman would have died, regardless."

"We know the perpetrator was a man, Sergeant. Did you see him? Did you see his face?" asked Beauviér.

Shaking his head, Martin opened his mouth slightly, though no words came out, closing his eyes in apparent frustration.

"It's all right, Sergeant," said Beauviér. "I understand. We have plenty of time... plenty of time."

Looking at the two firemen, Beauviér nodded toward the door, and with a compassion that men show to one of their own, they wheeled the fallen sergeant from the room. Police lamps had been brought in to illuminate the scene; their brilliant light followed the gurney into the hallway, pushing awkward shadows against the walls.

The gurney, too long to fit inside the elevator cage, was lowered down the staircase, a fireman on each side. Martin looked back at the Inspector from the first landing, his blackened eyes seeming to apologize, before disappearing down the staircase.

The telephone in the apartment sounded, its rattle piercing the quiet labor. Moving to the telephone, Beauviér hesitated before lifting the receiver, then in English, said, "Hello."

The line went dead.

Shrugging, his eyes drifted to some paper squares next to the telephone. "What is this?" he asked, picking them up.

A policeman in the corner replied, "Gambling markers, Inspector."

Beauviér looked carefully at each one. "This is a great deal of money, Corporal."

"And there are more," the officer informed him, removing an identical batch of papers from an open briefcase. "Almost three million francs here."

"And a half a million here," said Beauviér. "What do you make of it?"

The policeman lifted his shoulders and then let them drop. "I believe these people who work in the embassies are quite well paid."

Closing his fist around the markers, Beauviér whispered, "Not this well, they're not," and dropped them into his coat pocket. He moved back to the landing, near the bloodied spot where Sergeant Martin was found.

It was an ordinary murder, something Beauviér had seen before, yet this was somehow obscure. The dead Englishman by the door, now covered in black plastic, was part of a crime that began so simply and had escalated into something he did not understand. Resting his gloved forefinger on his tightly closed mouth, Beauviér thought back to the first sign of a crime.

It all started with the death of the art dealer in Namur, maybe of a cardiac, and maybe not, and then the appearance of the painting by Monet. The American, he reasoned, was the center of everything, though none around him could be dismissed—each one held a place on the trail leading to the Englishman's death. Then there was the meeting at Le Cerf, but to what purpose? The American, the Englishman and the owner of the suspicious bar, said to be an Irishman. What had they discussed? With one now dead, the other two were possibly in danger, and possibly, from each other. But why? And from where did the Monet originate?

That was where he would find the answer to the strange murder before him.

It all began with the Monet.

One of the police lamps was moved in the small apartment, its beam briefly illuminating the wall beside Beauviér. The corners of his eyes wrinkled. Reaching out his hand, he took a step forward, then another. Touching the wall with his forefinger, he remained motionless for a few seconds.

"Corporal," he bellowed.

The young policeman appeared at the open door of the apartment, his arms pressed to his side. "Yes, Inspector."

"How many rounds did Sergeant Martin fire?"

The policeman paused. "One, monsieur."

"You are certain?"

"Yes, monsieur. Quite certain."

Removing a glove, Beauviér took a penknife from his coat pocket. As the blade clicked into place, the hallway went dark.

"Get that light back on!" he said. "Now!"

The police lamp again flooded the landing and another was hurriedly moved closer to the open door. The doctor and an additional policeman gathered between the lights, no one stepping beyond the threshold.

Grunting, Beauviér pushed the blade of the knife into the wall before him. As he gently probed the black impression, small bits of plaster began to fall to his feet. His burrowing became more aggressive, then a black piece of the wall fell to the carpet. Dropping to one knee, he picked it up, raising his hand to catch the light.

"Where was the round from Martin's gun found?" he asked, to no one in particular.

"In the leg of the dining table," replied the young corporal.

Beauviér twisted his upper body, studying the carpet that led to the staircase, then dropped to all fours, slowly moving across the landing. The three men at the door looked at one another, then back at the Inspector.

"How did the Englishman die, Doctor?" asked Beauviér, not looking up.

One of the near apartment doors opened slightly. The face of an old woman appeared.

"Get back inside!" yelled Beauviér, glaring at the intrusive neighbor.

Hurriedly the door shut.

Cocking his head to face the doctor, Beauviér said, "Well?"

"The stomach wound, monsieur. He—"

"He bled to death?"

"Yes, I would say so."

"Then where was all the blood?"

"In the carpeting, monsieur. The padding underneath is like a sponge and quite absorbent."

"His face, Doctor," said Beauviér. "Did you see the Englishman's face?"

"I—I don't understand, monsieur."

Beauviér again looked at the carpet, moving slowly toward the stairs. Stopping, he poked at a smudge on the floor. "I mean he did not have the look of a man who died a slow death. The Englishman was killed outright. Would you please have another look at him," he said. It was not a question.

While Beauviér picked at the carpet, the doctor lifted the black plastic from the Englishman's body, revealing the upper torso.

A silent minute passed, then another.

Softly, the doctor said, "I found it, Inspector."

147

"What?" yelled Beauviér.

"He has been shot, monsieur. Quite a small caliber." The doctor indicated a minute hole in the Englishman's dark vest. "It went right through the heart, exiting out the left shoulder blade. His suit jacket hid the wound. I did not think to look for it after the bullet was found in the table leg. It seemed impossible for that to have been what killed the man."

"It wasn't, Doctor," said Beauviér, sounding exasperated. Sitting down on the carpet, his back to the wall, he held up the black bit removed from the plaster. "This is what killed the Englishman. A small caliber bullet, as you speculated."

"I don't understand." He looked away from the Inspector to the splintered leg of the dining table. "The doorman said there was but one gunshot."

"The old doorman, my dear Doctor," said Beauviér, gazing at the carpet by his shoes, "does not know what year this is."

Sounding uncertain, the doctor inquired, "Then Sergeant Martin fired twice?"

Another apartment door opened, though quickly closed following a harsh rebuke from Beauviér.

Again studying the lead bullet, he said, "No, of course not. You see, the Englishman opened his door for the assassin. He possibly knew him. The killer took two or three steps into the apartment, turning before the Englishman had time to close the door, and fired one shot at close range. The bullet went through the Englishman's heart and out his chest, coming to rest—" Beauviér pointed at the chipped wall above his head. "There."

Quickly the doctor said, "Then why the knife wound?"

Beauviér's brow wrinkled. "His belt was cut, was it not?"

"Yes," the doctor replied, dropping his gaze to the Englishman's waist. "In two pieces."

Beauviér said, "He was carrying something, secured by the belt. Probably in the small of his back."

"But what would he be carrying?"

"How should I know?" he blared, lifting himself from the floor. "Maybe jewels or money, or a Monet, for all I know."

"A Monet?"

Frowning at the doctor, Beauviér said, "We know these things: one, the killer is a man of average height, assuming the path of the bullet was not too altered as it passed through the body. Two, he is armed with a small caliber hand gun, equipped possibly with

148

something to silence the discharge; and three, he has been wounded." He quickly looked at the highest-ranking policeman. "Corporal, get on the radio and inform dispatch that all hospitals and clinics in each commune should be on alert for a gunshot wound or puncture wound or anything suspicious."

"Yes, monsieur," he said, reaching for the radio connected to his belt.

As the corporal gave his report, the static from the responding police operator filled the hallway. The doctor again covered the body with the black plastic and moved from the apartment onto the landing. He walked next to Beauviér, who appeared lost in thought.

"How do you know, monsieur?" he inquired.

Beauviér turned. "What? Know what?" He squinted at the white-jacketed man.

"That the assassin was wounded."

Sounding bored, as if the question were bothersome, Beauviér took a deep breath and said, "Martin surprised the killer, who had obviously put away his gun and carried only the knife he used to cut the Englishman's belt. The landing was poorly lighted, and the killer, advancing from the apartment, was certainly hard to make out." He then indicated the single bulb in the glass-covered wall sconce. "So, he was on the sergeant and slashed at his throat, the only available target, as Martin was crouching. But the thick collar of the ski jacket caught most of the damage from the blade and Martin was able to get off a round." Beauviér pointed at his feet with his forefinger, moving it slowly toward the stairway. "Those drops of blood are neither the Englishman's nor Martin's. They are from a third party. They belong to the assassin."

Cocking his head to the side, the doctor looked at the carpet and said, "I assumed that—"

"We all did, Doctor," Beauviér interrupted. "Now please collect some of the dried blood and let me know the type by morning. You are trained in such matters, are you not?"

"Yes, of course, monsieur."

"That's good. We might reduce the list of suspects to a few million as opposed to the entire male population."

The two policemen at the door stepped aside as Beauviér entered the apartment. Glancing at the covered body of Stuart Endfield, he moved to the window, pulling at the drawstring. The floor length drapes flew open and the black of night met his eyes.

It glittered. It all glittered—washed down by the winter rain, the city looked freshly scrubbed and its placid veneer was again in place. Beauviér's eyes wandered over the elegant city, finally coming to rest on the street below. The open end of *rue des Minimes* was sealed off by a police van, the roof light flashing its blue tint against the wet cobblestones. A policeman stood chatting with a single onlooker and each had a cigarette, the smoke hanging above their heads in the still night air. He saw a speeding police car in the distance, with another close behind, advancing on the scene. Their sirens echoed off the near Palais de Justice, its outline barely visible save the lone flood lamp on the domed roof, the light caressing the motionless Belgian flag. One hundred years earlier, Beauviér remembered being told, shackled prisoners made their way down the carriage route from that building. Many an evil man passed this way.

And nothing had changed.

Letting the spent bullet drop into the pocket of his topcoat, he slid the loose glove onto his hand and glanced at his watch. It was twenty-five minutes before midnight. In twenty-five minutes there would be but twenty-one days remaining at his post. He thought it not sufficient; he thought himself moving backward, and away from the truth of it all.

* * *

Looking through the French doors into the dark of the garden, Thomas Breck was mindful of the stillness. The rains and winds had stopped. Nothing moved in the darkness.

He stood frozen beside the hall telephone while the voice still resonated in his thoughts. The man had paused after answering, waiting for Tom to speak, and then his accented greeting rushed through the line like a cold wind.

Something was wrong. Endfield did not answer his telephone. Someone else had.

Tom walked into the living room and cautiously lowered himself into an overstuffed chair.

Nothing was going as planned. The few thousand francs he was able to acquire by the sale of his cars, and the useless bank accounts, left him all but bankrupt. He would have to sell his home and gather what equity there was. Sitting up, he grabbed a bottle of Cognac from the adjacent liquor cart and hurriedly poured a glass, taking a large drink. The alcohol seemed to calm him, so he drank until the glass was empty. Again he grabbed the bottle, but stopped, grinning awkwardly at his thoughts.

Only ten years earlier he had nothing—no cars, no fine house, no elegant clothes or safe-deposit boxes tucked into the shadows of scattered banks. Ten years before he had possessed nothing, yet somehow as he sat with his hand clutching the neck of the bottle, he remembered being happier. He remembered being more at peace.

Letting his hand fall, he looked into the dining room. He could see the chair where his wife last sat; he remembered their conversation, or exchange he would deem it, and the constant evasion. They shared the same language, but the words came out so differently—their meaning somehow lost in the battles—he wanting her so desperately, she wanting more than he had to give, more than he knew how to give.

Resting his face on his upturned palms, he closed his eyes. They watered slightly from the strain and from the emotion rushing through him. He fell back into the chair, his eyes shut tight as a fatigue came over him. The restless energy was now subsiding—he began to drift, and fell to sleep.

After some thirty minutes, he woke with a start. A ringing sound had brought him out of a dream, a terrible dream that his wife was gone forever, that she had found another.

The telephone in the hallway was clattering. He stood in his bare feet and walked into the foyer to stare at the vibrating machine.

Finally lifting the receiver, he cleared his throat and said, "Yes."

"Thomas, lad," came the accented voice.

"Yes," he said, trying to shake the dream, then repeated, "Yes, John."

"Listen to me carefully, Thomas," said John Clark. "The Englishman is dead."

"What?" he exclaimed. "How?"

"I don't know that, lad," answered the Irishman, his voice hushed. "Only that he is dead."

"But—"

"The police were here, at Le Cerf," John said. "They knew Endfield was here. They knew you were here."

"How?"

"Again, Thomas, I don't know that."

"They said nothing else?"

151

"No, not really. Only—" The Irishman paused. "Don't mistake me, Thomas, but I think it's best if I leave town for a while. There are things... There are skeletons that I don't wish to have disturbed, if you can understand."

"Of course. You must do what you feel is best," he said, trying to stay calm, trying to think. "What about the bar?"

"I'll turn it over to my nephew, for the time being."

"Nephew? You have a nephew?"

"Not actually, Thomas. As I said, there are things about me I don't wish to have discussed. I hope you can understand."

Tom's voice was sympathetic. "I understand you're a good friend, John. That's all that needs to be said."

"And you to me, Thomas... And you to me."

Tom asked, "Where will you be?"

"There is a village in Ireland, just a mile south of where the ferry from Holyhead lands," he whispered into the receiver. "It's called Dalkey. I've kept a cottage there all these years, in case I needed a place to hide myself."

"I can call you?"

"There's no telephone there, lad."

Tom swallowed. "I understand," he said softly.

"I knew you would," said the Irishman. "Oh, and one more thing."

"Yes."

"The policeman that I spoke with. He was not a city copper. He was a gendarme."

"A gendarme?"

"Yes. His name was Beauviér, Inspector Beauviér." John's voice sounded even more distant. "I must be going, lad... Good luck to you."

"Thank you, John. I—"

The line went dead.

Tom looked into the dining room, staring out to the garden as it lay motionless in the dark night. The dream returned to his thoughts and a pain ran into his heart; a pain that he had never felt before.

* * *

Standing at the painted window, Tatiana Gregòsh peered through a section scraped clear the evening before. She'd used a coin to make this peephole, allowing her to see the gravel drive of

152

the hotel and a portion of the Danube beyond. It looked different; it now felt different, and she sensed her captivity was coming to an end. One way or another, it would soon be over.

The door to the hallway was open, and had been for some time. Before dawn a policeman brought her coffee, leaving the door ajar when he left. The tobacco smoke from his cheap cigarette still hung in the room, as did the scent of his clothing—the cold air seeming to accent each smell. The wall radiator no longer worked and the room temperature had dropped, creating moisture on the painted window. Using the side of her hand to clear it away, she watched the changing scene below.

A black sedan pulled into the drive, coming to an abrupt stop. The driver hurriedly opened the rear door and took the hand of a man who emerged slowly. His eyes moved to the painted window on the second floor.

Turning away, Tatiana looked at the open door of her room. She took a step toward it, then another, listening to the sound of the sedan's engine shutting down and the quiet that followed. A door slammed closed and she heard footsteps on the staircase, the wood floor creaking under each step. The policeman, a cigarette hanging from his mouth, appeared in the doorway. His face expressionless, he motioned with his thick forefinger that she follow.

Kneeling before the fireplace in the hotel lobby, the policeman blew on the struggling embers, taking deep breaths that were causing him to cough. Gradually, gray-white smoke rose from a flame glimmering in the damp sticks; paper was added and gradually the wood began to snap.

Sitting in a near armchair, Tatiana watched him closely, avoiding any eye contact with the stranger on her left. The stranger and Tatiana sat in chairs half facing each other, half facing the fire.

Slumped back, he appeared irritated and said, "Why didn't you check the level of the oil before we took over this goddamn dump?"

Slowly turning his reddened face, the policeman shrugged.

"Damn," mumbled the stranger, pushing his hands back and forth on the arms of the chair as if to warm them.

The hotel's front door opened, then slammed shut behind the second policeman, who now leaned over the back of the stranger's chair, whispering in his ear. The conversation was brief and the policeman quickly moved back to the entrance. A cold wind pushed into the small lobby as he went outside, again slamming the door behind him.

The flame in the fireplace grew, but Tatiana could not feel any change in the room's temperature. Unfolding her hands, she placed them in the pockets of her coat, forcing her shoulders up, then glanced at the stranger. His eyes were closed and his head tipped slightly down. His face had a sickly pallor and was dotted with spots of perspiration, as if from fever. He grunted and raised his head. Tatiana looked away.

The policeman threw his spent cigarette into the fire and stood. Slapping his knees to clear the leavings of ash, he walked to the reception counter and grabbed a stool. Tatiana could hear him sigh as he sat behind her, followed by the heels of his shoes scraping the leg brace. The lid of a lighter clicked open, then closed. Gradually, the smoke from the Russian cigarette floated between her and the stranger, who said, "I hope you have not been too uncomfortable, mademoiselle?" while he gazed straight ahead.

Tatiana looked at him. "Why am I—"

"That's good," he said. "A bit of time away can be good; good to think about life and her little inconsistencies." He made a fist and coughed into it.

The fire was gathering strength. Tatiana removed her hands from her pockets and clasped them on her lap, remaining quiet, wishing the stranger would do the same.

After a half-minute he said, "My name is Mégot," and signaled the policeman with a raised hand. "I know your partner Thomas Breck."

Tatiana's mouth opened slightly, watching the policeman move into view.

"Bring me some water," said Mégot, his voice weak.

A cupboard squeaked open, then shut. Tatiana was about to speak when again the policeman appeared. He removed a cork from a bottle of flat water and pouring some into a wine glass, handed it to Mégot. She watched him gulp at the liquid. Small amounts of it ran out the corner of his mouth, dropping onto the lapel of his topcoat. The policeman attempted to pour additional water, but Mégot waved him off, handing him the empty glass.

Wiping at his chin, Mégot said, "I don't have much time, so if you will please listen closely." He calmly looked at Tatiana.

The little coloring he had, was uneven in his pale face. His eyes, like two black spots, studied her. Slowly, she nodded.

154

Folding his arms against his chest, he tipped his head back slightly. "This affair has gotten rather messy of late." His tone was strangely apologetic. "And I would like to get us back on the right path as quickly as possible." Coughing again into his closed fist, he mumbled a profanity and said, "Your partner, Monsieur Breck, has been less than agreeable in our dealings, but I am certain, after our little talk, you will be able to—"

"Thomas does what he wishes," she blurted, quickly sitting up.

Mégot held up his hand. "So I'm discovering, mademoiselle," he said faintly. "But there are no choices in this matter. Either do what I request or you will both end up in prison." He smirked. "You appear to have lost weight, mademoiselle. Have you enjoyed your stay here at the auberge?"

Slumping back into her chair, Tatiana didn't respond.

"I thought not," he said sharply. "Now, it is all very simple, so if you will please listen." He began loosening the scarf about his neck. "There is a machine in Belgium that I would like to have moved to North Africa." He stopped, as if waiting for her to protest.

Taking a deep breath, she said, "What kind of machine?"

"Oh, it's quite illegal, mademoiselle, if that's what you mean." He sounded pleased with her participation in the conversation.

"But I must know what it is," she demanded.

"What it is, is not your concern, mademoiselle. I only need to know if you are willing to do as I say."

Her eyes narrowed. "Where is Thomas?"

"In Brussels," he answered, growing more animated. "His wife left him, you know. In light of his financial problems, it's only natural. I don't know why there are not more women bankers; they can always tell when a man is running low on funds, no matter what he says. It's a sixth sense, really." He attempted to laugh, but only coughed loudly.

Placing her elbows on the arms of the chair, she clasped her hands, pressing her forefingers to her closed mouth. She did not understand; Thomas Breck should have no financial problems. For years they were successful, and now there were the two masterpieces. Money should not be an issue.

Mégot said, "It's gone, mademoiselle."

"What is gone?" she asked, breaking from her thoughts.

"Why, the painting, mademoiselle. The Monet is now in the hands of the police and the—" He did not finish the sentence.

155

"I don't know what you are talking about," she said, attempting to hide her shock at the news.

Mégot held out a newspaper clipping, but she didn't move. Moving quickly between them, the policeman took the paper, forcing it into her grip, followed by a whispered threat. She glared up at him, then slowly lowered her gaze and began to read. It was a week-old clipping from *Le Monde*, the report on the Claude Monet masterpiece found in the city of Namur. She leaned forward to catch the light of the fire, realizing the fortune that had been so close was now gone. Only the Renoir remained and that too, might be in the hands of the police. She'd spent all of her money to procure the two paintings and now she, like Tom, was bankrupt. There was no money to fight Mégot.

"Why me?" she asked.

"This job demands the best forger there is. And that is you, mademoiselle."

"And Thomas?" she asked, her voice trailing off.

Mégot grinned. "A smuggler who is not in prison, is also the best."

"And when this is done, what is to keep you from wanting something more?"

"At that point, mademoiselle, you will have more on me than anything I could have on you," he answered, his tone unwavering. "I am not greedy. This is all that I need."

Resigned to completing the conversation, she asked, "Where in North Africa?"

"To Algeria, and I would like—"

A knocking sound cut him off.

The second policeman was at the front door, an elderly man at his side. Mégot twisted his neck to glance at them as the door closed, then said to Tatiana, "You have until the end of the month to do what I ask."

"That is not enough time."

"You have no choice, mademoiselle," he said, slamming his hand down on the arm of the chair. "Your stay here will seem like a holiday compared to what will happen should you fail. Do you understand?" He stared at her, his black eyes waiting, until she reluctantly nodded.

"He will take you home now," he said, indicating the second policeman. "This is all you need to know about the machine." He held out a manila envelope.

"What's the date?" said Tatiana. "I don't even know what day it is."

"It is December tenth, mademoiselle."

"You are giving us only twenty-one days, monsieur," she complained.

Mégot shook the manila envelope, "Take this," he ordered, "or you will have even less."

Standing, Tatiana obeyed, then moved to the front door before Mégot mentioned additional orders, or changed his mind. The policeman opened the door and the cold of winter brushed against her face. It awakened her to the freedom a few steps ahead, but she hesitated, looking back over her shoulder at the man who seemingly controlled her life. He appeared to be in pain as he nodded at the elderly man who had already taken her vacated chair. The man was opening a black satchel, exposing its contents that sparkled from the light of the fire.

Tatiana and the policeman walked from the hotel to the waiting sedan. She climbed into the back seat, pulling the skirts of her coat about her knees. The door fell closed and the car began pulling forward, the Danube framed in her side window, gradually slipping away. It appeared frozen in the morning light, with no boats making their way across the world. Only patches of thin mist floated on the surface, like giant step stones to the other side. She watched the river until it disappeared behind a stand of trees, then let her gaze fall to the manila envelope on her lap. Removing the single slip of paper from inside, she began reading.

Abruptly, she said, "Wait! Stop! I must speak with him again. This is impossible."

Glancing in the mirror, the policeman pushed on the accelerator, as if he'd misunderstood.

CHAPTER FIVE

The drive from Brussels to Paris would take slightly less than three hours if traffic were moderate. Thomas Breck did it in two. The Jensen slowed only once for customs and immigration at the French frontier, and even then did not stop as the unconcerned guards waved him through.

The border was all but open, with the European community forging ahead by way of a common market and an impending common currency. In an effort to copy the economic success of the United States, a twelve-member coalition of European countries was uniting to do economic battle with the American upstarts. Whereas a man from Alabama might uproot his family in search of a better life in Montana, with no need to change money between states as he traveled, the European Community was choosing to adopt the same mechanism, the theory being that a family from Madrid might relocate to Dusseldorf or a Frenchman might move to Oslo.

However, the one issue never mentioned was the need to communicate. The twelve member states represented almost as many languages, let alone dialects, and the odds of any migration similar to one in America occurring were as remote as Sweden shutting down in observance of Bastille Day or West Germany in recognition of Armistice. Twelve different mentalities with competing parliaments in both Brussels and Strasbourg seemed ludicrous to Tom when he first heard of it, and clearly impossible. The centuries-old art of smuggling would be made moot as the soldiers and police manning the watchtowers were to be replaced by a twelve-star welcome mat.

The call from Budapest had come at eight-fifteen that morning. The conversation was brief and emotional as Tom listened to Yuri: Tatiana had been freed. The reason was not immediately

159

important since a rendezvous had been set in a place they all knew without mentioning—a small hotel south of Paris in the village of Barbizon. Yuri at first resisted, preferring to meet in Switzerland, but Tom insisted Barbizon was safe for Tatiana and he had personal reasons that were clouding his judgment.

Checking the rearview mirror, he pushed the Jensen faster. Traffic going into Paris was light and, driving onto the *périphérique* that encircled the city, he took the autoroute south toward Lyon. It was now only fifty kilometers to Barbizon, he would arrive before noon.

* * *

Inspector Jules Beauviér sat in the darkened room of the British Embassy as the projector shot bursts of light across the screen. Like snow coming out of the night, the scenes silently took shape while a man standing in the corner performed commentary.

"Here is Endfield replacing the file," he announced to his audience of one, "and he is completely oblivious to the camera."

Beauviér sat up in his chair. "What is this?" he asked.

"Endfield has plainly discovered the camera. The carpenters hadn't yet covered the exposed wiring with the proper molding and he merely followed it from his adjoining office."

"Then he knew he was caught?"

"Not necessarily. Had he not been murdered, we wouldn't have reviewed this tape and it would have eventually erased itself." The man cleared his throat. "Just a few hours following the call from you, the recording would have been lost."

There was a click and the screen went black.

Sitting back in his chair, Beauviér said, "But you telephoned me, monsieur."

Not responding to the contradiction, the man moved noisily across the room. Slowly, the floor length curtains running the length of the wall were drawn and Beauviér blinked his eyes against the incoming daylight.

"What was in the file?" he asked.

The man dropped something onto the table in front of Beauviér, said, "Look for yourself, Inspector," then sat in a near chair. "It's about the American, Thomas Allan Breck. Not much really; bits and pieces about his criminal activities in Britain during the early seventies and then his move to Belgium." The man produced a

160

package of cigarettes from his pocket, offering one to Beauviér while he continued, "He was small time, really. A bit of untaxed scotch and gin coming out of Rotterdam and then tobacco, sometimes as much as a container."

Beauviér glanced at the gesture and shaking his head, flipped open the file before him. "You say small time?"

The man lit his cigarette with a wooden match, and flicking his hand to extinguish it, said, "In the scope of things, quite small, Inspector. We are not a police operation, as you know, and he only came to our attention after being sighted repeatedly in Budapest and Prague and then sometime later in Warsaw. I'm embarrassed to say we thought him to be a spy of some sort, although that was Nigel Hathaway in charge then—everyone was an enemy operative to that poor sod."

With care, Beauviér read the paper before him, running the tip of his middle finger below each line, attempting to make sense of the words. The information appeared vague and offered little help to his case, save the final paragraph at the bottom of the paper.

"What do you know about this Alice Malinaud?" he asked.

Taking a long drag on his cigarette, the man finally exhaled, pushing the smoke out the corner of his mouth. "Well for one thing, that's not her name. It's actually Tatiana Gregòsh. Polish, I believe. Don't have that much on her and would not have this, were it not for her bodyguard."

"Bodyguard?" said Beauviér, observing the man through the veil of smoke.

"Something of that sort—been with her forever, best as we can make out. His first name is Yuri and I'm afraid that's all we have. Not related and somewhat older than she. Anyway, it seems he got into a spot of trouble with the French some years back and this Tatiana came to rescue him, and the frogs—" The man stopped himself. "Excuse me, Inspector."

Beauviér waved him off. "I'm Belgian, monsieur."

"Right, of course." He extinguished his cigarette in a coffee cup with an illustration of the Queen Mother on the side, then moved toward the bank of windows, his hands clasped behind his back. "Well, appears she forged some documents to get this Yuri chap freed up and the French police didn't find out for some time, or until they were out of the country in any case, and by then living in Budapest." Wearing a crooked smile, he turned to face Beauviér. "But Tatiana Gregòsh left behind a nice set of fingerprints."

His brow wrinkling, Beauviér said, "You had her fingerprints recorded?" and slowly closed the file.

"No, we didn't," he replied. "The Poles had them. Seems she was wanted on murder charges in Warsaw almost twenty years earlier."

"You work with the Communists?"

"On criminal affairs, yes, Inspector. But it's kept quite hush-hush, if you understand."

Beauviér did not understand, but said, "Of course, monsieur." Lifting himself from the chair, he went to the door, turning as he reached for the handle. "So I'm to understand this—this Tatiana Gregòsh committed a murder when she was a teenager?"

"She was fourteen years old. So, you understand the level of criminals you're dealing with, Inspector?"

"I see," said Beauviér. "Then why was Tatiana Gregòsh not arrested by the Hungarians when they discovered her identity?"

"I would only suppose she paid someone off. She is quite well-to-do."

"Then she is still in Budapest?"

"No, we've discovered she has recently returned to France."

"France?" he said, sounding surprised. "Why would she risk such a thing?"

"She is up to her old tricks, most assuredly, Inspector. She and the American," replied the man sharply. "And she will have forged a new identity for herself. That is, after all, what she does best."

"And the name she is using?"

"That I do not know."

"But you know where she is, monsieur?"

"Yes. The village of Barbizon; it's south of—"

"Yes, I know it." Beauviér removed a handkerchief from his topcoat pocket and dabbed at his forehead. "You seem to have a great deal more knowledge of these people than is written there," he said, indicating the file.

The man took a step forward. "These people must be brought to justice, Inspector."

"But—"

"The file on the American is being updated, Inspector. I merely had a peek at it."

Beauviér ran his fingers under his chin, his face quizzical. "Do you have anything else on him?"

"No, nothing else. Your guess is as good as mine, what he and the woman are up to." Moving across the room, the man held out his hand. "You'll telephone me, Inspector, if there are any developments, or if you need any further information?"

Beauviér took the man's hand, thinking the gesture flaccid. "Yes, of course, monsieur... Monsieur Mustard."

The man laughed loudly. "No, Inspector. That's Musters—Ian Musters."

Nodding, Beauviér opened the door and, without another word, left the room. Walking down the second floor hallway, he passed the office that once belonged to the Englishman, Stuart Endfield. It looked newly occupied.

* * *

Ian Musters stood at the open door studying a man in a ruffled pinstriped suit arrange things on a desk. He was positioning a penholder at the top edge of a writing pad and apparently dissatisfied, twice moved it the length of his thumb, finally nodding in approval. He then placed a framed photograph beside the telephone. Tipping his head to the side, he tapped it repeatedly with his forefinger, then sighed.

Musters' thin upper lip rose at one end. "Family?" he said to the man at the desk.

The man looked up, his face startled, his voice weak. "Pardon me?"

Musters waved his right hand in the direction of the picture and repeated, "Family?"

As if uncertain what the photograph was, the man glanced at it. "No, I mean yes. It's my daughter."

"How wonderful." Pointing at the metal threshold just beyond the toes of his shoes, Musters requested, "May I?"

"Of course. Of course," said the man.

Moving inside the small office, his arm extended, he said, "How do you do? Ian Musters here."

"Fine, thank you." He gripped Musters' hand. "Roger Catchpole is the name. Just arrived—first day."

"Well, welcome aboard." Bending forward to look at the photograph, Musters said, "Isn't she lovely. What? Sixteen—seventeen?"

Softly, Catchpole said, "Twelve, actually," and gently took his hand back.

163

"Right," said Musters, looking at him. "How they grow up on us. One day a little girl and the next a woman, what?"

The lids on Catchpole's large eyes lowered slightly. "You have children of your own?"

"No, can't say as I do, Roger—may I call you Roger?"

"Of course."

Both men slowly placed their arms behind their backs as if on parade.

"Found a place to live, Roger?" Musters asked, barely parting his thin lips.

Catchpole frowned. "Yes, a flat, other side of Brussels. Third floor walk-up."

"What a pity, Roger," he commiserated, his narrow eyes becoming narrower. "What say we don't find you something better—with a lift, anyway. You've made no long term commitment, I hope."

"I'm to sign this evening."

"Well don't, my good man. Come to think of it, I have a friend with a furnished two bedroom in a topnotch neighborhood: ground floor; even has a small garden. How does that sound to you?"

"I'm afraid I don't have much of a budget for—"

"I think we can get it for ten thousand a month," Musters interrupted.

Catchpole frowned.

Musters pushed a grin onto his thin lips. "That's two hundred quid, Roger."

His tone enthusiastic, Catchpole said, "Are you certain, Ian?"

"Quite certain, Roger. Spoke with him only yesterday about it." He glanced at his watch. "I have an idea. What say we go over there right now, have a look, and if it suits you, well, we can move you in this evening."

"I don't know—"

"Nonsense. It's almost time for lunch—we can be there and back before anyone notices you're gone."

"Well, if you think it's all right," said Catchpole, his voice falling off.

"Quite all right. Now let's be quick about it." He removed a bowler hat dangling from the coat stand and held it out. "Here you are."

"I must say, this is awfully good of you, Ian," Catchpole said, and taking the hat, carefully gripped the brim with both hands.

"Not at all." He placed his hand on Catchpole's shoulder. "I'm glad to help a countryman; after all, we must look out for one another, here on the continent."

"Yes, I suppose you're right."

As Musters politely let Catchpole move into the hallway ahead of him, he inquired casually, "Do you like to gamble, Roger?"

* * *

Uncertain of visitation hours, Jules Beauviér had entered the hospital through a back entrance, wishing to avoid any possible delay at reception. His time was too precious for detours, though for almost forty-five minutes, he had stood at the young sergeant's bedside. At unplanned intervals, he shifted his gaze between Martin and a clipboard hanging from its footboard. He studied the words on the attached paper, trying to understand their meaning, how they related to the sleeping man, but understood almost none of them.

From the doorway of the small room, a voice asked, "Who are you?"

Beauviér locked his eyes on an elderly nun in a floor-length habit as he held up his identification.

Stepping inside the room, she said, "So?"

"This is my sergeant, mademoiselle," he advised resolutely, as if to further justify his presence.

"Possibly," said the nun, moving toward the sleeping man. "But more importantly, he is *my* patient, monsieur."

Beauviér pushed his gloved hands into the pockets of his topcoat and asked, "How is he?"

The nun's green eyes regarded the stolid Inspector. "His larynx was cut in the attack, but it's healing, monsieur," she whispered, "as you are well aware."

"Yes, of course… Can he talk?"

"He can, but he shouldn't."

Beauviér grunted.

Taking two steps toward the Inspector, she said, "Is it all that important?"

"Yes, mademoiselle."

165

The elderly woman shook her head. "It's always the same with policemen. Everything must be done immediately and at the expense of the injured."

The bedcovers rustled as Martin's eyelids fluttered and a smile took over his face. Glancing at the nun, he then raised his arm to acknowledge his superior.

Beauviér moved past the nun, his hand gripping the headboard. "How are you, Sergeant?" he asked in a hushed voice.

Martin nodded, wrinkling the bandages that wrapped about his neck like a cheap white scarf. His eyes were still black at the edges—fatigue, thought Beauviér—but they were clear, and the color had returned to his face.

Lifting his arm again, Martin made a guttural sound, before rolling onto his side.

Beauviér implored, "You mustn't move, Sergeant."

The nun tugged on the Beauviér's sleeve. Turning, he saw she held a white board, the size of letter paper.

"He wants this," she said, frowning.

Beauviér took the board, handing it to Martin.

"And this also," she added, placing a large colored pencil in Martin's grip. "It's easier for him to write what he wants to say, monsieur."

"I see," said Beauviér, then repeated firmly, "I see," as if he were entirely familiar with such practices. He faced the nun. "I would like to be alone with the Sergeant."

The elderly woman glared disapprovingly, but slowly turned and left the room, closing the door behind her.

Beauviér watched Martin scribbling on the white board, mouthing the words as he wrote. Before Martin finished, he said, "I'm fine, Sergeant. Just fine."

Erasing the colored wax with his sleeve, Martin began writing again.

Beauviér put his hand flat on the white board. "Let me go first, Sergeant."

Martin nodded, and laying the pencil down, carefully folded his hands on his stomach.

His tone matter-of-fact, Beauviér began, "I had a meeting at the British Embassy this morning. It was with a man named Ian Musters, who works there as a secretary. He gave me everything he knew about the American—his history, what there was of it, and who he works with and where they are now." He was uncomfortable relating the story, in that he was uncomfortable with the man who told him, but Martin appeared eager, his expression changing with each new bit of information. "There was even a film. It was rather extraordinary, Sergeant."

Martin hurriedly scribbled on the white board.

Reading the words as they took shape, Beauviér said, "Is that normal? For them to be so candid? No, Sergeant, it isn't." He began to pace in the small room.

Martin's eyes followed him, like a slow-moving sporting event.

After one minute or more, the Inspector turned. "Fifteen years ago a man from the British Embassy was killed in Old Brussels by a prostitute. She stabbed him with a letter opener. Just once, mind you, but right through the heart." He gently tapped his left breast. "The hooker claimed self-defense when we found her."

Martin began writing.

Beauviér read the words, and said, "Was it self-defense? No, Sergeant. It was a simple robbery gone wrong. But when we asked for help regarding the murdered man from the British Embassy, they closed up like a tomb. Not one word about him. They eventually announced at a press conference that the fellow had had a heart attack—or that's the way it appeared in all the papers, and we were obliged to concur. The police commissioner at the time said it was out of our hands."

Martin quickly scrawled.

Beauviér said, "The hooker? Forget about the hooker!" Shaking his head, he walked slowly to the foot of the bed and placed his hands together on the metal rail, staring at his thumbs where they touched. "I telephoned the British Embassy after we found Stuart Endfield," he continued, his tone calm. "And again they shut down like it was an aerial blackout. They barely acknowledged his position at the embassy, asking if I hadn't made a mistake, as if it were another Stuart Endfield."

Beauviér lifted his gaze. "Then Musters telephones—he must have read my name in the papers—and informs me he has evidence linking the dead Englishman to an American named Thomas Allan Breck."

Martin cocked his head to the side, his eyes curious.

Understanding the sergeant's anticipation, the corners of Beauviér's mouth turned up. "It also appears there is a woman named Gregòsh, Tatiana Gregòsh, who works with the American—a forger, and quite ruthless I'm told." He relaxed his shoulders. "She is now in France, in the village of Barbizon. Do you know it?"

Martin nodded.

Beauviér let out a deep breath. "That is what Musters wanted to tell me, Sergeant. To keep me, or someone like me, on the trail of these people."

Martin wrote quickly, turning the white board to face the Inspector.

"The American? He is in Barbizon also, I'm certain," said Beauviér confidently. "I went by his house in Wolowe St. Pierre to question him about the Englishman, but the maid said he left town, and the owner of Le Cerf, an Irishman named John Clark, has also disappeared."

Hesitating, he went on, "I should telephone the French authorities and make them aware of this Tatiana. She is wanted there on forgery charges, according to Musters, but..." Beauviér looked sternly at Martin. "But there was no mention of the painting, Sergeant. The Monet was left out of the conversation and that's what I didn't understand. How could Musters know so much about the American, but be ignorant of the Monet, unless—"

There was a knock at the door and before Beauviér could respond, it opened halfway. Carrying a large tray with both hands, the elderly nun nudged the door open wider with her hip. She moved quietly to Martin's bedside.

Carefully placing the tray on the bedcovers, she methodically unwrapped a plastic straw, dropping it into a glass of orange juice. Addressing Beauviér, she said, "That will be all for today, monsieur," and handed Martin the glass, directing the straw to his mouth.

Beauviér scowled, though Martin grinned, causing some of the juice to run out the corner of his mouth.

Removing the white board and crayon, the nun pushed down gently on Martin's knees till his legs lay flat under the bedcovers. Lifting the large tray, she placed it on his lap, sliding it tight to his stomach. "I've brought you some playing cards, young man," she said, spreading them out nimbly with her aged fingers. "They will help to pass the time. Possibly a nice game of Solitaire."

168

Staring at the red cards, Beauviér did not notice the slight inferred by the woman, but rather his eyes narrowed, and reaching inside his topcoat, removed a small square of dark paper. It was one of the gambling markers discovered at the apartment of Stuart Endfield.

Slowly looking up, his eyes drifted to the small table by the bed. "I'll speak with you later, Sergeant."

Nodding at the nun, Beauviér left the room.

Martin glanced at the bedside table. It was empty, save for a half dozen sympathy cards surrounding a black telephone with no dial.

* * *

The village of Barbizon looked like an abandoned scene from a child's fairytale. It was off-season and the shops bordering the only commercial street were closed, leaving *la grande rue* void of traffic or pedestrians or any sign of life as it eventually vanished into the Fontainebleau forest. Holiday decorations were minimal, with an occasional flickering neon or tattered cardboard sign indicating the festive season and the end of another trying year. But on the whole, Barbizon's storybook appearance was intact, oblivious to any season. Its rich history of harboring painters like Claude Monet and Pierre Renoir was more important than any day-tourist or student on a field trip.

Thomas Breck thought of this as he turned the Jensen onto *la grande rue*, moving his car slowly up the quiet street. He knew the value of the masterpieces created by such men, masterpieces he once possessed.

Pulling to the curb, he looked at a sign attached to the near building that read: *Hotel Les Charmettes, French Lodging Association*. Underneath was stenciled a single white star. On each side of the star were blotches of dark green paint, recently applied in an attempt to match the original background. But they didn't, informing the curious observer that two stars had been removed, most certainly by order of government inspectors.

Smiling at the sight, Tom went inside the hotel, dropping his satchel on the chest-high reception desk. The foyer was quiet, save for a pendulum wall clock marking time in the silence, a seemingly hypnotic rhythm as Tom closed his eyes. Tired and strangely uneasy, he didn't want to be in Barbizon. He wanted to be away, though he couldn't imagine where. If it were anywhere but Brussels, he would be running; any other city in the world, he would be admitting defeat.

The swinging door into the foyer creaked. Tom opened his eyes to observe a man now standing at the end of the reception desk. It was Raymond Dreyfus, the proprietor of Les Charmettes, who stood dressed in kitchen whites and a chef's hat that almost touched the ceiling. Slender and middle-aged, he sported a large black mustache which hid any expression on his mouth, although his equally black eyes were cold.

"Well, well. What has it been? Two years, Monsieur Breck?" he said, lifting his arms almost perpendicular to his shoulders before letting them slap to his side. "Two years and not one word from a man I treated as a brother."

Tom was about to speak when Dreyfus continued, "What? Is Belgium too far away that you are unable to spend one night and take dinner with me? Or even telephone to see if I am still alive?" His expression unchanged, he walked slowly alongside the reception desk. "You forget that for over one month you lived here while you courted the young woman from Milly-La-Forêt. Both lunch and dinner, I spared no expense to make you look the *bon vivant extraordinaire*. Don't you remember my duck under glass, monsieur?"

The edges of Tom's mouth turned up. "You mean duck *with* glass, don't you, Raymond? I remember it as being somewhat crunchy."

His eyes remained cold, his tone somber. "That is not funny, monsieur."

Tom said nothing.

Dreyfus took another step forward and raising his arms, threw them around Tom. "My cooking is so bad, monsieur?" he questioned, embracing him harder. "You won the woman, did you not?"

The smile fell from Tom's face, his eyes ambiguous. "Yes, Raymond... I won her."

Letting his arms fall, Dreyfus took a step back, glancing at the entrance. "Is she still in the car, Thomas? Where is that beauty? I thought—" Then, looking at Tom, he did not finish.

"She is not with me, this time," Tom said, his tone unconcerned. "She is at her father's."

170

Dreyfus' brow furrowed. "Yes, of course," he said, rubbing his hands together. "All the better, Thomas. It will allow us more time together. Yes, yes, more time—Say, I have a new pastis that is made from twelve different herbs. They claim it is very good for the heart."

"I can imagine," Tom said, taking his satchel from the desk. "And how's business?"

"The same, Thomas. The only regular customer I have is the man from the bank. He shows up after dinner every evening to take the day's receipts," he replied with fatigue in his voice.

"And employees?"

"Also the same, Thomas. It is only I and Madame Bovary." He began tugging the ends of his mustache.

Tom remembered Raymond's timid wife. "That's good."

"Good, you say! She just turned every sheet in the house bright pink with her inventive washing."

Knowing the conversation might never end, Tom moved toward the staircase. "Please, excuse me, but I'm a bit tired. Is room thirty-six available?"

"Of course, Thomas. The key is in the door."

Climbing the steps, he said, "I will need two more rooms, Raymond. There will be three of us."

Dreyfus looked up at him. "They may have their choice when they arrive."

"They should be here around nine o'clock. Which reminds me, is that fish market in Melun open this time of year?"

Raymond's eyes brightened as he moved to the bottom of the stairs. "Yes, it is."

Tom removed a small roll of bank notes from his pocket and counted out seven hundred French francs, handing them to Dreyfus. "Make that lobster dish, will you? I think my friends would like it tonight."

"It's good to have you back, Thomas."

Without another word, Tom moved up the stairs to the second floor landing. He walked dolefully along the softly lighted corridor, stopping in front of a door with the number 36 painted on the frame. He hesitated, then turned the handle. The door creaked open to reveal a room he remembered well. Nothing had changed except the winter light through the windows. The writing desk and the wardrobe were the same, and the covers on the bed were as before.

He walked slowly to the windows, pulling the drapes shut without looking to the street below. It seemed better now, with the room darkened, though the memories were as vivid: Michelle, sitting cross-legged on the bed, combing her hair while she told him of a deer she had seen in the forest, how it had come up to her, how excited she had been, insisting they buy food for it, then laughing, wondering what on earth that might be.

Even in the dimness, it was all so clear.

He lay down on the bed, uncertain if he could sleep, staring at the plaster ceiling and listening to the quiet. Finally closing his eyes, he caught the faint scent of a familiar perfume. Then it was gone.

* * *

The alley was narrower than Jules Beauviér remembered. The walls of the surrounding buildings seeming to have crept closer, like a fissure sealing itself. The bricks and mortar, now covered in the black soot that cities emit, and the trash cans at his feet, ostensibly more numerous, all added to the alley's air of confinement. One or two streams of afternoon light broke through, but other than that it was dark, leaving a sense of nightfall; an eternal twilight.

Reaching the closed end of the alley, he found a door with the words *La Piste Royale*, *Members Only*, skillfully painted upon it, though beginning to fade. To the side was a glass fisheye, refracting the inner light like a tired flashlight.

Beauviér was pleased; La Piste Royale was open for business. He knocked on the door and waited, pushing his shoulders up against the wintry air.

La Piste Royale was one of the original off-track betting parlors in Brussels, dating back to the 1830's and the advent of the telegraph. In the beginning, the parlor sat on *rue Artan* and there was neither an alley to navigate, nor brick walls blocking out the sun. But progress came, along with new buildings and new addresses, each encroachment taking a piece of *rue Artan* and the overhead sky. The owner of the parlor refused to negotiate with the contractors, claiming they had no right to block his one and only door. They offered him money, then a different location, and finally both, but he refused, claiming historical preference. Princes, dukes and counts wagered their money at La Piste Royale, waiting for the results to come in from all over Europe, while sipping at overpriced champagne.

172

La Piste Royale was an institution, and those words echoed against the sounds of the carpenter's hammer as the buildings went up seemingly overnight. Only a narrow passage to the entrance remained, later to be called *L'allée de la Piste* and then, as the years passed, forgotten altogether.

The fisheye went dark. A lock clicked and the door opened slightly to reveal a man a few years older than Beauviér gazing into the dark alley.

Examining the stranger in the shadows, the man finally said, "Lieutenant Beauviér. Please, please come in," and, opening the door fully, stiffly raised his right arm.

Beauviér took the extended hand, grasping it gently, aware of the arthritis that had gnarled the fingers. "It has been a long time," he said, moving into the well-lighted room.

"Yes, Lieutenant. It has been," the man agreed, closing the door with his elbow.

Beauviér grinned. He now knew the man through the years that had altered his face and body. "And it is 'Inspector' now. I am no longer a lieutenant, Monsieur Mallraux."

Mallraux placed his hands together, as if to clap them, though there was no sound other than his tired voice. "Inspector, is it?" He turned slowly to look across the smoke-filled room. "Look who is here, Chrétien. It is *Inspector* Beauviér of the Gendarmerie."

A fat man, older than either Beauviér or Mallraux, sat behind the metal bars of the betting cage. He looked up from a hand of cards and lifted his large arm, then returned to his game without a word.

Mallraux spoke in a whisper. "Chrétien has not changed. He's still a bastard." Then, his tone excited, said, "What may I bring you, Inspector? Whiskey, Gin?"

Beauviér shook his head. "Nothing, thank you."

Mallraux's expression grew stern as the skin at the edges of his eyes, spotted from years of cigarettes and alcohol, began to crinkle.

Beauviér said, "Whiskey sounds nice," while removing his gloves. "Scotch if you have it."

Frowning, Mallraux mumbled, "If we have it," and slowly turned, moving across the room.

Beauviér watched him open a cupboard against the wall with a key attached to his belt by a piece of black string. As Mallraux removed a liter bottle of Scotch, a Teletype machine in the corner flew to life. Its loud rattle did not seem to disturb the few men inside the stuffy room, save for one, who unsteadily lifted himself from his chair, his back crooked from age. He grabbed the paper being spit from the Teletype, shoving it through the bars of the betting cage. The machine shut down and again it was quiet except for the clinking of ice cubes being dropped into a glass.

Beauviér took out his wallet.

"El Rey in the sixth looks good," came a voice from behind the betting window. It was Chrétien, still studying his hand of cards.

"Pardon me?" said Beauviér.

Sounding impatient, Chrétien repeated, "El Rey in the sixth looks good," and jerked his fat thumb at a large chalkboard on the wall. "It rained in Madrid today. He's good in the mud. You have ten minutes to place your bet."

Beauviér stared at the fat man, then glanced at the wallet in his hand. "No, I was just…" He stopped himself, looking at Mallraux, now standing before him.

"Here," said Mallraux, a glass clutched between his palms, his twisted fingers no longer useful.

Taking the whiskey, Beauviér nodded.

Bluntly, Mallraux said, "What's on your mind, Inspector?" and took a seat at a near card table.

Beauviér put his glass on the table beside Mallraux, a black marker next to that.

"Where is this from?" he asked.

Mallraux placed his hands on the table, one on top of the other. Leaning forward, he made no attempt to pick up the marker, but said, "I don't know. Looks like a French casino marker." Unblinking, he cocked his head to the side. "Near the Swiss frontier, would be my guess. You see the English written on the bottom. They want everybody to know just how much trouble they're in." He laughed and then coughed repeatedly, lifting the back of his withered hand to his mouth.

Beauviér pointed at the marker. "But the watermark in the corner, that must mean something."

Looking up with his filmy eyes, Mallraux shrugged.

Beauviér was returning the marker to his wallet when a voice said, "The casino Le Cheval Noir." It was Chrétien, still motionless in the betting cage, staring at Beauviér from under his puffy, half-open eyelids.

Beauviér took a step toward him, holding the marker up. "But you haven't seen it."

Waving his chubby hand, Chrétien said, "I can see it, Inspector—I can see it."

Beauviér's brow furrowed. "Le Cheval Noir in Paris?"

"No, no—in Brussels. It's off *rue Jourdan* near Charleroi," said Chrétien as if his patience were being tried. "The front half is a gentleman's club, Eastern European girls, North African girls, and high prices—you know, Inspector. The casino is in the back, but…"

The Teletype machine clicked on, cutting him off. It clattered for a few seconds and again shut down. No one in the room had moved toward it.

Taking a deep breath, he continued, "It's only for foreigners, because they don't complain to the police if there's trouble. No Belgians allowed."

"What!" said Beauviér. "Can they do that?"

Chrétien's corpulent cheeks pushed out as he frowned. "You're the cop. You tell me."

Beauviér said, "Then what is the watermark?"

"It's in the shape of a cowboy. Or at least, it used to be. Like John Wayne; they think they're clever; they think they're cowboys," he replied, returning to his game.

"What kind of foreigners?"

Chrétien began shuffling the cards. "You only have three minutes for El Rey in the sixth, Inspector," he said, glancing at the large clock above the chalkboard. "It rained in Spain and he's a mudder."

Moving toward the betting cage, Beauviér removed a bank note from his wallet. Slipping it though the opening at the base of the bars, he said, "Five hundred on El Rey in the sixth," and stepped back, letting his arms fall.

Motionless, Chrétien stared at the azure-colored note.

Removing another five hundred franc note, Beauviér slid it through the window. "One thousand on El Rey in the sixth," he said, his tone immodest.

"One thousand on El Rey in the sixth at Patagonia," bellowed Chrétien. "Win, place or show, monsieur?"

Softly, Beauviér answered, "To win, monsieur."

Chrétien filled out the ticket and, sliding it through the window, confided to Beauviér, "Americans, Japanese, Swedes and Germans—lots of Germans at Le Cheval Noir."

"English?" Beauviér asked.

"Sure. English, South Africans, Australians. You get the idea, Inspector."

Dropping the ticket into his pocket, Beauviér asked, "Why have I never heard of this place?"

The man lowered his bulbous face until it almost touched the bars of the cage. His eyes locked on to Beauviér's. "Because the house is crooked, Inspector. The croupiers, the maitre d'hôtel, the director, the owners and the city cops that watch it every night," he replied, his voice unfaltering. "They're all crooked, and you're not. That's why you've never heard of it."

Beauviér kept his face impassive as he stepped back from the betting cage. The two men stared at each other, neither speaking. For almost thirty seconds, they remained motionless in the stone-quiet room. Someone in the far corner struck a match and Mallraux coughed. Then the Teletype returned to life, the metal arms slapping loudly against the vibrating carriage. Its clattering broke the uneasy stillness.

The man with the crooked back lifted himself from his chair, moving between Beauviér and the betting cage. As the printed-paper was torn free and the machine again shut down, Beauviér moved to the door, his black gloves gripped in his hand.

Again Chrétien bellowed from behind the bars. "Messieurs and mesdames," he said, although no women were present. "We have a winner in the sixth race at Patagonia. Who has ticket number four-two-two? I repeat, who carries ticket number four-two-two?"

Beauviér turned, glaring. Slowly, he made his way to the cage and, removing the ticket from his pocket, slid it under the bars. "Let me see the results," he demanded, nodding at the Teletype paper beside Chrétien's hand.

Not looking up, Chrétien slid the paper to Beauviér who read the two lines of type. He did not speak Spanish, but was able to determine a horse named El Rey, in a field of twelve, came first in the sixth race at La Patagonia racetrack just outside of Madrid. The time printed in the corner of the paper indicated the results were but two minutes old.

Crumpling the paper, he watched the fat fingers of Chrétien slowly count out the winnings.

"At thirty-to-one, you have done well, monsieur," said Chrétien, pushing the six five-thousand franc notes toward the bars. "Yes, very well indeed."

He protested, "I can't take that."

176

"But you can. It's yours." Chrétien pushed his face forward. "Don't you see how easy it is, Inspector? Do you see how they do it? What does this represent compared to your salary each week— each month, for that matter? The man whose signature is on the marker from Le Cheval Noir most certainly played a similar winning horse, or hand of cards. All he needed was a little more credit and he would win big again, just like this." He pulled his head back. "If you ask him, he will tell you as much."

"He is dead," said Beauviér. "That is why I'm here."

Chrétien's large jowls shook as he nodded. "I thought as much. And I also knew you wouldn't take the money, because if you take the money they will own you. Though I could use a man like you on the payroll."

Looking at the blackboard, Beauviér casually put on his gloves. "Who in the third race at Milan?" he asked.

Chrétien did not answer.

"You asked me if I understood?" he said, placing his hand on the money.

A grin contorted Chrétien's puffy mouth. "There's nothing in the third, but... there's Tedesco in the fourth, and he's due."

"Tedesco it is," said Beauviér, pushing his winnings toward the fat man.

"All of it?" said Chrétien.

Mindful of one half-month's salary but an arm's length away, Beauviér walked away. Taking his whiskey from the table, he nodded at Mallraux, and finished it with one gulp.

"All of it," he said, moving to the entrance. "And to win."

Stepping into the cold alley, he slowly looked up to the strip of pale blue sky between the shadowed walls. Though he didn't know why, he had a sense of melancholy, knowing that he would never return to this place.

* * *

Tom Breck was the only customer in the dining room and had been for the entire evening. The wife of the owner, affectionately known as Madame Bovary, for reasons no one could remember, would occasionally peek in from the bar. It was her way of being unobtrusive, but it had the opposite effect, as Tom preferred the empty room and its solitude. A fireplace provided most of the light, and also most of the heat, burning what appeared to be furniture.

Against the opposite wall, surrounded by hunting artifacts, sat a tired grandfather clock, its pendulum groaning between movements, but it kept the hour sufficiently. It read fifteen minutes before ten in the evening, and soon Yuri and Tatiana would arrive, and Tom was becoming anxious.

What Tatiana had been through, he could only imagine. Where she was taken and what had happened to her, he still did not know. Yuri said she was fine, considering, but Tom needed to see her. He looked again to the clock; one minute had passed.

Lighting a cigarette, he paced about the room, finally stopping before a window looking upon *la grande rue*. The gas street lamps flickered from uneven fuel as the cobblestones glistened from an earlier shower. Unbothered by pedestrians or traffic, the street seemed from an earlier time. If a horse-drawn carriage were to pass, followed by mounted soldiers in Napoleonic dress, it would not seem out of place.

The fire in the corner crackled. Turning, he saw Madame Bovary peering in.

"Everything is fine, madame," he said, "My friends should be along shortly."

Nervously, she took a step into the room. "But you haven't touched your wine. May I bring you—" She stopped. There was a commotion coming from the other side of the bar. "That must be them," she said, tipping her head to the side. "Yes, most certainly, monsieur—that must be them." She moved hurriedly away.

Tom put out his cigarette. Placing his hands behind his back, he lifted his eyes, gazing at the dining room entrance. The sound from reception was louder. A door slammed closed, followed by voices, speaking softly as strangers arriving late will do. Although Dreyfus was boisterous, his voice clear in the distant foyer, offering to take everyone's luggage and to hurry along, dinner was about to be served.

Tom remained still, his eyes fixed on the door. The voices advanced into the bar, then he recognized the faint accent of someone he knew well. Tatiana appeared at the door. She stopped when she saw him, her soft blue eyes looking back. Without speaking, they moved forward to embrace, kissing the other's cheek twice, as was their custom.

Tom was elated to see her, more than he had imagined. Placing his hand on the side of her face, he gently lifted her head to look at him.

"How are you?" he asked.

"I am fine… Now I am fine, Thomas Breck."

He did not speak for a few seconds, studying her face. She looked thinner. "They did not hurt you?"

She shook her head. "No, they didn't."

Leading her to the table, he said, "You must be tired."

"A little, but I am quite hungry," she said cheerfully. "The chef said there is something special tonight?"

"Yes, I suppose there is." His eyes narrowed, watching her.

She was adjusting the napkin on her lap with her head bowed. Even after what she had been through, there was an ease and simple beauty about her that he rarely thought about—it was not an issue, they were partners and nothing more.

He sat beside her. "You had no trouble finding this place?"

She placed her hands on the table. "It was as you said all those years ago; if there is trouble and we cannot speak on the telephone, we are to meet at Les Charmettes in Barbizon. It was neither hard to remember, nor hard to find."

His tone became serious. "There is still trouble, isn't there?" he asked, uncertain if she knew of the machine.

"Yes, Thomas," she said ruefully, "but first I'd like a drink of wine."

Pouring her a glass, Tom glanced to the door. "Where is Yuri?" he asked, as if only just remembering.

"He's putting the car away in the back garage, then taking the luggage to the room and—you remember," she answered, lifting her wine from the table. "He likes to take care of things; he likes to take care of me, even more so since—" She stopped herself, gently clinking her wine glass against his. "To us."

"To us," he said.

They each took a drink and returning their glasses to the table, neither spoke, both seeming to wait for the other. Then Tom said, "You had no trouble getting into France?"

"No," she replied. "Yuri and I are now Swiss. I had two blank passports hidden. I was saving them for something like this."

"Will you return to Budapest?"

"No. I can never return."

Staring at his glass, he asked, "Will you tell me about it now? Tell me what happened?"

Tatiana took another sip of wine. Her blue eyes watered, reflecting the light of the fire.

Scooting his chair closer, Tom gently placed his hand on her shoulder. "We'll talk about it another time," he whispered.

Tatiana sat up straight, blinking to clear her eyes, and said, "No, you need to know."

Madame Bovary stepped into the room and Tom waved her away, looking again at Tatiana, who seemed unaware of the intrusion as she started to speak. Softly at first, she talked of the early morning when the police arrived, then her voice became firm and unfaltering. She told of the room in the empty hotel; about the policemen who would never speak; about how the uncertainty was the worst of it, and the hours that seemed like days. Glancing at the fire, she talked sometimes as if to herself, trying to remember each detail of the kidnapping until, ultimately, the morning when the man called Mégot released her.

Watching Tatiana, he sensed she'd left some things incomplete, and inquired, "Did Mégot tell you why he was letting you go?"

She answered calmly, "No, only that things were getting messy, that he wanted to get it back on the right path. I believe those were the words."

"You spoke in French?"

"Yes."

"What was his accent?"

"Belgian, I believe," she replied, glancing at the doorway. "And he told me about the Monet."

Through his teeth, Tom said, "Then he knew it was ours."

She nodded.

"How?"

"I don't know."

Wearily, he said, "The police found the Monet at Buchon's gallery. He died of a cardiac, and they discovered it during the investigation."

As if she already knew the answer, she asked, "And the Renoir?"

Tom was feeling uneasy. Clearing his throat, he said, "When I went to see Buchon, before I knew he was dead, I was attacked by someone, obviously Mégot, if he knew about the other painting— and he took the Renoir."

Casually lifting her hand, she touched the side of his head where the hair had been cut back for the stitches. "Is that where you got this?" she asked.

"I'm sorry. I should have been more cautious."

"But how?" she asked, seemingly resigned to the dire news. "How could you have known about Mégot? He is dangerous."

"More than you know," he agreed. "He is a murderer."

"What are you saying? You said Buchon died of a cardiac."

"No, not him... there was an Englishman who worked for Mégot. He was the one who demanded the ransom. He was killed the evening I paid him—certainly by Mégot."

Tatiana looked troubled. "Why?"

"I don't know. But he was working for Mégot against his will. He was being blackmailed."

"Then there was a ransom and... and he would have killed me also." Her voice trailed off.

Tom took hold of her shoulders, forcing her to look at him. "No," he exclaimed. "It would never have happened. A ransom was demanded and it was paid. If they had wanted the Monet or the Renoir, or anything else, they could have had it. Nothing was going to happen, Tatiana—nothing."

Letting his hands drop, he fell silent as the fireplace pitched its faint yellow glow on them. It was then that Tom knew they *had* hurt her—not physically, for which he was thankful, but her confidence, always so apparent, so clear, had retreated and been replaced by fear. It is always so easy to gamble with freedom, until it is lost.

Madame Bovary moved quietly into the room, placing a basket of bread on the table. In her other hand she carried two plates, with another balanced on her forearm. She carefully laid the plates before each of the three settings then cleared her throat, looking at the empty place at the table.

Tom glanced at her, then moved his eyes to the vacant chair. "He'll be here, madame."

With her gaze fixed on the flickering candle, Tatiana said, "Yuri takes his time, I'm afraid. You do not need to wait for him."

Bowing slightly, Madame Bovary left.

"What was his name?" asked Tatiana.

Tom's eyes narrowed. "You mean—"

"The Englishman. What was his name?"

"Stuart Endfield. He was a secretary with the British Embassy."

"And what was he like?"

"I don't know, Tatiana," he replied, sitting up in his chair. "Was he good? Was he bad? I only spoke with him once and it wasn't very pleasant. I hated him. Then I understood he was in trouble and only trying to survive. But he wasn't very competent at it. He was too frightened to be."

Softly, as if to herself, she said, "Then there is no difference."

"What do you mean?"

"Between you and me, and Stuart Endfield," she said, locking her eyes onto his. "We are also trying to survive, and I am frightened."

Tom wanted to tell her not to be afraid, that there was no reason, but it would be a lie and she would know it. She would hear it in his voice.

"What else did Mégot tell you?" he asked, hoping to find something, anything that might help.

She tapped the base of her wine glass with her forefinger, seemingly reluctant to answer, then said, "He told me Michelle left you."

"What?" he blurted. "How? How would he know?"

"Then it is true, Thomas?"

"Yes," he answered, growling.

She reached out her hand, lightly touching his. "You see why I'm frightened."

Glaring, he rose and went to the window, looking again to the cobblestone street. It was the same: a photograph of another time, but its serene appearance was darkening. The wind had begun to bluster, pushing against the limbs of the leafless trees that lined the street. A storm was moving in and hail fell in bursts from the black sky, sporadically tapping against the window.

Lowering his gaze, he felt Tatiana next to him, brushing her arm against his.

She said, "It was snowing in Budapest when we left this morning."

Tom remained silent.

"Yuri bought a new car—well, it's secondhand, really, but they hadn't begun salting the roads and he was concerned we'd slide into a tree or something." Slowly lifting her hand, she touched the pane of glass with her forefinger. "There are no mountains until you reach Austria, so we were—"

Tom cut her off. "He knows everything about us Tatiana."

She said nothing. Her hand fell away from the window.

Still staring into the night, he said, "The knowledge of my wife, and the Monet... the state police kidnapping you, and then Stuart Endfield blackmailed to be used as a carrier pigeon. It was all for one reason and it wasn't for the ransom. It was to show his power. So we'd do a job for him and not refuse." He looked at Tatiana. "Mégot told you about the machine?"

"Yes," she whispered.

"What did he say?"

"That he wants it moved to North Africa... to Algeria. We have until the end of the month." Reaching into the side pocket of her blazer, she retrieved a piece of paper and handed it to Tom. "This is what he gave me."

As he read the paper, his eyes narrowed. "Where is the machine now?"

"In Belgium, the town of Mons. Its location is written in the corner of the paper with a series of numbers underneath, but I don't know what they mean."

He looked up. "These measurements can't be accurate," he said, his voice unsteady.

"But they are. Look at the weight. It corresponds."

He dropped his arms, the paper slapping against his leg. "It's larger than this room. Did he tell you what it is?

"No," she answered, returning to her seat. "He said it wasn't our concern."

Tom pulled his chair close to her and asked, "How much money do you have?"

She shrugged. "After buying the Renoir—"

"How much?" he repeated.

"Maybe twenty thousand American dollars."

"That includes Yuri?"

"Yes."

"Okay," he said, dropping the paper onto the table as if it was no longer relevant. "If I sell off the equity in my home and everything else, for that matter, I should be able to raise two hundred thousand dollars. Unfortunately the Belgian frank is weak right now, but I will give you half of what I collect."

"Why?"

"So you can get away."

"You mean run?" she demanded. "And to where? Where would I go?"

"I have a friend in South America, in Buenos Aires. He can set everything up."

"I don't speak Spanish," she said angrily.

He pulled his head back. "What does that mean?"

She did not respond and appeared impatient, as if forcing herself not to answer. Then she said, "I have been running and hiding for most of my life. I don't think you know what that means. To spend each day thinking twice about where to go, so by chance I would not see someone from my past, or be seen by someone still searching me out; always looking over my shoulder..."

"But—"

She held her hand up. "These last few years in Budapest have been the most peaceful of my life. You see, living in a police state has its advantages, Thomas. I was able to buy the upper level of equality with my fellow Communists, so when I was arrested I merely thought I had been outbid, so to speak. But I accepted it. Then, to find it was this man Mégot and that it had nothing to do with my past—I was angry. But that, too, has passed." She fixed her eyes on his. "I will tell you that I am not going to start running again, jumping every time the telephone rings or there is a knock at the door, because that in itself is a prison. Mégot is more dangerous than all the policemen I have ever feared and, if we flee, he will find us and kill us for what we know."

Tom was apprehensive. This was not the response he'd expected. "Then you will have to do it without me," he said.

Her eyes became troubled, her face sullen. She asked bluntly, "Is your wife in the village nearby?"

"Yes, she is in Milly-La-Forêt with her father."

"And she will go with you to Argentina? To Brazil maybe?"

"I don't know."

"Then you would leave without her?"

Tom did not answer.

"And when the money is gone? Will she be with you?"

He blurted, "You are saying my wife is for sale?"

Softly, she replied, "We are all for sale. Only the price varies."

"And what is your price?" he demanded sharply.

Tatiana looked away.

And Tom looked away also, knowing he had been unkind to someone who wished him no harm—to one of the few people he could trust. Leaning forward, he whispered, "I am sorry."

Casually folding her hands, she said, "It took six months to acquire the Monet from the old Russian soldier and then again as long to get the Renoir. Do you remember, Thomas?"

"Of course."

With her gaze fixed on the candle, she continued. "The Monet would have been enough, really. It is valued at over two million dollars." Grinning, she repeated slowly, "Two million dollars... Well, we didn't know, so we bought the Renoir, thinking that would be it. The Monet and the Renoir, and we would be finished. Who could need more money than that? Do you remember?"

Watching Tatiana reach for her wine, Tom said nothing. It was quiet in the room, with only the hail tapping at the window. She took a sip, then slowly returned the glass to the table, and said, "But I wonder if we would have stopped. There were rumors of a Matisse in St. Petersburg and a—oh I can't remember the artist's name, but it doesn't matter. We would have convinced each other to smuggle it across all the same, saying it was the last time and never again." She reached out her hand to touch his. "What we do separates us from everyone else. We cannot speak to anyone about what we do or who we are, or what we are thinking—truly thinking that is— because if we do, we are putting ourselves at risk." She looked at him. "We cannot have the things that other people have."

"So we must continue on this carousel?"

"No. I just don't want us to start running," she protested in a tired voice. "Me, in one direction trying to get away, and you in another, chasing after something you can never have."

He rose, standing quite still before bending down to kiss her cheek. "I'm sorry, but I can't," he whispered.

Tatiana appeared about to speak when there was a commotion in the bar. Loud voices were moving toward the dining room. She turned her gaze on the far window.

The conversation entered the room before the two men. Raymond Dreyfus was describing the necessary skills for preparing seafood to Yuri, who reluctantly agreed on the condition that sufficient salt was used. They were speaking like old friends when they appeared at the door of the dining room—Raymond's arms waved in the air to make a point as Yuri's head bowed, contemplating the facts.

Both men stopped speaking, seemingly aware of the pensive mood in the room. Yuri glanced at Tatiana as he moved toward Tom, his hand extended. "Please excuse me, but I had to make some calls to Budapest on the sale of the house. It is good to see you, Thomas."

The two men shook hands vigorously.

"And you, Yuri," said Tom, noticing the man's once-dark hair had grayed. "It's been some time."

"Two years, anyway."

"That long?"

Yuri did not reply but looked at Tatiana and then, as if it were an afterthought, said, "Yes, I believe so." Taking his hand from Tom, he placed it on Tatiana's shoulder and slowly bent forward, briefly kissing her on the top of her head. "Doesn't she look beautiful?"

"Yes, Yuri. She looks wonderful."

Staring at her from behind, waiting for a response, Yuri's forehead wrinkled. Then Dreyfus bellowed, "If everyone would please take a seat, dinner service can begin."

Moving to his chair, Yuri again looked at Tatiana. She remained silent.

Tom asked, "So tell us, Chef Raymond, what do you have for us this evening?"

Proudly, Dreyfus said, "For our first course we have a green salad with vinaigrette," and then signaled at Madame Bovary who cautiously entered the room, a large wooden bowl in her hands.

"Green salad with vinaigrette," repeated Tom. "How on earth did you think of something so daring?"

Dreyfus' eyes frowned over his large mustache.

Tom asked, "And for the next course, Chef?"

Clapping his hands together, he answered, "We have fresh lobster, messieurs and mademoiselle, which I call *Homard aux Charmettes*."

Tatiana, a glint in her eye, said, "What does that mean?"

Leaning forward to whisper in her ear, Dreyfus said, "That means, mademoiselle, I have steamed some lobster and it shall be served with freshly melted butter."

Tatiana grinned. "Well, that is even more adventurous than your salad, monsieur."

Standing upright, Dreyfus placed his hands on his hips. Studying his three guests, he began to laugh. It started in his stomach, growing louder as he tipped his head back and clapped his hands.

* * *

Inspector Jules Beauviér sat at the corner end of the bar. It was the least appealing seat in the lounge at Le Cheval Noir, but it allowed him a certain privacy as the shadows seemed to converge at that point, leaving only a candle to illuminate his hands while he fiddled with the straw in his drink. Unable to read his watch clearly in the meager light, he thought it to be just after ten as Le Cheval Noir had just opened for the evening. And as yet, he was the only legitimate customer.

Beside the candle sat a recently opened bottle of Dewar's Scotch, the name Van Rops written on it in black felt pen. There was no first name, because Beauviér had not been asked for one. Le Cheval Noir was a private club and he was obliged to purchase the bottle—the house would also sell him a glass to drink it from, and the ice to make it potable. If the new member wished some soda, that would be an additional charge. Beauviér drank his whiskey straight.

The name Van Rops came to Beauviér in an awkward moment when the barman abruptly asked. Aware that membership was limited to foreigners, he decided to become Dutch, though he now wondered why, since he did not speak the language.

The dark lounge contained two-dozen tables, though only one was occupied with four young women in evening dress— Hospitality Girls, he imagined them to be, and working for the house. The seats at the bar were empty except for the one occupied by Beauviér, who was alone with a cocktail waitress of twenty or twenty-one, preparing her tray. She wore a white blouse covered by a red vest, a matching short skirt, and white American style cowboy boots that went just below her calves.

Soft jazz began to fill the room as Beauviér admired her costume. Sipping on his glass of scotch, he felt he was becoming slightly more comfortable than he should.

Le Cheval Noir was an overpriced saloon with bad lighting and arguable taste, but it offered privileges to its members, one being the young women at the near table, who were available for conversation or dreams, and another being privacy. Two large men guarded the front door and another stood in the lounge beside a curtain with the words *Gaming Room* in blue neon just above. That hidden room was the privilege that most interested Jules Beauviér as he watched the four young women stand, straightening out their ill-fitted gowns, before forming an erratic line facing the door. Three well-dressed men had entered the lounge and without hesitation moved by the young women, straight to the bar. They spoke German amongst themselves; one of them, in broken French, asked for his private bottle of whiskey. The barman obliged, following it with three empty glasses and a liter bottle of soda. Still ignoring the young women, the Germans each consumed a glass of whiskey, then, as if on cue, moved to the casino entrance and went inside.

The barman returned the bottle of whiskey to the shelf and the young women returned to their table, though they did not sit. Two men were now entering, speaking in whispers. Something about them seemed familiar to Beauviér. Letting himself slump into the shadows, he watched them chat briefly with one of the girls before proceeding to the bar. Their words were still indiscernible, but the manner with which one of the men moved was clear. It was the secretary from the British Embassy. The man called Ian Musters.

Beauviér quickly pulled his hands off the bar, resting them on his lap. He was now all but invisible, watching Musters make a toast to something that was most certainly a lie.

* * *

Le Cheval Noir had become full of customers, all seemingly drunk and increasingly bothersome, in a matter of two hours. There were no seats available at the bar and each table was full, and it was loud. Pushing his nearly full bottle of scotch toward the barman, Beauviér asked the hour and finding it to be just after midnight, felt sufficient time had passed.

A small man, nearly Beauviér's age, sat on his stool as quickly as he vacated it. The movement irritated him, reaching to collect the remains of a five thousand franc note. That expense agitated him further—knowing the bursar wouldn't compensate such an expense from gendarme accounts. He pushed through the thick crowd to the casino entrance, where a man, almost a head taller than Beauviér, wearing a black patch across one eye, blocked his path. The corners of Beauviér's mouth turned down. "I would like to go inside," he said over the competing noise.

With his good eye, the man studied him. "Your membership card, monsieur."

"I don't have one."

"Then I can't help you."

Beauviér supposed a gratuity was expected, but he had little money remaining and even less patience. "I would like to go inside," he repeated.

The man folded his arms across his chest, indicating the request had been denied.

Beauviér was tired of the noise and even more so of the charade. Reaching into his coat pocket, he removed his gendarme identification, placing it in front of the man's face. "Here is my membership card," he said, standing on the balls of his feet, his mouth next to the man's ear. "How does that look to you?"

His lips separating slightly, the man let his arms fall. "I'm sorry, monsieur. I didn't know. We have an understanding with the police."

Beauviér suggested, "Well now you and I have an understanding," and nudged the man out of his way.

The lounge noise followed him through the curtain, into a small anteroom. An attractive young girl sat behind a waist-high counter, selling cigars and cigarettes. Immediately she moved through a small opening, taking the handle of an inner door.

"Monsieur," she said in a breathy voice.

Beauviér handed her a one hundred franc note.

"Thank you, monsieur," she said, turning the handle. "And good luck."

Grabbing the edge of the door before it fully opened, Beauviér observed the room beyond.

Reassuringly, the young girl said, "There are only members in the casino this evening, monsieur... no wives."

"How considerate," he commented, squinting against the bright lights.

The casino was twice the size of the lounge, and brilliantly illuminated by overhead chandeliers that ran its length. Near Beauviér were four blackjack tables, each full of gamblers, followed by a roulette table, equally congested. However most of the activity was concentrated at a crap table by the back wall. It was the loudest, most spirited game in the room, and was completely surrounded by frenzied players.

Glancing at the young woman, he said, "You're right, mademoiselle. My wife doesn't seem to be here," and moved inside, stopping at the first blackjack table, standing by the last chair of six. Observing the far end of the room, he did not hear the words of the near dealer, but felt a tug on his sleeve and turning quickly saw each player at the table staring back.

The dealer, dressed smartly in black tuxedo, repeated, "Are you going to place a bet, monsieur?" and pointed at the painted square by Beauviér's fingers.

Beauviér pulled back his hand. "I—" He stopped and, not wishing to draw attention to himself, hurriedly placed all his remaining money on the painted square.

The dealer said, "There is a one thousand franc minimum, monsieur."

Beauviér looked at the six crumpled one hundred franc notes, but before he could respond, one of the gamblers, a cigarette dangling from his mouth, said, "Let him bet. I could use a change of luck," and placed a small stack of chips on his own painted square.

"Very well, monsieur," assented the dealer, reaching for the shoe.

Beauviér did not pay attention to the cards being dealt, only looking again to the far end of the room.

There was another tug on Beauviér's sleeve. Glancing at the dealer, then at the two cards before him, he saw he had a red ace showing. Lifting the hidden card, he let it fall backward into view. It was also an ace.

"Do you wish to split them, monsieur?" asked the dealer indifferently.

Out of curiosity Beauviér nodded, and the dealer swiftly dealt a king—one red, one black—on each ace.

The man with the cigarette hanging from his mouth mumbled a profanity as his chips were removed and placed in front of Beauviér.

Beauviér stared at the winnings before him, thinking back to La Piste Royale and the words of Chrétien.

Don't you see how easy it is? Do you see how they do it?

Glancing at the casino entrance, Beauviér noticed the man with the black patch, his arms again folded, and his face impassive, like a director in the wings. Looking at the money on the table, Beauviér again heard the words of Chrétien over the sound of shuffling cards.

If you take the money they will own you.

Beauviér took a step back.

The dealer said, "Your winnings, monsieur. Don't forget your winnings."

He forced a smile. "Why don't you turn it all into chips, I'll be back."

"Very good, monsieur," the dealer agreed.

Beauviér turned away, his expression again serious, and made his way to the craps table in the back of the room. There were some thirty people around it, though the mood was now dispirited. The house was winning. Examining each face, he at last found the profile of the person he sought—Ian Musters was at the dice end of the table, speaking with the man who had accompanied him into Le Cheval Noir two hours earlier. Beauviér moved closer.

With the dice landing in their favor, a cry rose from the gamblers. Bets were hurriedly placed as the shooter raised his fist in the air. Calling out in German, he brought his arm down, pitching the dice against the far rail. A collective moan sounded as the croupier shouted, "Nine showing, messieurs," and cleared the chips and bank notes with a table rake.

Using the gamblers as a shield, Beauviér moved cautiously toward Musters and his associate who were now but an arm's length away. Cocking his head to the side, Beauviér listened for any part of their conversation—it was at first muffled under the chants of the crowd, then became clear: "But you must remember, Roger, you were over one hundred thousand ahead. You can do it again, I'm certain." It was Muster's speaking, thought Beauviér—it was the same voice.

"But I am now four hundred thousand down, Ian. I don't know where I can find that kind of money. Like you, I am only a secretary," replied the unfortunate man. His voice was unsteady.

Listening to the conversation repeat itself, Beauviér peered over the shoulder of the gambler in front of him and caught a glimpse of the man speaking, a man who looked familiar.

He wore a rumpled dark blue suit with white piping, a white shirt and dark polka-dot tie. The apparel was almost identical to that of the Englishman found dead on *rue des Minimes* a few days before. Except for the full head of hair and slight age difference, the man conversing with Musters could have easily been Stuart Endfield. However this man was alive and quite animated, stammering in a sense of hopelessness as he repeatedly wiped his brow with the sleeve of his jacket. And that was when Beauviér saw it: a gambling marker gripped tightly in his hand.

Having heard and seen all he needed, Beauviér moved back to the blackjack table and without breaking stride, picked up his winnings, dropping them into his pocket. Entering the anteroom, he stopped, his eyes opaque as he studied the cigars for sale in a glass case.

"May I help you with something, monsieur?" inquired the young woman behind the counter.

He glanced at her but did not reply, instead moved toward the curtain, pulling it back. The man with the eye patch still stood watch. Over the pounding music, Beauviér said, "May I have a word with you, monsieur?"

The man turned, grinning stupidly.

Grabbing the outside of his jacket pocket, Beauviér shook it twice, jingling the loose chips. "I did well tonight, monsieur. I wanted to thank you and have a word, if possible?"

The man waved his arm and shortly there was a changing of the guard.

"Okay," said the one-eyed man. "This way, Inspector."

Pushing his shoulder against those customers not quick enough, the man cleared a path toward the far side of the bar with Beauviér right behind. Stopping at door marked 'Office,' the man threw it open.

"After you, Inspector," he said, nodding at the unlit interior.

Beauviér took four steps inside before turning. The door shut and the overhead lights blazed in a small room. The man moved toward a desk. Beauviér's expression hardened and the corners of his eyes turned up sharply. Spreading out his stance a half step, he grabbed the man's left wrist with one hand and the left thumb with the other before pulling straight up. Dropping to his knees, the man let out a cry as Beauviér drove his knee into the small of the man's back, forcing him face down on the carpet.

"Shut up," yelled Beauviér.

There was momentary silence, then the large man whimpered slightly. Beauviér, his knees bent slightly, held his place and his grip, watching the large man blubber against the floor. Again the room was silent. Seeming to acquiesce, the man let out a deep breath and as quickly began struggling. Beauviér drew back his lips and gradually turned his grip clockwise. The man's wailing intensified, forcing spittle down the side of his chin.

There was sharp pain in Beauviér's shoulder, although it was nothing the man had done, but rather his aged body rebelling as he used parts of his body long since retired.

Taking a deep breath, he said calmly, "I am sorry to resort to such methods, but I knew you would understand this type of opening dialogue."

Not expecting a reply, he straightened his legs, trying to push blood into his ankles, which were beginning to ache. The movement seemed to help, turning his shoulders one way, then the other, he attempted to reduce the tension in his back.

With his grip still tight, he again bent his knees and said, "Normally when I find an operation such as yours, I arrange surveillance and undercover operatives or other such mundane things, but that could take weeks, even months, monsieur—excuse me, but I didn't catch your name."

The man mumbled something inaudible into the carpet.

"Let's try one more time," said Beauviér, twisting the man's wrist.

The man yelled, "Bernard."

Beauviér said mildly, "But I don't have the time, Bernard. So I have an offer to make, and it is this. There is an Englishman in your casino named Ian Musters and I would like to have everything you know about him. For this, I will allow you to stay in business. However, if for some reason I feel you are lying to me…" He again twisted Bernard's wrist, who wailed briefly. In the ensuing silence, Beauviér continued, "Well then, I will have to shut you down and you will go to prison for a year or two. Now, does all of that seem fair?"

Attempting to nod, Bernard's head moved in circles against the carpet.

"That's good. Very good," said Beauviér, straightening his legs. "Now I am going to let you up, but if you try anything naughty, then we will be right back here again, and next time my offer won't be so attractive. Do you understand?" He released his grip, taking a step back. His eyes steady on the motionless man, he wiped at his brow with a handkerchief.

Initially Bernard did not move, his face pressed to the carpet. Then, cautiously rolling onto his back, he sat up, immediately clutching his arm. "You broke it! You broke my arm!"

Beauviér shook his head. "No, Bernard, it is not broken." He watched Bernard attempt to stand, and said, "Hold it! I think I prefer you on the ground for the moment. Until our business is completed, anyway."

Bernard obeyed, cautiously glancing at Beauviér, who was grinning fiercely. The eye patch, now pushed to the side, proved unnecessary as two identical bloodshot eyes looked back at Beauviér.

"Can you see me all right?" asked Beauviér.

Blinking repeatedly, Bernard removed the useless patch.

"Why do you wear that?" asked Beauviér, sounding bothered. "Does it make you look tough?"

"I suppose," he replied, wiping at the saliva around his mouth.

Beauviér sat against the edge of the near desk, casually folding his hands. "So, you know Ian Musters, Bernard?"

Bernard did not immediately respond, then murmured, "Yes."

"How long has he been coming into Le Cheval Noir?"

"I don't know. Three months, maybe longer."

"You two have an arrangement, don't you?"

Sitting cross-legged, he carefully placed the injured arm on his lap, then whispered, "Yes."

"And do you know a Stuart Endfield?"

Bernard looked sideways at the Inspector. "The name is familiar."

"I thought we had an understanding, Bernard," complained Beauviér, unclasping his hands.

"Okay, okay," he said quickly. "I know him."

Refolding his hands, Beauviér said, "He's dead. What can you tell me about that?"

Bernard stammered, "N—n—nothing. I—I don't know anything about that killing."

"I didn't say he was murdered, Bernard."

"I saw it in the evening paper," he exclaimed, grimacing as he inadvertently put weight on his tender arm. "It was in the paper."

Beauviér nodded. "So it was. So it was." Reaching into his pocket, he removed his winnings from blackjack. "But you appear just a bully, Bernard, and I really didn't think you a murderer. Now, I believe these belong to you." Glaring, he threw the chips at the cowering man, and said, "So, why don't we just start at the beginning. For example, tell me about the first time you came across the man, Ian Musters…"

* * *

194

The wind and the hail stopped as if a switch had been thrown somewhere in the darkness. A quiet settled in, the quiet of the countryside. But the night air was still cold, keeping the thick layer of hailstones in a single white sheet, coating the far unlit house and encircling woods. The black strip of the nearby river, emerging briefly between the house and the drive, appeared fluorescent under the creeping three-quarter moon. It all looked unreal, like a beautiful hand-toy that could be picked up and shaken to make the hail fall again.

Sitting in his parked car, Tom Breck remembered the serenity and the river plodding through the valley until the forest swallowed it up; he remembered the fishermen waiting patiently in their boats, rarely speaking, as the sun reflected off the water.

But that was three years ago and a different time. It had been summer, the month of August, and there were few worries. Tom had courted Michelle at this house at the end of the winding drive—her father's home, and where she'd been born. He had stayed at Les Charmettes, in room 36, waking each morning to drive the six kilometers and take breakfast with her in a small grove on the bank of the river. They explored the countryside each day and then, as the afternoon fell away, returned to the house for cocktails and conversation with her father before the three of them dined overlooking the now black river.

It had all been so perfect.

Pushing away the cold, his arms tight about his chest, Tom glanced at the clock on the dash. It was twenty-seven minutes past midnight. He'd received no response when he knocked on the door of the far house some minutes earlier and had considered leaving, to return in the morning, but he wanted to see his wife. A few minutes more would bother him little.

Glancing at the passenger seat, he saw the bouquet of flowers he had stolen from the foyer at Les Charmettes. They were old, slightly brown, but he hoped they would do; he hoped she would understand. He needed to let her know things were different, that they would be different. He had decided to involve her more in his life, to share with her his deepest feelings, feelings that he had always kept to himself. It wasn't much, but it was a start and just maybe, she would offer the same.

195

Placing the flowers on his lap, he let his head fall back on the headrest. Michelle could be home soon. He thought to close his eyes for a minute or two.

Headlights flashed through the driver's window of Tom's car and he awoke with a start. Running his hands down his face, he blinked in the darkness, glancing at the luminous hands of the dashboard clock. It was five minutes before two.

Sitting up, he noticed the house and driveway and the river beyond had vanished. Jerking his head to the right, he could see the trees of the surrounding woods clearly enough. Then he understood. While he slept it had snowed, blanketing the windshield.

He flicked the switch for the wipers but they only groaned, unable to move against the frozen layer of snow. Climbing out of the car, the bouquet on his lap fell to the snow-covered ground and stooping to pick it up, he noticed Michelle's car pulling into the garage of her father's house.

Hearing the motor shut down, he wondered why she had not stopped upon seeing his car at the top of the drive. Then he saw the reason—the snowfall had hidden the Jensen under its layer, the black tires blending nicely with the near woods.

Michelle's car door opened, the interior light revealing someone beside her, most certainly her father. Then the passenger door opened and Tom became still, realizing it was not her father. The man getting out was taller, clearly more agile, and it sounded as if he were speaking English, or possibly Dutch, but that was impossible as Michelle spoke neither. The man waited at the end of the car before taking her arm, leading her toward the house.

Still motionless, Tom was uncertain what to do, standing in the cold as white clouds floated out his mouth. He watched Michelle rummaging in her purse at the front door, when it happened. The man had bent forward, kissing her on her mouth, and she made no effort to resist.

Tom suddenly felt the bitter night cut into his body. Pressing his arms tight to his side, he did his best to remain motionless—he did not want to be seen, he could not be seen.

Michelle was again searching her purse. A word was spoken and the sound of laughter rushed up the drive as the front door opened. The two figures entered and a light in the foyer went on, then another illuminated the outside snow with a warped square of light. Abruptly the light in the foyer went out, followed by the second. The house was again dark; it seemed so harmless, coated in the glistening snow.

Tom felt like running, but he didn't know where, he didn't know if he could even move. He stared at the passing river, now seemingly at rest, and it appeared like a black hole that he could easily step into, falling, never to land. The cold was biting at his face as his breathing became labored. Slowly, he turned and began clearing the windshield of snow. It came off in frozen chunks, revealing his reflection in the glass and it seemed a stranger looking back. Up and down he rubbed, pushing harder. His right foot slipped and he tried to keep his balance but was unable, collapsing onto the ground.

He raised his trembling hand and opened the car door, climbing inside. His fingers, seemingly too cold to bend, turned the key and the engine let out a muffled roar. The headlights flew to life as the Jensen rolled onto the road which appeared distorted in the streaked glass. It lay ahead in awkward curves, though he knew it to be straight. Leaning forward, his chest almost touching the steering wheel, he tried to warm himself, but still shivered. He pushed down on the accelerator and the needle of the speedometer began to climb.

The trees, framed in the side window, fell away to open fields. The car moved faster. He glanced at his side mirror, the moonlit countryside behind—the trailing snow shot up in a rooster-tail as if the road were of sand and he was suddenly crossing a barren desert.

Abruptly, he took the road into the Fontainebleau forest. A canopy of trees immediately engulfed him and the asphalt road was again clear. He was traveling in a black and white tube, the beams of the headlights seemingly ineffectual against the darkness, reflecting off the woods into his eyes. He pushed the car faster still. The road weaved left, then right, descending deeper into the darkness, then gradually the cover of trees fell away. The lights of Barbizon took shape in the distance and the moon again lighted the sky. Tom lifted his foot from the accelerator and the car began to slow.

As he entered the village, his face was hard and his eyes unblinking. The buildings rushed up as he slowed to a crawl on *la grande rue* and pulling in front of Les Charmettes, let the Jensen roll to a stop. He stared straight ahead, the headlights still showing the way, as if he should keep going, as if he should never stop.

He then looked at his hands resting on the wheel. They no longer trembled.

Shutting the car down, he went inside the darkened hotel. The only light in the cavernous structure came from the dining room fireplace, still flickering its yellow glow. For quite a while Tom stared into the struggling flames, all the time wondering how long it would take to forget about this evening, to forget about what he'd seen. Taking a seat in the near chair, his gaze was constant, watching the flames creep back and forth, and the smoke rise.

Tom heard the timbers of the staircase creak—the old building, speaking in the night—and then sensed someone entering the small room. Recognizing Tatiana out the corner of his eye, he looked again to the smoldering fire. Quietly, she knelt beside him and placed a small log on the embers. The pendulum clock sounded the half-hour and not a word was spoken.

There was no need.

CHAPTER SIX

Moving through the entrance of the small park, Jules Beauviér walked to a bench beside a rather small statue of King Léopold the First. The statue and the bench, and the park itself, were all covered in a fine layer of snow. It had fallen earlier that morning in contradiction to the man on the radio who had promised clear skies and not to worry. Beauviér wondered how someone could be wrong so consistently as he pushed the snow off the bench seat with his gloved hand. A policeman could not afford to be wrong or he'd end up in a hospital bed, and that's if he's lucky. Meteorologists! Beauviér thought. Why don't they just do that? Study the damn meteors, and let the weather be. Producing a newspaper from his topcoat pocket, he laid it on the bench seat, turned and sat down. He shivered briefly before lifting his wrist to see the time. It was three minutes before eight in the morning. He was on time.

Trying to ignore the cold, and hoping he would not have to wait long, he watched the pedestrians hastily shoot by the narrow park entrance. Most were on their way to work at the nearby hospital and paid him no mind—a man sitting on a park bench in the middle of winter was certainly to be avoided. And this was why he chose such a place, wanting the certain privacy it afforded. That, and the crisp winter air that allowed him to think more clearly, to sort out those things that needed sorting.

The simple case of the dead art dealer in Namur and the discovered Monet was developing into something of greater proportions than he ever imagined. With each fact gathered, an unknown would appear. The American and the Polish woman seemed to be slipping away, though the murderer of the Englishman, Stuart Endfield, was the most troubling. That man must be put away, and he would be, it was just a matter of time and this is what concerned him most. Taking the other half of the

199

newspaper from his pocket, he observed the date in the top right corner—though he already knew the answer, there was need for confirmation. It was Thursday, December 20, 1984, leaving him but twelve days as Chief Inspector. The Gendarmerie would allow no grace period for almost solving a crime.

His gaze and thoughts drifted to the snow about his feet, and he didn't notice an approaching man until he stood beside the bench. Startled, Beauviér lifted his head.

"Good morning, Sergeant," he said in good humor.

His voice hoarse and barely audible, Martin said, "Good morning, Inspector."

Beauviér brushed away the snow next to him on the bench. "Sit here," he said, laying out additional newsprint.

Taking the seat, Martin stared straight ahead at the ivy-covered wall that surrounded the small park.

Beauviér said, "How do you feel, Sergeant?"

Speaking in a whisper, he replied, "Fine, monsieur."

"So when do they let you out of the hospital?"

"Two days, maybe three."

"Oh, that's nice."

Martin glanced at Beauviér, then looked again at the far wall. "When you telephoned, Inspector, you said there had been a development."

Beauviér clapped his hands together. "Yes, yes, Sergeant, there are a couple of new players in the affair which I will tell you about." Quickly his demeanor calmed and his voice lowered. "But first I wanted to ask you about something... When you found the American in Namur, you felt the attacker had meant to humiliate him. Do you still think that?"

"Yes," Martin answered firmly.

"And that something was stolen. Though he had all of his possessions, you thought there had been a robbery." He paused, waiting for confirmation.

Martin nodded.

"Well, I believe you were right," he acknowledged, lowering his head to study his folded hands.

Neither man spoke for a few seconds, then Beauviér said, "I had the American's home searched."

Martin turned to look at Beauviér. "And you found something?"

"No, Sergeant. Nothing."

"Oh," said Martin faintly.

"But we spoke with his maid."

"She discovered you?"

"Not quite, Sergeant," Beauviér reassured him. "We had a magistrate's paper to search the premises and seize anything relevant, but there was nothing, except, well, the maid thinks quite highly of our Monsieur Breck. She said he is a kind man, and painted a much different picture of him than I would have imagined."

Martin's brow wrinkled. "So?"

Beauviér took a deep breath. "It is all a part of it, part of this miserable affair. At the beginning everything was black and white. We had a smuggler to track down, and any accomplices, of course," he added as if to remind himself, then his voice became somber. "It seems the American's wife left him some days back."

"The maid told you this?"

"Yes. However, I already knew about it."

"You did? How?"

"It started with the gambling markers, Sergeant. You see, I traced them to a casino in town, Le Cheval Noir. Do you know it?"

Adjusting his jacket about his neck, Martin shook his head.

Beauviér said, "I went there on a hunch last evening and stumbled upon a fellow named Bernard Fouchét. He is the manager. We had an interesting conversation."

"He willingly spoke with you?"

"In a fashion, Sergeant. Now listen, as this is where the black and white starts to cloud."

Martin said nothing as he waited.

Beauviér asked, "Do you remember the name, Ian Musters?"

"Yes," he answered without hesitation. "The Englishman that showed you the film of Stuart Endfield stealing the file at the British Embassy and told you where to find the American and the Polish woman in France. In… In Barbizon."

"That's correct," said Beauviér, pleased with the sergeant's recall. "Well, it seems that Ian Musters himself started going into Le Cheval Noir some months back, ingratiating himself with the local gangsters in an effort to gain favor."

"He was able to do this?" asked Martin skeptically.

"No, not at first. They found him bothersome, evidently, as did I. But then he claimed to have knowledge on the whereabouts of a famous painting, worth millions of francs."

"The Monet," said Martin quickly. "And before it was discovered in Namur?"

"Yes," said Beauviér.

"Then it was he who attacked the American and—"

Beauviér held his hand up. "No, it's not that simple, Sergeant. The gangsters still did not believe him completely and it took some prodding on his part to finally convince one of them."

"But why didn't he just go get it himself?"

"Why should he, if he can get someone else to do his dirty work, Sergeant? And he might have been scared. Who knows?"

"But if this one gangster was finally convinced... What went wrong?"

"The gallery owner dropped dead, is what went wrong, Sergeant," Beauviér explained. "The fellow was on his way to Namur the day Buchon was found crumpled in the doorway. It was a case of bad timing, otherwise it would have never come to our attention."

"This Bernard Fouchét told you all this?"

"Yes."

"Why?"

"The murder of Stuart Endfield had him somewhat nervous, among other things."

Martin was about to speak when a group of schoolchildren appeared at the entrance of the park. A brief snowball fight ensued, then they departed, taking their noise with them.

As it became quiet, Martin said, "So, this Ian Musters was just going to *give* this gangster the Monet?"

"No, of course not. He wanted half of the money after the sale, and something else."

"Why would the gangster give it up? I mean, if he had the Monet, what's to force him to share with the Englishman?"

"Because there was the promise of another painting—one even more valuable."

"I don't understand."

"But you told me, Sergeant," recalled Beauviér. "When you found the American in Namur after the attack. Although nothing appeared missing, you said there had been a robbery, didn't you?"

"Yes," he answered as his eyes narrowed. "So there was another painting. Ian Musters stole the second painting."

Beauviér shrugged. "He may have, but it's out of character. The gangster from Le Cheval Noir didn't get it, of this I am certain, and as I said, Musters would probably not have the courage on his own."

"You believe this—this Bernard Fouchét?"

"Yes, I do."

"Why, Inspector? Why would you believe such a man?"

"Because the gangster from Le Cheval Noir that agreed to work with Musters… is Bernard Fouchét's brother."

Martin pulled his head back. "He turned in his own brother?"

"Not exactly."

His face quizzical, Martin said, "How? Not exactly?"

"Well first, his brother will be difficult to find because he is now using another name."

"And you know it?"

"Yes, it is Mégot. No first name."

"Mégot?" repeated Martin, and laughed. "What a strange name."

"Gangsters are not known for their imagination, Sergeant," Beauviér said curtly.

"No, no of course not, Inspector," Martin agreed as the grin fell from his face. "But he can't hide forever, regardless of the name."

"He doesn't need to, Sergeant. You see he is evidently dying. He may not make it to the end of the year, according to his brother."

"Of what?" asked Martin, sounding doubtful.

"Of advanced syphilis, Sergeant." Beauviér's tone was strangely sympathetic. "Evidently his organs are giving out on him. He may already be dead, for all I know."

"And if he's not?"

"Then we need to find him."

"Then this Mégot killed Stuart Endfield and attacked me?" said Martin angrily, touching his bandaged neck lightly with the tips of his fingers.

"When his name came up, I imagined that also. But he wouldn't have had the strength." Leaning forward, Beauviér placed his forearms on his upper legs, casually folding his hands together. "Shooting Stuart Endfield would have been no problem, but the attack on you would have demanded someone able-bodied, and Mégot could not have done it."

"Then that only leaves Ian Musters—and you still feel it is not in his character?"

"Now, I'm not so sure."

Martin's weak voice grew weaker as he said, "You mentioned Musters demanded one-half of the proceeds from the sale of the Monet, and something else—that he wanted something else."

Still leaning forward, Beauviér spoke to the snow-covered ground. "This is one of the most bothersome things I have discovered in this affair and I find it... well..." He took a deep breath. "You said the American had been attacked with an unnecessary vengeance when you found him. At the time I didn't know what you meant; I thought you were being overly dramatic, as this was your first assignment." He sat up, placing his palms on the bench seat, as if he were going to stand. With his gaze steady on the ivy-covered wall, he continued. "On any given evening in Le Cheval Noir there are gamblers, most of them mobsters, and pickpockets employed by the house. There are city cops on the take and the felons who pay them, and then, of course, the prostitutes and their pimps. It was through Mégot that Musters met with one of these pimps. He wanted to hire a prostitute, but it wasn't for himself."

The breeze lifted the lapel on Beauviér's topcoat, slapping it gently against the side of his face. He did not seem aware of it as Martin folded his arms, waiting for him to continue.

Finally, Beauviér said, "Musters hired a male prostitute, or gigolo, I suppose you'd call him. Some exiled count or duke from Rumanian royalty. Quite young and handsome, I'm told, with education, breeding and title, but no money. So Ian Musters fixed him up with the necessary funds, then sent him on his way." Beauviér looked at Martin. "He sent him after the wife of the American. To seduce her with promises of golden palaces with Lippizaner drawn carriages and evidently it worked. Shortly after the Rumanian was given his marching orders, she left for France to meet him. So you see, Sergeant. The black and white is graying."

"Why?" whispered Martin. "Why does Musters hate the American so?"

His eyes distant, Beauviér looked at the sergeant. "What? Oh, we'll find out. Along with everything else in due time." Pulling his gloves tight to his fingers, he said, "I asked the French authorities to pick up the Rumanian."

"On what charges?" asked Martin.

Beauviér glared. "On charges of being a son-of-a-bitch, Sergeant. Those are the charges." Pushing his hands into his topcoat pockets, he said, "And I mentioned to them something about an unsolved murder and the Monet. The French have petitioned for its return, you know."

Martin sat up straight. "What would you like me to do, Inspector?"

"But don't they want you back at the hospital?"

"They're being overly cautious. I'm really quite fit, monsieur."

"Are you really?" he commented. "All right then, Sergeant. I want you to get on Ian Musters and find out everything you can. Where he lives, what kind of car he drives, the color of his favorite shirt and most importantly, where he was before he arrived in Belgium." Cautiously, he lifted himself from the bench. "Also, there's a man who works for the British Embassy—his name is Roger Catchpole. He is in trouble with gambling markers, compliments of Ian Musters and Le Cheval Noir, and I would like you to find out about him. He's, well, just find out about him."

Beauviér moved toward the entrance of the park.

"And where will you be, Inspector?" Martin called, his voice struggling.

As if the answer were obvious, Beauviér replied over his shoulder, "Why, I'll be in Barbizon, Sergeant."

* * *

The flight from Paris had departed on time and the pilot reported visibility to be good. There was even mention of a tailwind over the North Atlantic, however, Air Lingus 904 to Dublin, Ireland, was still behind schedule. Tom Breck checked his watch to confirm it as he refused additional champagne from the stewardess. Though he did not have an appointment, and no set hour for arrival, he was pressed for time nonetheless. He had only ten days to complete something that, even under normal circumstances, would demand three months, maybe longer. But in ten days he needed to smuggle a gun, something just smaller than the commuter plane he was on, to Algeria in North Africa. For this, he required assistance. And for the first time in his career, he considered the real possibility of failure.

Leaning back in his seat, he thought of a telephone call made earlier that morning. It had been to his home, to speak with Chantal, his maid. She acted as his secretary when he was away, keeping record of all guests and callers, and what she told him was worse than he could have imagined.

205

Almost hysterical, she had reported a visit by the police—though gendarmes she later called them—and they spent the early morning searching the house and grounds, though apparently took nothing. They talked with her at length about Tom's daily routine, his behavior, habits, and what type of man she felt him to be. They talked with her about his wife, Michelle. At this point Chantal had begun to cry, feeling remorse at having told the gendarmes about Madame Breck's departure. She knew it was none of their affair, but she'd been frightened. There were ten of them, she explained between sobs, or maybe more. They seemed to be everywhere—in the bedrooms and about the garden, with more in the garage. There was even one standing guard at the gate, and he had a gun.

Tom had tried to console her, without success. The news of the gendarmes' appearance was overwhelming and he told her to close up the house, that he would telephone after the first of the year when things settled down, but she refused, saying she'd stay until he returned and if the gendarmes appeared again, would watch them and give him a full report.

Thinking of her words, Tom allowed himself a crooked grin. Loyalty had surfaced in the form of a woman who cleaned his home, did his laundry and prepared his meals for a handful of francs in an envelope each Friday. Such loyalty was rare.

Abruptly, the airplane banked and the green of Ireland filled his window. There was no snow to be seen, but rather looked a spring day, the gentle façade of a place with few worries. The farms, outlined by their rock fences—not one seeming to run in a straight line—slowly gave way to the concrete sprawl of urban Dublin as the plane touched down.

Having no luggage, Tom moved quickly through customs, following the overhead signs for ground transport. There were more than a dozen taxis in line, each one an Austin and each painted olive green. The one at the head of the line started its engine as Tom climbed into the back seat.

"Dalkey, please," he said to the driver and the car lurched forward.

Tom cranked his window down a full turn and removing a package of cigarettes from his pocket, offered one to the driver, who refused with a wave of the hand.

Lighting his cigarette, Tom glanced at the driver in the mirror and commented, "It's warm today."

"Is it?" said the driver.

"I guess I wouldn't know, it's just—" He did not finish the sentence.

The taxi raced forward, climbing above the airport's protective berm, revealing multi-story apartment blocks pressed together in dull gray lines. The buildings became greater in number, as did the traffic that pushed into the outskirts of Dublin.

Unexpectedly, the driver said, "We're called the Mediterranean of the north, we are."

"I'm sorry?"

"The weather, you spoke of the weather. Balmy it is, and can be like this right up to summer next," the driver announced. "Then she'll bluster. Do you have family in Dalkey?"

"What? Oh, no. I'm just going to find a friend."

"Find a friend," repeated the driver, moving his eyes between the mirror and the road ahead. "You don't have any luggage, sir."

"No, I'm here for the day. I'll be catching an evening flight out."

"After you've found your friend," the driver restated, reaffirming the purpose of his trip.

Tom took a drag on his cigarette. "Yes."

"You've come all the way from America to be here a few hours?"

"I live in Brussels."

"But you're a Yank, aren't you?"

"Yes."

"I thought so," said the driver proudly. "It's fifteen quid to Dalkey, sir."

Tom caught the man's eyes in the mirror, but said nothing.

"We're not a third world country, you know," the driver continued. "Things are quite dear these days. Homes are going for over fifty thousand, but everyone seems to think we run around like wild Indians with hatchets swinging about."

Crushing his cigarette out in the ashtray, Tom said, "I don't believe I had such an opinion."

"Didn't you now?"

He grinned. "No, I didn't."

"Now, there's a phone box," said the driver, indicating the near intersection. "Would you like to give your friend a call?"

"No, thank you."

"But you know where he lives?"

"Yes."

"Well, what's the address? Possibly there's a shorter route."

Tom squinted. "I thought Dalkey was a village. How could there be a shorter way?"

"Well, you never know now, do you? Say, might I take you up on that cigarette now?"

They journeyed some forty-five minutes, the driver's conversation incessant. He covered everything from the Norman invasion of the twelfth century to the civil war of the twentieth, only stopping his monologue as the coastal road they were traveling abruptly narrowed and a village took shape. Two-and three-story shops clung together, almost tenuously, as if a loud noise might bring them crashing down. The wooden facades were intact, though battered by salt air and time. A mason's stone above the green grocer's shop read *Dalkey*, followed by a chiseled date no longer legible. There were few pedestrians and no cars to be seen.

Tom suddenly felt he had made a mistake—that he would not find what he needed in this place.

The taxi came to a stop, the engine gently rocking the car.

"Here we are, sir," said the driver.

"Is there a city hall?"

The driver laughed. "In Dalkey? I shouldn't think so, sir."

Glancing at his watch, Tom considered returning to the airport.

The driver said, "Are you looking for your friend's name all written down nice and neat, with a postal marking next to it?"

Tom didn't reply.

"This is Ireland," the man went on. "We don't take note of a man's whereabouts until he's gone, if you take my meaning. It's only then we mark somewhere he was once alive, the only exception being if he owes money, or you fancy his wife. No sir, you won't be finding the name of your friend in any book unless he happens to be in jail and then it'll do you little good." Lifting his arm, he pointed to the near corner. "If you're looking for a man, and he wishes to be found, then that's where he'll be."

The driver was indicating a public house at the corner. It had neatly curtained windows and a name painted above the doorway that read, *The Rose and Thistle*.

"You know this place?" asked Tom.

"I know of it, sir. Though never been inside, as I don't feel I'd be all that welcome." The driver turned in his seat to look at Tom. "But with your accent you'll be all right, and if what you're saying is true."

Producing a handful of pound notes from his pocket, Tom said, "Would you wait for me?"

Counting the money handed him, the driver said, "No, sir. I'm afraid a Dublin taxi parked on this street for an extended period would be of service to no one. Someone'll come for you if you call, minding it's not too late in the day."

Though not understanding the refusal, Tom got out as the driver turned the wheel sharply, making a U-turn in the narrow street. The front wheels jumped the far curb, falling back on the asphalt with a clatter and accelerating quickly, the taxi disappeared round the first bend.

The street was now vacant. No people, no cars, no more sounds, nothing, and Tom remembered there was a two-thirty flight to Paris, imagining he would be on it. He made his way to the entrance of The Rose and Thistle, briefly hesitating before going inside.

Although as quiet as the street outside, the pub appeared ready for business. Brilliantly lighted by glass fixtures screwed into the ceiling, it appeared particularly well maintained. The walls, the floor and the furniture were of mahogany, and all appeared recently polished. A young boy was preparing the tables along the far wall with fresh tablecloths and a small 'Reserved' sign on each. The only customers were two men at the end of the long wooden bar in conversation with the bartender.

Tom took the last stool at opposite end of the bar, the bartender slowly walking toward him.

"I'll have a glass of that, please," said Tom, pointing at the draught handle of an unfamiliar beer.

The bartender repeated, "A glass, is it?"

Tom nodded and, watching the bartender draw the beer, said, "I'm looking for a friend. His name is John Clark. Would you know him?"

"John Clark, is it?" Again repeating Tom's words. "That's quite a common name. A friend, is he?"

"Yes," Tom answered, lighting a cigarette. "From Brussels."

"In Germany?"

Tom pinched a piece of tobacco off the end of his tongue. "No, that's in Belgium," he replied, sensing a futility in their conversation. "How much do I owe you?"

Placing the beer in front of Tom, the bartender ignored the question. "Is he a good friend?"

"Yes." Tom placed a five-pound note on the bar. "He is."

"And he lives in Dalkey?"

Taking a sip of the lukewarm beer, Tom nodded.

Loudly, the bartender addressed the two men at the opposite end of the bar. The words were clear, though unintelligible, as they were in Gaelic. One of the men mumbled and the other snickered. The young boy setting the tables said something and Tom was certain he heard the name John Clark mentioned in the accented words. The two men laughed loudly as the bartender smiled, tipping his head in the direction of the young boy. "The lad thinks John Clark is the real name of Superman and he's quite certain he wouldn't live in these parts, with it being so unsafe and all."

Taking a drag of his cigarette, Tom remained silent, watching the smoke float away.

The bartender said, "I'm sorry I can't be of more help to you, sir."

Looking up from under his eyelids, Tom said, "That's all right," and pushed the five pound note toward the bartender. "Could you take out what I owe you?"

"The special today is cottage pie, sir," he said, seemingly oblivious to the money near his fingers. "And it will be for the last time, as Molly in the kitchen is off to America in a week's time." He leaned his stomach against the bar, pushing his face close to Tom's. "To Massachusetts, she's going. Have you been there, sir?"

Tom pulled back slightly. "No, I haven't."

"But you're American aren't you?"

"Yes."

"And what's your name?"

The corners of Tom's mouth fell straight. Crushing his cigarette out in the ashtray, he reached for the glass of beer, said, "Tom Breck," and then drank the remainder in one swallow. Standing, he nodded at the bank note on the bar. "You can keep the change."

The bartender bellowed, "Thomas Breck, all the way from America is with us." He then whispered to Tom, "And there'll be no change from that, sir, as your money's no good in here. So return the fiver to your pocketbook, if you'd be so kind."

Tom's brow wrinkled. Looking to the end of the bar, he saw the two men were gone, as was the young boy. Taking a step backward, he was about to turn when arms embraced his upper body from behind, pressing his own tight to his side. Someone breathed heavily near his left ear. He struggled to break the grip around him but the hands against his stomach were locked tight. Gradually, the breathing in his ear turned into a voice and words he could understand. "What brings a lost soul such as yourself to a tear-stained isle as this, young Thomas Breck? I suspect you'll be wanting full refund from your travel agent upon return."

Tom stopped struggling, letting his arms hang limp. "They promised the package tour. And all the risks that go with it."

The grip fell away and Tom felt hands on his shoulders that gently turned him around. He was now looking at John Clark, who said, "When they told me someone with an American accent was searching me out, I was hoping against hope it might be you, Thomas. But I never really imagined." He smiled broadly. "How are you?"

"I'm fine," he replied, knowing his tone did not match the words. "It's good to see you, John."

The edges of the Irishman's smile dropped. "You have news, Thomas, and whether it's good or not, let's first get comfortable," he advised, and taking Tom's arm, directed him across the room.

The young boy had returned and was sliding out a table to expose a leather bench set that ran the length of the wall. John Clark and Tom sat, side by side, facing the bar. A clamor inside the kitchen had commenced and the pub was taking on life as customers entered. A clock behind the bar struck twelve times announcing that luncheon, at The Rose and Thistle, had begun.

Speaking to the young boy over the gathering din, John Clark said, "Bring out my wine, a dozen oysters and two salmon filets with something green on the side, lad, and in that particular order if it wouldn't be a bother."

Watching the boy disappear through the kitchen door, John Clark said, "It's either fish or the cottage pie, and that wouldn't be right."

Tom glanced at John Clark. "The taxi that brought me from the airport wouldn't wait."

Taking a cigar from the breast pocket of his tweed jacket, John said, "No, I suppose he wouldn't." He struck a wooden match, holding the flame against the end of the cigar, waiting for it to catch, before placing it in his mouth. With smoke floating between them, he continued, "There was a bold robbery at Gatwick a short time back. They got away clean with millions, but the Brits knew it was Irish that did it and they want a little cooperation with the local Garda." Removing the cigar from his mouth, he grinned. "That's Gaelic for the demons in blue, but then you knew that, Thomas."

The young boy appeared at the table, gripping a bottle of red wine and two glasses. He hurriedly placed all three on the table. Taking a corkscrew from his back pocket, he removed the cork and filled both glasses to the top. Putting the bottle on the table, he turned and left.

Cautiously placing one of the glasses in front of Tom, John Clark said, "Don't you find the lack of formality rather refreshing, Thomas?"

Taking a sip of wine, Tom smiled.

After an extended drag on his cigar, John Clark said, "The rumor is that the Garda have narrowed the manhunt to this end of county Dublin and the villages Dún Laoghaire to the north and Bray to the south. Arrests are expected any moment and everyone's at the end of their rope, waiting. No outsider is to be trusted—not that they really ever are, but it's a bit more stressful than usual."

Tom placed his package of cigarettes on the table, removing one as John Clark struck a match, and said, "I know you're too much of a gentleman to ask, Thomas, but no, I' m not involved in the affair, neither do I know those responsible. I've been away too long and I'm no longer privy to such matters. It's much easier for someone to keep a secret if they don't know what it is."

Producing a white envelope from his inside coat pocket, Tom laid it on the tablecloth beside John Clark's hand. "That's the money I owe you. There are thirty-one Swiss, thousand franc notes inside."

He tapped the envelope with his forefinger, and said, "I'm not in need of the money at the moment, and something tells me you are."

"Take it, John. I'm all right."

Folding the envelope, John Clark dropped it in the side pocket of his jacket. "I'm listening, Thomas."

"The gendarmes searched my home yesterday," he declared.

"Did they find anything?"

"No, there was nothing to find."

"Were you there?"

Tom shook his head. "No, the maid told me about it."

Gripping the cigar with his thumb and forefinger, John began turning it in his mouth. "Did you use your own passport to come here?"

"Yes."

"Well then, they don't want you as yet," he said as if to himself. "But they searched your home. They know something and they're waiting." He looked at Tom. "What do they have?"

"It must be about the murder of Stuart Endfield."

"No. They were watching us that evening; they know you couldn't have done it. Then what is it?"

"I don't know."

John Clark leaned back, and, sounding disinterested, said, "You tell me whatever it is you want, Thomas, nothing more."

Tom took a large drink of wine, then lifted his cigarette from the ashtray. He held it for an instant before crushing it out, and said, "Do you remember the Monet found in Namur?"

The edges of John Clark's eyes wrinkled. "I do."

"Well, the painting was mine before it was discovered, and possibly the police are aware of that. I just don't know."

Rubbing his hands together, John Clark commended, "I knew you were a man of destiny, Thomas Breck. But to such a level I wouldn't have dreamt."

His tone serious, Tom said, "If it were nothing more than losing a painting, there would be no reason for us to talk. But I need your help."

John Clark faced Tom. "I'm still listening."

"About a year ago we were speaking at Le Cerf late one evening, and you mentioned your time in the air force and that you were a pilot and I—"

John Clark raised his hand, then ruefully said, "It was a story, Thomas. Just a story. I have never been in an air force or any other flying circus. I'm sorry, but it was just a tale."

"But the incident of the parachutists…"

He shook his head. "It was something to entertain you and anyone listening. It made you laugh, as was intended. If I thought for a moment I was misleading you, I would have never told it. I'm sorry."

Tilting his head back, Tom said, "I am a fool."

John Clark placed his hand on Tom's forearm. "You came here today and told me something that could put you in danger. You trust me and I' m not going to let you down, Thomas, of that you can be sure. Now tell me why you need a man who can fly a plane."

Tom presented a folded piece of paper. "This is why."

Lifting his hand from Tom's forearm, John Clark took the paper and began to read.

After just more than a minute, he said, "You need to move this somewhere, is that it?"

"Yes."

"Where?"

"Algeria."

John Clark opened his mouth to speak, then stopped as the young boy, carrying a large platter of oysters, placed it on the table between them.

"Bring me some paper and something to write with, lad," John Clark instructed the young boy who obliged, returning shortly with a pencil and stack of white coasters.

"Perfect," said John, and pressing one of the coasters flat to the tablecloth, began to write. He started mumbling, the timbre varying as the scribbling became more intense. Filling up one coaster, he removed another from the pile. His hand slid back and forth in a mechanical movement that covered the second coaster with numbers and connecting lines showing span and weight. Each figure on the white paper was factored, one after the other, until five coasters were used up. Leaning back, he let the pencil fall from his hand. "You don't know what this is, do you, Thomas?"

Tom touched one of the coasters. "Why would you say that?"

"Because if you did know when you gave me that paper," he advised, "then your hand would've trembled."

"Then tell me what it is."

"I shall, soon enough… In the old days, before the killing became a business and there were no benefactors to modernize our wretched ways," he began. "We were forced to innovate. We scavenged like beasts in the wood, searching out discarded pipes, gauge wire and the like. And those things we couldn't find, we'd steal.

"I was put in charge of engineering because I could add. I'd go to Trinity University and spend hours in the library finding what I needed." He touched the stack of coasters, running his thumb up the side like a deck of playing cards. "What I'm trying to say, Thomas, is the mathematics is the same. Whether you're building a mortar out of tin cans and just trying to keep it from blowing up in your

214

face, or the rabid thing we have before us here." Abruptly, he looked up. "This is a gun, Thomas. As big a gun as there ever was. The breech alone outweighs anything out there and it could throw a shell the size of a small car over a hundred miles, probably more."

Tom was silent, staring at the table.

John Clark asked, "What have you got yourself into, Thomas?"

The young boy appeared, carrying a plate in each hand. Appearing to study the untouched oysters, he said, "What? Don't you like 'em?"

John Clark waved his hand. "Take them away, lad. We'll just have the salmon."

The boy handed one of the plates he carried to John Clark. "Yeah, sure," he said, picking up the platter of oysters. "Can I have 'em, then?"

John Clark nodded.

The young boy placed the other dish in front of Tom, looked to John Clark for approval, and hurried away.

Tom picked up his fork, held it for a few seconds, then placed it back on the table. "I have no choice, John. I need to move this thing to Algeria."

"What?" John exclaimed. "What do you mean, you have no choice?"

"It's Mégot."

"He's forcing you?"

"Yes."

John Clark removed his cigar from the ashtray, puffing deliberately to get the ember up. With smoke rolling out his mouth, he said, "Give me thirty days and this Mégot will bother you no longer."

Tom shook his head. "There is someone out there directing Mégot and I don't know who. And the gendarmes are too close now. I even thought about... No. We go through with it. We have ten days to get this done, John."

"Ten days?"

"Yes, that's why I considered a plane. I didn't know if one or two trips would be needed, considering the weight, but we could finish quickly and be done with it."

"How?"

There was a brief silence, then briskly, as if from rote, he said, "I'd lease a cargo plane from an *aerodrome* I know of near La Rochelle and create a manifest with a suitable explanation of the freight. The first leg would be to Malta; I've done it before—Malta that is—and it's no problem. And then to Algeria. A landing strip would be easy enough to find in the desert, close enough to the destination. Then truck it on from there."

"You'd have a lorry and driver waiting?"

"Yes, I have a man I can trust."

"And a crane to move it from the airplane to the lorry?"

"If it's needed, then yes."

"I see," John said, trimming the cigar ember on the lip of the ashtray. "And while all of this is going on, there won't be any blanket-headed gentlemen on camels taking shots at you with long rifles."

"I need only one hour."

John Clark gently shook his head. "In the desert you don't have one hour. You can find the most remote airstrip, circling forever to be certain, and when you land there will be people, and everywhere. In thirty minutes it'll seem like an open-air bazaar. I know this. A desert is not what the word implies unless you're in the middle of the Sahara, then the plane and the lorry will never find the other. You'd all die out there."

Impatiently, Tom said, "Then we'd create a false bill of lading and arrange an Algerian buyer of the incoming cargo. We'd fly the plane straight into Algiers or Constantine."

"And then? What is the final destination?"

"I don't know. We're to be told later."

John Clark chewed the cigar on his back teeth. "Why? Why would he wait to tell you?"

"Because once I have possession of the cargo, then I could go around Mégot and straight to the buyer myself."

"It's no longer just cargo, Thomas… It's a gun."

Reluctantly, Tom nodded.

John Clark asked, "And where is it now?"

"By the French border, in Mons."

"So when you pick the gun up, you will each effectively have one-half of the treasure map."

"You could say that." He glanced at the Irishman. "I know what you're thinking."

"No, Thomas. You don't know what I'm thinking, but I shall tell you." Pushing the table away, he added, "You wait here. I'll be back," then moved quickly to the entrance and disappeared out the front door.

The young boy appeared at the table, said, "Have you finished then?" and pointed at the plates.

"I suppose," replied Tom.

Hurriedly clearing up, the boy asked, "Would you like an after lunch drink, sir?"

Tom glanced at the clock above the bar—it read four minutes to one. "No, thanks."

The boy turned and left.

Leaning back, Tom watched the crowd begin dispersing as the minute hand on the clock jumped straight up. The bell struck once and before the sound finished resonating, half the customers were gone. The clatter of lunch fell into hushed voices with two tables still occupied and a half-dozen men at the bar. Loudly, a round of drinks was ordered up, glasses were clinked together, and the conversations again fell to broken whispers.

A large man entered the pub as the clock's bell sounded four times, but it wasn't John Clark. Then two more men entered, followed by a third. The bar was again almost full, though now a red-haired girl tended the tables. She had deep green eyes, which rarely looked up, even when asking Tom if there was something more. But he wanted nothing. No more wine, no more food. He was feeling tired, and now claustrophobic as the crowd grew. Placing a twenty-pound note under his wine glass, he pushed the table away and moving to the entrance, went outside. It was dusk and the powder-white stars blinked, struggling in the clear sky. And the temperature was still strangely warm, with a slight breeze that smelled brackish. He could also taste it, the salt on his tongue as he made his way to the seawall and looked out to the blue-black Irish Sea. A half-dozen fishing boats were tethered to their buoys and a small island, empty of life, lay just beyond.

The clatter of a car's engine broke the calm and headlights streamed from the bend on the harbor side, advancing quickly on the narrow road. Tom pushed himself closer to the wall as brakes screeched and car doors opened, then closed. Tom heard voices over the sound of the car's engine, when suddenly it shut down and the headlights went out. Two figures appeared in the meager light, moving toward him.

"I'm sorry to have kept you waiting so long, Thomas." It was John Clark. "I'd like you to meet Francis Dwyer. Francis, this is Thomas Breck."

217

Tom took a step forward. "Hello."

The man said, "Pleased to meet you," and could have gestured, though it was difficult to know in the darkness that had pushed away the remaining daylight.

John Clark cleared his throat. "I want you to listen to me, Thomas, before you say anything. I want to tell you a little tale, a true tale it is."

Glancing at one man, then the other, Tom did as he was bidden.

John Clark moved closer. "I've known Francis twenty-five years—all his life, in fact. His father and I worked together in the sixties when the real trouble in the northern counties began. We did things together that put us as close as two men could be. We shared everything, good and bad, and one night when things went wrong and Benny—" John Clark stopped talking as if he were trying to catch his breath.

Leaning against the wall, Tom lit a cigarette as John Clark continued, "One night the RUC grabbed him and locked him up on a charge he had nothing to do with. They gave him five years and were to give him five more when that was done, so we broke him out. We got him away, across the border, and all would have been well except for what they did to him in there. He wasn't a strong man to begin with—having had consumption as a boy—and he died a short while later. That's when I left for Brussels, hoping to get it all behind me... Running I was, really. But then there was Francis and he needed looking after." He turned to face the young man standing by the front of the car. "So we sent you to that Anglican school in Wexford, didn't we?"

"Yes," Francis replied affectionately. "That you did, John."

"And six years later you were off to England and school in Somersetshire... Yes, those were wonderful days." John Clark turned to face Tom. "Francis didn't need me anymore then. He received funding on account of his marks being as they were; first or second in his form each fortnight, Thomas. We were all proud and—"

A car, advancing from the Dalkey side of the harbor road, interrupted him. The headlights bounced up and down, illuminating the three men in the roadway as the car came to an unsteady stop. Leaning across the passenger seat, the driver cranked the window down and exclaimed, "What are you doing? Get moving will you, you're blocking the way."

John Clark took a step toward the car's open window.

The driver repeated, "Don't make me get out of this—"

Tom could see the belligerence leaving the face of the driver, who then said, "I didn't see it was you, Johnny Clark. I—I thought it was those lads from Bray playing their little jokes. You don't disturb yourself, Johnny. No, no… I think I'll be taking the other way. It's a beautiful evening for a drive, don't you think?"

John Clark did not answer the man, nor was he given the time as the driver sat up and jerked the car backward, the headlights quickly disappearing round the bend.

A frustrated expression on his face and his tone impatient, John Clark said, "The school in England that Francis attended was merchant marine, Thomas. He is the pilot you are looking for. He'll take you and the cargo to Algeria, and before ten days are up."

"In a boat?" said Tom nervously.

"A ship, Thomas. A ship."

Stepping away from the wall, Tom began pacing in short steps. "Going through Gibraltar," he said softly. "We'd be in Spanish waters and they could board at any time, without warning."

"Is that the best you can come up with?" John Clark asked.

"For the moment, yes. You caught me off guard with this."

"Have you never smuggled anything on the ocean, Thomas?"

"No."

"And why not?"

Tom stopped his pacing and blurted, "Because I get seasick. Just motoring in the harbor I get ill. And that's why."

John Clark moved closer to Tom, their faces but a hand length apart. "You follow Francis here and you'll not be worrying about the Strait of Gibraltar and the Spanish Armada, or puking out your guts because your feet are confused," he whispered, his tone resolute.

Tom said, "There's more to this than you're saying, isn't there?"

"There is."

"But you have a ship in mind?"

John Clark looked at Francis, who said, "Yes, she's British registry out of Aberdeen and carries one hundred tons. Her name's the *Ondine*."

Tom asked, "How much is this going to cost?"

Francis lifted his hand. In it he held a white envelope—the same white envelope that Tom gave John Clark a few hours earlier. "I have already been paid," he said.

"Thank you, John," said Tom, pausing, then asked Francis, "And what about a crew?"

"Coming out of Scotland I'll have help to the north coast, but from Antwerp on, it'll be just the three of us."

Tom looked at John Clark. "You're coming along?"

"I am. You forget I'm here because of this Mégot, and my blood is up. I don't like people pushing me about."

"So you'll tell me what else you're thinking?"

"Yes, Thomas. How long do you have?"

"I have the eight o'clock to Paris."

"Good, that'll do. Now, let's sit down with a bottle of whiskey and I'll tell you what's on my mind."

The three men climbed into the car, Tom sitting alone in the back seat, staring through his window at the blue-black Irish Sea. He thought of Brussels and of home. He thought of Michelle.

* * *

Sergeant Henri Martin stood quite still as he stared at the man hanging from the ceiling, a rope about his neck. Although it was the first corpse Martin had ever seen, he felt there was something not right. The man's contorted features contrasted with the hair that was neatly parted and combed. It appeared he had groomed himself prior to his leap from the shipping box, knowing his feet would never reach the ground.

Only slightly thicker than string, the rope left a curious pattern of soft colors where it disappeared into the flesh, resurfacing at the nape. Attached to the overhead chandelier by a series of knots, the securing of the rope appeared to have taken some time. The suicide had been well planned, leaving little chance of failure.

Lowering his gaze, Martin walked to a partially open closet door, gently pushing it shut with his elbow. He then viewed the studio apartment.

There was no furniture, only a dozen unopened boxes near the kitchen entrance where a dining table and chairs would normally be. A built-in counter that opened into the kitchen was clear. Having searched the closets, he now concluded the apartment contained only the boxes, the chandelier, and the dead man.

As he reached for the radio attached to his belt, something caught his attention. Moving to the shipping box under the dead man, he removed a piece of black paper wedged between it and the floor. It was a gambling marker from Le Cheval Noir and the name Roger Catchpole was written neatly in the corner. Below the signature, across the center of the paper, was the amount of five hundred thousand francs, written both in words and numbers, with a watermark just opposite.

On the backside, inscribed in pencil or weak ink, was a series of letters. Martin studied them briefly, but unable to determine their meaning, simply dropped the marker into the side pocket of his jacket. Looking again at the box, he laid it on its side, nodding at what he saw.

It appeared that before Roger Catchpole attached the rope about his neck, he thoughtfully placed the contents of his pockets on top of the box, only to have everything slide after him when he stepped from the edge. The box then jumped forward as the heavy weight lifted, concealing the odd bits and pieces that Martin, now sitting cross-legged on the floor, was studying.

They were mostly personal items: a plastic comb, metal fingernail clippers, an inexpensive pen, three twenty-franc coins, a small brass medal of obscure origin, a business card from Le Cheval Noir with the name Bernard Fouchét prominently displayed, and two additional gambling markers. Roger Catchpole's signature was on each, as was the amount of five hundred thousand francs written just underneath.

Turning the markers over, Martin found a similar series of letters, but they were different from the first and from each other.

He pocketed the gambling markers, leaving all else where he found it, and again stood the box upright. Exhaling deeply, he raised his arms and began patting the pockets of the dead man. Taking his time, he searched each one, eventually standing on his toes to check the breast and cigarette pockets. He then moved to the trousers and, as he had found some fifteen minutes earlier, each pocket was empty.

Removing the radio from his belt, he hesitated momentarily, touching the bandage on his neck before saying in a gravelly voice, "Inspector Beauviér. Can you hear me?"

The response was uneven in its volume, the sounds garbled. He moved closer to the curtained windows as the voice at the other end became clear.

"Yes, Sergeant," said Beauviér

"Where are you, Inspector?"

"I'm outside of Lille, on my way to Barbizon. So make it quick. I'm not certain the distance these radios will carry."

Inhaling deeply, he said, "The man you asked me to check on. The man called Roger Catchpole... he is dead."

The static fell into a steady hum. For a moment, he was uncertain if his message got through.

Abruptly, Beauviér said, "How, Sergeant? How did he die?"

"It appears a suicide."

"Appears?"

"Yes, monsieur. I am not trained in such things, but there are some inconsistencies in his death."

"I understand. How was it done?"

"He is hanging by the neck from the chandelier in his apartment. That is where I am."

"Who else knows of this?"

"No one. I thought I should speak with you first, Inspector."

"That's good, Sergeant, very good. Now I want you to search the apartment and his person for anything that might help us."

"I already have, monsieur."

"Did you find anything?"

"Maybe—I'm not sure."

For a moment there was silence, then Beauviér said, "I want you to arrest Ian Musters on suspicion of murder, Sergeant. It is just after four o'clock so he should still be at the British Embassy."

Martin checked his watch for confirmation as Beauviér continued, "You cannot go on the embassy grounds, of course, but I want you waiting out front when he leaves for the day. You should have men in uniform and I want at least two cars and a wagon. When you take him into custody use handcuffs, and keep him on the sidewalk. Turn on every light on every vehicle. Make it last—put on a spectacle, Sergeant. We don't know who else is caught up in his web, but if it is suicide then maybe we can stop another from happening. Do you understand, Sergeant?"

"Yes, Inspector."

The static swelled until Beauviér's voice finally broke through. "Notify the city police, but only tell them you were checking on Roger Catchpole in connection with the murder of Stuart Endfield, nothing more. No mention of the American or the paintings or anything further. We can't have them intruding, Sergeant—not now."

222

Martin's lips brushed against the mouthpiece as he said faintly, "Very good, monsieur."

He was about to shut down the radio when Beauviér said, "And Sergeant, I would like—" A loud hissing commenced, continuing for over a minute. Beauviér was most certainly out of range, Martin reasoned, returning the radio to his belt and moved out the front door.

Stepping into the causeway that ran to the sidewalk, he unlocked the door, leaving it as he had found it some twenty minutes earlier. He then stood motionless, still gripping the handle, thinking of the unlocked door and the feel of his heart beating against his chest when he had entered. He'd turned on the chandelier to see the Englishman hanging, almost comically, like an inept scarecrow. He'd been unable to contain a cry and embarrassed at the outburst, although thankful to be alone. Then, forcing a mechanical demeanor on himself—a dead man's aplomb, he'd heard it called—he'd gone about his job.

His radio flew to life, the sudden sound startling him. He moved quickly from the crime scene toward the street and reaching the sidewalk, jerked the radio from his belt.

"Yes, Inspector," he said, his breathing strained.

"You can hear me, Sergeant. That's good. I turned the car around and headed back until… well, I want you to be at my office tomorrow morning."

"At *your* office?"

"Yes. Be there by eight o'clock. I will call you then. All right?"

Martin stood stiffly, his left arm pressed to his side. "Yes, Inspector, at eight o'clock."

"You are doing well, Sergeant. I'm very pleased."

"Thank you, Inspector," he said, holding the radio tight to his ear, although Beauviér was gone.

Discovering a telephone booth at the near corner, Martin went inside and dialed a number he knew well. When the line engaged, he demanded to speak with the officer on duty, then patiently waited. He thought again of the dead Englishman—while reaching to touch the bandage about his own neck—and of the man's blanched pallor, the closed eyes still watering under the lights of the chandelier. Abruptly, the receiver dropped from Martin's grip. He felt his sense of balance failing and stumbling from the booth, collapsed onto the sidewalk, gasping for breath. He then cried out before vomiting onto the black ground.

223

* * *

Thomas Breck sat in the corner of his darkened room, his elbows resting on the arms of the overstuffed chair. He appeared lifeless, save for the occasional movement of his wrist so he might check the hour. It was now sixteen minutes before seven in the morning and just beyond the near window, daybreak was illuminating a sign attached to the exterior wall of the building. The words *Les Charmettes* were becoming clear, the clinging snow causing the letters to glitter like tired sequins, half of them missing.

He again turned his wrist to check the time. Six minutes had passed.

He would still wait.

Returning to the hotel just after midnight, Tom did not feel it was too late to speak with Tatiana, but felt it was too soon. He'd now convinced himself against speaking with her so that she might sleep longer, so she might rest, although that was not truly a concern. He simply wanted to put off the lies.

The morning light was becoming more brilliant, now creeping across the floor toward him. Like a slow burning fuse it inched its way up the side of the chair then finally, into his eyes. He stood and pulling the drawstring on his bathrobe tighter, walked barefoot to the door, opening it gradually. He checked to see the hallway was clear before stepping to the next door and knocking softly.

"Yes?" came a voice.

Opening the door a crack, he said into the darkness, "I'm sorry to wake you, Tatiana, but I need to speak with you."

"Certainly, Thomas. May I have a few minutes?"

"Of course," he replied. "I'll see you downstairs when you are ready."

"Thomas?" she said, sleep in her voice.

"Yes?"

"Are you okay?"

He answered, "I'm fine," and closed the door.

Moving to the next room, he knocked twice with the knuckle of his forefinger, then again. There was no response. Turning the handle of the door, he pushed it open.

He whispered, "Yuri, are you awake?" and entered the room.

224

It was stuffy inside and he could hear labored breathing. Barely able to distinguish the sleeping man in the weak light, Tom reached out, touching him on the shoulder.

Yuri awoke with a start, swinging his arm wildly from his chest.

Tom jumped back. "It's me," he said loudly.

Sitting up in the bed, Yuri looked dazed. He was silent for a few seconds, then said, "I'm sorry, Thomas. I was having a bad dream."

"That's understandable… but I didn't mean to startle you," he apologized, walking toward the door. "But I'd like to speak with you downstairs."

Pulling his knees up to his chest, Yuri placed the blanket over his shoulders and said, "Yes, I'll be ready in a few minutes."

"That's fine."

Returning to his room, Tom went straight to the bathroom sink and turning the faucet, his eyes suddenly widened. On the finger tips of his right hand were dark spots, almost a black liquid that was drying and beginning to flake. A small piece broke away, floating against the white porcelain of the sink. It was unmistakable to him what it was—it was blood, and not his own.

* * *

A small metal Christmas tree, powered by an electric motor, sat on the end of the downstairs bar. It rotated once every minute or so and a red light on top fluttered to life almost as often. Taking a sip of coffee, Tom watched his reflection in the passing silver foil leaves—his face was distorted, almost comically in the gleaming metal, appearing as if he were smiling, but he wasn't.

The floorboards above him began creaking, the sound moving slowly across the ceiling. Taking another sip of coffee, he heard the staircase groan, briefly falling silent as a word or two was whispered.

Turning, he saw Tatiana and Yuri standing in the doorway of the bar.

They moved toward him and sleepily exchanged pleasantries. Tatiana and Tom kissed each other's cheek twice; the men shook hands. Yuri poured two cups of coffee from the tray on the bar, added milk and sugar, then led them all toward the near corner where they sat at a small round table.

225

Tom's gaze moved between the two people opposite him. "Did you hurt yourself, Yuri?" he asked calmly.

Yuri's brow wrinkled. "What do you mean, Thomas?"

"When I touched you on your shoulder this morning, I got blood on my hand."

Yuri grinned. "Oh, that," he said, glancing at Tatiana. "When I was clearing out the drawers of the house in Budapest, we were in such a hurry I forgot to close one of the overhead cabinet doors. When I stood, the corner of it went into my shoulder. It was deep. There was blood everywhere."

Tom suggested, "Possibly you should see a doctor. It may need stitches."

"I tried already, Thomas," complained Tatiana. "He won't listen. He has always been like that."

"Well, I might ask you to have it looked at, Yuri," said Tom. "We can't afford to have it getting infected. Not now."

Still grinning, Yuri said nothing.

Tatiana inquired, "Tell us about your trip, Thomas. What did you find out?"

"It was a good trip. I've told you about John Clark, the best that I could; he is a man we can trust and has agreed to help us move the machine."

Tatiana said, "Do you know what it is? Did John Clark know?"

Looking into her eyes, Tom replied, "No, he did not."

His tone determined, Yuri said, "Thomas, can't you please talk her out of this thing? It's all crazy. She said you mentioned the possibility of South America, of Argentina. You knew a man that could help us to get started again."

"I do."

"Well then, we should take advantage of it and get away from here. He won't be able to find us there and—and why would he bother?"

Tom stared at his fingers where they rested on the edge of the table. "I understand, but first of all it's not just Mégot that we're dealing with. If it were, then I might agree, but it's not," he said, lifting his eyes. "Secondly, how far do we run? Buenos Aires? Is that sufficient, or should we hide in the pampas grass until we die of old age? No, Yuri. Tatiana is right. We must go through with this."

Yuri loudly returned his cup to its saucer.

Ignoring the detraction, Tom said, "We are all under terrible stress, but the only thing we can do is go forward. Soon we will be finished, and we can start looking for some part of the lives we used to have. It will never be like it was, but we'll succeed in this—we must succeed."

No one spoke for a few moments, then Tatiana said, "What are we going to do, Thomas?"

Tom leaned closer to his two friends. "We are going by boat."

"Boat?" said Tatiana and Yuri at the same time.

"Yes."

Tatiana said, "But you get sick on the water."

"I know, but I'll be all right."

Yuri asked, "What type of boat?"

"It's a freighter called the *Ondine* out of Scotland. It will be off the Belgian coast in three days."

"There is a captain and crew?"

"There is a captain, Yuri. You and I, and John Clark will be the crew."

"On a freighter?"

Tom nodded. "Yes."

Skeptically, Yuri said, "And we will sail this enormous thing all the way to Algeria?"

"It's mostly automated," Tom assured him. "Almost everything is done from the wheelhouse."

"And you feel confident with this?"

"I am."

Tatiana asked, "What would you like us to do, Thomas?"

"I need two documents from you. First, if by chance we are stopped on the road between Mons and the coast, we will need a temporary importation form. Something that says the machine may be in the country for... I don't know... thirty days, let's say, and it's simply a prototype. A cop reading this will not feel the need to get overly concerned with the machine, as it will be moving out of the country soon enough. He would also be unfamiliar with such a form. Have the document say it was fabricated in... Austria. That sounds sufficiently innocuous."

Tom reached into his pocket for his package of cigarettes, giving one to Yuri. Both men searched their pockets for matches. Tatiana removed a lighter from her purse and carefully lit each man's cigarette.

Tom took a drag and as the smoke emptied from his mouth, he said, "Second, we'll need a Belgian export document. It is basically identical to the one used for bringing in the paintings. World

Express will be the freight forwarder and the destination will be Great Britain. The British regulations for import are so strict that Belgian customs should be more lax in letting it out of the country, and may not say a word... and the stamps. Can you make the necessary stamps?"

Tatiana said, "How much time do I have?"

"Two days."

"I thought you said three days before the boat is off the coast."

"Yes, but we need to be there in two, and prepared, just in case."

Tatiana nodded. "Yes, I can do it," she said. "But what do we say it is?"

Exhaling deeply, Tom said, "Do you remember the earthquake in Italy last year?"

Her tone quizzical, she replied, "Yes, I do."

Slowly crushing his cigarette out in the ashtray, he said, "Just after it happened, the European Community began demanding that any new construction be more resistant to earthquakes. They decided that a sort of shock absorber should be incorporated in the base of buildings to take the brunt of the shake."

"A shock absorber?" questioned Tatiana.

"Yes. It would be placed at each corner of the taller buildings and could survive a six- or seven-point magnitude quake."

"Magnitude?"

Tom nodded. "That's what it's called."

"Where did you hear of such a thing?" asked Yuri.

Uneasily, Tom replied, "A copy of *Paris Match*."

"You saw it in a magazine?"

"Yes, a magazine," he said defensively.

Frowning, Yuri asked, "There were pictures in the magazine of this... shock absorber?"

Tom leaned forward, locking his eyes onto Yuri's. His tone was firm and unapologetic. "No, there were no pictures, and that's the point. Nobody knows what it looks like. It hasn't been built yet."

Yuri sat back in his chair, his eyes curious. "So the machine could pass for this—"

"It can. And it will," he promised. "You must understand that a customs officer only knows what he sees. Anything abstract must be immediately categorized. Tobacco, alcohol, pelts, diamonds, automobiles—he knows these things, and no matter how you try, you will never be able to convince him differently. When we brought in paintings, we said they were paintings, only changing the artist and thus the value. When I brought in liquor in the old days, I *said* it was liquor. There's no point in hiding it if the tax stamps are done well enough, and the same with cigarettes. You present it up front and obvious, even put a little spotlight on it for him and stand right there, calmly, as if you're thinking about what a clever fellow he is: 'Yes, sir—no, sir,' to any of the questions. When you start hiding things, that's when you get caught—eventually anyway—and it's the same with this machine. We'll present it as... Tremor Suppressant Columns, and we'll stencil those very words all over the machine. In French and Dutch, German and English, with little warnings in red for the eventual building contractor about placement in the buildings explaining suitable concrete mix requirements for the foundation and excessive payload imbalance."

Yuri asked, "What is payload imbalance?"

Tom shrugged. "How should I know," he replied casually. "I have a degree in French literature. But neither will the customs man, and he'll see it and he'll write it down on his piece of paper. He needs to be able to complete his form so it can be appropriately filed when we've gone. And there must be an identification number. Any number will do, but it is essential." He grinned. "I'm only sorry we don't have time for a full-color brochure." Abruptly the grin dropped from his face. "The point is, the customs agent will never acknowledge he doesn't know what he's looking at. It's a widget, a gadget, a gizmo; everyone understands the word but no one knows what it is."

Yuri said, "You make it sound easy."

"Easy? Sure. Sitting here, it's very easy. But when the moment comes, you will age one year for every minute the agent takes in filling out his little form," he advised. "Would you prefer I tell you we don't have a chance?"

The three sat in silence when he finished speaking. Only the sound of the metal tree's electric motor, grinding in spurts and starts, could be heard in the still room.

After almost a minute, Tatiana said, "May I have some more coffee, Yuri?"

Yuri stood and moved toward the bar.

Tom took a cigarette from the package on the table and glanced at Tatiana. She was looking into his eyes while she removed the lighter from her purse. Igniting the lighter with a sharp thrust of her thumb, she moved the flame toward him. With the cigarette pursed

Josef Kraus

in his lips, he smiled awkwardly through the smoke rising between them.

In a half-whisper, she said, "Is there anything else I should know, Thomas?"

Though wanting to tell her everything he knew and everything he felt, he only said, "No. Unless there's something minor I've forgotten."

Returning the lighter to her purse, she dropped her gaze and said nothing more. He sensed she had accepted the lie.

Yuri returned with a fresh cup of coffee, the milk and the sugar added.

Tom took a drag on his cigarette as Tatiana folded her hands on her lap. Yuri sat again at the table and looking at Tatiana, said, "Now you don't want the coffee?"

"Yes," she said, unfolding her hands. "I was letting it cool."

Yuri's brow wrinkled.

Tom said, "I want you to go to Paris, Yuri."

Still looking at Tatiana, he said, "Paris?" He turned to face Tom and repeated, "Paris?"

"That's right, we need a truck. Can you get us a truck?"

Yuri replied enthusiastically, "Yes, of course."

Tom nodded his appreciation, albeit reluctantly. Yuri had never been asked to help in any of their operations before, although he'd offered many times. There had been an unwillingness because of his simple manner, and his inability to speak either French or English sufficiently to understand each detail of conversations around him. There had also never been a place, or a necessity, until now.

Tom said, "It needs to be a secondhand tractor and trailer capable of carrying thirty thousand kilos. When they ask you what it's for, tell them you'll need it for hauling scrap metal. That will alleviate any need for a fixed address or specific area of operation, as you're simply a scavenger—a night crawler."

"But it won't be any of their business what it's for," said Yuri firmly.

"Yes, but they will ask you all the same and it's best to have something ready for them. They might suspect you'll be using the thing to transport stolen cars or God knows if the answer you give them isn't believable. Somebody's brother-in-law could be a cop, you never know. Play along with them, be their friend, though tell them nothing more than necessary, and then get the hell out."

"Okay, Thomas. I understand."

Exhaling deeply, Tom said, "The truck shouldn't be more than six or seven years old. Buy it from a licensed dealer, no gypsies—we're not looking for a bargain. Check the body and make certain there's no salt rust and that it looks professional. Remember you are going to be hauling the latest component in building design, and be certain the gray card matches the identification plates and that it's passed the current safety... What do you call it?"

"Road worthiness test," said Yuri proudly.

"Right—Now, the license plates can be any EU country except Spain or Britain."

Sounding puzzled, Yuri asked, "Why is that?"

"Because the Spanish are notorious hashish smugglers and we don't need that problem. Also, we will be supposedly shipping the machine to England by boat. If customs sees British plates on the truck they might wonder why we aren't just putting it on a ferry and driving it there."

Quickly, Yuri said, "Oh, of course."

"And don't worry too much about the amount of kilometers on the engine. If the truck goes around the block then it will probably survive the few hundred kilometers we'll be driving it. Okay?"

"Okay," Yuri agreed.

Tom slowly moved his eyes to Tatiana. She looked back, her face expressionless. Her deep blue eyes said nothing of what she was thinking.

He took a drink of coffee. It was now cold and tasted bitter. Returning the cup to its saucer, he said, "The truck should cost around one hundred thousand French francs, Tatiana."

She pushed her lips together as if to wet them, then said, "I will go with Yuri to Paris and take care of it. There are also things there that I need for the documents. I had to leave my pens and blotting tools behind. I didn't want them to be found if we were searched coming out of Hungary." She lowered her eyes. "Also... there were some clothes I saw on a Swedish woman one evening. They were from Paris, I'm sure." She laughed, running her fingers down the sleeve of her jacket. "I mean, look at this thing. If I continue to wear it in public, I might be taken for a vagabond."

Tom looked at the black velveteen jacket she wore. The cuffs were beginning to wear, as were the buttonholes, and the color was fading. Her white cotton blouse was simply made by a peasant's needle. He had not noticed before, but her clothing was from the Communist bloc and lacked the quality so commonplace in the west. Tatiana's natural beauty distracted the eye from the flaws of whatever thing she wore; he knew she would never be mistaken for a vagabond.

He said, "Why don't we take an early lunch and go over everything again, then you can have the afternoon in Paris to get all you need."

"Then we will next see you in Mons, Thomas?" she asked.

"Yes, as soon as you can. We'll meet at the Hotel Metropole. It's in the town center and large enough for us not to be noticed. With the holidays coming there will not be many other guests."

"Yes," said Tatiana. "It's almost Christmas."

Tom's eyes gradually moved across the room to the metal tree on the bar. It had tilted slightly and now turned in an elliptical rotation while the electric motor churned like a pointless timepiece.

Returning his gaze to the table and the cup of cold coffee before him, he whispered, "So it is."

* * *

The pharmacy sat on the opposite end of *la grande rue* from Les Charmettes. Its small interior was outlined by a series of floor lamps, although only one was illuminated. An elderly woman sat behind a waist-high counter and a man, approximately the same age, stood beside her in the dim, sluggishly putting on a long white jacket. Just above their heads, beside a poster introducing the latest in toothpastes, was a wall clock that read fifteen minutes before nine. Tom confirmed the time with his watch as he stepped back from the window of the pharmacy, noting the hours of operation painted in its corner. It read: Nine to five, Monday through Friday, and Tom thought in the interim to have coffee at an auberge immediately opposite. It appeared to be serving breakfast as just beyond its plate glass window a single man sat inside, a croissant in one hand and newspaper in the other.

Crossing the street, Tom stopped in between two parked cars as something caught his eye. The license plate on one of the cars was Belgian and had no distinguishing characteristics other than its brevity—the red and white plate had but three numbers. As license plates were maintained by their owners until death, the few numbers indicated someone extremely old or, like the government, wistfully immortal. Curiously, he stepped back on the sidewalk and glanced into the driver's window of the black Peugeot with the Belgian plates.

There was nothing inside the car that might announce the bureaucracy it represented, save for a rectangular red box sitting on the console between the front seats. It was strangely familiar to him and he tried to remember why.

Lifting his gaze, he noticed the man who had been reading the newspaper in the window of the auberge was now staring back, and Tom suddenly recalled where he had once seen the red box. It had been attached to the belt of the gendarme who found him at the gallery in Namur, a sergeant called Henri Martin. Tom remembered clearly now: there'd been the holstered pistol and the rectangular radio beside it.

The man in the window was still there, still staring, and Tom thought back to the telephone call from John Clark after the gendarmes had visited him. He'd mentioned an Inspector being present—an Inspector Beauviér of the Gendarmerie, and to hold that rank he would certainly be over fifty years old. The man in the window, with the salt and pepper hair, could be that man. The car was certainly his, and the two-way radio, now probably out of range and left behind, confirmed it. It was the other half of the one attached to Sergeant Martin's belt.

Tom looked again at the man in the window. His demeanor had changed; the possible concern of a petty thief ransacking his car was gone, replaced by one of surprise. It was as if he also knew the person he was watching, with no need of introduction and the shaking of hands.

The formalities complete, each appeared uncertain of what to do next.

Tom lowered his gaze and, casually turning, walked toward Les Charmettes. He kept his pace unhurried, trying to appear calm, watching his feet move over the cobblestones. He tried to imagine what Beauviér might have on him; maybe nothing or maybe everything, but even if he were only taken in for questioning, he could be kept for hours or even days.

He didn't have time for such a detour.

His breathing was becoming more rapid and picking up his pace, turned his head slightly, listening for any sounds behind. He thought he heard a car starting, but it was only a door closing

Josef Kraus

somewhere on the street. He could see the entrance to Les Charmettes just ahead. The time for any pretense of calm was over.

He began to run. His arms swung wildly as his legs pushed him faster, moving quickly through the open gate of the hotel, onto the gravel entry to the front door, pushing it open. The foyer was empty. Running for the stairs, he called out, "Tatiana! Yuri!" Not waiting for a response, he climbed the staircase, again calling, "Tatiana! Yuri!" and still there was nothing.

He ran down the hallway to Yuri's room, though found it vacant, the door to the bath wide open. Moving to Tatiana's room, he also found it empty—only her open suitcase on the bed.

Glancing back down the hallway, he went to his room and grabbing the car keys from the nightstand, stepped back into the hallway to find Yuri and Tatiana coming toward him.

"What is it, Thomas?" asked Tatiana.

"The Belgian gendarme is here," he said, breathing heavily. "The one investigating the Englishman's murder. He's on to us. You must get away."

Yuri countered, "He can't hurt us here."

"He can't?" said Tom. "He might be telephoning the French police right now."

Tatiana grabbed his arm. "How did he find us?"

"I don't know, but we don't have time to speculate. You must get away and now. Leave everything. Take nothing—you have no time." He looked at Yuri. "He's driving a new Peugeot 604 sedan. It's black with Belgian plates. Can your car outrun it?"

"Yes, easily," he replied.

"Be certain he doesn't follow, no matter what," said Tom, cautiously pushing them toward the staircase. "You both know what you have to do. We'll meet again in Mons. Get there as soon as you can."

"Will you be all right, Thomas?" asked Tatiana.

Tom's eyes narrowed, placing the palm of his hand tenderly on her cheek. "Yes, I'll be fine," he replied, leading them down the stairs. "He appears to be alone but I don't know for certain. I'll try and get him to follow me. Your car is still out back?"

"Yes," said Yuri.

"Good. Now don't wait to see what happens to me, just get going. Oh hell, do you have your car keys on you, Yuri?"

"Yes, I do."

As they reached the front door of the hotel, Tom said, "Okay, I'll go first, but don't wait more than half a minute before following."

Tatiana kissed Tom quickly on the mouth and stepped back. Looking at Yuri, then Tatiana, he moved out the doorway to the sidewalk.

The black Peugeot, Beauviér behind the wheel, was speeding down the center of the street toward Tom as he ran to his car. Climbing in, he glanced in the rearview mirror to see the Peugeot's reflection becoming larger. He pushed on the accelerator and the tires spun, spewing black smoke into the air. The Jensen jerked away from the curb, the rear end swinging wildly. He struggled to maintain control, the Peugeot moving in and out of his side mirror, until finally the rear end straightened out. Now but a car length behind, the Peugeot's siren let out a wail. Tom gripped the wheel with both hands and pushing the accelerator to the floor, the engine howled. The Jensen shifted up one gear as it entered the canopy of the Fontainebleau forest, the Peugeot right behind. The asphalt road was free of lingering snow and traffic, and the Peugeot had fallen back, though Tom did not let up. He held the accelerator down.

The sound of the siren began to fade and the black car's image in the rearview mirror grew smaller. Tom wiped at his mouth with his wrist, hurriedly returning his hand to the wheel. The speedometer crept to one hundred fifty kilometers an hour and climbing.

The turnoff to the village of Milly-La-Forêt was not far ahead. Tom would take it, soon losing the trailing gendarme in the labyrinth of unmarked side streets and back roads. It would not be difficult. He knew the village well.

CHAPTER SEVEN

Sitting at a small table in the captain's quarters, the two men appeared oblivious to the outside weather. Berthed at the mouth of Aberdeen harbor, the freighter *Mary Celeste* was struggling against a high wind off the North Sea. The sound of the mooring lines slackening, then growing taut, drifted through the cabin's sealed porthole. A rainstorm was commencing, its first drops tapping at the glass.

Taking a package of English cigarettes from his pocket, Francis Dwyer offered one to the man opposite him who stared at the gesture before removing one. He then watched Dwyer strike a match against the edge of the table, and said, "I understand what you're saying, Francis, and there isn't much I wouldn't do for the money, but it all seems a bit mad."

Lighting his cigarette first, Dwyer casually moved the flame across the narrow table. The man puffed repeatedly, exhaling out the side of his mouth, then sat up straight in his chair. The large vessel tipped slightly to starboard as Dwyer silently watched the cork from an opened bottle of port slowly roll against the edge of the ashtray. He then took a sip from his glass and swallowing slowly, suggested, "But it's what you've been looking for Liam, after all this time sitting here with your ship's belly as empty as your own. You'll be done with your troubles and remember, a rich cargo of this type doesn't come along every day."

The man picked up his glass of port. "I know," he said, tipping his hand slightly as if to study the dark red liquid. "She's a good ship, the *Mary Celeste*. You know that, don't you, Francis?"

"Yes, Liam. I know."

"It just seems such a terrible thing I'll be asking of her."

Dwyer leaned forward. His eyes and voice steady. "So you'd rather she die a slow death here in harbor? All safe and tethered for the man from the bank to come and gather. Is that what you want? Or would you rather take her out to sea where she belongs, and do something bold. Something that'll free you of your worries."

"But the risks are great."

"They are."

"And such a betrayal of—"

"Betrayal, is it? Is that what you're thinking?" Dwyer said, crushing out his cigarette in the ashtray. "Life's not a melodic poem with a happy ending or anything to do with the dreams we once had. You and I are the same, Liam. We wanted only one thing in the beginning. To be captains of our own ships and masters of the sea—romantic ports spilling with adventure one after the other. That is what we envisioned and I remember well our talking about the way it would be. Don't you remember?"

Liam nodded. "That I do."

"Well then, it hasn't been like that, has it? And now is your chance to begin anew. In a few days' time you'll be able to choose a different path."

"But my own ship is all I want, Francis."

"Then this is what it'll be, but without the sheriff knocking at your door with one fist, clutching the bank's delinquency papers with the other. Listen well, Liam, and tell me. How much time do you have remaining before your creditors lose their patience and demand payment in full?"

"They've already started coming round. You know that."

"But the *Mary Celeste* is still yours, isn't she?"

"She is."

"Well then, make up your mind. Will you do it?"

Liam took the last of his port down in one swallow. "I'll do it," he said. His tired eyes locked onto Dwyer's. "But I'll be needing eight thousand quid to get her out of harbor."

Removing a white envelope from the inside of his double-breasted coat, Dwyer laid it on the table. "That will take care of everything."

Liam opened the envelope and removing the contents, asked, "And what is this?"

"Those are Swiss franc notes and they're worth six hundred quid apiece."

The man grinned. "You don't say."

"Now get to your bank and change them as soon as you can. I want you to be off the Belgian coast no later than tomorrow's sunset."

Glancing at an overhead clock, Liam said, "It's almost noon and they'll be closed until two. I'll do it then."

"And tomorrow evening will pose no problem for you?"

He shook his head. "I'll be there."

"And you understand exactly what you're to do?"

"I do."

Dwyer lifted his glass. "To our success."

Liam raised his glass but didn't drink. Returning it to the table, he said, "We both know the one thing we're saying and I want to hear it again so later there'll be no bewildered faces or words." He leaned forward, his voice falling to a whisper. "Anyone on board the ship… every one of them, will be killed. Tell me you know that, Francis."

Lowering his glass, Dwyer said, "There are to be no survivors, Liam, and that is understood."

Seeming to think on the words just spoken, both men became still in the small cabin as the *Mary Celeste* tugged at her moorings.

* * *

Sergeant Henri Martin looked studiously at a paper jutting from the typewriter before him. At the top of the paper were the words *Police Report*, which were followed by questions and spaces for answers that such a report would contain. All of the particulars had been filled out concerning location, time of day, what was discovered at the above location, reason for the discovering officer to be present, and then specifics within the specifics, inquiring if the officer had been in uniform or not—and why not—and whether a gendarmerie vehicle was used—and was it damaged, considering everything from a paint scratch to a bullet hole, and their number.

Martin had answered each one dutifully, within the space provided, save for the final question before the required signature. It asked if the officer filling out the report had altered or removed anything from the crime scene. There were two boxes following the question with one word under each, *No* and *Yes*, respectively. It was very straightforward and very troubling.

Beside the typewriter were the three gambling markers Martin had taken from under the suspended body of Roger Catchpole, though now he wondered why. They offered nothing that he didn't already know. The reason for the suicide, or possible murder, was these acknowledged debts and in possessing them, he hindered the further investigation by the city police.

He lifted his eyes, looking at a document on the wall opposite. The articles of the Gendarmerie were neatly framed and hung before him like a silent warning. They were titled, *La Mission De La Gendarmerie*, and each one began with two words: *Without prejudice...*

But Martin was prejudiced, and angry, and wanted to find the man who had attacked him and killed Stuart Endfield. Martin had taken the gambling markers hoping they contained something to bring him closer to that end, but there was nothing other than some randomly written letters and numbers which made no sense. They could be anything, from a pretty girl's telephone number drunkenly scrawled or the address of another casino to be visited.

Tapping the typewriter's spacebar to mark the *Yes* box, thus unleashing certain inquiry by Internal Affairs, he heard voices coming down the hallway. He recognized one as Beauviér's, speaking loudly to the desk officer.

"It's called a Jensen Interceptor, Corporal, and yes, I'm quite certain of the spelling," Beauviér shouted as he appeared in the doorway. "You have the license number, now get it out to every gendarme garrison along the frontier between France and Luxembourg."

The corporal, unseen at the other end of the hallway, could be vaguely heard to agree with the Inspector, who turned to see Martin standing by his desk.

Beauviér said, "As you were, Sergeant," and then moved into the office, removing his topcoat. "I'm sorry I didn't telephone or use the radio, but I had a rather unpleasant morning."

"I did not expect you back so soon, monsieur."

Beauviér grumbled, "Nor did I."

Martin started to move from the desk when Beauviér lifted his hand. "Stay where you are, Sergeant," he said, taking one of the two chairs facing him. "How are you feeling?"

Briefly touching his bandaged throat, he answered, "Much better, monsieur. Thank you."

Beauviér nodded once but said nothing, seeming to be off in thought. He crossed his legs, then uncrossed them and, sitting up straight, slammed his fist on the edge of the desk. "He saw me, Sergeant. He knew who I was and fled."

"The American?"

"Yes, the American and his conspirators: the Polish woman and her bodyguard. They were all there, Sergeant, and I let them get away."

"But how did he know who you were?"

"I don't know… then again, I do," he replied. "We both knew who the other was."

"He fled on foot?'

"No, that car of his… You were right about it. He lost me easily."

"But you discovered something in Barbizon, monsieur?"

Beauviér sat back in his chair. "No, nothing. I even spoke with the owner of the hotel where they were staying. His name was Dreyfus and he pretended to be unaware of them, searching the registry as if he'd never heard the names—but they were the only guests he had."

"You spoke with the local police?"

Beauviér sighed. "Yes, that is where I've been this morning. There is a gendarmerie brigade in Melun. They arrested the Rumanian gigolo and held him for twelve hours, but let him go. He knew nothing about the Monet painting as I had led them to believe, so they were quite upset and not very cooperative."

"They did nothing?"

"Next to that, Sergeant. They put out a description of the American's car on radio and sent a cruiser to search the Fontainebleau forest where I lost him. But he's well gone and I don't know where." He glanced at the calendar on the wall and shook his head. "I am a fool. I have tried to solve this without assistance and now am paying the price. I thought they would take the case away from me, with such little time remaining at my post. I was too vain in thinking I could do it alone. It all seems such a muddle…" His voice trailed off, then said, "I need to have a word with Ian Musters, Sergeant. Where are you holding him?"

Martin replied, "I am afraid I have some more bad news, Inspector. He is gone also."

"What do you mean?"

241

"I mean he has fled, monsieur. Like the American, he is gone and no one seems to know where."

"He quit his job at the British Embassy?"

"They wouldn't say. But he wasn't there yesterday afternoon when I went to arrest him and when we went to his apartment it was empty. We searched it thoroughly though found nothing. He left no following address with the concierge, who himself wasn't aware that Musters had vacated."

Looking down, Beauviér said, "I see… and that is exactly what we have, isn't it? After all of this we have next to nothing, and have also managed to tip off everyone involved in the case of our presence. They are probably having a good laugh."

Quickly Martin said, "I doubt if anyone is laughing, Inspector."

"No, I suppose not," he said, lifting his eyes. "Tell me about the death of Roger Catchpole."

Martin paused, then said, "It looked very much a suicide when I found him, Inspector. There appeared to be no foul play. No bruising about the face where he might have been beaten or any marks about his arms or wrists where he might have been restrained. As you know I have no real training in such—"

"Don't underestimate yourself, Sergeant," Beauviér interrupted. "You have sufficient training and, more importantly, you have common sense. Now please, do you suspect it wasn't suicide?"

Martin shook his head. "I'm not sure. I feel someone was there, searching for something. There were inconsistencies in the dead man's personal items."

"Yes?"

"First, there were no keys found to the apartment."

"I see. How did you get in? Was the door unlocked?"

"Yes, and possibly Roger Catchpole found it that way also, but it seems unlikely. All of his possessions had been recently moved into the apartment. I can't imagine him leaving it unsecured or not having a key."

Seemingly unimpressed, Beauviér said, "And what else?"

"He had neither a wallet nor pocketbook on him."

The corners of Beauviér's eyes went up. "You are certain?"

"Yes, monsieur. However, I did not search any of the packing boxes, as they were all sealed with the original shipper's tape."

Beauviér nodded. "When you radioed me last evening you mentioned finding something. Was that it?"

242

"Not exactly, monsieur," he said, and picking up the crumpled gambling markers, he handed them across the desk to Beauviér. "I found these."

"You took them from the scene?"

"Yes, monsieur."

"Why?" he asked, studying the markers.

"Because of the writing on them, Inspector. It is barely legible, but I imagined there might be something to explain Roger Catchpole's involvement."

"And was there?"

"No, I'm afraid not. Just some numbers and letters which appear pointless. Written when he was drunk, I suppose. Could be anything."

Beauviér laid the three markers on the edge of the desk, looking at each one before placing them in a line. "It is the handwriting of more than one person," he said, switching the marker in the middle with the one on the end. "One appears hurried and the other seems quite calm... It is two different hands—one is Belgian, or French it seems, and the other is English."

Martin's forehead wrinkled. "How do you know this?" he asked.

Moving the markers lengthwise, Beauviér pushed the edges together. "Because of the letter K that is written by the calm hand. First, the letter is in our French alphabet but we don't in fact use it."

"Kilometer, kilogram, monsieur."

"Yes? And?"

Putting his hand to his chin, Martin said proudly, "Kaleidoscope."

"Very good, Sergeant, but you have now basically exhausted the letter except maybe kiosk or Kremlin, and not likely subject matter."

"Then it might be weight or distance?"

"Possibly, Sergeant, except when I write the letter K, I first make a V at a slight angle and then attach a simple line straight down," he said, demonstrating to Martin on a piece of note paper. "You see, like that. And you, how do you do it?"

"Yes, monsieur. I write it the same."

"Precisely, it's how a French or Belgian would write it. However, an Englishman would first make a straight line and then attach the letter *V* lying on its side." Again Beauviér demonstrated on the paper. "We come up with the same thing but the look is much different."

"So then, it's Roger Catchpole's writing?"

"Or more importantly, Ian Musters," Sergeant."

"So you would cover the letters written by the French hand and read only those in English," he said excitedly.

"Yes," replied Beauviér, scratching on a marker with the pencil.

"Then what about the numbers?" he asked, leaning closer.

Beauviér explained, "It's the same," and pointed at the upper corner of a marker. "What number is this?"

"It's a one," Martin answered quickly.

Beauviér shook his head. "Standing alone it appears as such, but it is the number seven. You and I would put a line horizontal on the down stroke to distinguish it from our number one; however, an English writer would not. Their number one is merely an up and down line with no stroke at the top like ours. Also the number four underneath is closed. Our number four is always open at the top— like a goal post with one leg. So we can determine that this line of numbers was written by an English hand."

"Or American?"

"I suppose, Sergeant. But let's not complicate this any further."

"Yes, monsieur."

Beauviér said nothing more as he wrote on the markers, pushing them together, then separating them, attempting to make out the written words. He continued quietly for over five minutes.

Martin looked to the clock above the open doorway. It was three minutes before noon. Opening the drawer of the desk, he removed a folded newspaper as quietly as possible, but the noise seemed to irritate Beauviér, who said, "What are you fiddling with, Sergeant?"

"Pardon me, Inspector, but when you asked me to be here by eight this morning because you might possibly telephone—"

"You know I was occupied, Sergeant," said Beauviér, laying his pencil down.

"No, monsieur. It's not that. It's only, well, when I arrived the Director General was here. I mean, he was sitting at your desk, waiting."

Beauviér grunted. "What did he want?"

"He didn't really say, though his mood was quite bad and gave me this." Martin handed Beauviér the morning edition of *Le Figaro*. "It's in the corner, monsieur, by the—"

"I see it, Sergeant," he said angrily. "I see it."

It was a two-column article with the headline *British Counsel Demands End To Belgian Plague*, and read:

'Sir Benjamin Howell, a lesser British chargé d'affaires, has referred to the unexplained deaths of two employees from their embassy in Brussels as a 'Belgian Plague,' and demanded full cooperation from the Gendarmerie National. The Gendarmerie, he claims, has been negligent in its duties, the first and foremost being the protection of each and every citizen of Britain serving honorably on Belgian soil.'

The article continued for an additional five paragraphs, repeating the term 'Belgian Plague' as many times, before ending on a conciliatory note, referencing the two countries' common struggle against communism and artificial beef pricing.

He mumbled, "Plague, is it?"

Martin said nothing.

Beauviér laid the newspaper on his lap. "You know what this means, Sergeant?"

"I know the Director General was unhappy, monsieur."

"Unhappy, was he?" mused Beauviér. "No, he is not unhappy. He is afraid, afraid for his job, and he will take mine to protect his. The next time I see the Director General it will be to remove me from my post as Inspector."

"But you could have done nothing to prevent the death of either man."

"Couldn't I, Sergeant?" he countered, turning his chair so that he might cross his legs. "In regard to Stuart Endfield, you are right; there was no way of knowing. But with Roger Catchpole, I knew he was in trouble. I recognized the danger that evening at Le Cheval Noir. Had I spoken with him, had I warned him, he would most certainly still be alive." Lifting the newspaper from his lap, he let it fall to the floor.

Uncertain how to respond, but sensing Beauviér's resignation, Martin inquired, "Did you discover anything with the gambling markers, Inspector?"

He turned to look at Martin. "No. It's only incomplete names and numbers, nothing more."

"Oh." Martin nodded slowly, then suddenly he brightened. "You asked me to find out what I could on Ian Musters, Inspector." Hurriedly removing a small notebook from his pocket, he flipped it open. "Let's see... He supposedly wore the same gray suit each day, even on the weekends. He had no friends to speak of," he read aloud, glancing at Beauviér, who sat motionless and apparently uninterested. "And owned a new Jaguar sedan but drove it rarely—"

"Did you get a license number?" asked Beauviér idly.

"Yes, however, the car was left parked in the underground of the apartment house. I had it towed to the police garage."

"And you searched it?"

"Yes, monsieur. Nothing."

Sardonically, he said, "It's nice to see each person we have interest in is so tidy, cleaning up after themselves as they do."

Again studying the notebook, Martin added, "They found an unopened package of chewing gum, and a newspaper wedged between the front seats of the Jaguar."

"Now we're getting somewhere," grumbled Beauviér. "And what newspaper did Monsieur Musters prefer?"

Martin glanced at the notebook. "*De Gazet*, monsieur."

Beauviér uncrossed his legs and sat up, his gaze still directed at the corner of the room. "A Flemish newspaper? Could he read Flemish?"

"According to his apartment house concierge, where I received most of the information on him, no. He only spoke English."

Beauviér looked at Martin, his expression quizzical. "Then what would he want with a paper he couldn't read?"

Martin suggested, "Some things are the same in any language, Inspector. Scores for football matches or other sports, or maybe the weather in Martinique."

Beauviér shook his head. "It is almost Christmas, Sergeant. There are no sports this week, and I can tell you from here, the weather in Martinique is sunny with a cloud or two. No, there is something more."

Skeptically, Martin said, "It may have been left behind by someone he had given a lift, monsieur."

"But you told me yourself he had no friends and took the car out only rarely, and why a Flemish newspaper from Antwerp? Why not *De Standaard* or *Het Volk* newspapers? A Flemish speaker from

Brussels would read those first." He sat back, resting his elbows on the arms of the chair. "Then again, it may be as simple as you say. Does it sound as if I am grabbing at straws, Sergeant?"

"I don't know, Inspector. Maybe there's something, or maybe it's like the gambling markers. I was quite certain I had a lead of some sort."

Lazily, Beauvièr asked, "Where again did you get this information on Musters?"

"From the apartment house concierge," he replied, flipping to the next page of his notebook. "He was quite eager and—"

"What is it you have there, Sergeant?" Beauvièr interjected, nodding at the typewriter.

"It's the police report, monsieur. On the death of Roger Catchpole."

Staring at two pieces of black carbon paper in the carriage, Beauvièr asked, "In triplicate?"

Martin grinned. "It's a habit picked up when I was a desk sergeant. I keep one for my own files—you never know, monsieur."

"No, you do not," he agreed. "Now excuse me, you were saying, Sergeant?"

"Yes, monsieur... The concierge told me where Ian Musters had moved from, just before Brussels, that is."

"Yes?"

"He was in Hungary. He worked for the British embassy in Budapest."

Beauvièr sat up quickly. "Then that means—" He stopped himself. Staring at the typewriter, he then looked at the gambling markers before him. "That's it," he said, clearly oblivious to Martin's last words.

"Monsieur?"

Beauvièr gripped the pencil and said, "The other day I placed a bet at La Piste Royale gambling parlor off *rue Artan...* do you know it? Never mind, it doesn't matter. It's only that when I received my copy of the betting ticket I noticed the man behind the cage used no carbon paper. That is to say, if you write firmly enough the inscription will transfer to a second ticket underneath." He pointed at a blank sheet of typing paper. "Hand that to me, Sergeant."

Martin did as requested, watching Beauvièr lay the paper on the desk, carefully placing each gambling marker on top of it. "You see, no one actually wrote on the gambling markers with a weak pencil

Josef Kraus

in some sort of obscure code. They were merely underneath whatever was being written on and the chemicals impregnated into the markers made them darken, picking up any numbers or letters when sufficient pressure was applied. When the pressure lessened only the item under the markers, like a table or clipboard or whatever, received the image. That means everything that was written is still here."

Martin asked, "But how can you possibly make them reappear?"

Holding up a marker to catch the light from the window, he said, "I'm not quite certain, Sergeant," while slowly turning his wrist. He then placed the marker back on the typing paper and began writing directly below it. "We have the word *rue*, which was clear enough from the beginning, and the letter *p* just after it. Then there is a blank followed by the letter *k* and the number 38."

He stopped writing. Tapping at the gambling marker with the end of the pencil, he said, "I assumed the letter *k* denoted kilograms or kilometers or simply the words 'one thousand.' And the number 38 was the exact weight or distance or…" Turning the pencil on end, he pushed the eraser gently over the marker. "The chemicals around those letters or numbers already written will still be intact and should leave a stain on this paper underneath, but it will remain white where they have been broken down—in theory, anyway."

Gently pushing the eraser a half dozen more times, he then cautiously lifted a marker. His brows raised as he placed his forefinger under the dark smudges left on the white paper. "You see, Sergeant, in the center of each mark is our missing character."

Martin moved around the desk. "What are they, Inspector?" he asked excitedly.

Beauviér answered, "We had the word *rue* and the letter *p*. Now we have uncovered the letters *a* and *r* following it, and then the letter *k*, as we already knew."

Martin said, "Rue Park?" and leaned forward, pointing at the black marks. "Why, it's *rue du parc*, Inspector."

"Exactly," confirmed Beauviér. "*Parc* is spelled with a *k* in English and the preposition was ignored by the writer. So we have *rue du parc*, number 38 as our address, Sergeant."

Sounding discouraged, Martin said, "There is a *rue du parc* in every French-speaking town and village in Europe, monsieur."

"Hold on, Sergeant," said Beauviér, pushing the eraser against the next marker. "So we'll go to this line. It appears to be a

248

combination or telephone number or... We have the numbers 65, 48, 42..." He again lifted the marker to see the impression left. "There is now a zero before the number 65. Why, it's a telephone prefix. Where is that, Sergeant?"

Martin opened a directory, flipping to one page, then another, and finally said, "It's the province of Hainaut, monsieur."

"No specific town?"

Studying the page, he shook his head. "No, it's the entire province."

His voice still calm, Beauviér said, "And the last two digits of the number are missing. They were written below the bottom edge of the gambling marker." He again began pushing with the eraser. "On the next line there are the letters *e* and *r*, with nothing before or after except—" As he lifted the marker, his voice was no longer calm. "There is now the letter *b* at the beginning and then the letter *g* after the *r*; another *e*, and finally the letter *n*."

Martin's eyes widened. "Bergen," he exclaimed.

Beauviér clapped his hands as Martin said loudly, "Mons!"

Beauviér stood. "We have found them, Sergeant. They are in Mons."

"Do we go after them, monsieur?"

"Absolutely, Sergeant."

"But what about the Director General?"

"I can't be relieved from my post until I'm informed."

"Of course. When do we leave, monsieur?"

"Why, immediately, Sergeant."

* * *

A story is told of a Spanish businessman who had an appointment in the town of Anvers in northern Belgium. One morning he left his hotel in Brussels for the drive he'd been told would take less than an hour. The appointment was to be brief and he could easily be back to his hotel before noon.

However, returning to Brussels late in the evening, he informed the hotel concierge that Anvers had vanished. When he was within thirty kilometers of the town, according to all the road signs, it was then no longer mentioned on any further signs and any pedestrian he asked simply shrugged their shoulders. He approached the town from three different directions, and it was always the same.

The concierge informed the Spaniard that the name Anvers was French, but the town was located in the Flemish region of the country where it was called Antwerpen, and anyone in the surrounding countryside could be as innocently lost as he regarding the whereabouts of Anvers.

The Spaniard naturally asked why the road signs did not give both spellings, although for this the concierge had no suitable answer except Anvers was called Antwerpen and the traveler must be aware.

Yet, the most noteworthy such instance, the Spaniard was warned, is the town of Bergen in the south. There, the French-speaking inhabitants referred to it simply as Mons.

* * *

The magazine stand at *Place Léopold* afforded little protection from the bitter morning wind. The frigid air, entitled 'The Hamburg Express,' referring to its supposed point of origin, rolled across southeastern Belgium and into the town of Mons, sometimes lingering for days. Ian Musters had heard this term before, and only grunted upon having it repeated by the man in the magazine stand. The air bit at his fingers as Musters counted out the coins for his purchase before returning to the waiting taxi, climbing into the back seat. He shivered briefly, then began flipping through the pages of that morning's *De Gazet.* Reaching the second to the last page, he ran his finger down a column of names, mumbled a profanity and, crumpling as much as folding, threw the newspaper onto the floor.

Patting the pockets of his topcoat, he removed a pack of chewing gum, then stopped, replaced the gum and took out a package of cigarettes. Patting his pockets again, he said to the taxi driver, "Do you have a match?"

As he engaged the dash lighter, the driver glanced in the rearview mirror and advised, "I need to get fuel, monsieur."

"Why didn't you get it earlier?" he complained, pinching the cigarette between his thin lips.

The driver turned in his seat, holding the heated lighter for his passenger. "Because when we began the trip, monsieur, I had plenty of fuel. You said you wished to come to Mons, which is merely seventy kilometers from Brussels, but you mentioned nothing about waiting for two hours in front of this church with the motor running."

Musters puffed on the cigarette. "Well then, why don't you shut the damn motor off," he suggested out the corner of his mouth.

His tone impatient, the driver replied, "Because it is two degrees centigrade outside, monsieur. Now, either we get some fuel or you pay me what is owed."

Musters was about to speak when he noticed something out the front window. Glancing at the meter screwed to the dash, he paid the fare and got out.

Over his shoulder, the driver shouted, "Do you want your newspaper?"

Ignoring the question, Musters slammed the door and moving up the first half-dozen steps of the church, fell in behind a man who walked cautiously, gripping the handrail equally so. Musters followed him, step for step, then leaning forward, his mouth just below the rim of the man's hat, said, "Hello, Fouchét."

The man stopped and stood as if at attention, his unsteady hand still tight to the wood railing.

Musters grinned. "Or should I say, Mégot?" He didn't wait for an answer. "That's quite a *nom de guerre* you chose for yourself. It's the name given the third man crucified on Calvary that sad day. He was the good thief, I have been told. Is that you, Fouchét? The good thief? Hardly a threatening moniker, my dear fellow. However, it worked sufficiently in the case of our departed Stuart Endfield." He walked up a step, to stand next to Mégot. "Though you could have called yourself 'Mary Quite Contrary,' and he would have been equally terrified."

Moving up another step, he now looked down on Mégot whose face was shadowed by the large brim of his hat. Throwing his cigarette to the ground, Musters leaned against the railing and said, "Your brother told me where I might find you. Not in so many words, but he did, nonetheless. He admitted that you'd found religion, and where else would you be but Sainte Waudru cathedral? They say just touching the gilded wagon of Saint George they have inside can cure a man of all that ails him." He smirked. "I read that in a brochure. I found you with some tourist propaganda, Fouchét."

His voice weak, Mégot said, "I am not well, monsieur. I need to be left alone."

Musters ignored him. "You are both from this valley, he informed me, although I suspected something of the sort when you insisted we hide the gun here. Lovely little out of the way place, you said, and no one would be the wiser."

251

"Please, monsieur, it is cold," Mégot murmured.

"I wish you'd told me about your sickness, Fouchét. Your brother asked that I leave you be, as though you were some sort of wounded elephant heading off to the family plot. But we have some catching up to do, don't we now? You were supposed to be in Brussels yesterday, and the day before that, to tell me all about your trip to Budapest. Did you have the *fois gras* at the Hotel Gellert as I recommended?"

He did not answer, but slowly raised his head. The grin fell from Musters' face and his eyes widened. Then slowly the grin returned and his eyes became hard as they studied the man below. "Well, I must say your brother didn't exaggerate, Fouchét. You do look a sight," he commented. "I'm surprised I recognized you at all, my dear man. In your current state, you should qualify for some type of government assistance." He laughed. "Perhaps they'll put you in some sort of colony and drop food for you every fortnight. But you'll have your peace and quiet. That is what you want, isn't it my dear Fouchét? To be alone?"

Mégot had lowered his head while Musters spoke and now stood motionless. "I need to sit down, monsieur," he implored.

"Yes, yes, of course. Take a seat and have a fag if you like." Musters held out the package of cigarettes. "Here you are, man. Go ahead, take it. And maybe we can have one of the birds from Le Cheval Noir give you a full body massage while you gaze up to the beautiful gray sky. You were quite the *bon vivant* when we met, weren't you, Fouchét? But now what? You've had a spot of bad luck, it appears. What is it? Your kidneys don't work like they're supposed to, or is it your liver? Doesn't matter much, I always get them confused." He bent slightly, pushing his face closer to Mégot's. "Yes, that's it, I get confused. Is that what happened to you, my dear man? I asked you to speak to Stuart Endfield and give him a simple order, and the next thing I hear is you've added a little something for yourself. A little honey to sweeten the pot, as it were." His voice became hard. "Well, not bloody likely. Then some sort of time limit was implemented; the end of the month, I gather. Didn't you think you'd be alive long enough to collect? Listen to me, you little fool. I kidnapped the Polish woman so she and the American would help me move the gun. That was it. Scare them a little bit and then they'd do exactly what I asked, but you had to ask for money. How much was it? A million francs? That's what your brother thought it to be."

Mégot lifted his head slightly, then as quickly lowered it, but said nothing.

"And then you killed Stuart Endfield so it wouldn't get out, didn't you?"

His voice weak and barely audible, Mégot said, "I didn't kill him."

"No, of course not, and the million francs just evaporated along with the mystery killer. Is that it?"

"I didn't kill him," he repeated. "I didn't kill anybody,"

Slowly, Musters stood up straight. He watched an elderly couple ascend the steps using the handrail opposite. Speaking softly, he said, "You know, in the beginning it was always a bit of a toss-up who was thicker—you or your brother. The things that used to come out of your mouths…" He slowly shook his head. "Now mind you, I haven't had the pleasure of meeting the rest of the family, but it seems you have won the silver cup, my dear Fouchét."

Mégot again pleaded, "Please, monsieur."

"Shut up," ordered Musters. He casually looked at a group of schoolchildren gathering at the far corner of the steps. "There would have been all the money you could have needed if you hadn't become so greedy. The American would have done all the work. No risk, and very little effort, Fouchét. But you got greedy, and now the coppers are after me. Does that make you happy?"

Mégot cried, "But, you told the police—" He began to cough, wiping at his mouth with the back of his hand. "You told them about the Polish woman and the American. They might have let you alone, but you put them on to everyone—on to the entire plan."

Musters stared at Mégot. His thin upper lip began to twitch. "And who put that bright idea into your head?"

Mégot tilted his head up. A rash covered parts of his gaunt face, oddly coloring the skin and accenting his bloodshot eyes. His voice was weak, but the words were clear. "You did, monsieur. You told me you spoke with the Inspector from the Gendarmerie, that he interrogated you. But why you? Why not the others in the embassy? There was nothing to put you and Stuart Endfield together. And then the Inspector appeared in Barbizon. How, if you revealed nothing as you claimed? Only

253

you or I could have told of the meeting there, and I know I said nothing, monsieur."

"So, you know about Barbizon," Musters said, staring straight ahead. "You are a clever little tick, Fouchét."

"Clever, monsieur?" he asked. "No, I am not clever. If I were, then I would never have agreed to do your bidding for dreams. You promised me one half of the proceeds from the sale of a gun that collects dust, and from paintings we do not have. The Monet is with the government and the Renoir stolen from under our eyes. I have fifty percent of nothing."

"Someone else knew about the Renoir, Fouchét. There is another player, that is all."

Mégot attempted to laugh, but only coughed. "Another player? Is that what you think? Now who is the stupid one, monsieur?"

"You don't know what you're talking about."

"Don't I, monsieur? Listen to me. The two state policemen you hired to kidnap the Polish woman are dead."

"What? What are you saying?"

"I was being treated by a doctor at the hotel on the Danube and he put me in one of the rooms to rest. When I awoke later that afternoon, I went downstairs and found their bodies by the fireplace. They had both been shot."

"That's impossible," Musters exclaimed.

"Is it? Just think about it." He leaned forward slightly as if to catch his breath, then said, "The Monet was stolen just before we got to the American, then Stuart Endfield was robbed of the blackmail money and killed, most certainly to silence him." He stared at Musters until he finally faced him. "Look at me, monsieur. I did not have the strength to kill a man."

"But he was shot," Musters said excitedly. "You could have pulled a trigger."

"I have never owned a gun in my life, monsieur," he professed. "My brother and I convinced you we were gangsters and a necessary murder or two was not beyond our means, but we are only petty crooks and have never killed anyone. It is only my brother's size that makes you think he is a tough, but he is not. We are frauds, monsieur. Even the eye patch Bernard wears is a fake. It was all part of the show at Le Cheval Noir, and you bought it all. I was going to grab what I could, so I thought up the blackmail money because I knew then there would be no millions from the sale of any gun."

Musters protested, "But the gun is real, you've seen it. You've touched it."

"Yes, I have, and if it were that simple I might believe you would give me my share when it was finished, but there is something more to this than you told me, monsieur," he said, cautiously taking a step up. "I am afraid we have all had our little secrets in this, right from the beginning. For example, why did you have Stuart Endfield steal the file on the American? You already knew everything."

"I had to be certain the informer was telling the truth, Fouchét."

"And was he? Is he still?"

Musters said nothing.

"I thought so, monsieur," sneered Mégot. "What a shame; unable to trust anyone. Now if you would please get out of my way."

Still shaken by the news of the dead policemen in Budapest and his impotence in any further control over Mégot, Musters stepped from the railing. He stared blankly down the stairs before gradually turning to watch Mégot make his way to the cathedral entrance and disappear inside. Musters shoved his fists into the pockets of his topcoat, only to remove them, running the palm of one hand down his face. He stared at the perspiration that came away on his hand, slowly drawing his fingers apart before clenching them. Abruptly, he climbed to the cathedral entrance and went inside. He felt the warmth of the dark interior push against him as the door silently shut behind. Though difficult to see in the shadows, he was keenly aware the cathedral had no parishioners other than Mégot who had just finished crossing himself in the far aisle. Musters moved toward him.

The priest at the altar, giving direction to an acolyte, had not seemingly noticed the arrival of the two men who now sat together in the last pew.

Musters whispered, "Did you leave the message for the American?"

"I said I would," replied Mégot.

"Then you know where he is staying."

"Yes, at the Hotel Metropole."

"But he might not have used his name, with the police now after him."

"He will get the message, monsieur," Mégot assured him as he removed his hat.

Looking about the deserted cathedral, Musters said, "You know the police will eventually find you, Fouchét. What will you say to them?"

"You ask this because I have nothing to lose—is that it, monsieur?" His eyes fixed on the far altar. "You are right, I have lost. I have lost everything, but somehow, I am no longer frightened. It is you who should be frightened."

Mégot wore a rueful grin as he continued, "Did you ever hear the story of the Ten Little Indians? You must have—an Englishman wrote it. You see, in the story, the ten Indians strangely die, murdered really, one after the other until there are only two standing. Well, that is us, monsieur. The others are all dead. They have all been silenced. The art dealer in Namur, the two policemen in Budapest, Stuart Endfield, and then the poor man you recently attempted to conscript—Roger Catchpole wasn't it? Did he really hang himself? That's not important now I suppose, though I did wonder when I heard." Mégot lowered his gaze. "You thought I was the killer and I, you. But since we never trusted each other to begin with, it makes no real difference anymore."

He slowly lowered his hand, placing it on top of the pew in front of him. "Now if you would let me be," he said, and gradually knelt on the padded hassock.

A Bach fugue commenced from the organ loft; softly at first, then progressively louder, until its sound filled the enormous sanctuary, the interwoven melodies discordant amid the interior calm. Musters looked at the man beside him, then at the priest and acolyte before the altar—their backs to the congregation of two.

The organ music was now at a crescendo as Musters removed the red scarf from his neck, gripping an end in each hand. With a quick movement, he dropped it around Mégot's neck and crossing his hands, pulled with all his strength. In his weak state, Mégot had no chance against such an attack and put up little resistance, lightly touching the woolen scarf that was cutting off air to his lungs. He tried to look at Musters through his drooping eyelids, but the tightening scarf kept his face forward. Then, as if the overhead music had put him to sleep, he slumped into a pose little different than the one he'd maintained while praying. His chin resting on the back of the pew, he faced the altar as his dangling arms became still.

Musters withdrew his woolen scarf and stood, his footsteps unnoticed as he moved to the entrance and opened the large wooden door, escaping into the gray afternoon.

* * *

Thomas Breck sat opposite John Clark in the ground floor café of the Hotel Metropole just off Place Léopold. They spoke softly in half-whispers, as they had been doing for over twenty minutes. Both men's faces showed little emotion except when the waitress appeared at their table, attempting to pour additional wine into glasses they had barely touched. They would stop speaking, offering restrained smiles, then continue with their conversation once she moved out of earshot.

Rolling the ember of his cigar inside the edge of the ashtray, John Clark said, "Where did you leave your car?"

"Paris, in an underground garage."

"You took the train here?"

"No, it was too dangerous. I bought a used car and crossed the frontier north of Metz."

"And the gun—how far is it from here?"

"A little over a kilometer," Tom replied. "It's in an abandoned factory."

"You've seen it?"

"The building, yes; but I didn't go inside."

"I'm inquiring of these things Thomas, so that we—"

Lifting his hand, he said, "I understand."

John Clark paused, then asked, "How will you stack it onto the lorry?"

Moving his wine glass to the side, Tom leaned forward. "A factory of that size should have an overhead winch and pulley system."

"Assuming there's still power into the building."

"Look, they obviously trucked it to the abandoned factory and I'm hoping it's still on a trailer," he answered patiently. "I understand you want me to be prepared, John, but I've thought it through. I'll be at the coast as planned."

"I know you will, Thomas," he said, clenching the cigar in his back teeth. "Let me see the note again."

Tom took a folded envelope from his coat pocket, handing it across the table.

John Clark asked, "When the man at the reception desk gave you this, did he act peculiar in any way?"

"No. It was very matter of fact. I tipped him and that was it."

"And I don't want to be repeating myself, but who else knew you'd be checking in here and the name you'd be using?"

"No one but you, Tatiana and I."

"You've never used this name before?"

"Never."

"And the writing on the note, you don't know this hand?"

"No."

Placing the square of paper on the table, John Clark casually removed the cigar from his mouth. "It says you're to go to the Hotel Idou Anfa in Algiers and ask for a message left under the alias you are now using," he said, running his finger along the words written on the paper. "Do you know this hotel?"

Tom shook his head.

"And you must do this no later than December thirty-first." He returned the note to the envelope, dropping it in the center of the table. "This was written to let you know you're being watched," he said, tapping the envelope with his thumb. "And if you're being watched and Mégot knows everything you're doing, then he'll know when you get to Algeria, regardless. So why the note?"

"To keep his whip on my back. It's part of the game—a game that must be brought to an end."

"And maybe Inspector Beauviér's also been told you're here," he added pensively. "As in Barbizon. Someone told him where to find you."

"I don't believe Beauviér knows. I've thought about that a great deal—particularly when he was chasing me," Tom said, gazing at his wine glass. "Beauviér is an unusual man. He was alone in Barbizon with no gendarme backup and I got away easily. He only wanted to follow me, not arrest me, and simply overreacted when I spotted him. If he knew where I was going next, he would have gone back to his coffee that morning and not bothered with a high-speed pursuit. No, he thought he would never see me again. I'd like to think he was right."

"You sound confident."

"Do I?"

"So we go with our plan?"

258

"We go with our plan."

Unsmiling, John Clark said, "There's another way—an easier way, Thomas. You know that now, don't you?"

"Easier is it? I've never killed a man in my life, John, and I'm not going to start now."

"But the plan might fail."

"Yes, though it's the only way... if we are to be completely finished with it all."

Looking out the window alongside their table, John Clark blew out a long plume of smoke. "The *Ondine* is three miles out and waiting on word from me. I best get to the coast and let the captain know to come in." He glanced at his watch. "My return ticket's for the two-thirty-five train; that'll get me there by six. I should be on my way."

"How do you contact the *Ondine*?"

"A short-wave radio. It's hidden in a room I let in Zeebrugge for the week. That's the telephone number I gave you." He grinned. "It has a lovely view of the sea."

Tom put his hand on the Irishman's wrist and said, "Everything depends on the ship's captain, John. He must follow his instructions. Can he be trusted to do this?"

"He can," John replied, his eyes narrowing.

"I hope you're right."

After taking a long drink of wine, John said, "Have you heard from Tatiana or Yuri?"

"No, but they'll be here soon."

"We all have to follow instructions, Thomas."

"Pardon me, John. I didn't mean—"

A siren just outside cut him off and he hurriedly looked out the window.

"It's an ambulance, Thomas."

"I'm a little tired. I'll be okay."

"Well, get some rest," John Clark said and stood. "There's nothing you can do until they arrive with the lorry. So you might as—"

Another siren passed the window, followed by a third.

"What is it?" asked Tom, watching John Clark lean toward the window.

"I'm not sure, but it's something, all right. There are three copper wagons and an ambulance. They're in front of the

259

cathedral on the other side of the square." He put his hand on Tom's shoulder. "Well, at least it has nothing to do with us."

* * *

Jules Beauviér stood in the narrow street opposite a buzzing neon sign, the words *Hotel de la Gare* barely visible in the afternoon light. His gaze moved between the fluttering sign and the address just below, rechecking the street numbers, comparing them to those he had written down earlier that day. They were identical.

Henri Martin appeared at the hotel entrance, walking quickly toward him.

"Well?" said Beauviér.

"Yes, that's number 38 *rue du parc* and they had a reservation under the name Roger Catchpole," he said, catching his breath. "It was for the twenty-third and he was going to stay three nights."

"And the telephone number?"

"The same as on the markers, with the missing last two digits being a six and an eight," he said, extending his arm. "Here is the hotel's business card."

Beauviér frowned, dropping the card into his topcoat pocket without looking at it. "I don't suppose the American or the Polish woman are there?"

"No, Inspector. There are only four rooms rented and none of the guests fit their descriptions."

"But they are here in Mons, I know it. They are all here and we don't have much time," he said, walking toward the hotel entrance. "I want you to telephone the city police and have them send over as many men as they can. I want every hotel in this town searched for the American and the Polish woman, Mégot and Ian Musters."

Martin asked, "What charges do I say they are wanted on?"

Opening the door of the hotel, Beauviér said softly, "On suspicion of smuggling and murder—wait, leave out the word suspicion. Just say they are wanted for smuggling and murder. That should do it, Sergeant." Stepping into the foyer, he nodded toward the corner. "There's a telephone. Tell them to be quick."

Digging in his pocket for coins, Martin went to the telephone as Beauviér walked to the reception desk and addressed the young girl behind it. She confirmed what Martin had just relayed, but seemed to know nothing more. The hotel contained only fifteen rooms and she could not recall the last time an English-speaking person had stayed there. There was no record, going back over two months, of an Ian Musters, a Fouchét or Mégot, or an American named Thomas Breck.

The hotel appeared to have been chosen at random.

Thanking her, he turned to see Martin moving toward him and asked, "How many men are they sending?"

His face doleful, Martin said, "None, Inspector."

"What?" he exclaimed. "Give me a coin. I'll speak with them."

"It won't do any good, Inspector."

"And why not?"

"They have no officers available, monsieur. There was a murder discovered just an hour ago and every extra man is on that," the sergeant explained. "It's Christmas Eve. They're working with a limited force."

"A murder?"

"Yes. It was in the cathedral on Place Léopold."

"Sainte Waudru?"

"I believe he said that name."

Beauviér lowered his gaze. "I have not heard of such a thing, not in years."

"Neither had the Captain I spoke with. He was very upset and asked why we didn't contact the gendarme garrison for assistance."

Beauviér said nothing.

Martin cleared his throat, and asked, "You are concerned that the Director General will find out and remove you from the case, monsieur?"

"Yes, Sergeant," he admitted. "But maybe that's best. We have nothing other than a hunch that they are here, and even if we find them we don't know what they are up to, and have no real evidence on any of the charges. We have nothing."

"But the American, for smuggling."

Beauviér shook his head. "His name was crudely deciphered on the frame of a painting discovered in the gallery of a man who died of natural causes. Arguably, they did business together and it could have been there for any reason."

"Then the Polish woman; she is wanted on charges of murder."

"So says Ian Musters. I want nothing to do with sending someone to a Communist country because of something that may or may not have happened, twenty years back."

Sounding frustrated, Martin said, "But the murder of Stuart Endfield, monsieur. We must bring them in."

"You forget, Sergeant. We had the American under surveillance at the time. That only leaves Mégot, who was incapable, or Ian Musters, who showed me the film of Stuart Endfield to keep me going forward. He wouldn't have done that if he were the murderer of the Englishman. And we do not have the evidence, Sergeant. We need the murder weapon; we need its owner," he said, pushing his hands into his coat pockets. "No, our only hope was to find them and to follow them. We had to uncover what they are doing, though I do not understand why they continue."

Martin appeared about to speak, but only returned to the telephone in the corner.

Beauviér looked away, toward the front door. Standing in the lobby of the small hotel, he sensed the end of his career approaching. Forty years of being a policeman, his only real life, now wasted with a final defeat. Such an ignoble end made him wince.

There was a rustling sound behind him.

"Inspector?" said Martin.

He turned. "Yes?"

"This is not Brussels, Inspector. There are only twenty-two hotels in the center of Mons." He held out a piece of paper. "This is the page from the telephone book. Since this hotel has been eliminated, that leaves ten for you to search and eleven for me. They are all within reasonable walking distance and I can't see this taking more than two or three hours, can you?"

Beauviér took the page, studying the hotel names.

Martin said, "If we come up with nothing, then we can speak to the local gendarme brigade. We must try this, monsieur."

"How many hotels do I have here, Sergeant?" asked Beauviér, shaking the paper.

"Ten, monsieur."

Swapping pages with Martin, he said, "I'll take the eleven, Sergeant," and headed for the front door of the hotel. "Let's be off. We don't have much time."

* * *

The lobby of the Hotel Metropole had the appearance of a ghost town. The reception desk had been vacated, as had the concierge desk, the porter's stand and even the rent-a-car counter tucked into the corner of the lobby was void of any life. Each employee responsible for these posts at the two-star accommodation had some five minutes earlier made a great dash to the sidewalk, just outside the entrance. They were now loitering there, staring and pointing as if a great fire were engulfing the cathedral on the opposite side of Place Léopold, but there were neither flames nor smoke to be seen.

The Cathedral of Sainte Waudru was merely blocked off with makeshift barricades and portable fencing brought in by the police. An ambulance had left some minutes earlier, though it appeared in no great hurry with its lights and siren shut down. There was no reason evidently, as their sole passenger was already dead.

Tom Breck overheard the story from the hotel porter and the bellman immediately confirmed that someone had been murdered, strangled to death it was suggested. The porter stated the victim was a stranger, a nameless stranger.

Normally, Tom would have ignored such an event, but this was somehow different. There had not been a murder in the town of Mons for years—the porter recalled more than eight, the doorman thought more than ten. Standing in the center of the crowd, Tom listened to a few more comments, each one contradicting the next, before deciding he had heard enough, and went back into the hotel.

Standing at the empty reception desk, he looked at his key box, hoping a message had been left, as Tatiana and Yuri were overdue. But there was nothing, not even his key, which he had kept with him.

One of the desk clerks, possibly having lost interest in the outside spectacle, had slipped behind the desk and was moving toward Tom when the telephone rang. Though the clerk had a look of ambivalence when placing the receiver to his ear, this quickly changed to one of attentiveness. The clerk was silent, listening to the caller, and then said, "How do you spell that, monsieur?" as he wrote carefully on a piece of paper, attempting to nod with the receiver pressed between his shoulder and ear.

Leaning forward, Tom watched the letters being written. Gradually, they formed two words, which were upside down to him, but quite clear nonetheless. The man behind the desk had written the name *Thomas Breck*.

Josef Kraus

Tom pulled back, wondering if he had already been recognized. But the clerk gave no indication of this as he again nodded, and said, "Yes, Inspector."

Tom felt unsteady. He began moving toward the elevator, but changed his mind and went to the stairs, quickly climbing them to the first floor. He picked up his pace, running down the hallway to his room. Throwing open the door, he went into the bathroom, grabbed his shaving kit and robe, stuffing them all into the satchel at his feet. Anything else remaining in the room had suddenly become unimportant and would be left behind. He ran out the door to the stairs and reaching the lobby, noticed there was now a young woman behind reception, trying to get his attention. She called out, "Monsieur."

Tom stopped, staring at the front door of the hotel.

"Monsieur, I have a message for you," she repeated.

Slowly turning, he looked at the young woman, then the clerk next to her who was still on the telephone, his eyes fixed on the reservation book.

The young woman held out a square of paper. "A Madame Malinaud telephoned earlier for you, monsieur. I'm sorry in being so late getting this to you." Briefly lowering her eyes, she blushed. "I went out to see all of the excitement in the square. Please excuse me, however, it was no more than ten minutes ago that she called. Madame said she has had car difficulties and is on the outskirts of town. I have written down the address. Can you read it, monsieur?"

Taking the paper, Tom said, "Yes, it's quite legible."

"Again, please excuse me, monsieur," she said.

"Believe me, mademoiselle," he said, glancing at the clerk still on the telephone, "it is no problem at all," and walked away, pushing through the revolving door into the crowd.

There was no thought in retrieving his recently purchased car from the hotel garage. It was now useless with its make and plate number recorded. Throwing the strap of his satchel over his shoulder, he moved away from the Hotel Metropole and Place Léopold. He cut across one intersection to the next, unconcerned if he was going toward the address on the paper he held—it was not important, wanting only to distance himself from Beauviér. It was Christmas Eve and he was running.

He covered over five blocks before finding an available taxi. Climbing into the back seat, he slowly caught his breath, scanning the urban scene beyond his window with troubled eyes. Through the emptied streets, past the closed storefronts, the taxi moved, the driver talking incessantly of the murder at the cathedral. Tom didn't listen. He was only aware of his trembling fingers when he lifted a cigarette to his mouth, the match flame dancing in his unsteady hand.

Sitting back in the seat, he realized how little time he had and the need to keep Beauviér at bay, wondering why there were not more gendarmes after him. He imagined except for Sergeant Martin, the Inspector was still working alone. This appeared to be his best advantage—the opening he needed to smuggle the gun out.

The taxi slowed to a stop. The driver said, "This is the address, monsieur."

They were at a crossroads in what appeared to be the industrial section of town, no pedestrians or cars to be seen.

Tom asked, "This is the address I gave you?"

Turning in his seat, the driver replied, "It is, but everything is closed for the holidays. It must be a mistake."

"No, this will do," he said, and paying the fare climbed out of the taxi.

Pulling away, the driver called out through his open window, "Merry Christmas, monsieur," and disappeared around the first corner.

Standing on the empty sidewalk, Tom whispered, "Merry Christmas."

There was no sign of Tatiana or Yuri, and no broken-down car. For a moment Tom thought he had been set up when a large truck appeared at the far end of the street. The sound of its diesel engine cut though the quiet; the side pipes pushing out plumes of black smoke. Its size became more apparent as it advanced, occupying the better of both lanes while moving slowly down the center of the road. It was enormous, Tom thought, then noticed an arm emerge from the passenger window.

It was Tatiana with Yuri behind the wheel, who gradually brought the truck to a stop beside Tom. Climbing down from the cab, Tatiana ran around the front of the truck and threw her arms around him.

"You're all right," she exclaimed.

"Of course," he countered. "Why wouldn't I be?"

Pressing the side of her face against his chest, she explained, "When I tried to drive to the Hotel Metropole in Yuri's car, the police wouldn't let me into the square. There was a murder, Thomas."

"I know. In the cathedral," he said reassuringly. "Why would you think it had something to do with me?"

"Oh, I don't know. Now I feel so foolish, but the policeman that stopped me said a man from Brussels had been killed. And I remembered Mégot's threats... I just got frightened, Thomas."

He grew somber. "From Brussels? The man murdered was from Brussels?"

"Yes," she replied. "And they couldn't find you when I called the hotel. So I thought..." She stepped back from her embrace. "We always said that if something happened to one of us the other should get away."

"You didn't get very far, did you?"

"That's when I became truly frightened," she whispered. "Thinking that you may be gone." Her voice became unsteady. "I knew I had no place to go."

"You must never think like that."

Lowering her eyes, she nodded, then lifted her gaze, smiling. "Did you see the new truck?"

Tom laughed. "It's hard to miss," he said, looking up at Yuri who was still in the driver's seat, his window rolled down. "Hello, Yuri."

"Thomas," he responded, lifting his hand slightly. "What do you think? It's American. It's a Freightliner."

"So I see. Was it expensive?"

"No, no. Not at all," he said proudly, climbing down from the cab. "It's the only one in Europe. It even has a bed and air conditioning. They were going to import them, I guess. Anyway, the man we bought it from said it would be difficult to get parts, so we got it cheap."

"Really?"

"Yes." He stared admiringly at the towering vehicle.

"Where is your car?" asked Tom.

"Tatiana put it in a garage not far from here," he answered. "Do we need it?"

"Depends." Tom turned to face Tatiana. "Where are your things?"

"I have everything here," she replied.

"Good," he said. "We are going to get the cargo."

"But, the hotel," she demurred. "I would like to get cleaned up."

"I'm sorry, but we can't."

"Why?" asked Yuri.

Tom lowered his satchel to the ground. "Because Beauviér is here. He tracked me to the hotel."

The three people stood silently, oblivious to the cold wind blowing about them. Yuri's face had become ashen. Tatiana said, "How is that possible?"

"Beauviér's a policeman," Tom replied. "I think he found us by doing his job. He discovered that we were to be in Mons, but there's no way he could have known exactly where, unless somebody told him."

"Who?" asked Yuri.

"Mégot knew we would be in Mons," Tatiana said.

"But not where—he didn't know we would meet at the Hotel Metropole," said Tom. "Somehow he found out." Solemnly, he handed the envelope he'd received at the hotel to Tatiana.

"This is from Mégot?" she said, taking the envelope. "It's on Hotel Metropole stationary and the alias you used is written on it."

"Then Mégot told Beauviér," asserted Yuri, "and he told him you'd be in Barbizon, as well."

"No. He has no reason to put himself at such risk. If he wanted to see us in jail there are easier ways, and remember: he didn't know the alias I was to use."

Tatiana looked up from the note. "There is someone else working with Mégot?"

Tom shrugged. "Someone knows our every move."

"We are being watched," she said.

Tom picked up his bag, returning the strap to his shoulder. "Yes, there is. But now we have a small jump on them and must take advantage of it."

"Let's call this off and get away from here," Yuri urged. "Somewhere, anywhere."

Tom struck a match, holding the flame steady under the corner of the envelope. "There are some things that are unexplainable and this is why we must go through with this to the end. I understand your fear, Yuri, but if we once thought there was the option of fleeing, that is now gone."

"Then we better get to the cargo," said Tatiana.

Letting the ashes of the envelope drift to the ground, Tom crushed it underfoot. "Let's go," he said, and they moved toward the open doors of the truck.

* * *

The building stood three stories high and covered enough land for three football fields. Its upper face consisted of glass panes, hundreds of them, though none were larger than the width of a man's hand, and each framed in steel. The remainder of the structure was of concrete, save for two doors. The first stood one story in height, was of metal, and faced the near road. The second was of brushed steel, of conventional height, though it had no handle and the hinges, assuming they existed, were concealed. Adjacent to the second door, screwed into the concrete façade of the building was a sign that read: *Mons Cement Works, Established 1919.* Directly under the sign was a small plastic box, which, like the near door, was not part of the original construction. And it was this plastic box that had Tom Breck's attention as he tapped it with the tip of his forefinger.

"How do we get in?" asked Tatiana.

"I'm not sure," he replied, twisting his neck to look underneath the box. He then lowered his hand and pulled up on the bottom edge. Its face lifted easily, locking in place to reveal a numerical keyboard constructed flush to the wall. It was made of metal and surrounded by metal.

"Do you know the code?" asked Yuri, studying the keyboard.

Tom removed a piece of paper from his pocket. "On the bottom of the instructions from Mégot is a series of numbers. They could be the combination."

Tatiana pointed to a pole abutting the road. "The wires to the building have all been cut. There's no electricity."

Tom said, "Let's find out," and began to type in the numbers.

No sounds were emitted and no lights flashed as Tom pushed the metal keys one at a time. He moved slowly, twisting the paper slightly to catch the fading afternoon light. After punching in the final number, he was about to speak when a simple clicking sound came from the box.

"Hurry," exclaimed Yuri.

Both men pushed on the door. It would not budge. Winter rime had collected round the edges, forming an adhesive between the jamb and the door. The box continued to click.

Taking a step back, Tom kicked repeatedly at the center of the door with all his strength when suddenly it flew open, releasing a plume of fine gray powder into the air. Squinting to see, he moved inside, Tatiana and Yuri following.

As the dust settled, the interior of the abandoned factory took shape. Spreading the length of the building, dormant machinery rose up like skyscrapers to the ceiling. Steel ladders climbed three stories to walkways that switchbacked, supporting a labyrinth of connecting pipes and conveyer belts that still carried their final load.

From the near corner, Yuri said, "Here, Thomas. It's these that allowed the door to work," indicating a wall of batteries approximately his height, and again as long. "Maybe they're connected to the lights."

He threw the near wall switch as overhead flood lamps came to life, illuminating the factory floor and specifically a loaded trailer against the far wall. At first, the freight appeared to be pipes used to move oil, but there was something different about them. Moving closer, Tom could see the interior of the four long tubes glisten as the metal had been finished to a luster.

"Yuri, shut off some of these lights," he said.

The lights went out, save for one section above the trailer.

Yuri called, "Can you see well enough with only these?"

"I can," he replied softly, touching one of the steel tubes, then called out, "We're in luck. Cargo is still on a trailer." He looked to the entrance of the building. "Open the overhead door and get the Freightliner in here and out of sight, Yuri."

"Should I leave the other trailer outside?"

"Yes, hide it on the opposite side of the building. We'll remove the license plates later."

Looking again at one of the steel tubes, his eyes narrowed. Stenciled in white paint were the words *Magellan Armaments, Belgium*. The gun had been overtly manufactured and proudly advertised the fact.

Tatiana moved toward the trailer. "You have no suspicion of what this is?" she asked.

269

Tom didn't reply.

She said, "When you returned from Ireland, I asked if you and John Clark knew what we would be smuggling. You said no, Thomas."

He was still silent.

"We've known each other a long time. What we do is lie to people, and we do it very well, but we do not lie to each other." Stepping closer to the trailer, her eyes moved to the stenciled words when abruptly she lifted her hand to her mouth. Turning to look at him, she lowered her hand and said, "This was fabricated at a plant that makes armaments. What is this?"

Taking a deep breath, he said, "It's what you're possibly imagining. It's a gun."

"A weapon?"

"Yes."

"We—we agreed to never deal with such things!" she stammered.

"It's what has been dealt to us, Tatiana. There was no choice."

"But why?" she demanded. "Why did you lie to me?"

"Because you never would have agreed if you had known."

She took a step back. "And what makes you think I will now? Now that I know?"

He went to her, attempting to take her hand, but she resisted.

Embarrassed at being rebuffed, he said, "Please forgive me, but you must trust me."

She shook her head. "Why?"

"Because I am asking you, Tatiana. We've known each other so long, I've always looked out for you."

"By lying?"

Tom stumbled with his words. "In a way…I have, yes…I've kept things from you that might have caused you needless concern; I've kept you clear of those things that were dangerous, but I have never lied to you."

"Until now."

He looked at her steadily, but said apologetically, "Until now."

"Then tell me what it is I'm supposed to trust you with?"

"I can't."

Angrily, she said, "I'm going to be with you in that truck as we cross the country, then on the freighter to Algeria, and you have a secret, Thomas?"

"But you are not," he said quickly.

Tatiana squinted. "What? I don't understand."

"You're not going to be with me in the truck and you won't be going to Algeria." He took her hand—this time she did not resist. "When you finish with the paperwork and documents we need for the gun, you will get as far away from here as you can," he said resolutely. "I want you to go to Argentina, as we spoke about before. You are not to worry about anyone coming after you."

Her eyes softened. "But—"

"Yuri will go with me to the coast and then on to Algeria. When we leave here you will take Yuri's car to Luxembourg and take a flight out from there." He handed her a folded paper from his pocket. "This is the name and address in Buenos Aires. I wrote my friend a few days back, telling him you would be coming. You will be safe there and I will follow as soon as I can."

Tatiana stared at the folded paper but did not open it. "And Yuri?"

"Of course. Yuri and I will both be there."

She stared at him. "Why didn't you tell me these things before?" The anger in her voice was gone; she sounded unsure.

"I thought I was doing the right thing."

"And do you still think you are doing the right thing?

"I do," he answered.

With resignation in her voice, she said, "I must trust you, I always have."

"Thank you," he said.

She did not speak for few seconds, then said, "But there's nothing more I can do?"

"No, Tatiana. I want you away."

"You have always controlled that end of our business. All right, Thomas."

Glancing at the door, he said in a half-whisper, "I think it's best if this stays between us."

"You mean not tell Yuri?"

"Yes."

"Why?"

"Because this is his first time working with us," he explained. "He'll be nervous enough without the knowledge he's smuggling a gun."

"I understand."

Tom was about to speak when he noticed Yuri enter the building, moving toward the large overhead door. "The trailer was

271

tough to get unhooked," he said, pulling on a looped chain that ran up the wall. As he did, the door began to lift, letting in the sound of the Freightliner's idling engine just outside.

Tom called, "Do you need any help?"

"No, I'm fine," he yelled, continuing to pull on the chain.

Tatiana shivered.

Tom said, "You're cold."

"Yes," she replied, her hands pressed into the pockets of her coat. "Though I think it's colder in here than outside."

"Come on," he said.

They moved across the concrete floor to the open door of a small office and went in. There was only a battered desk inside, nothing else. No chairs or file cabinets, nor anything on the walls but spotted and fading paint. Tom knelt by a baseboard heater and turning a dial on the end, tried to listen over the sound of the Freightliner entering the building. There was a faint tapping. He said, "Good, it works," and standing, flipped the switch for the overhead light. It didn't work. He faced Tatiana. "Can you see well enough?"

"When I was a little girl I used candlelight. I'll be fine," she replied, kneeling by the radiator to warm her hands.

Tom went out of the office though returned shortly, carrying a wooden box and some empty sacks used to bag cement. He put the box on end, the folded sacks on top. "I'm sorry, but this was all I could find."

"It looks very comfortable, Thomas."

Yuri entered the office carrying three shopping bags that he placed on the desk. "Here are the things you bought in Paris."

"Oh, good," said Tatiana, reaching in one of the bags.

Tom said, "Maybe you should begin with the stencils so Yuri and I can get started."

"Yes, yes. But first, these are for you." She held two small packages, handing one to Yuri and the other to Tom. "Merry Christmas."

Both men looked at the gesture they'd been given, then at each other before their eyes slowly moved back to Tatiana.

"It's all right, gentlemen. I know you didn't get me anything." As Tom began to speak, she held up her hand. "Please, just open them."

The two men obliged her request, removing their contents.

Tatiana smiled. "They are Swiss Army knives, and look—they even have little toothpicks. Isn't that clever?" she mused. "And the woman who sold them to me said they were terribly practical, because you never know when you might find yourself far from home, and in trouble."

Her eyes sparkled as she began to laugh.

* * *

Inspector Beauviér and Sergeant Martin walked side by side along the sidewalk, the passing storefronts closed and darkened. Their mood was equally somber and they had not spoken in the last fifteen minutes. The spirit of their chase was fading like the afternoon light in Mons, and it was quiet, only the occasional car going by, the stoplights clicking their colors to empty streets.

They continued for another block when Martin lifted his arm, pointing ahead. "There it is, monsieur."

With these words their pace did not speed up, but rather slowed till they found themselves at a foot of stairs, a dozen or so steps in total. At the top of the stairs was an unremarkable door with an attached sign that read, *Police-La Morgue*.

The two men trudged up the stairs and, with Martin leading the way, entered the attached building. The poorly lighted foyer was empty, as if the sign outside had alternately read 'Unfurnished Office To Let.' There were no chairs or tables, no lamps or even pictures on the wall. There was only a wooden counter that ran the width of the small room, a painted arrow indicating an electric button screwed into its frame. Glancing at Beauviér, Martin pushed the button.

Somewhere in the back of the room, a buzzer rang faintly. There was the sound of footsteps and a slender man appeared from behind a partition. He wore a full-length white coat that was undone, as was his tie. Seeming to have just awakened, he rubbed at each eye and said, "Is one of you Beauviér?"

"Yes," he said. "Are you the coroner?"

The man grunted. "Of course I am. You're late," he added, glancing at his bare wrist.

Quickly Martin responded, "We were called to the other side of Mons, thinking it possibly related, monsieur."

The coroner complained, "It's Christmas Eve, messieurs." He adjusted his tie. "Wait there, I'll just be a minute."

As the man disappeared behind the partition, Martin turned to look at Beauviér who stood near the door, his hands clasped behind his back, and said cautiously, "It was just bad luck, Inspector, the American standing at the desk when you telephoned the hotel. It would've been impossible to have known."

Beauviér remained motionless except for his eyes, which moved toward Martin. "I should have personally gone to the Hotel Metropole, Sergeant. It was only a five-minute walk from where I was. Now we have lost him and again have nothing."

"But the message the desk clerk took for the American, it was from a Madame Malinaud," he said, sounding hopeful. "That is a name the Polish woman uses. Now we know she is also in Mons, and we have the address in the industrial zone where her car broke down. She was certainly there."

Beauviér looked away. "But there was no broken-down car, Sergeant. Nor were the American or the Polish woman anywhere to be found. That means we still have nothing."

"But the building janitor you found," Martin reminded him. "He said a young man was standing at the corner and was picked up by a large, dark-colored truck."

"A large truck—what does that mean? And besides, the janitor smelled of whiskey."

Martin briefly chewed on his lower lip, then asked, "What was the alias the American was using at the hotel? You didn't say."

His eyes became hard, and he growled, "He used my name, Sergeant. He checked in under the name of Jules Beauviér."

Martin lowered his gaze. "Oh, I see."

There was a noise on the other side of the partition and the coroner reappeared. He lifted a hinged section of the counter over his head and, struggling to hold it in place, said, "Come in, messieurs."

A moment later they were descending a staircase into darkness.

"It has been nine years since we've had a murder of this sort in Mons," commented the coroner.

"There's another sort?" asked Martin.

"Well, yes, of course. Those of passion are quite popular. A husband killing the wife's lover or the lover killing the husband, or the wife killing them both and running off with the money," the

274

coroner replied, sounding bored. "About one every ten months, I'd say. Otherwise I would be unemployed."

"That would be a pity," said Beauviér.

"Yes, quite," the man concurred. "Now watch your step, messieurs."

At the bottom of the stairs the three men stopped and waited. There was a click and a white-tiled room abruptly blazed with lights. It was a spotless room, appearing unused. The floor, the walls, and the ceiling could be interchangeable, save the wall on the left. Flush to the tiles were two-dozen stainless steel drawers with stainless steel handles. Each drawer was twice the width of a man's shoulders and three times the height.

Moving to the near drawer, the coroner unhooked a red bag from the handle and handed it to Beauviér. "This is what was in his pockets," he said, then jerked his bony thumb toward the corner. "And that is what he was wearing."

As Beauviér looked into the bag, Martin retrieved the clothing. "That too?" he asked, pointing at a large-brimmed hat at his feet.

"Yes, all of it," grumbled the coroner, pulling on the handle of the drawer. "Normally I would have it boxed and filed, but it's a holiday and I'm alone here."

"Of course, monsieur," said Beauviér, poking in the bag. "Is this all he had on him?"

"I'm afraid so," he confirmed, sliding the long drawer out from the wall. "There was no wallet or money found."

"No identification?"

Staring at the black sheet covering the corpse, the coroner shook his head. "No, nothing," he said apologetically. "A local pickpocket was seen in the cathedral about the time the body was found. But as this man won't be filing a complaint, it's impossible to know if he carried anything more. He might just be a vagabond."

Beauviér glanced at the clothes Martin held. "A vagabond wears a cashmere topcoat and a freshly laundered shirt?"

The coroner shrugged. "I'm not a policeman, monsieur."

"Then why was I told that he was from Brussels?" Beauviér asked.

"If you look in the bag," replied the coroner impatiently, "you will see a pass for the Brussels underground and it's good for six months. Hardly something one would purchase if they're just passing through."

Beauviér poked his hand into the bag and then looked up. "Bring that over here, Sergeant," he said, indicating a metal stretcher with wheeled legs in the corner. When Martin complied, Beauviér dumped the bag's contents onto it, spreading the items apart with his forefinger.

"Let's see him," he said to the coroner.

The coroner folded the sheet back, exposing the cadaver. "Well, do you know him?" he asked.

Beauviér took a step forward. "Sergeant?"

Martin moved next to Beauviér. He did not speak for a few seconds, then said, "No, monsieur. I do not recognize him."

"What is his height?" asked Beauviér.

"One meter, sixty," answered the coroner from rote. "Quite a short fellow... so, do you know him?"

Beauviér did not reply, but turned to look at the items on the stretcher. There lay the pass for the underground as the coroner mentioned, and a few personal items of no significance. Beauviér picked up a ballpoint pen emblazoned with an advertiser's name that was no longer legible, then used it to poke at the victim's possessions: a plastic comb, what appeared to be a latch key, one half of a blue pill, a package of cigarettes with two or three missing, a book of matches, a business card from a flower shop in Brussels, and a small tube of ointment. Bending forward to read the side of the tube, he said, "The rash the man has on his body, monsieur. What is it?"

The coroner cocked his head to the side, studying the affliction. "Hard to say. An allergy of sorts, I would imagine."

"A reaction that extreme in the middle of winter?"

"Certainly. It needn't be a common allergy. He might have been sensitive to cold weather, monsieur."

Beauviér picked up the business card. Turning it over, he asked, "Could it be syphilis?"

The coroner laughed. "What a thing to ask, monsieur. But that would be impossible to know without a blood test. Are you suggesting—"

"No, I was just thinking out loud, monsieur. You're the professional in such matters, I'm sure." He dropped the business card into his side pocket. "You told me on the telephone that he had been strangled. Do you have anything more?"

The man nodded. "If you look closely at the man's neck you will see some red fibers embedded in the skin. But they are not cotton or hemp, as I imagined. They are wool."

"Wool?" said Beauviér.

"Yes, monsieur."

Beauviér tapped his forefinger on the edge of his chin. "A scarf, possibly," he said as if to himself.

The coroner grinned. "Yes, that's very possible, monsieur. Of course, it wouldn't be socks—they're too short; or a jacket—too bulky…Yes, it was a scarf."

Frowning, Beauviér looked across the stretcher at Martin who was studying the dead man's hat, running his index finger along the inside of the band. His eyes darted toward the occupied coroner as he pulled out a small slip of paper and quickly put it into his jacket pocket.

Beauviér cleared his throat. "I'm sorry we could not have been of any help, monsieur. There is an affair that brought us here to Mons and I thought this man might be possibly related, but I was wrong."

Preoccupied, the coroner said, "A red scarf…I'll be certain to tell the captain of police, monsieur."

"By all means," Beauviér said and, looking at Martin, tipped his head toward the entrance.

"Of course I'll say you first mentioned the possibility," the coroner said as the two men moved to the door.

Beauviér glanced at him. "That might be best, because it certainly could have been a wool sock; possibly a pair of them tied together. Or then again, the jacket as you stated, but the killer used only the sleeve, possibly with his arm still in it," he suggested. "Good evening, monsieur." He and Martin disappeared up the dark staircase.

The two men moved quickly through the office to the front door of the morgue and outside. Standing on the stoop, Beauviér adjusted his gloves tight over his hands. "What did you discover, Sergeant?"

Martin held up the slip of paper. "It's a claim ticket for the hat. It's from Le Cheval Noir."

"Well, that confirms the dead man was Fouchét's brother, Sergeant."

"But you thought that all along, Inspector."

"I suspected it, yes," said Beauviér, walking slowly down the steps.

"Then why didn't you tell the coroner of your suspicions?"

"Because you might have noticed that he is a man of peculiar efficiencies," he replied, stepping onto the sidewalk. "He would be on the phone to Brussels right now with the information and, no matter what I feel about Fouchét, he cared for his brother. To tell the man of his brother's death on Christmas Eve, well, struck me as unnecessary." He took a deep breath. "A day or two will make no difference."

As the two men walked casually along the sidewalk, Martin said, "Who do you imagine killed him?"

"For the moment I am uncertain. It could be any one of them. They're all here, and motives seem to be abundant."

"But there is no sign of Ian Musters."

"Oh, he's here, Sergeant. You can't have theater of this level without the director in the wings."

The two men came to an intersection and, though there was no traffic, they stopped at the corner.

Martin said, "And you found something in the dead man's possessions, Inspector?"

Removing the business card from his side pocket, he handed it to Martin. "Only this, Sergeant. It looked interesting."

Studying the card, Martin asked, "You intend to see where he might have sent flowers, monsieur?"

Beauviér grinned. "No, Sergeant. Our dead man is just as likely to send some flowers this evening as he ever was in the past." He turned to face Martin. "That card was simply handy when he needed to write something down. Look on the back."

"Well, I did notice that, monsieur, but it meant nothing to me."

"What does it say?"

"December twenty-fifth."

"Right, and that's tomorrow, so it hasn't happened yet."

"What hasn't happened?"

"Look at the word below the date."

"*Ondine*. What is that?"

"I don't know, Sergeant." Beauviér stepped off the curb. "I only said it looked interesting, I didn't say I knew what it meant. Come with me."

Walking briskly to the middle of the next block, the two men stopped in front of a small hotel. Without a word, Beauviér walked inside. Martin followed.

The small lobby was empty. A wood-burning heater in the corner warmed the room; in the opposite corner sat a Christmas tree laden with pulsating lights. A porcelain nativity scene covered a table next to the reception desk and next to that was a hall tree holding two coats.

Beauviér went to the desk. "Is anyone there?" he called.

A door closed, then footsteps shuffled along the wooden floor. A middle-aged man appeared at the end of the desk, moving cautiously toward him. The man seemed as wide as he was tall. He skated forward, never entirely lifting either foot from the floor. He lifted his hands slightly from his side, the palms turned up, as he said, "Messieurs, good evening. A room is it? Or two? I have a lovely top floor—"

Beauviér held up his hand. "I would like a newspaper. You sell them?"

The desk clerk's enthusiasm did not diminish as he replied, "I do, monsieur, but I'm afraid I have received nothing since Saturday. All of the papers are... expired, I guess you'd say." He chuckled.

"That's all right," said Beauviér. "Would you have a copy of *De Gazet?*"

The clerk leaned under the counter. "I'm certain I do," he said, speaking to the floor. Slowly lifting a stack of newspapers from under the counter, he let them fall onto the desk. "They only give me one copy when they deliver, but I rarely sell it, or any of the Flemish papers, for that matter." He licked the tip of his plump forefinger, but kept it in the air as if to dry, using his middle finger to push back the corners of the newspapers. "*De Gazet*, is it?"

"Please."

Sliding a newspaper from the pile, the clerk spun it on the desk to present the masthead. "There you are," he said jovially. "You see, however, it's from last Saturday. Perhaps you'd like to see the local journal?"

"No," Beauviér replied, lifting the newspaper from the desk. "This will be fine."

"I'm sorry, but I must charge you, monsieur, as I am still liable for it."

Beauviér nodded. "Sergeant," he called.

Removing change from his pocket, Martin moved to the desk. He counted out thirty-five francs and handing it to the large man, turned to see Beauviér seated on a small couch by the wood heater. As it was the only place to sit in the small lobby, Martin stood by the arm of the couch, his hands folded behind his back.

"I want you to tell me the difference between this newspaper and *Le Soir*, or *Le Figaro*, or *The London Times*, for that matter," said Beauviér, laying it on the coffee table before him.

"Monsieur?"

Opening the newspaper, Beauviér tried to make sense of a language he did not speak. "It has been troubling me since a copy of this newspaper was found inside Ian Musters' car," he said, flipping to the next page. "Now, I know you feel it was simply left there accidentally by someone, though I don't think so. I believe he purchased a copy of *De Gazet* and I would like to find out why."

Martin said, "I'm able to count to fifty in Flemish, and I know the days of the week, I believe, though that's all, I'm afraid."

"But we have determined Ian Musters does not speak it either, Sergeant," he said gruffly. "We are getting away from the point. There is something different here and I would like to find it."

"Yes, monsieur." He leaned forward to study the newsprint.

Beauviér flipped to another page. Pointing at the top corner, he asked, "What is that?"

Martin lowered himself to one knee. "I am really not certain of the second and third words, but it appears to be publicity for a flower exposition in Holland, monsieur."

Beauviér grunted and flipped to the next page.

Martin said, "Have you considered the personal advertisements, Inspector?"

"Of course, Sergeant, that was my first thought. However, that makes little sense. First, no one in this affair appears to be either Flemish or Dutch. A clandestine message to Ian Musters would do him no good written in Flemish, and in English it would stand out too much. No, they would then use the *International Herald Tribune* or a British paper, and certainly one more accessible than *De Gazet*."

Turning each page slowly, he reached the last one and sighed, looking again to the headlines. He was about to speak when the corpulent desk clerk appeared beside them carrying a tray, half in his hands and half on his stomach.

"Messieurs, I thought I might bring you a coffee," said the fleshy man and gently placed the tray in the center of the newspaper.

"That's very nice of you," said Martin.

"Not at all." The large man pointed his thick finger at the two cordial glasses next to the cups of coffee and said proudly, "That is some pastis my wife and I make every Noël. It's all from our garden." He pushed his pudgy hands together and grinned. "But it is made with only anise, some herbs, and there is no wormwood that might cause hallucinations or addiction. This, I can assure you."

Leaning back in the couch, Beauviér said solemnly, "But it is nevertheless illegal in Belgium to fabricate your own pastis, monsieur."

The man's puffy eyes widened. "You called him a sergeant, didn't you?" he said to Beauviér.

"I did. And I, am Inspector Beauviér."

Staring at the two men, the heavy man stood motionless.

"Monsieur?" said Beauviér.

"Yes, Inspector?" inquired the desk clerk nervously.

"Does the name, *Ondine* mean anything to you?"

"*Ondine?*"

"Yes, monsieur, *Ondine*. Possibly it's the name of a business here in Mons or on the outskirts of town. Or possibly it's the name of an auberge, or hotel like yours for that matter."

The large man considered the question for some time, glancing occasionally at the cordial glass in front of Beauviér. "No, Inspector," he replied, finally. "There is no business I am aware of in Mons, or her environs, called that. It is quite unusual, and I would most certainly remember the name, *Ondine*."

"Yes, I thought as much, monsieur. Thank you for your time and for the—" Beauviér lifted the cordial glass from the tray and ran it under his nose. "That is very nice, but you might want to consider adding the wormwood next year," he said indifferently. "It gives it an extra sense of taboo that seems to be lacking."

Apparently uncertain what to do or say, the fat man took a step backward and mumbled, "Yes, monsieur."

Beauviér said, "My father made it that way and we were very popular this time of the year."

"Yes, monsieur," he repeated, taking another step backward, "I'll remember that," and shuffled from the room.

Martin lifted his cordial glass from the tray. "Your father made absinthe, monsieur?"

Beauviér shook his head. "No, he didn't. But by confessing to a crime, the desk clerk knows I'll not pursue his. And besides, that would make me a hypocrite." He tapped the edge of his glass against Martin's. "Merry Christmas, Sergeant."

"Merry Christmas, Inspector," Martin said, grinning.

After taking a drink, Beauviér placed his glass on the exposed corner of the newspaper, its damp base forming a small ring next to a Flemish word—a word that would eventually lead them to what they were searching, and distinguished *De Gazet* from every other newspaper in the world.

* * *

Tom Breck stood in front of the tired mirror, its aluminum backing all but gone. Searching for pieces of his reflection, he was darkening his sideburns with hair oil, creating the man he would be for the next twenty-four hours. There was the blue jumpsuit and beret tilted neatly to the side, though somehow they seemed less believable. He questioned that it would allow him an edge with the Belgian border police; he wondered if such a disguise would fool anyone.

Adjusting the collar of the jumpsuit, he knew that either way, this would be the final performance of Jean-Paul Van der Elst, delivery driver for *World Express Transport,* freight carriers and customs brokers centered in Brussels, Belgium, with offices worldwide. It was the last act of a sordid play.

His image in the peeling foil was increasingly bothersome; the looming apparatus of the cement works just behind him. Its reflection appeared like a maze, the gray steel pipes twisting like cockatrice that he must turn and face. But it represented nothing more than his fears, the possibility of failure. He turned quickly, his footsteps echoing off the dormant machinery as he made his way to the waiting cargo, the black boots slapping the concrete floor like those of a soldier, or a customs man. He then heard the Freightliner's diesel engine idling and beneath its clatter, the voices of two people speaking. Rounding a stream of conveyer belts, he saw Yuri and Tatiana standing by the trailer.

Turning to look at him, she said, "I did not recognize you, Thomas."

He didn't respond to her comment. "Have we checked everything?" he asked. "Are we ready?"

Yuri replied, "Yes, I checked those things you asked me."

"Good." He looked to the newly painted stencils on each section of the gun. They stated that each tube was one of four, beside identification numbers corresponding to the documents Tatiana had fabricated. After the string of numbers, the words *Tremor Suppressant Column* were written in English, French, Dutch, and then German, as the item was presumably manufactured in Austria. The name of *Magellan Armaments-Belgium* had been meticulously removed, then painted over. The breech was covered with a tarpaulin, though could easily be inspected by customs with no serious concern as its design was only slightly different from the remainder of the gun. The polished interior of the tubes had been coated with handfuls of dirt to reduce the luster and any unnecessary questions. The original intent of the four black pipes had been masked, though Tom knew any elaborate scrutiny could end all that, along with everything else.

"You've double-checked that the identification numbers match the documents?" he asked Tatiana.

"I have and they do, Thomas."

He put his hand on one of the stenciled numbers. "Even though they are contrived, as are the documents, they must agree. If they don't, customs will not let it go and we'll have trouble."

Gripping the documents, she asked, "Would you like me to check again?"

Tom nodded. "Please." He then asked Yuri, "The wheels and tires on the Freightliner and trailer are all fine?"

"Yes, Thomas, you know they are. We both checked them."

"I know, but we must be certain of those things we can control—there will be enough we can't," he said, over the sound of the idling engine. "A simple thing like a flat tire could be disastrous."

Sounding fatigued, Yuri asked, "Would you like me to look at them again?"

"There's an additional trailer we can cannibalize," he said, pulling on the cable that held the gun in place. "So, yes."

Yuri began checking the eighteen wheels and tires.

Tom threw his satchel between the seats of the cab and climbed inside. Pressing on the brake pedal, he called through the open window, "Do the brake lights work?"

"Yes," yelled Tatiana.

He flipped on the turn signals, watching them reflect off the walls, then checked the headlights, Yuri and Tatiana moving toward him in their wake.

"The tires are good," called Yuri.

"And the numbers match," said Tatiana, handing Tom the documents.

He took a deep breath and said, "Then let's go. Yuri, get the door."

Tatiana climbed into the passenger seat beside Tom, but neither spoke as they watched the bay door slowly rise, the morning light creeping in. It was muddy outside, with a layer of fog that cut off visibility any further than the passing road. A good morning for moving bad things, reasoned Tom as he engaged the transmission, edging the Freightliner out of the abandoned factory into the pale of the winter day.

Bringing the truck to a stop just clear of the bay door, he looked at Tatiana, her face somber as she gripped his forearm with her hand.

"I'll see you soon?" she asked, seeming to know the question useless.

"Very soon," he replied.

"You'll call me in Buenos Aires when all is well? I mean, even if you can't come straight away, just to let me know."

"I will. I promise."

The passenger door opened. Tatiana lifted herself from the seat, making room for Yuri, who said, "Everything is secure."

Tatiana then sat on his lap, her feet dangling between the two seats. "It doesn't seem like Christmas," she said softly, staring out the windshield into the fog. "It doesn't seem like anything at all."

The air brakes let out a muffled groan, loosening their hold as the Freightliner rolled forward, down the drive to the road.

* * *

Pacing nervously by his parked car, Francis Dwyer glanced at the captain of the *Mary Celeste* through the early morning fog. The two men were on the narrow canal road connecting the seaports of Zeebrugge to Oostende. A rarely used road, no car had gone by in the last forty minutes and there were no distinguishable sounds save the distant foghorns of the North

284

Sea. If their presence in this lonely place had earlier instilled calm, it was now gone.

The captain of the *Mary Celeste* took a long drag on his cigarette, then called, "Do you think they're coming, Francis?"

"I do, Liam," he replied, guardedly, staring into the mist. "They'll be along."

"We've been waiting over an hour."

"I know, but the road's not that easy to find even without this soup hanging about our eyes."

"And you're certain this is the place?"

Francis nodded, though his movements were all but concealed in the fog. Squinting down the canal road, he exclaimed, "There's a car."

Headlights had appeared, looking like distant fires, bobbing as they advanced. The beams crept along the black asphalt, slowly drifting across the two men and into their eyes. Stepping forward, Francis lifted his arm in a greeting, but there was no response from the car's occupants.

Liam said softly, "It mightn't be them, Francis."

"It must be."

"But there's another one coming," Liam cried, the cigarette dropping from his hand.

Facing the opposite direction, Francis saw more advancing headlights. This car's pace was also unhurried and an American make like the first.

Biting on his upper lip, he took a step back as the second car came to a stop, its headlights on him. A door opened, then voices spoke in whispers. The first car backed up, quickly falling from sight. Then a door closed.

A tall figure appeared on the passenger side of the stationary vehicle. "Is that you, Mr. Dwyer?" called a man's voice.

Francis recognized the unusual accent. "It is. Are you Aram?"

"I am. Who is with you, Mr. Dwyer?" he asked sternly.

Francis stammered, "It's—it's the captain of the *Mary Celeste*."

"You were to be alone, Mr. Dwyer."

Francis glanced at Liam. "But you never told me that on the telephone. You never said nothing about being alone."

"It was understood, Mr. Dwyer."

"Well, he can leave then. I mean he's seen nothing. Would you like that?"

There were more whispers in the fog. Another door opened, then closed. Suddenly another man appeared, wearing a brimmed hat that shadowed his face; he carried something about his shoulder. Squinting, Francis saw that it was the strap to an automatic weapon, its barrel pointed toward the canal.

Aram called, "What is his involvement with this affair, Mr. Dwyer?"

"I told you that," he said anxiously. "I mean, I told you what he'd be doing."

"Humor me, Mr. Dwyer."

Nervously, he ran his tongue across his lips and said, "He'll be helping me pirate the gun onto the *Mary Celeste*."

Aram took a step forward, his face still concealed in the mist. "They'll most certainly try and stop you, Mr. Dwyer."

"Yes, but we have the advantage of surprise."

"That doesn't sound like much of an advantage, Mr. Dwyer."

Lowering his eyes, he said somberly, "We'll do whatever is required to get the gun."

"And then who will the gun belong to, Mr. Dwyer?" Aram inquired, cutting across the headlights to the near shoulder of the road.

"You," Francis replied.

Aram walked along the gravel shoulder, gripping a large duffel bag with one hand, a briefcase with the other. Stopping beside Dwyer's car, he said, "That is correct, and I think it very important that, like us, the captain of the *Mary Celeste* understands the gravity of this affair."

Glancing at the man with the automatic weapon, Francis then looked at Liam, who was clearly uncomfortable. "If he didn't, he does now."

"That's good. Very good," said Aram, letting the duffel bag fall onto the hood of the car. "Open that, if you would, Mr. Dwyer."

Francis now saw the man clearly for the first time. He thought the face handsome, the tanned skin accenting light green eyes that were gentler than the words the man spoke. He stood a head above Francis, who was himself taller than most men. But it was the demeanor of the man that made him most intimidating and equally, convincing.

"Open that, Mr. Dwyer," Aram repeated.

Unzipping the bag, Francis spread out the sides and stared at the contents.

Aram said, "The advantage of surprise can be very useful, Mr. Dwyer," and reached into the bag, removing a white rectangular brick slightly larger than his hand. "But this is more tangible than being light on your feet." He tossed it to Francis. "It is made in Czechoslovakia and is considered the most reliable. I requisitioned this from a nasty little man who lost his bearing, among other things. It is Semtex, a plastic explosive that can be detonated by electrical impulse, or fuse if you prefer, and I would like you to use this to heighten your advantage, as it were."

Studying the white explosive, Francis nodded. "We were to do it another way."

"I understand that, however, failure in this affair would be unacceptable and this gives a certain closure, if you will. You'll find the fuses and batteries underneath the Semtex." Taking the brick from Francis, he then lifted the briefcase at his feet and placed it on the hood beside the bag. "Open that, Mr. Dwyer."

Francis ran his palms down the front of his pea coat, then slowly reached out, sliding the latch buttons of the briefcase with his thumbs. The lid jumped open slightly and he gripped it, pushing it back completely.

Aram said, "As per our agreement, there is eight hundred thousand American dollars. You may count it if you wish, but if I were going to deceive you, Mr. Dwyer, there are certainly other ways." Picking up one of the bundles of hundred dollar bills, he ran his thumb down the end as if along a deck of cards. "You will see the numbers are sequential, but that should not be a concern, as they were drawn from a friendly bank and I' m not about to inform the police as to their whereabouts."

Francis lifted a bundle from the briefcase and glanced at Liam, whose nervousness appeared to lessen at the sight of the money.

Aram then added, "Which brings me to a necessary request."

Returning the money to the briefcase, Francis said, "I'm listening."

"Unfortunately the police have been rather persistent in their pursuit of the gun and of those involved. I was hoping they would have faded away by this point, but it seems there are two gendarmes that have nothing better to do."

Francis squinted at the tall man. "Yes?"

"As we discussed, it is essential to rid ourselves of all those concerned with the gun so in the future there will be no need wasting time looking over our shoulders, so to speak," Aram said calmly. "Though sadly, the police have become a part of the equation, Mr. Dwyer. So to fulfill your obligation to me it is necessary that the two gendarmes be eliminated."

Francis' narrowed eyes widened. "You want me to kill them?"

"I want them to go away, Mr. Dwyer. How you accomplish that is your responsibility from this point on. Do you understand?"

He looked down at his feet and said, "Two coppers."

"You've received a great deal of money for services not yet rendered," Aram said firmly. "So I expect full compliance with our original arrangement. Well, Mr. Dwyer?"

Francis studied the briefcase on the hood of the car, then the duffel bag behind. He faced Aram. "Very well."

"Good, that is very good." Aram clasped his hands behind his back. "Now there is one final issue and then I will leave you."

Francis took a breath and exhaled deeply. "What is it?"

Aram smiled for the first time, revealing his perfect white teeth, and said confidently, "This will be the one and only time we shall meet, Mr. Dwyer and Mister..." Still smiling, he looked at the captain of the *Mary Celeste*. "It is Liam isn't it? Liam Campbell, I've been led to believe... Well, gentlemen, if you ever see me again it will be because you have failed in your duties and our next meeting will be very brief." Raising his arm, he pointed at the near canal.

The man carrying the automatic weapon fired a volley into the still water. A dozen shots cut a straight path to the opposite shore, their sound muted by an extension on the barrel, which added to the simplicity of the demonstration.

Aram turned and walked away. Moving from the shoulder of the road to his waiting car, he neither spoke nor glanced back at the two men who were only just looking away from the canal. Doors opened and closed on both sides of them as they stood motionless, but only one car came into view, moving quickly by.

A distant foghorn sounded, then all was again quiet.

* * *

Jules Beauviér sat on the edge of the disheveled bed, his elbow resting against his closed suitcase. A chest of drawers sat opposite him, a placard of holiday greetings from the hotel management sat on top beside an alarm clock the guest was obliged to wind. It read either five minutes before noon or midnight, both of which were wrong. Taking an impatient breath, he glanced at his watch. It was one minute after ten o'clock Christmas morning and Sergeant Martin was now late, though Beauviér did not mind. Bending forward, his forearms on his knees, he rubbed the top of one hand with the palm of the other, gazing at the worn carpet at his feet. He was troubled, knowing he would have to inform the Gendarme Brigade in Brussels the state of the affair he'd been tracking. The brigade would in turn inform the Director General, who'd then relieve Beauviér of his duties. And there was nothing he could do to prevent it. He had failed.

There were the smugglers and the forgers and a murderer or two, but he had nothing but trails leading nowhere. If he could only have found the common denominator keeping these people together—but time was up. He had informed Martin that if they did not find something tangible by last evening they would then report all they knew and face the inevitable. It was Christmas day and Beauviér's career was over.

A low voice spoke at the open door of the room. He lifted his gaze to see Sergeant Martin standing in the hallway, his overnight bag draped from his shoulder.

"Did you hear me, Inspector? I'm sorry I'm late," he said, "but I thought it best to try and retrieve the car from the garage. The man at the desk mentioned I might have difficulty, with it being Christmas and all. But I didn't. It was automated; everything is becoming automated these days. So, monsieur, shall we go? The car's right out front."

Without a word, Beauviér dragged his suitcase from the bed, nodding at Martin to go ahead. The two men descended the stairs, went through the lobby and out the front door of the hotel to their car.

Martin placed both suitcases in the trunk as he glanced at Beauviér who appeared distracted. "Is there something the matter, Inspector?" he asked sympathetically.

His head cocked slightly to the side, he said, "They're gone, Sergeant. They're all gone."

"Inspector?"

"The American, the Polish woman, Ian Musters... They were all here, and now they're gone."

Martin's brow wrinkled. "Yes, Inspector."

"So if I know so much, why don't I know where they are? Is that what you're thinking, Sergeant?"

Josef Kraus

"No, monsieur," he answered quickly. "It's just that you shouldn't be so hard on yourself. We were dealing with professional criminals and—"

"And they got the better of the professional cop, is that what you want to say?"

"No, Inspector, of course not," he said resolutely, "and you should never think like that. After all, it was you the Gendarmerie called to bring in *Les Maudits*, and you did. They had the finest of the police and military, and they still brought you out of retirement. Would they have done that if you were not considered the best?" His eyes narrowed. "Though unfortunately, we went against those with unlimited resources, their crimes are quite ordinary until you put them all together."

"And they continue," Beauviér grumbled, putting on his gloves, "so, come on, Sergeant. Let's be on our way," and climbed in the passenger side.

As Martin started the engine, Beauviér said, "I have never seen a criminal in my life who did not stop the crime when he knew there was a police presence. But these people keep on like they were simply going to market for a bottle of wine. What is it they need to do? And what makes them so brazen?"

"The money must be great, Inspector," he suggested, pulling away from the curb.

"Possibly."

"Well if not, then what?"

"I don't know, Sergeant. I don't know."

Martin drove them onto Place Léopold, past the gothic cathedral of Sainte Waudru. The police barricades were now down, leaving no indication a murder had been recently committed, though Beauviér refrained from looking, his eyes fixed on the road ahead. They continued, through the empty streets, following the signs that would take them back to Brussels and the end of an affair which began with the death of an art dealer in Namur.

Beauviér was thinking to all of it, from the very beginning. He was back in his office, the telex from the prefect of police in Namur before him. Might be worth looking into, he had written to Beauviér, though again, might be nothing at all. Maybe the painting's a forgery; maybe this Breck fellow is wholly innocent; and just maybe a Chief Inspector of the gendarmerie would have more pressing issues before him: a man dropping dead of a cardiac, bits of dirt coming to the surface—why it happens all the time.

Beauviér shook his head as their car stopped at a red light, the autoroute to Brussels just ahead. There was a sense of anger in him, and of embarrassment. He had failed so completely, stumbling like the old man he suddenly felt he was. When he was younger none of this would have transpired and nodded at the thought: a younger man should have been on the case. In a few years that might well be Sergeant Martin directing such an investigation. But now there was only the return to Brussels, empty-handed, imagining the final words spoken between him and Martin; they would be full of good-byes and feeble wishes of future happiness. Not wishing their relationship to end on such a note, he was about to speak when Martin accelerated through the red light, turning the wheel sharply to bring the car round.

They were now heading in the opposite direction, and moving quickly.

"What are you doing, Sergeant?" demanded Beauviér.

Pushing the car faster still, he said, "That car ahead, the silver Mercedes. That's the same one I saw in Namur and then again in front of Stuart Endfield's apartment."

"Which one?" Beauviér asked, leaning forward slightly.

"The silver Mercedes, two cars ahead."

Beauviér's eyes narrowed. "But it's just a typical Mercedes, and you said you didn't get the license number that night."

Martin shook his head. "But you're wrong, Inspector," he said excitedly. "That is a 450 SEL body, but it has a seven liter engine—don't you see? There are the two numbers on the trunk lid."

"Yes, I do see it."

"They are extremely rare," Martin said, veering right as the car just behind the Mercedes turned off. "That's the same one, I'm certain."

"Don't get too close, Sergeant," said Beauviér, rubbing his gloved hands together. "Where's he heading?"

"I'm not—"Martin lifted his hand from the steering wheel to point at a passing sign. "He's taking the autoroute east, it looks like... Yes, there he goes."

Their black Peugeot sedan settled in, remaining five car lengths behind the Mercedes as they moved onto the autoroute east, hugging the far right lane.

"If he decides to accelerate, we've had it, Inspector," said Martin.

Beauviér glanced at the speedometer. "I understand, Sergeant. But he appears to be doing the limit."

"For the moment," he murmured.

"Can you see who's driving?" asked Beauviér, scribbling down the license number.

"No, his headrest is up too high. I can't tell. Should I get closer?"

"No. Stay as you are. Do we have plenty of fuel?"

"Yes, almost a full tank."

"Good, stay with him, Sergeant." The corners of Beauviér's eyes crept up. "We just might have something."

The two men then fell into an understanding of silence, speaking infrequently during the next forty minutes as the Peugeot kept pace with the silver Mercedes, always maintaining a distance of five to six car lengths, though slightly more when there were long sections with no exits. The Mercedes going no faster than the posted signs, its driver being reluctant to break the law, or was in no immediate hurry.

As they approached the border with Luxembourg, Beauviér wondered aloud, "Now where?"

"I don't know," replied Martin, glancing at a road sign, apparently weighing the endless possibilities: Germany, France, Luxembourg; north again to Holland, the cities of Basil, Strasbourg—even Vienna was mentioned.

"His license plates are French," commented Beauviér.

"I don't think that means anything."

"No, I suppose not" Beauviér agreed, then exclaimed, "He's got his turn signal on."

"I see, Inspector, I see."

"It looks like Luxembourg."

"Yes, but not the city."

Grunting his agreement, Beauviér said, "He's on the roundabout, Sergeant. Not too close."

"But I must see the exit he takes."

Beauviér scooted forward, watching car after car fall away, disappearing into one or the other exits on the roundabout, but the Mercedes kept to the inside lane, taking none.

"What's he doing?" said Beauviér, lifting his hands, palms up.

"I don't—look, he's now heading west, back toward Mons."

"Did he see us, Sergeant? Is he playing a game?"

"I don't know. I don't think so.

All right, drop back," ordered Beauviér. "We'll see what he's up to."

Cautiously accelerating the Peugeot, Martin let the Mercedes gain on them as both cars gradually picked up speed on the westbound autoroute. The traffic was now sparse, with little to conceal the trailing black car except for a light rain that had commenced. After a minute, Martin turned on the windshield wipers. The driver of the Mercedes did the same.

For more than an hour the two cars moved along the autoroute, their speed varying only slightly as the rain turned briefly to hail and visibility worsened. The Mercedes remained in the center lane, the Peugeot in the far right.

They moved past Namur and the turnoff to Mons with little comment. As they entered the highway ring that encircled Brussels, traffic became heavier. The Peugeot moved closer to the Mercedes, the additional cars aiding in its concealment and exits becoming more numerous. The Mercedes drove past each, continuing on the autoroute, again heading due west.

"Now what's he up to?" asked Beauviér.

Martin exhaled deeply. "I don't know, Inspector. There is Ghent coming up."

"Right, and if he were heading to either Holland or France he would have certainly taken the roads out of Brussels," Beauviér said, tapping the window button to let in fresh air.

"Unless he's going to Lille or Calais," considered Martin, loosening his grip on the steering wheel for the first time.

Beauviér sat back in his seat, his eyes fixed on the silver Mercedes.

After twenty minutes the two cars moved past the town of Ghent, the speed and the distance between them constant; five to six car lengths, 130 kilometers an hour, as it had been for over two hours. The rain had become a steady drizzle; the windshield wipers slid intermittently across the glass to interrupt the monotonous view, though neither man was bored.

Suddenly, the Mercedes accelerated.

"What's happening?" cried Beauviér, sitting up.

Martin did not speak, but pushed the gas pedal to the floor.

"He's pulling away from us, Sergeant!"

"There's nothing we can do, Inspector. The Mercedes is too fast."

Beauviér glanced at the speedometer; it was creeping up to 160, then 170. "He's going to lose us!"

Reluctantly Martin said, "He's lost us, Inspector," and slowly lifted his foot from the accelerator, the needle of the speedometer touching 190 before beginning to fall.

"What are you doing?" Beauviér yelled, rapidly moving his eyes between Martin and the road ahead.

"The tachometer was in the red, Inspector," he answered. "Another minute at that speed and the engine would have exploded."

"I don't care about the engine, Sergeant!"

Martin did not speak for thirty seconds, then said, "We still would have lost him, Inspector." He glanced at Beauviér. "That Mercedes can do 250 kilometers an hour if it needs to. And it can do it all day long. We didn't have a chance."

Beauviér stared out the windshield to the seemingly eternal asphalt. The Mercedes was gone. "Pull over, Sergeant," he demanded.

Martin did not immediately stop the car, but continued on for another kilometer to a small rest area. Pulling off, he drove into the first parking space and shut off the engine. Without a word Beauviér got out.

Martin looked at the Inspector through the rain-streaked glass, well knowing the loss of the Mercedes had been devastating to him. It was the one last connection with those they were chasing. Everything else they knew, now seemed of no help.

The gun used to kill Stuart Endfield was .223 caliber, according to ballistics, and the killer's blood, or that of the man wounded at the scene, was type O. Both facts were useless with neither the murder weapon nor a suspect in custody. The links with Le Cheval Noir seemed all but exhausted with the death of Fouchét's brother, the man called Mégot. The deaths were so different; the murderer might not be the same, as Roger Catchpole was now presumed a suicide. And the gambling markers had become worthless, with their only connection to the town of Mons thoroughly investigated. But the silver Mercedes was something different. It had been in Mons, Brussels and Namur, and it was certainly on its way to the next crime. It had taken the two gendarmes across Belgium on a fool's errand, to end up in Flanders, just a few kilometers from the coast.

Martin's eyes became thin slits as he remembered the item found in Ian Musters' car. A newspaper from Antwerp called *De Gazet*; it fit in nowhere, and was inexplicable, but Beauviér thought it meant something; it was too obscure an item to be purchased by chance.

A flock of seagulls landed in the parking area. Through the mist, Martin watched them gather on an island of grass, searching for food round a trash bin. His eyes widened and, climbing out of the car, called out the Inspector's name, quickly walking toward him. Martin waved his arms to express a point as Beauviér removed something from his topcoat pocket.

Returning to their car, the mood of both men had changed.

Excitedly, Beauviér said, "Take us deeper into Flanders, Sergeant. We must find an open market."

Martin obliged, racing the Peugeot back onto the autoroute, passed the scattering seagulls and toward the heart of Flemish Belgium.

* * *

At the crest of a knoll overlooking the coastal town of Zeebrugge, Tom Breck brought the Freightliner to a stop, its diesel engine clattering as he stared through the windshield to the bottle-shaped harbor below. There were few ships moored and but one crane in operation, a handful of longshoremen working underneath. Only a skeleton crew had been deployed to work the docks this day—after all, it was Christmas.

Taking a package of cigarettes from the dash, he offered one to Yuri, though his gaze never drifted from the harbor.

The two men had driven from Mons to the coast with only a few words spoken between them. Shaken by the departure of Tatiana, Yuri initially seemed inconsolable, asking repeatedly why she could not be with them, constantly rubbing his eyes to hide their watering. Then for the last hour, he had gazed out the side window and said nothing more.

As the cigarette smoke floated out his open wind-wing, Tom thought of the fog-shrouded street corner in Mons earlier that morning, then of Tatiana and Yuri. They had stood outside the garage where Yuri's car was hidden, embracing each other while speaking in whispers. He held her like a man holding his wife and she, like a woman holding a brother. The differences to Tom had been clear, though they seemed unaware. He wondered about Michelle, did she hold *him* like a brother?

Tom took a long drag on his cigarette, his eyes moving along the cyclone fence that ran the perimeter of the wharf. It had but one entrance, a large retractable gate beside a one-story building with numerous parking places adjacent, all of them vacant.

He said softly, "Customs is empty."

Yuri did not immediately respond, then finally asked, "Is it closed today?"

"No, it's just not busy."

"Should we return later?"

"I don't think it's going to get any busier," he replied, studying the tranquil wharf. "They'll have all the time in the world to inspect the cargo. This is not good."

He considered aborting the attempt with such little traffic, but that was impossible. All had been planned for this day and nothing could be altered regardless of added risk. He must think of a way to improve his odds.

Lifting his foot from the brake pedal, he inched the Freightliner down the knoll, onto the perimeter road. Straight ahead and behind, the road was empty, only the looming customs house just ahead. Painted a brilliant yellow, like a warning signal, the one-story building crept toward them as Tom turned in the entrance, immediately shutting down the engine. Restarting the engine, he again shut it down. He repeated this practice three more times and said, "I'm going to unlock the hood, Yuri. I want you to get under it and stare at the motor like you know what you're doing, all right?"

Not questioning the order, Yuri jumped out, climbing onto the bumper. Tom adjusted the beret on his head, hesitating at the reflection of Jean-Paul Van der Elst in the side mirror. He wondered briefly if he had it in him, if he had the strength to spew any more lies. And would anyone believe him, regardless. He took a deep breath and jumping from the cab ran up the ramp to the front door of the customs house, another deep breath, and went inside.

Gently closing the door behind him, he studied the quiet room. There were eight desks in a single line, each flush to the far wall, though only one was occupied. A man in a dark red customs uniform sat in a chair, his feet on another, reading what looked like a movie magazine. A cigarette burned in a near ashtray while somewhere in the background, a radio chattered in Dutch. A telephone on one of the desks rang once.

Slowly lifting his eyes, the customs man glanced at Tom, then looked to the row of windows just behind him as if searching for a truck with cargo to inspect.

In French, Tom said, "Good afternoon."

The customs man did not reply.

Clearing his throat, he then repeated his greeting, but in accented English.

The customs man grinned, and also in English said, "Good afternoon."

Having found the officer's preferred language, Tom moved to the counter separating the desks from the entry and asked, "Are you open all day?"

Expending little effort, the customs man nodded. "Twenty-four hours a day, like every day."

"Oh," Tom said, sounding pleased. "Of course, I was uncertain with it being Christmas."

The customs man squinted. "Your first time dropping cargo at the port?"

"Yes, sir."

Letting his magazine fall onto the desk, he asked, "Well, where is it?" and crushed out his cigarette in the ashtray.

"I'm having a little trouble with my truck. But it's just outside." He pointed over his shoulder. "Could you have a look?"

The customs man stood and moving around the counter went up to the bank of windows. He stared at the Freightliner with its hood up. "I heard it dying on you out there. American truck, is it?"

"Yes, sir," he replied, sounding frustrated. "I can't get it going. It just won't start. Could you check the cargo where it is?"

Shaking his head, he said, "Nope," and pointed at a large painted rectangle on the asphalt directly in front of the customs office. "You see that yellow box?"

"Yes, sir."

"Well that is where the truck must be parked before I can inspect it," he said apologetically. "It marks the beginning of no-man's land." He waved his arm toward the docks. "Like the wharf, but anything before the yellow box, well, is out of my jurisdiction."

"Is that right?" said Tom, sounding impressed.

297

"I'm afraid it is. So you'll just have to get your truck started." The customs man studied Tom's clothing and the name sewn by the breast pocket. "I'm sorry, Jean-Paul, but... Say, you could have it towed up to the inspection mark and from there to your ship if you're behind schedule. Would you like me to give a call?"

"No, no that won't be necessary," Tom said quickly, unprepared for such accommodation. "But it's very kind of you. I'll just work on it for a while and see what happens. You're open all day, so we'll be all right."

The customs man kneaded his lips with his fingers. "I forgot to say customs will close at two o'clock. I'm alone today and it's Christmas. That's my break."

"Of course. You must have a break," he agreed, moving toward the door. "At two o'clock, is it?"

"Yes, for about an hour."

Tom went outside and, giving the customs man a guarded wave through the glass, moved quickly down the ramp to the Freightliner.

Standing beneath Yuri, who was almost on top of the engine, he said, "Did any tools come with this truck?"

Yuri squatted on the edge of the bumper. "Yes, I believe so."

"Good, then get them and spread them out on the ground." Tom glanced at his watch. "We need to look busy for an hour and ten minutes."

With the pretense of repairing the troubled engine, as much as keeping out of the rain, Tom and Yuri sat underneath the front fender of the Freightliner while they waited. In the last hour only one truck had entered the harbor. It carried cargo of stacked flowers, and the customs man had taken his time with it, inspecting several of the wooden flats; questioning the driver incessantly. If given too much time, the agent was clearly dangerous.

Tom wiped away the mist that had collected on the crystal of his watch. It was eleven minutes before two o'clock. He would still wait before starting up the Freightliner, before moving it into the yellow box for dissection. The customs man would be obliged to inspect the cargo, although with less scrutiny so as not to interfere with his upcoming break—a quick peek under the tarpaulin, a few checks on the export form, a passing comment about the weather, and that would be it.

Tom glanced again at his watch. It was eight minutes before two o'clock. Now was the time.

"Pick up all the tools, Yuri," he called, sliding out from underneath the fender. "Don't bother wrapping it up, just throw everything on the floorboard and get inside."

Pushing the hood closed, Tom climbed inside the cab and started the engine. Black plumes shot out the exhaust pipes, carried by an offshore breeze they rolled across the hood of the truck, temporarily clouding the view. Through the clearing smoke, he saw the agent coming out the doorway as he accelerated, rolling the Freightliner into the yellow box. He jumped from the cab and ran to the covered stoop where the customs man stood.

"What luck," he said, clapping his hands together. "I got it started in time."

Looking down, the agent's brow wrinkled. "In time for what?"

"Why, in time for inspection," he reminded the customs man. "You said you would be open until two o'clock."

"I did," the man agreed, tapping his left wrist with his forefinger. "But it is now after two, so I'll see you in about an hour."

Pushing the rain from his eyes, Tom looked at the wall clock inside the customs office. It was not yet two o'clock, though it would do him no good to contradict the agent's sense of time, and only replied, "Yes, sir."

Moving to the harbor gate, the customs man walked it closed before securing it with a padlock. "But you'll be first in line when I return, Jean-Paul," he said encouragingly

Tom gave a dry grin. "So I will," he whispered, watching the customs man climb into a yellow Fiat and drive away.

Angrily, Tom looked at Yuri in passenger seat of the truck, his face quizzical as if waiting for an explanation. But Tom had none other than he'd pressed his luck too far; cut the time too close and he knew better. A customs man likes breathing room, time to look around, ask those silly little questions that Tom had answered a thousand times before. It wasn't difficult if handled properly. Just say, 'Yes, sir,' or 'No, sir,' even shine a little light on it for them. 'What are we smuggling today, Mr. Breck? Is it a giant gun? Why how lovely.' They'd never say that, they'd never know what you had, not really. Follow them around like a big dumb puppy; let them think they're clever, let them think you're impressed with every word they utter. Tom knew the rules, but he didn't apply them and now he understood why. Thomas Breck had been scared. He didn't know if it was because of the gun or he'd simply lost his nerve, or just maybe come to his senses. That would be the cheap excuse, the one for confessional, but he hadn't seen a light, some vision requiring a drastic change in lifestyle—an option being to find a job come Monday morning, assuming anyone would hire him. 'We notice a little gap in your résumé, Mr. Breck. The last fifteen years seem to be unaccounted for, would you mind elaborating? You haven't been in prison by chance?' Prison, thought Tom. Sure, why not? After all, that's what a job was, a prison of measured time. He could return to school and in six years be a doctor or in just two a lawyer, 'Your Honor, on behalf of my obviously guilty client...' No, it wouldn't do, even if he embraced such a thought. Tom Breck was in too deep and the only honest alternative to his current dilemma was to run. An alternative he found extremely unacceptable.

The rain was falling harder now, the closed gate before him with an attached sign *All Trucks Must Stop For Inspection.* His eyes moved across it, then to an opening just before the cyclone fencing commenced. He glanced back at the truck and as he took step toward the opening a horn sounded, startling him. A car had turned into the entry and without stopping, drove quickly through the opening in the fence.

It was suddenly clear: authorized cars had unlimited access to the harbor, but no truck would dare drive through this opening with customs open twenty-four hours a day, every day.

Except this Christmas day.

Tom ran to the Freightliner and scrambling inside the cab, engaged the transmission, moving the truck forward.

"What's happening?" cried Yuri, his eyes fixed on the narrow gap in the fence they were approaching.

Tom said loudly, "We've just been cleared by customs. Hold on." Accelerating, he shifted up one gear.

Yuri grabbed the door handle with both hands, saying nothing more.

The Freightliner cleared the fence poles by no more than the width of a man's hand. However the trailer's sides, being disproportionately wide, scraped against the metal barrier and the truck began slowing. Tom quickly downshifted as the front end of the Freightliner began bucking, though gradually advancing, black smoke rising from both the exhaust and the rear tires. Then it broke free, at last through the opening and onto the wharf. Racing along the creosoted timbers, Tom glanced about the harbor. There appeared to be no witnesses, he prayed there were none, and said, "Look for our ship, Yuri."

The two men studied the names of each moored vessel they passed. They were of varying nationalities and tonnage, but none was the one they were searching. Then on the stern of a towering freighter, a Scottish flag came into view, and on the bow, sloppily painted in white, was the name *Ondine*. Tom pulled the Freightliner beside it. A man stood on the stairs leading to its elevated wheelhouse, watching Tom jump onto the dock. Walking toward the vessel, he called into the rain, "Who are you?"

The man yelled, "My name is Liam Campbell. I'm here to help you load the cargo. Are you Thomas?"

"I am. Where is Francis Dwyer?"

"He couldn't be here, though you're not to worry. Everything is all right."

Tom stared at the man, recalling his accent, the Irish accent. It was similar to Francis Dwyer's but quite different from John Clark's. "Well, here it is!" he cried.

Abruptly, the whistle of the *Ondine* sounded three times—two long, one short.

Yuri climbed out of the Freightliner, falling in behind Tom as they made their way up the ship's stairs that draped the hull like a high-rise fire escape. Reaching the deck's gunnel, they looked out across the docks to see an elongated flat truck with an attached crane moving rapidly toward them. The driver was exposed to the rain, as were the four men directly behind him. They all wore metal helmets and were dressed in the bright yellow of the stevedore.

Liam Campbell called from the stairs of the Captain's bridge, "There's nothing more for you to do, Thomas. Those men below will take care of everything and there's no need for you to stand in this weather."

Tom had turned to look up at him, but said nothing.

"The second door from the aft on your side of the ship, you'll find the galley, Thomas," he continued. "There's food and drink and you can dry yourselves. I'll be along shortly, after all's secure."

Tom looked to Yuri who was drenched, looking like a lost dog on the ship's open deck. "Let's get inside, Yuri," he advised.

The two men followed Liam Campbell's direction and finding the galley, shut the door behind them. Although the room was quite large, the ceiling was low and all was painted in white. The only furnishings were a rectangular table in the middle of the room, a dozen chairs placed neatly around it. The table itself was clear save for an unopened liter bottle of Scotch at the near end.

Tom grabbed it and took a long drink. Briefly shivering, he moved to the near porthole. Through the rain-streaked glass he could see the longshoremen, their yellow jackets dancing like confused bees as they adjusted two cables around a section of the gun. Soon it would be out of the way; soon the first part of the journey would be complete.

Lighting a cigarette, he used the match to ignite the now useless documents that Tatiana had meticulously prepared. They burned quickly, turning to flecks of ash on the steel floor, and he looked again to the longshoremen working the crane, watching them lower the first section of the gun gracefully into the ship's hold. The second followed, then the third. In the thirty minutes that followed, Tom smoked an additional cigarette before the final steel tube was hoisted from the trailer and placed out of sight. There was a crashing sound as the cargo hatch sealed tight against the weather and sea, and any prying eyes. The longshoremen then departed, waving at the bridge of the *Ondine* as they drove away, rapidly vanishing into the fading light of the day.

Continuing to gaze out the porthole, watching the harbor lights sparkle in the falling mist and darkness, Tom asked abruptly, "How does your shoulder feel, Yuri?"

The whiskey bottle slid along the wooden table. "My shoulder?" he asked with surprise in his voice.

"Yes," he said. "Where you hit it on the open cupboard door. Has it healed?"

As if just understanding the question, he replied, "Oh yes, Thomas, it's much better."

"That's good. I noticed you favoring your other arm, and I was concerned if I could count on you."

"You can count on me, Thomas," he said reassuringly. "I won't let you down."

"Won't you?" Tom questioned lazily. He paused, then said, "You know the newspaper reported the man had been injured and that all hospitals should be on the lookout for a gunshot wound."

"What are you talking about?"

Shutting the small curtain on the porthole, Tom turned to face Yuri. "Why, the man who killed the Englishman on *rue des Minimes* is what I'm talking about. The assassin was wounded, they said. Shot by a gendarme," he said angrily. "You are that man, aren't you, Yuri? You killed Stuart Endfield."

CHAPTER EIGHT

Through the raindrops off the car's passenger window, Inspector Beauviér watched Sergeant Martin moving about in the small shop. After forty minutes of searching in Flanders it was the first store they had found open, though not originally. The owner simply lived on the floor above the shop, a sign on the door indicated that for emergencies he could be contacted by ringing a bell. And concluding this was an emergency, the bell had been sounded—though now Martin seemed to be taking forever, thought Beauviér as he watched the rain form little rivers on the passing road. He exhaled deeply. The hunt had again proved frustrating, especially if their guess was correct.

Appearing at the doorway of the shop, Martin moved quickly to the car and climbing in, said, "It's today's *De Gazet*, Inspector," as he produced a newspaper from under his jacket.

"Well, open it then, Sergeant."

Flipping the pages, Martin then pointed at something. "That word means *Maritime*, Inspector," he said, running his forefinger down a list of printed names. "The shop owner confirmed it. This is the one thing the Brussels newspapers do not have. Let me see the card please."

Handing him the business card found in Mégot's possessions, Beauviér said, "The name is *Ondine*, Sergeant. Is it there, or isn't it?"

Martin was using the card to underline the names when suddenly he exclaimed, "Yes, here it is."

"Where?" asked Beauviér excitedly.

Martin jabbed at the name with his finger. "The port of Zeebrugge, monsieur," he said, moving his eyes to the top of the page. "Yes, that's where it is, the inner harbor. The *Ondine* arrived last evening at five minutes before midnight, from Aberdeen."

Beauviér clapped his gloved hands. "How far are we away?"

"Forty, maybe forty-five minutes," Martin replied, shoving the newspaper between the front seats.

"Well, let's get going." He glanced at his watch. "And try and get there before dark."

Martin pulled away from the curb. "Should I use the siren?"

"That's what it's for, Sergeant."

The braying sound filled the rain-soaked streets as Martin pushed the Peugeot into the first curve, flashing the headlights to clear the way. The tires slipped against the wet surface, though Beauviér said nothing while the speed increased almost recklessly. The final opportunity had presented itself and he would not let it escape. This was what he had been looking for.

The forty-five minute drive from northern Flanders to the port of Zeebrugge took less than thirty. As the Peugeot came onto a knoll overlooking the harbor, Beauviér said, "Shut down the siren."

It was now quiet except for the faint hum of the engine and the moan of the windshield wipers against the glass.

"There is the outer harbor, Inspector," said Martin, indicating the ocean side of the port, its lights glittering in the dusk. "The locks to get to the inner harbor are just beyond."

"All right, Sergeant. But now let's keep our speed down."

The Peugeot rolled down the knoll and as they reached the road that ran parallel with the harbor, Martin's eyes drifted to the cyclone fencing just alongside. Suddenly braking, he pulled to the shoulder of the road.

"What are you doing, Sergeant?" demanded Beauviér, grabbing the dashboard to keep from falling forward.

"There it is, monsieur," exclaimed Martin, pointing toward the wharf.

"Is what?"

"The *Ondine*, monsieur."

"That's not the inner harbor."

"I know. But there it is, nevertheless," he repeated, indicating a distant freighter, the name *Ondine* clearly painted on her bow.

"So it is." Beauviér studied the cyclone fence. "There's an entry by customs."

Martin drove to the customs building, stopping at the entrance. "Should we let customs know we're here, Inspector?" he asked.

"It appears closed. Keep moving, Sergeant," he ordered, pointing to a gap in the fence. "Go in there."

Martin cautiously advanced the car through the opening and onto the pier, the rain adding to the darkness as the daylight diminished. "Look, Inspector," he said, squinting in the gloom. "There's a large dark-colored truck like the janitor in Mons recalled. It's an American truck."

Beauviér stared at the parked Freightliner. "Maybe the old man wasn't so intoxicated after all," he admitted. "Move next to it, Sergeant."

Pulling alongside the trailer, Martin shut off the engine. The Peugeot was now concealed from the *Ondine*, but the two men could still make out her stern to midship.

"What did they bring here on this truck?" said Beauviér as if to himself. Then looking to the freighter, he observed, "There's someone in the wheelhouse."

Martin glanced at Beauviér. "I'm not familiar with boats, Inspector."

"The top of the ship," he explained, pointing at the bridge. "And there are also lights on the main deck toward the rear. That appears to be all."

Martin stared at the dark vessel and swallowed. "What do we do, Inspector?"

Beauviér reached for the door handle. "Let's go see who's home, Sergeant."

"But, Inspector, shouldn't we call for assistance?"

"Assistance for what? Because a business card we stole from a dead man out of our jurisdiction had the name of some ship written on it? Is that sufficient? What's an *Ondine*, Sergeant?" he demanded, slapping the newspaper between their seats. "For all we know it might be the name of a hospitality girl at Le Cheval Noir which Mégot fancied, or possibly a horse full of drugs in the third race at Milan. No, we have nothing to call assistance on, Sergeant."

As if he were going to disagree, Martin looked again to the ominous freighter, but only said, "Yes, monsieur."

Both men got out of the car and, hunching forward, quietly shut their doors. Beauviér went to the front of the Freightliner, briefly looking about the dock, then moved toward the stairs pressed to the freighter's hull with Martin following two paces back. The nightfall was complete and the rain now fell in a steady drizzle, obscuring the men as they made their way up the steps. Pressing their hands against the frigid hull, they struggled to keep the suspended stairs from knocking against the ship. Neither spoke as the metal treads under their feet moaned with each step.

Reaching the deck, they moved toward the stern, their backs tight against the bulkhead, stopping short of a curtained porthole. Aware of the muted voices on the other side of the glass, Beauviér ducked his head and moving underneath the porthole, pressed his ear against the near door. He listened briefly, then indicated that Martin should follow. The two men moved to the next door and as Beauviér had done with other, placed his ear against it. He listened for over one minute, then carefully opened the door, revealing a cabin that was pitch dark. Cautiously entering, he whispered to Martin, "Do you have a match?"

"No."

"Shut the door."

Gently, Martin obliged. The two men then stood motionless, listening to the muffled voices in the adjacent cabin.

As his eyes adjusted to the darkness, Beauviér could distinguish two portholes, each an arm's length apart, though they brought in no discernible light. Quickly removing the glove from his right hand, he pressed his bare palm to the bulkhead connecting the next cabin and moved it slowly across the surface. He touched a vertical row of rivets, then a protruding plate of steel. Using the tips of his fingers to feel his way, he walked slowly alongside the bulkhead and deeper into the cabin.

Feeling an indentation just above his head, he squatted, following it with his fingers until it stopped just above the floor. Removing his other glove, he used both hands to touch the face of the indentation until he discovered a doorknob. It was round, unlike the outside handle, and he imagined it might go unnoticed if it were gently turned. Glancing at Martin, whose features were lost shadows, he felt the door ease away from the jamb. The muted voices were becoming clear as he placed his ear to the narrow aperture. Martin moved beside him, their movements guarded while they listened.

Suddenly the voices stopped. There was the sound of an object scraping along the floor, then something struck an apparently hollow object.

A man's voice cried, "Why!"

"To end it," replied a second man's voice. "To end it all, Thomas."

Beauviér's eyes narrowed when he heard the name. It was the American.

"You kill a man so easily, Yuri?" bellowed Tom Breck.

Beauviér's jaw tightened. The Polish woman's bodyguard was also just beyond the door. Now, he had at least two of them.

Yuri pleaded, "They were destroying us. I had no choice."

"Who was destroying us, Yuri? Who?"

"Mégot and... and the Englishman."

"Stuart Endfield was a pawn, blackmailed into his position. He wanted out as much as any of us. There was no reason to kill him."

"I didn't want to," he protested. "I wanted Mégot, but I couldn't get to him. He was sick and only wanted the ransom money."

"The million francs?"

"Yes."

"You took it from Stuart Endfield?"

"Yes, yes... But I didn't spend any of it. I only took it so they wouldn't have it."

"They? You mean Mégot?"

"I mean all of them."

"Who else is there, Yuri?"

There was a pause before he replied, "The kidnappers... the ones that took Tatiana."

"Who took her?"

"The police. The Hungarian state police took her," he cried. "But I found them, and I stopped them."

"How did you stop them, Yuri?"

The room became quiet.

In a weak voice, Yuri said, "When Tatiana was freed by the kidnappers, she told me what had happened; how she was treated and their ways with her. I saw the weight she had lost and how scared she still was. Then she told me where they had taken her— the hotel on the Danube. It was only thirty minutes away. All the time she was so close." He cleared his throat and his voice became less timid. "But I knew the hotel and when I put her to bed that morning I got in my car and drove there. I wanted to find Mégot, to make him pay for what he had done."

"Kill him, like you did Stuart Endfield?"

"Yes!" he cried. "They had taken her away from me and that was not the..." He did not finish the sentence.

309

"The what, Yuri? What was it not? What else had they done?"

Ignoring the questions, he said, "When I arrived at the hotel I looked for Mégot but he was gone. There were only the two policemen. They were still there, drinking wine in front of the fireplace like they were on holiday." There was a loud noise, as if a fist had slammed on a table. "And when I asked them why they had taken her, they laughed."

"Then you knew them, Yuri? Or did they know you?"

Again ignoring the questions, he continued, "I asked them to leave her alone; to leave us alone, but they said they would do what they wished. That they were the police and the decision was theirs when it would be over."

"And what did you do when you heard this, Yuri?"

The room was again quiet. Then Yuri said, "Do?"

"Yes, what did you do?"

"The skinny one told me to get out—to go home and stay with my Polish whore," he answered, his voice shaky. "So I shot them; both of them—once in the head and once through the heart. I had to be certain."

"Of course you did, Yuri," said Tom Breck calmly, as if he concurred. "And Mégot?"

"I… After I killed them, I became frightened and ran away. I drove around for a while, an hour or so, or maybe longer, I don't know—I had forgotten why I went to the hotel, then I remembered Mégot. I knew I had to find him, so I went back and found the two policemen as I had left them, but their sedan was gone," he said, his voice mechanical. "Mégot *had* been there, but he got away."

Still motionless, Beauviér listened intently to the confession describing the deaths of three men, knowing he must be patient.

Tom Breck asked, "But the Englishman, Stuart Endfield. How did you know he was to collect the money?"

"Mégot told me."

"Why would he tell you this?"

"I don't know. To keep me informed."

"Then you were working together?"

There was no audible response and Beauviér let the door ease toward him. He tried to see either of the men in the next room, but he saw nothing more than the vacant end of a table.

Finally, Tom Breck said, "Who came to you about this, Yuri?"

"Came to me?"

"Yes, about the smuggling of the gun. You know it's a gun, don't you?"

Beauviér scowled when he heard these words, thinking again to the large truck parked on the pier.

"Oh, it wasn't like that at all, Thomas. No, it was—" He paused. "But you already know, don't you, Thomas?"

"I know some things, but I would like you to tell me about it, Yuri."

"No, I want you to tell *me*! How do you know?"

Something scraped against the floor, possibly a chair, then Tom Breck said, "Though John Clark suspected you from the beginning, I refused to believe it. He didn't know you like I did, but it was in Barbizon that I understood. When Tatiana and I were in the dining room and you were supposedly busy putting away your car, it took you almost thirty minutes to join us, your excuse being you had made a call to Budapest about the house. That you had it for sale."

"But, I did," he protested.

"Yes, you did, and I imagined you thought yourself clever, if by chance I had seen you on the telephone. But the next morning, when I paid the bill, there were three telephone numbers written on the bottom. The owner of Les Charmettes noted them when you made your calls from the booth by reception. You had paid in cash, but the numbers were still there and the owner pointed them out to me. He told me they were taken care of—I wasn't to concern myself.

"I wasn't to concern myself," he repeated, seeming to mock the words. "There was one call to Budapest, like you said, then two to Brussels. One was to the home of a man named Fouchét. I discovered he's a petty crook and assumed, after not too much thought, that he was also the man called Mégot, as no one would be born with such a name. But it was the other number which truly frightened me. It was to the telephone of a man named Ian Musters. Someone I knew a very long time ago. Was he the man that came to you, Yuri? Did he offer you something you didn't have?"

Something fell to the floor, and Beauviér let the door creep open further, observing a chair on its side but neither of the men inside.

Yuri cried, "He offered me what was mine! There was to be nothing new I wanted, but what I once had."

"You mean Tatiana, don't you?"

Another chair crashed to the floor. "Yes," he exclaimed.

"But she would never leave you."

311

"You don't understand," said Yuri, moving into Beauviér's line of sight.

"I understand that she loves you."

"Is it me she loves, Thomas?" he demanded. "No, it is not me. It is you she speaks of in such ways. I have just become someone who carries the luggage and shops at the market like a servant, and for no other purpose am I tolerated. She would never consider me for her lover as long as—" He stopped his reproach, mumbling something inaudible.

"You don't believe that?"

"I do."

"So you decided to get rid of me, is that it?"

"No, not at first. It was not like that. It was only jokes in the beginning."

Tom Breck's voice was unsteady. "Jokes?"

"Yes, jokes. A practical joke, he called it."

"You mean Ian Musters?"

Yuri nodded. "One evening, or late afternoon I guess it was, we met by accident in Budapest at the Hotel Gellert; in the bar, the one downstairs by the baths. We got to talking about things and places, and he mentioned Brussels. He asked me if I knew the city, but I didn't really. Just said I knew a man who lived there and told him your name. He acted surprised, telling me what good friends you had been in Canada, but somehow you'd lost touch—I think that's what he said, lost touch. And we spoke about how we would get together and wouldn't it be fun if we surprised you. You know, play a trick on you. He came up with all of these funny games to do to you… They were funny at first anyway, and then as we drank more they weren't so funny. They were dangerous and cruel, and I knew it," he said calmly, as if in penitence.

Then leaning forward, he picked up one of the fallen chairs, gripping the back with both hands. "I knew then that we both wanted the same thing. There were no more jokes. I wanted you to go away and he… I don't know. He wanted more than that, but I didn't care as long as you were gone."

"It was not by accident you met, Yuri. But you know that now," said Tom. "So you told him about the paintings?"

Looking to the floor, he replied, "I knew not to, but then later, it was days later, I mentioned something about them."

"Why, Yuri?"

"Because without the paintings you'd be gone. There would be nothing to keep you and Tatiana together, and she would stop waiting for you—that is what she was doing all these years. She was waiting for you to change your mind about her." He ran the palm of his hand across his eyes before gripping the chair again. "Tatiana told me why you married the French woman. She said it was because of her beauty and one day you'd see the mistake. And she spoke of the way you surrounded yourself with the expensive home and the cars and all of those things that don't matter." He lifted his eyes. "Don't you see how she loves you? And she was willing to wait forever until you did."

There was long silence. "You are right. I did not understand."

Sitting down in the chair, Yuri said, "I'm very tired."

Tom Breck moved beside him and righting the other chair, sat down. He then spoke softly, the words hard to make out. Beauviér let the door open yet further.

"Were you going to divide the money from the sale of the paintings?" Tom asked.

Yuri jerked his head up. "No, no, no," he cried. "Don't you see anything? I didn't want the money. I didn't want any of it. Ian Musters could keep everything as long as you were gone."

"But then you and Tatiana would have nothing."

"Nothing? No, you are wrong. We would've had each other, like before, and no Thomas Breck appearing without warning to discuss the newest crime." He shook his head. "The way she changed when you were about. Preparing herself and the house as if..." He paused, lowering his eyes, then looked up and said firmly, "We would have nothing? Is that what you see? No, I would then look out for her because I knew a man like you wouldn't be interested in a penniless Polish girl. All that kept you in our lives would be gone."

"You think that of me? You think I would allow Tatiana to be poor? Or you, if I could prevent it?" Tom said. "Listen to me, Yuri. I never meant to intrude."

"But you did," he yelled.

Tom Breck slowly stood, walking out of Beauviér's line of sight. There was the sound of something knocking, then a bottle of whiskey slid along the table, stopping near Yuri's hand.

313

Tom spoke, though the words were barely audible, as if he were facing away: "Was it Ian Musters who stole the Renoir from me in Namur? Was he the one who attacked me?"

Yuri touched the label of the whiskey bottle with the tip of his forefinger, before gripping the bottle's neck. "No," he replied and hurriedly took a drink.

"But Mégot was ill, you told me this much. How was he capable?"

Returning the bottle to the table, he replied, "He wasn't," then wiped at his mouth with the back of his hand. "He began this just like me, only wanting one simple thing, but then it dropped from our hands."

"Then who? Who took the painting?"

As if he were discussing nothing more serious than the falling rain, Yuri said, "I did, Thomas. I took the Renoir and I was the one who attacked you."

"You, Yuri? Why? Why would you?"

"Because Ian Musters kidnapped Tatiana. He betrayed me so I had to get the painting away from all of you. It was safer with me."

"But why did you attack me the way you did?"

Yuri sat back in his chair. "Because I blamed you. Because I hated you."

"I would have gone away at any time, had I known—had you told me. Do you see what you have done? We are all running, and for what? For jealousy and a practical joke that leaves men dead?"

Sitting motionless, Yuri said nothing.

"Why didn't you kill me too, Yuri?" asked Tom, his voice breaking. "You had the chance in Namur. You had me on the ground in the art gallery and you're stronger. You were going to, weren't you?"

"Yes, Thomas, you're right. I was going to, but they still held Tatiana and I was uncertain if they would free her with you dead. It would've been easier for them to simply drop her in the river, once she was no longer important. No one would care if a Polish girl were found floating in the Danube." He turned to face Tom Breck. "There was just me, so I let you live."

"And now?"

"Now, Thomas? I'm not sure," he replied, reaching into his jacket pocket, though his exact movements were hidden from Beauviér. There was a thud on the table that could have been the whiskey bottle, but it hadn't been touched.

Tom Breck said, "Is that what you used to kill Stuart Endfield?"

Before Yuri responded, Beauviér softly closed the door and turned toward Martin's shadow in the darkness. "Give me your gun, Sergeant," he whispered.

There was a rustling sound, then Beauviér felt the cold steel press into his hand. Instinctively, he pushed the release to free the clip, but stopped before it fell from the handle and asked quietly, "Is it fully loaded?"

"Yes."

Beauviér struck the butt of the semi-automatic with his palm, then facing the door, brought it back till Yuri was again in view. He had turned in his chair and was now gripping a black pistol in his right hand, seeming to admire it.

"It is only a .223 caliber, Thomas, but it's very effective," commented Yuri, "and not as loud as you might think."

"How many more people are you going to kill?" Tom asked, his voice strangely calm.

"I can't have Tatiana find out what I've done, Thomas. After the kidnapping was over I could have told you what I knew, but Ian Musters threatened to expose my involvement unless I continued keeping him informed."

"What makes you think she doesn't already know?"

Slamming his fist on the table, Yuri bellowed, "You think I am a fool?" He stood, pushing the chair away with the back of his knees. "That is why you sent her away, and she agreed because it came from you, but not a word to me. You didn't ask what I thought. You both treat me like I'm stupid—the taxi driver from Warsaw who gave a little girl a ride and that is all you think of me. Someone who can chauffeur and stow the luggage properly."

"You are wrong, Yuri. You are wrong about all of it."

He didn't respond, only stood motionless, the black pistol dangling in his hand.

Beauviér ran his tongue across his lips. He was waiting for the right moment to throw open the door and disarm Yuri, one way or the other. Suddenly his dark cabin filled with lights from the pier below. He closed the door and murmured, "Go see what that is."

Quickly, Martin moved to the porthole, though just as he looked through the glass, the lights shut down. He remained there for a few seconds, then, returning to Beauviér, whispered, "It's the silver Mercedes."

"What?"

"Yes. The driver's coming toward the ship."

Beauviér closed the door before him, then moved rapidly to the porthole.

Into the night, through the rain that now fell in sheets, he watched the driver of the silver Mercedes appear at the top of the boarding stairs. The man hesitated, then seemingly drawn by the lights from the galley, stepped toward the covered walkway. He was slight, much smaller than Beauviér would have imagined, although there was something familiar. He squinted at the advancing figure, then quickly fell away from the porthole, his back to the bulkhead. Searching for Martin in the shadows, Beauviér said softly, "It's the Polish woman."

* * *

Shivering by the yet unanswered door, Tatiana announced herself, then twice more in brisk succession. She folded her arms about her chest, glancing down the narrow walkway as the delay was making her nervous. She thought she'd heard Yuri's voice on the other side of the door, but now she was uncertain. He would not keep her waiting.

About to call out her name again, the brass handle drooped, then turned down fully as the door crept open, the galley's lights streaming into her eyes. She stepped cautiously over the raised threshold and into the galley, the door closing quickly behind her. She now found herself face to face with Tom Breck, his hand still pressed to the handle. His expression was somber and showed a curious displeasure. She expected a word of admonishment for disobeying his wishes to flee the country, but nothing to match the look on his face.

She gave an innocent smile, which he didn't return, and was about to speak when she noticed Yuri, his back to her at the far end of a long dining table. He stood motionless, his arms at his side and his head bowed.

"Yuri." She took a step toward him. "What are you doing that you can't say hello to me?"

He made a noise, a clucking sound in his throat as if he were grasping for air, but didn't turn to face her.

Tipping her head to the side, she took another step forward. Her mouth opened slightly, wanting to speak, but then closed. She looked back at Tom.

When their eyes met, he said, "What are you doing here, Tatiana?"

"I—I don't understand," she said sharply. "What is happening?"

He ignored her words. "You're supposed to be away. You were to be on a plane by now, Tatiana. We had agreed."

"Agreed? Yes, I agreed, and it was for my safety—or that is what you led me to believe." She looked again at Yuri, still stationary at the far end of the table. "But there is something else going on here. What is it?"

Neither man replied.

Letting his hand fall from the door handle, Tom said, "Would you like to tell her, Yuri?"

His bowed head nodded slightly.

"You knew you'd have to sometime. One day it would come out," Tom continued. His tone became loud and unsteady. "You must tell her, Yuri."

"I…" Yuri's voice trailed off.

"Tell her!"

Slowly lifting his head, he said, "I betrayed you." The words were soft and barely audible.

"What?" She flashed an awkward look at Tom, then again faced Yuri. "What are you talking about?"

Yuri turned, offering his profile to her. "I only wanted us to be together, Tatiana."

"Together, Yuri? But we are together," she said, desperately trying to understand.

Yuri cried, "No, we are not! Not like I wanted," and then faced her.

"This is crazy," she said, looking at one man, then the other. "Are you—" She was staring at the pistol in Yuri's hand. "What is that?" she asked, pointing at the black weapon. "What do you have there?"

Yuri lowered his dark eyes.

Tom said softly, "That is the gun he used to kill the Englishman, Stuart Endfield."

"Shut up," cried Yuri. "Just shut up."

Tatiana said to Tom, "You're wrong," then turned to address Yuri. "He is wrong, isn't he? Tell him he's wrong."

Yuri said nothing.

Staring at her friend of twenty years, she felt lost, unable to speak. The man who saved her, the man who protected her, now looked so different—his shoulders slumped from the weight of the pistol and a terrible crime admitted with his silence.

Tom said, "He didn't want to, Tatiana. He only wanted to protect you, but it became too much. He was coerced by a man who wanted vengeance on me, a man who tricked Yuri into it."

Yuri shouted, "You see? You see what you think of me? You believe I'm stupid and didn't know what I was doing, but I did. I understood everything." He stepped away from the table. "I was not tricked by Ian Musters, I knew what needed to be done."

Tatiana said, "And what was that, Yuri? What needed to be done?"

"Him," he cried, pointing the gun at Tom. "He was taking you away from me."

"No, Yuri!" she said, stepping between the two men. "Tom isn't taking me from you. We will always be together."

"But you love him, don't you?"

"As I love you, Yuri. I care for you both."

"It's not the same."

"But it is. It is the same."

Yuri moved another step from the table, removing Tatiana from the line of fire.

"You would kill him?" she demanded. "You would kill him!"

Yuri kept the pistol pointed at Tom's chest. "Yes, I would," he said softly.

"Then it will be finished between us. You will never see me again." Her voice trembled. "Is that what you want?"

"But it's over anyway," he protested. "I killed all of those men."

318

Tatiana gasped. "What men? There are others?"

"Yes, the policemen in Budapest," he answered. "The ones that took you. They are both dead."

"Oh, no," choked Tatiana, turning to look at Tom, her eyes filling with tears. "You can get him away from here, Thomas. I'll prepare the papers. We'll get him away from here, won't we?"

Tom was silent, his eyes hard as he stared past her.

Tatiana exclaimed, "Yuri!" and quickly faced him.

The barrel of the gun wavered. He said, "You would help me?"

"Yes," she answered.

"After I betrayed you?"

"You didn't want to, Yuri. Thomas said it was someone after him, not you."

As Yuri wiped his mouth with the back of his free hand, the gun began to shake harder, his right arm jerking at the elbow. Slowly, as his control of the pistol worsened, he lowered his arm and, pointing the barrel down, began to weep.

No one moved for almost half a minute. The gun tumbled from Yuri's hand, striking the steel floor with a clatter that caused Tatiana to cry out. Suddenly, a door flew open. Two men ran in, shouting commands. Tatiana understood what was happening, but Yuri looked confused. His eyes glistening, watching the advancing men, he knelt and grabbed the black pistol.

One of the men jumped on Yuri, forcing him to the floor. They began wrestling for control of the weapon. Moving quickly, the second intruder raised a semi-automatic, bringing its butt down hard against Yuri's wounded shoulder.

He wailed, and relinquishing his hold on the pistol, rolled to his side, his right hand twitching as droplets of blood gathered within his cupped fingers.

"Stay as you are," Beauviér shouted, pointing the semi-automatic weapon at Tom and Tatiana.

She tried not to move, but failed. Her legs weakened and slowly folded, her body falling onto the floor only an arm's reach from Yuri.

* * *

John Clark turned to look at one of the two men in the shadows of the galley storeroom.

"They're all in now," he whispered. "Are you ready?"

"Yes," replied Liam Campbell.

"Well this is it," he said. "Before the coppers get a chance to organize."

He let the storeroom door open slightly to reveal the brightly lit galley. Studying the placement of each of the armed men, he paused briefly, then said, "Now," and shoving the door open, ran into the galley, a sawed-off shotgun in his grasp. He moved quickly behind Martin, who was attending to the fallen Tatiana, and pressing the two barrels against his neck, said, "Drop the pistol and stand if you will, young man."

Martin didn't obey.

John Clark repeated, "Drop the pistol and stand. I won't ask again."

Beauviér and Martin shared a glance, then the black pistol fell from his hand, striking the floor like the blow from a blacksmith's hammer.

"And you'll be wanting to do the same with your automatic," John Clark ordered Beauviér. "It would be preventing a great deal of bloodshed."

Looking into the eyes of his sergeant, he let the semi-automatic fall to the floor.

Liam Campbell ran to pick up the pistol dropped by the younger man, then moved to the open door the gendarmes had used to enter the galley. Disappearing inside the darkened cabin, he returned momentarily and said, "It's all clear."

"Wonderful," said John Clark, looking at Beauviér. "We saw you come on board from the wheelhouse and we've been waiting patiently in the room opposite, as you've now gathered, for your inevitable entry. Wasn't sure of your exact number though, and it took some time, I dare say. I thought for a moment you were taking a light supper before your gallant entrance, which was thoroughly professional, I must admit."

Liam Campbell stooped near Beauviér's feet and picked up the semi-automatic. He then backed up, his eyes fixed on the gendarmes, to stand beside John Clark.

"One gun for two coppers," John Clark said, glancing at the pistol. "Well, you're most certainly not Irish, gentlemen. Now if you would be so kind as to press your Belgian bums against the near wall, it would be greatly appreciated."

The two gendarmes walked toward the curtained porthole, placing their backs to the bulkhead.

320

"You may lower your arms, monsieur," said John Clark, lowering his shotgun. "And what is your name?"

"Martin, Sergeant Henri Martin," he replied proudly.

"How do you do, Sergeant? The Inspector and I have already had the pleasure at my bar one evening." Nodding at Beauviér, he said, "Inspector."

Beauviér scowled but said nothing.

Tom took a step forward. "John, I—" He stared at the shotgun now pointed at his stomach.

"I'd prefer if you stayed where you were, Thomas," John Clark said, his tone no longer amiable. "You see, since we last spoke, there has been, well, a turn of events."

"What are you—"

"One thing at a time, Thomas," John grumbled. "Now against the wall with the coppers, if you will."

"John—"

"Now! I'll not ask again!"

Tom did as he was bidden and said nothing more.

John Clark turned toward Yuri and signaling with the shotgun, said, "Come here."

Yuri did not move, other than to rub his shoulder.

John Clark's face hardened and he repeated, "Come here!"

Exhaling deeply, Yuri walked the few steps to John Clark, who tilted his head and whispered in his ear. Yuri's expression remained unchanged as he nodded.

"Very nice," said John Clark, whispering in his ear a second time.

Yuri said, "All right."

"Then you understand what I say is true?"

"Yes."

"Well then?"

"It's in my car."

"The silver Mercedes?"

"Yes, in the fender. The left rear fender."

"How perfectly lovely. And the money?"

"It's there also. Welded between the two plates."

John Clark smiled. "Do you see, gentlemen," he proclaimed loudly, "how two potential enemies can quickly become the best of friends? I mean this really is becoming the perfect Christmas." He then nodded at Liam Campbell. "Give him back his gun."

321

Liam Campbell handed Yuri the black pistol as Beauviér and Martin glanced at one another.

"I have traded my dear new friend, Yuri, his freedom in exchange for the whereabouts of the evasive Renoir," bragged John Clark. "It seems it has been neatly cached in the fender of his car all this time, along with the million francs liberated from the recumbent body of Stuart Endfield. How clever." He glanced at Yuri. "Where did you learn such a method, my dear man?"

Seeming to study the gun in his hand, he replied, "Thomas taught me. It was to be used if Tatiana and I needed to get out of Hungary quickly with our money. He showed me how to separate the weld spots and replace them with liquid solder."

"Oh dear, Thomas," said John Clark, laughing. "Another student gone bad. How perfectly dreadful." He then faced Yuri. "Now don't go shooting anyone with that thing. Do you understand?"

Yuri let the hand gripping the black pistol fall to his side.

Taking a step back, John Clark looked down at Tatiana curled on the floor. Her left arm pillowed her head and her eyes were closed loosely, like she was simply dozing. "Is the young lady all right?" he asked to no one in particular, then addressed Yuri: "Help the lass up before she catches her death from the cold of this place."

Yuri's gaze moved slowly to her. His eyes were distant, as if he had only just noticed the fallen woman, but didn't yet recognize her. He dropped the black pistol into his coat pocket and kneeling beside Tatiana, pushed a lock of hair from her face.

John Clark shrugged, looking at each of the three men against the near wall. The two gendarmes stood on either side of the curtained porthole and beside them, Thomas Breck, his back to the outside door. None of them displayed any noticeable fear from the shotgun pointed in their direction.

John Clark said, "Which at last brings us to the point of our being together this Christmas night," and moved two paces forward. "The gun in the hold of this ship." His eyes moved toward Tom. "Did you really think I would risk my life to help you rid yourself of this thing and receive nothing in return? Well, did you, Thomas?"

Tom said nothing.

"Friendship is wonderful, but it doesn't jingle in your pocket and I've always considered it a touch overrated for anything greater than sharing a pint," complained John Clark. "So I felt the need to search out a qualified buyer of the treasure you'd presented to me and, if the price were sufficient, to then sell it on my own. And that's where we find ourselves today. You see, I did find someone sufficiently well-heeled to make it all worthwhile." He addressed Liam Campbell, who stood just behind him, "How much were we offered?"

"Eight hundred thousand dollars, John," he answered briskly, as if waiting for the question.

"Did you hear that, Thomas? Over a half million guineas for a bit of reworked metal," he said excitedly. "Can you imagine me passing up such an offer? And with you doing all of the heavy lifting, it was all too perfect."

He turned toward a moaning sound followed by words spoken in whispers. Tatiana was coming to. With Yuri supporting her, she sat upright on the floor.

"Put her on a chair," ordered John Clark, "and get her a glass of water or some of the whiskey on the table there. Be quick about it."

Yuri helped her walk the few steps to a chair and as she laid her arms on the table, he said, "Would you like some water?"

As if she did not hear him, she reached out and took his hand, now coated in blood from the shoulder wound. "Are you all right?" she asked.

"Yes," he answered, "I—" and lowered his head.

She lifted her gaze to the wall where the two gendarmes and Tom Breck stood.

"Thomas?" she said weakly.

"Don't move, Tatiana. Stay where you are," he said. "This is John Clark, the man who was going to help, but has instead double crossed us and is taking the gun." He did not introduce anyone else in the room.

John Clark bowed slightly. "The pleasure is all mine, young lady." He then returned his attention to the men against the wall. "And of that, I am certain. But do not despair. You haven't missed all that much and awakened in time for the really big news. Now where was I? Oh yes, right.

"If they were willing to pay that much money for one gun, why not two guns? Or three? Or... Well, you get the idea, Thomas. A sort of package deal was in the making. But I had a little bit of a problem as there was only one available and where on earth would I find the others? Initially it was quite a dilemma, till I realized I might as well go to the source." He motioned toward the open storeroom door. "Go find him will you? This is really no time for the man to be bashful."

Liam Campbell went inside the darkened room. After a moment there was the sound of men's voices—both were indistinct, though one was louder than the other.

Abruptly, Liam Campbell reappeared, a smaller man following. Beauviér appeared to recognize him; a moment later, Tom Breck did as well.

John Clark glanced at the two advancing men. "There you are, Mr. Musters. I wondered if you'd possibly lost interest and gone home." He lifted his free arm like a ringmaster presenting the final act. "I'd like you to meet my newest partner in this affair. Some of you know him, some of you don't, but Mr. Musters will be acquiring the additional guns currently being manufactured by Magellan Armaments for the thirsting clients. Ours will be a fruitful, albeit brief, collaboration. So Thomas, you are hereby relieved and no longer required to deliver the gun. You see? There's a silver lining in everything if you look hard enough." He laughed.

Ian Musters grumbled, "I don't see any need for these theatrics, Mr. Clark."

"Theatrics, Mr. Musters? I thought it more informative than that," John Clark rejoined. "Keeping everyone abreast of our little changes."

His tone angry, Musters said, "You've managed to inform the police and everyone involved exactly what we are doing. Do you think that wise?"

"But Mr. Musters," he protested, "if I'm not mistaken you've had your little chat with our dear Inspector Beauviér yourself, and at your invitation. There was even a film provided so it might be easier to follow along." He sneered. "You must tell me about that sometime."

Angrily, Musters asked, "Why aren't these people tied up?" glancing at the two gendarmes and Tatiana, though avoiding any eye contact with Yuri and Tom Breck.

"I thought this prevented any nonessential movement on their part," John Clark commented, waving his shotgun. "However, if it would make you feel more secure." He called over his shoulder, "Get something to secure their hands. In the kitchen storeroom—cut the chords from the appliances if you don't see anything else."

Liam Campbell moved back into the darkened room, returning almost immediately with a large ball of twine. He went up to

Inspector Beauviér, then turned to look at John Clark, who shook his head; he moved to Sergeant Martin, and John Clark again shook his head. When Campbell stood in front of Tom Breck, John Clark lowered his eyes.

"Why aren't those other men being tied up?" demanded Musters, watching Liam Campbell wrap Tom's wrists with the twine.

"Because," John Clark answered curtly, "I don't feel it's necessary, Ian."

"All right, very well. But I want Breck's hands behind his back."

John Clark nodded, and pulling Tom's arms back so that his wrists again crossed, Liam Campbell wrapped the twine tightly in short jerking circles. Finally he gave Tom's shoulder a hard shove that pushed him against the bulkhead.

"Is it secure?" demanded Musters.

Liam Campbell taunted him. "It is. He's of no danger to you now."

Running his tongue across his thin lips, Musters moved toward the outside door. His steps at first were cautious, then more confident. He raised his hand above his head and struck Tom across the face, knocking him to his knees. He quickly stood, blood already running from the corner of his mouth. Tatiana cried out as Ian Musters swung his fist again. Tom ducked to the left, swiftly lifting his right knee. It connected with Musters' crotch with enough force that both men fell backward onto the floor.

Tom struggled to stand, but Liam Campbell pressed down on his shoulders, his large hands holding him in place.

"How perfectly delightful," shouted John Clark, glancing at Ian Musters, who was on all fours, gasping for breath. "I was wondering how long it would be until you two flew into each other's arms. So after all these years, the flame is still there." He laughed, nodding at Liam Campbell who jerked Tom to his feet.

Slowly, Ian Musters stood. Hunched forward at the waist, he lifted his head and again moved toward Tom. Liam Campbell blocked his path.

John Clark said, "That'll be enough of that, Mr. Musters. You have a long sea voyage ahead and there'll be plenty of opportunity for auld lang syne. Besides, it appears necessary that we bind Thomas' legs in order there be a fair scrimmage, if you catch my meaning. Didn't your mum let you play outside with the other children, Mr. Musters?"

His face flushed with anger, Musters shook his arms free from Liam Campbell's hold and began unbuttoning his topcoat.

Sergeant Martin nudged Beauviér, motioning with his head toward Musters as the man slowly removed a bright red scarf from his neck.

Noticing the gendarmes' interest in the scarf, John Clark smiled. "Well, I'm sure you'll all agree that this has been a perfect evening, but it's now time to be on our way." He glanced at Liam Campbell. "Get ready to cast off," he ordered, and moving toward the two gendarmes, said, "Let's go."

"What are you doing?" demanded Musters.

"I'm taking the coppers off the ship."

"But you're returning?"

"No, Mr. Musters, I'm not."

"That was not our arrangement."

"And the coppers were not in the arrangement either. Would you prefer that they come along or should we be done with them here?"

"I... I'm not sure."

"There's been a change of plans, Mr. Musters, and it's necessary that you adapt."

"I don't like it."

"Listen to me," John Clark said. "The captain is armed, as is Yuri, who has wisely decided to join ranks with us. He has been given his freedom and may take the young woman with him if he chooses when you reach port. Now this is the only option he has, Mr. Musters, and he'll do anything to protect her, you must know this by now. Please don't forget that being rid of Thomas Breck was as much his idea as it was yours. We're also talking about a great deal of money here. You saw the first installment we received, the eight hundred thousand dollars. Do you think I'd risk many times that amount if I weren't certain of everyone's behavior?"

Musters stammered, "But... but I want Breck locked up. I don't want him loose to talk with anyone."

John Clark called to Liam Campbell, "Is there a brig?"

"No, but there's the storeroom, and I can seal the outer door."

"Well, put Thomas in it."

Musters demanded, "And I'll want the key."

"You'll have it," said Liam Campbell, walking Tom across the galley to the open door.

"It's getting late and it might be best if you got some sleep, Mr. Musters," advised John Clark, pushing the two gendarmes toward the outside door with the barrel of the shotgun. "You may have the captain's cabin; he'll be at the helm all night and won't have use of it himself. It's the next cabin down."

"I—"

"Whatever you want, Mr. Musters. She's your ship till we meet again."

"And where will that be?"

As Inspector Beauviér and Sergeant Martin moved out the door, he said, "The captain knows and he'll inform you in due course, as there just might be a change of port. Good evening to you," and followed the gendarmes into the covered passage.

The storage room door slammed closed.

Walking toward Ian Musters, Liam Campbell tossed him a metal key. "That's the only one to that. The other hatch is battened from the outside. He'll be going nowhere." He turned toward the long table. "You'll help me throw off the lines, Yuri?"

Yuri was caressing Tatiana's head. She was sobbing, her face pressed into her folded arms. "Yes, I'll be right there," he replied.

"And Mr. Musters," said Liam Campbell, opening the outside door. "Would you care to lend a hand?"

Clearing his throat, Musters glanced at his watch. "No, I don't think so. It's getting late and I should get some sleep as Mr. Clark recommended."

Shrugging, Liam Campbell moved outside.

Musters quickly followed only to find the covered walkway empty, the rain blowing up from the docks into his eyes. Hurrying through the darkness, he found the captain's cabin. As he reached for the handle, he heard a voice from just off mid-ship.

"Take good care of yourself, Francis," yelled John Clark into the night.

There was no immediate response, then finally Liam Campbell called out from the stairs of the wheelhouse: "That I shall, John. That I shall."

Musters' forehead wrinkled when he heard the exchange. Shaking his head, he went inside the captain's cabin, locking the door behind him.

Josef Kraus

* * *

By order of John Clark, Jules Beauviér and Henri Martin sat in the front seats of the black Peugeot with their doors locked and their hands folded on their laps. Both men were motionless, staring through the windshield at the *Ondine*.

John Clark possessed the keys to their car and sat playing with them in the back seat. "I noticed some gloves in your pocket, Inspector," he said as he lit a cigar. "You're welcome to put them on."

Still motionless in the driver's seat, Beauviér said nothing.

"As you wish, Inspector," Clark said, lowering his window a turn. "But I'd like you gentlemen to listen to me very carefully, in that your lives depend on following my instructions."

The pier vibrated as the engines of the *Ondine* began to pound. A man moved quickly along the vessel's port side, cutting the mooring lines with a dual-bladed ax. Silently, one line fell into the water, then another, each unheard over the hammering engines. Yellow lights and blue lights fluttered to life, then a flood lamp attached to the wheelhouse came ablaze, searching the water off starboard.

"Soon she'll be gone," John Clark said over the clamor, "and then you'll have a story to tell, gentlemen. Oh yes, you'll thrill the little ones with the tale of the devil ship *Ondine* and her flight from justice." He laughed, coughing briefly on smoke from his glowing cigar. "Now all you have to do is sit as you are and try nothing foolish. We'll need to give her time to clear harbor, then a bit of a head start into the North Sea should do it."

Glancing into the rearview mirror, Beauviér said, "So we won't cause you any problems, you lead us to believe that we will be freed?"

"And you will be."

"But we know everything you've done and everything you've planned."

Adjusting the shotgun on his lap, John Clark took a long drag on his cigar. "No, Inspector," he said confidently. "You know absolutely nothing and that is what allows me to be so benevolent. So, if you'd be so kind as to follow my instructions, gentlemen, let us relax and enjoy the show."

The pilings under the pier started to creak as the rudder on the *Ondine* turned to hold back the flow from the churning prop.

Seawater shot up like a geyser, spraying the docks and the black police car. Direction was then reversed as the ship's bow began to turn away, easing toward the mouth of the outer harbor.

* * *

Ian Musters woke with a start. Sitting up in bed, he rubbed at his eyes to clear them of sleep and peered in the darkness of the small cabin. He listened intently, trying to determine the reason for his sudden waking, but heard nothing other than the groans of the freighter about him.

Throwing his legs off the side of the elevated bed, he stepped into a pair of slippers and shivering briefly, quickly put on a cotton bathrobe, cinching it tight about his waist.

A clock screwed into the bulkhead read three minutes after six in the morning. He had slept a full eight hours and felt rested, crediting the sea air's calming properties for the peaceful night. Still feeling a chill, he wrapped the red scarf about his neck before pulling the cabin door open. He looked both ways down the empty walkway, then moved to the gunwale, placing his forearms on the rail.

The clouds of the evening before were gone along with the rain they carried. Out on the open sea, the dawn light was brilliant on the blue water. The ocean was flat, almost becalmed as it disappeared into the horizon. A cold breeze ran up the freighter's side, tousling his uncombed hair and pushing it across his narrowed eyes. He imagined himself well clear of land and his troubles. Eight hours they had been underway, traveling at twelve to thirteen knots, placing the *Ondine* well beyond the rule of Belgian law.

Turning away from the cold wind, his eyes drifted to a ring-shaped life preserver hanging by the open cabin door. Printed boldly on it was the word *Ondine*, in bright red letters. It had been recently painted and he was pleased to find the captain so fastidious with the ship's maintenance. However, behind the life preserver, the bulkhead paint was peeling and showing rust. The walkway was also heavily oxidized, with large brown-orange spots that ran the entire length of the passage like an advancing disease. The freighter's only sign of upkeep appeared limited to the nearby life ring. Studying the newly painted ring, he pulled at a small edge of attached white fiber. It came off easily in his hand, revealing another fiber strip that was now loose, flapping in the breeze. It was affixed like *papier-mâché*, the gumming solution yet to harden.

He pulled on the strip, then the one under that. The word *Ondine* tore away and another gradually took its place. Taking a step back, he stared at the name *Mary Celeste*. He thought it curious and moving to another life preserver in the walkway, he scraped at the freshly painted letters with his fingernails. Again the name *Mary Celeste* appeared.

Turning in place, he observed a storage bin, the ship's name once more freshly painted and without looking, knew that underneath was the name *Mary Celeste*. He tried to make sense of a ship that would change its name. He thought it against all rules of maritime superstition to do such a thing; a ship must never change her name.

His concern for such a strange event abruptly became unimportant as he realized the reason he'd awaken earlier with such a start. It was not any noise or commotion that unsettled him, but the lack of it. The silence had awakened him. The engines on the freighter were no longer running and the *Ondine*—or the *Mary Celeste*, whatever her name—was adrift.

He thought to run to the wheelhouse but instead went to the door of the galley and threw it open.

There, sitting at the end of the long dining table, was Yuri. His arm hung from the back of his chair, the bottle of Scotch whiskey by his shoulder, empty and on its side.

"Welcome, Mr. Musters," he bellowed, looking back with half-open eyes. "Come in and close the door. It's cold out."

Musters stepped into the white room, shutting the door behind him. About to ask the reason for the silent engines, he saw the door of the storage room wide open. Lights inside it revealed nothing more than shelves containing canned goods and stacked burlap bags.

"Where are they?" he demanded.

"Who?" said Yuri, his tone jovial.

"Breck and Tatiana. Where are they?"

"Oh, they're gone."

Musters noticed beside the overturned whiskey bottle were remnants of twine and a blue Swiss Army knife, its blade exposed. "Gone? What do you mean, gone? That's impossible."

Yuri shook his head in an awkward circle. "No, you are wrong. It is very possible."

"How? How did they leave?" he said skeptically.

"In a boat."

"A boat?"

"Yes, one of the lifeboats."

Musters laughed. "Do you mean to tell me Breck is going to sail them safely all the way to shore in a small boat like... like Captain Bligh?"

Yuri tilted his head to the side as if not understanding the question, then said, "That's it. You're right. They took the captain."

"The captain is gone?" screamed Musters.

Nodding, Yuri smiled. "Yes, the captain sailed them, Mr. Musters. It's now just you and me."

"This is mad," he cried. "Why—why did you let them go?"

Yuri's face became somber. "I had no choice. I had to let them go."

"What? They forced you, is that it?"

"Oh, no. We had a long talk about it and we all agreed. It was for the best."

"The best? But what about the gun? They left it behind with us. We'll... we'll have to try and move this ship ourselves."

"But there's no fuel, Mr. Musters. The engines have taken the last of it."

"No fuel?"

Sitting up straight, Yuri confirmed softly, "No fuel and little time."

"What does that mean?"

Taking a deep breath, Yuri removed a piece of paper from his coat pocket. "That means the buyer of the gun," he paused, unfolding the paper, then began to read, " 'The owner of the gun does not wish to take possession of it.' "

"What are you talking about? What do you have there?"

"Oh," he said, lifting the paper slightly. "I wrote it down as they told me. I didn't want to make any mistakes when we talked. Like right now, I mean."

Musters' voice trembled. "Mistakes?"

"Yes, mistakes." Looking again to the paper, he carefully read aloud, " 'The people that bought the gun were not the ones John Clark led you to believe.' "

"What do I care *who* bought the gun?"

"Oh, I think that makes quite a difference, Mr. Musters. Yes, you see it was not an agent from a third world country like John Clark told you, but the people who bought the gun were from Israel. They were Israeli policemen. They were Mossad."

Musters gripped the handle of the door. "Mossad," he whispered.

"And they don't want the gun—but I already told you that." He lowered his head, using his finger to follow the words written on the paper. "No, they want it to be destroyed and they bought it for eight hundred thousand dollars so it would be. 'It was cheaper and less dangerous for them this way than to launch an aerial attack at a later date.' " He lifted his eyes. "Did you get that?"

"But—but you don't—you don't understand," stammered Musters.

Yuri's eyebrows went up. "Oh yes, I think I understand."

"No, no," he cried, stepping toward Yuri. "It's the gun—it doesn't work! It buckles in the center when it's joined. The weight of the steel is too great and it won't fire. That's why I kept Beauviér on Breck's trail. I mean, think about it. I wanted him to be caught trying to smuggle it so he'd go to jail for twenty years. That's all. But it doesn't really work. It was an experiment by a Canadian gunsmith for the Iraqis and it failed. Just ask them! Magellan Armaments originally made the thing and they're making five more because I asked them, and for next to nothing... Because it doesn't work! Are you listening?"

As if in deep thought, Yuri said, "Maybe you should have mentioned this to someone."

Musters lifted his arms, letting them fall to his side. "What? This is completely mad. Are they intending to let us float out here forever? Or..." His eyes became white circles, terrified. "Are they going to board the ship?"

"Who?"

"The Israelis."

"Oh, I don't think they're that stupid."

"What do you mean? Look, we have to get to the ship's radio and call someone."

"There is no radio, Mr. Musters. The captain took out the little diamond thing that makes it work. No, like I said, it's just you and me until..." Lowering his head, a sad look came over his face. "I wish there were some more whiskey," he whispered.

"Until what?" screamed Musters. "Until what?"

332

Yuri lifted his glassy eyes. "The Semtex."

"Semtex? What is that?"

"An explosive, Mr. Musters; a plastic explosive. It's all around the ship and it's set to go off in…" He glanced at his watch. "In thirty-two minutes."

"What? Thirty-two minutes? That can't be true." But then he knew it to be. "We have to get to it and disarm it! Yes, that's it." Musters moved quickly for the door, stopping as he gripped the handle. "No, no. The lifeboats. Like Breck and the others. Come on, let's get to a lifeboat."

"They took the other one," said Yuri quickly. "They took them both."

Musters stared at him. "Then we get to the explosives. We have time—thirty-two minutes, you said. Yes, that's plenty of time."

"I can't let you do that, Mr. Musters," Yuri declared, removing the black pistol from his coat pocket. "I'd prefer if you stayed here with me."

"Well I'm not going to, you stupid Pole," he screamed. "Stay here like the fool you are."

Yuri pointed the pistol at Musters and pulled the trigger. There was a simple click as the hammer struck the firing pin and nothing more.

"Ha!" said Musters. "You see. They didn't even trust you with a loaded gun. Now what do you think of them—your friends!"

Musters threw the door open and ran into the covered passage, disappearing from sight.

Staring at the black pistol, Yuri pushed a small lever by the trigger. The cylinder fell from the action; it was empty. With his face emotionless, he casually removed a small bag from his coat pocket, dumping its contents on the table. Three bullets rolled about on the uneven wood surface. He picked up one and placed it inside the cylinder, then in seeming afterthought, loaded the other two before moving onto the covered walkway and toward the ship's bow. He quickly descended the ladder leading to the hold. Beside the neatly stacked gun, Ian Musters stood in the shadows, struggling with a series of white squares attached to the hull.

Closing one eye, Yuri lifted the black pistol and cautiously taking aim, pulled the trigger. The sound of the gun firing was weak, but its impact was great. Ian Musters screamed and grabbing his leg, tumbled into the ankle-high water of the freighter's bilge.

"No, no!" he cried, spitting the foul water from his mouth. "Are you mad?"

His arms at his side, Yuri walked deeper into the hold till he stood opposite Ian Musters. For a few seconds Yuri remained motionless, then leaning his back against the hull, slid down it until he was squatting, his forearms resting on his knees. The gun dangled from his hand just above the icy pool that was soaking into his clothing. Neither man seemed aware of the freezing seawater they were in—Ian Musters' painful wound made it unimportant, as did Yuri's drunkenness.

"Look!" said Musters, gripping a clump of black wires in his bloodstained hand. "We can get them. We can get them all!"

Yuri said, "No, you can't. They're everywhere, even in the engine room." His brow furrowed. "They are placed below the waterline and all it takes is one... I think that's what he said."

"We must try," shouted Musters, and attempting to stand let out a cry, falling back into the water. Grabbing his knee with both hands, he lifted his leg to reveal the wound. It was still hemorrhaging. "You shot me."

Yuri glanced at his watch with half open eyes.

"Do you *want* to die?" yelled Musters.

"There are only thirteen minutes remaining, Mr. Musters. I don't believe I have a choice."

Musters' hands fell from his wound, splashing into the water. He stared at the row of white squares attached to the rusted hull, suddenly knowing he also had no choice. In less than thirteen minutes he would be dead.

"Breck," he whispered.

Yuri jerked his head up and glared at Musters. "You blame him for who you are? Is this his fault?" he said angrily. "You blame him for everything bad in your life, don't you? Tell me, what is it he did that made you hate him so?"

Musters cried, "He contrived I be thrown out of school. I was humiliated."

"And you did nothing to provoke this? He did it for fun, Mr. Musters?"

"I was his prefect. His superior! I had a right to—"

Quietly, Yuri said, "I don't think you're superior to anyone."

With his blood-covered hands, Musters tightened the red scarf before pulling his bathrobe fast about his chest to keep out the cold. He was trembling, lifting his gaze to the exposed light bulb over his head. It was a hold lamp that had no switch and was never turned off—burning day and night, it struggled against the creeping humidity of the sea.

He said softly, "Watchmaker."

Yuri jerked his head up, gradually opening his drunken eyes. "What did you say?"

Musters cleared his throat. "How many minutes are left?"

"Not many, Mr. Musters, not many…"

"We are to be blown to pieces? Is that it?" he demanded, nodding at the black pistol in Yuri's hand. "Are there still bullets in that?"

Slowly lifting the revolver, Yuri stared at it briefly before letting it fall from his grip, into the water at his feet. "It was empty." He lied. "There was only the one bullet."

Musters looked to the small bubbles rising from the submerged pistol. Watching them collect on the black water, he said, "I had to crawl on my belly just to get this far. Just to be a secretary with the Embassy. A clerk really, that's all I am and all I'd ever be because of Breck. I didn't have the proper schools in my résumé to be considered for anything more, anything better than a paper pusher with no responsibilities and never any respect… And no corporation would have me. How I tried, oh God, how I tried." He lifted his gaze toward Yuri, his thoughts drifting. "You know my father died when I was nine years old. We said it was heart failure, being Catholic and all, but he had in reality put a bullet in his own head. He only thought of himself and his own humiliation, not ours—my mother and myself."

He coughed, spitting out remnants of the oily water. Then, leaning against the pallets supporting the gun, he took a deep breath and grinned uneasily. "When I was ten my mother married Mr. Black and he took us to Lyme Regis in the southwest of England. He was a simple man but he treated me like his own son; even after my expulsion from school, he told me I could work with him. I wasn't to worry, he said, he'd teach me the trade."

He laughed. "But do you know what he did? He had a little shop on a side street in Lyme Regis, where he repaired vacuum cleaners for the fat old cows that would call. The little tin bell rang each time the door opened and they would cackle about this and that, always complaining about the charges. Can you imagine spending your life doing such a thing? Home every night at six with your hands still filthy from their work as you ate boiled potatoes, commenting that they were boiled much better than the evening before." He looked at Yuri, concerned he would be unable to finish his final account. "How much time is left?"

With his chin balanced on his chest, Yuri mumbled something unclear. His eyes fluttered.

Musters nodded as if an answer had been given, and though he knew no one listened, he continued, "In the window of the shop were some clocks my new father had for sale. He had repaired them and cleaned them and they kept perfect time." His voice fell to a whisper. "Some of them were beautiful, Yuri... the polished wood and silver. And so I called him the Watchmaker because I couldn't face what he really was, who he really was.

"Now you see that when the wealthy boys at school asked what he did for a living, I didn't tell them he fixed dirty vacuums for sodden hens. Oh no, I told them he was a master in his field, a watchmaker. And I kept the lie going because I knew I needed to get as far away from him and what he represented as I could. If I were on the other side of the world, I'd be safe." He lifted his eyes, blurred from tears, and tried to make out the man opposite him. "But you know the irony of all this? It was his savings I used to buy the people and things of these last few years. He allowed me to be the man I am now. It was the watchmaker that gave me a second chance, but I still resented him. Ultimately we all have someone, or something we're fleeing, however foolish. We all have our watchmaker... don't we?"

Yuri said nothing, though an explosion in the freighter's stern would have muted any reply. It was not loud like Musters imagined it would be, but rather like a tire had burst somewhere in the distance. Then there was another and another as the explosions ran down the length of the hull toward him.

Pulling the edges of the bathrobe ever tighter about his neck, he looked again to the exposed light bulb, now swinging overhead. And then, as if a surge of electricity rushed into the element, it became as bright as the sun and he no longer felt cold.

* * *

Both men had awakened at the same time, startled by something that took them from their dreamless sleep, but it was Sergeant Martin who spoke first after cautiously glancing at the seat behind him.

"He's gone, Inspector," he said, sounding greatly relieved.

Staring out the windshield of the black Peugeot, Beauviér faithfully put on his gloves. "Do you know what time you fell asleep, Sergeant?"

"Some time after you, monsieur. I think around two-thirty, or maybe it was three." He looked at the vacant mooring in the dawn light. "I tried to stay awake as long as I could. I thought if I could outlast the Irishman—if he dozed—then we had him. But he just kept playing with the car keys and smoking those cigars."

"Did he say anything more to you?"

"No, monsieur. Nothing. Like I said, he just kept playing with the... look, Inspector. There are the keys on the back seat, and—and my gun. He had my gun and he left it."

"A policeman should never lose his gun, Sergeant. That is always a difficult thing to explain, should it happen."

"Yes, monsieur." He grabbed the keys before hurriedly returning the semi-automatic to its holster. "But it was dangerous for him to have left these things. What if we had seen him leave?"

"But we didn't, Sergeant," said Beauviér as he opened his door and got out. With his hands clasped behind his back, he walked to the edge of the pier where it met the water and gazed out on the calm harbor, then to the sea beyond. The mooring lines were still tied to the cleats on each side of him; their frayed ends bobbing against the creosote-coated pilings. They had been cut away from the freighter to speed up its flight, but there was something more permanent about their crude removal, indicating a ship that would never return to this, or any other harbor.

A car door closed behind him and presently Martin stood at his side.

"Shouldn't we call the harbor patrol?" he asked, a sense of urgency in his voice.

"It has been over eight hours since the freighter left, Sergeant. They are well safe of our navy."

"But they must return to port at some time. I mean, eventually they will be in the jurisdiction of law, Inspector."

Beauviér glanced again at the sliced ends of the freighter's lines, but said nothing.

"The American truck is still here, though the silver Mercedes is gone, monsieur," said Martin, standing with his back to the harbor.

Already aware of the sergeant's observations, Beauviér said, "The Renoir and the million francs were hidden in it. It was not likely to have been left behind by the Irishman, Sergeant."

"I have the license number; shouldn't we report it right away?"

"That registration plate was certainly stolen and probably by now it has another, and is well out of the country, regardless."

Martin said, "He didn't kill us, Inspector. He told us about the gun and even the armaments company in Belgium... Magellan, he said."

"Yes, so he did."

"Well then, we have them. They'll never be able to pick the other guns up. We'll be waiting for them."

"Waiting for them? Yes, Sergeant. Of that I am certain."

Following a brief silence, Martin asked, "Did you think he was going to kill us?"

"At first, Sergeant, yes," he said, thinking back to the shotgun pointed at his chest. "Yet, there was something more than a group of smugglers on that ship last night."

"I don't understand, I—" Martin paused and, raising his arm, pointed toward the cloudless horizon. "Look at that, Inspector. It looks like a great fire on the North Sea. Do you see the smoke?"

Beauviér quietly observed a large gray-black plume rising up on the distant ocean.

"There are no oil rigs out that direction, are there, monsieur?"

Beauviér shook his head. "No, there're not."

"Then what could it be?"

"I don't know, Sergeant," he replied, turning to face the pier. "It could be anything, and we have more pressing issues. Let's get to a telephone. I need to speak with the Director General."

Returning to their car, Beauviér climbed in the driver's side. Placing the keys in the ignition, his eyes narrowed and he said, "He didn't bind our hands, Sergeant."

"Monsieur?"

"The ship's captain stood there holding the twine, ready to lash our wrists together, but the Irishman wouldn't let him," he recalled, turning to look at Martin. "At the time I thought he was hoping we might try something, so he'd have an excuse to shoot us, but it wasn't that at all. And he left the keys and your pistol behind when he fled. It was as if..." Beauviér didn't finish the sentence and Martin didn't ask him to explain further. They were both tired.

Nothing To Declare

* * *

From Dunkirk to Calais, the French coastline is a flat, horizontal line. There are no cliffs or places higher in elevation than a one-story building. Sand dunes are followed by more sand dunes, like overdone silent policemen as if to keep the seabirds in check, though little else. This part of France being considered indefensible, an open door for passing marauders, whereas only in the last fifty years had anything been done to change all that. At the end of 1941 heavy coastal batteries, along with the odd U-Boat pen, were emplaced by the German Army for the shelling of England. However, as the worm turned, these offensive placements needed defensive partners which manifested in the form of concrete pillboxes. Originally placed every 250 meters, they allowed an unhindered view of the coast between them. And at seven meters in height, they made the perfect crow's nest. This is what John Clark determined as he climbed on top of his third pillbox that morning. Raising a pair of military binoculars to his eyes, he again scoured the shore like he had been doing for over two hours. He could see almost ten kilometers to the north and better than fifteen to the south. The topography lay clear in the morning sun like a child's relief map, everything properly colored in blues and browns. Though he saw little more than the seemingly endless beach. There was no sign of life and slight movement save for the ocean tide advancing against the thin strip of land; the sea grass whipping before the onshore breeze as if to distract his view, as if in a false sign of hope.

Refocusing the binoculars, he studied the one lane asphalt road that ran parallel to the beach, the silver Mercedes parked on its shoulder. There were no homes or any traffic, nothing to indicate any human life had ever been to this beach save the pillbox at his feet. And that was why the location on the French coast had been chosen, but now it seemed too remote, and possibly a mistake.

Letting the field glasses dangle by a leather strap about his neck, he again checked his watch. It had been dawn for over twenty minutes. The advantages of time and cover were fading. Removing a cigar from the breast pocket of his jacket, he gripped it in his back teeth but didn't light it, only returning the glasses to his eyes.

To the south, there was suddenly a great explosion of colors on the beach. He turned on his heels, the cigar falling from his mouth as he adjusted the focus, watching the colored smoke climb. It went

339

straight up at first, then began to swirl in ever increasing circles along the sand. The colors were brilliant yellows and reds that pushed along the white beach like the vapor trail of a celebrating jet fighter. It was the signal flare he had been waiting for.

Returning to the Mercedes, he pushed the accelerator to floor, grinning as he watched the colored smoke rise. It was much further south than anyone had foreseen, though it didn't matter now. They had made it.

The Mercedes was traveling almost 200 kilometers an hour when it began to slow. The lifeboat was now in view, as were her three occupants. They jumped on the beach, waving their arms in the surging colors of the flares.

Through an opening in the berm, John Clark drove onto the sand, bringing the car to a stop beside the lifeboat. He jumped out, spreading his arms like a father receiving his children.

Tatiana reached him first, wrapping her arms about his waist. "We made it, John! We made it!" She then kissed him.

The hard Irishman blushed slightly at the gesture and said, "So you did, lass. So you did."

"Were you worried for us, John?" asked Tom, putting a hand on his shoulder.

"Not in the slightest, Thomas. In fact, I was taking breakfast when I happened to see all the pretty colors and simply came to investigate."

"Sure you were," he said, pointing at Liam Campbell. "The captain brought us in and didn't mention the struggle he was having until we got on the beach."

Apologetically, Liam Campbell said, "The tides were greater than I anticipated, John. I didn't think we'd be this far south."

John Clark shook his head. "I'd be hard pressed to find a captain anywhere who could have done a better job, Liam. It's an honor working with you. Now, everyone, we must get going. There's no knowing who else saw these flares. Will you scuttle the boat, Liam?"

"Yes, John. She's all set with the tiller secured. All we need is a wee hole in her bottom."

John Clark quickly removed the sawed-off shotgun from the trunk of the Mercedes. Pumping the action, he moved to the lifeboat and placing the butt to his shoulder, fired. The single blast took out one of the bench seats and a good section of the boat's bottom.

"I hope she'll get far enough out with a hole in her like that," said Liam Campbell, restarting the outboard engine. "I meant a *small*, wee hole."

"Give her some throttle, she'll get out far enough, Liam. The sea and a bit of time will do the rest," he advised, moving back toward the Mercedes. "Now everyone get in the car. We must get away from here. Thomas, will you drive please."

Liam Campbell directed the lifeboat back into the mild surf, then kicked sand over the flares before climbing into the back seat beside Tatiana. Tom sat behind the wheel next to John Clark, who said, "Go south and not too fast, there's no point in getting nicked for speeding."

Circling the car on the hard sand, Tom pointed it through the berm onto the road.

"There's a depot not ten kilometers from here, Thomas," said John Clark, lighting a cigar. "Liam will be taking a train north, and I'll be wanting one south." He turned in his seat to look at Tatiana. "It was the appearance of the coppers that made it all so difficult, young lady. I don't know what Thomas has had time to tell you, but I felt terrible putting you through all of that. I mean, without you knowing the truth of it all."

"Where are they now?" she asked.

"The gendarmes? I suspect they're on their way back to Brussels," he replied. "No harm came to them, if that's your concern."

Quietly, she said, "I just didn't know."

"Of course you didn't and again, I'm sorry." He glanced out the windshield, then again faced the back seat. "You see, Thomas had a hard time accepting my fears about Yuri, but he arranged to have you well away if my suspicions were proven right. And you understand, with Yuri being capable of betrayal and murder, we knew we'd have to do something, although uncertain of what, exactly. It was *why* he did all those things that made me go from disfavoring him like I did, to a sort of sympathy for the way he deceived himself and was so readily taken in by Ian Musters."

John reached out his hand to touch Tatiana as her eyes began to tear. "He did it because he loved you in a way that never comes to any good. But it was love, nevertheless. So I whispered in his ear and asked him if he'd like to save you and free us all from the terrible things he'd done. He didn't hesitate for a second in wanting to redeem himself in your eyes."

Glancing at Tom, he said, "Avoid the road going into Calais. Head east as soon as you can, then follow the tracks," and turned again to face Tatiana.

"When he told us about the Renoir and the million francs, I knew money was never the reason for any of it. So we gave him back his pistol, though Liam had removed the bullets in case his anger toward Musters got the best of him. It didn't. He played along right to the end, knowing he was to go down with the ship and make certain that the gun, along with its owner, was there for the ride. Yuri understood there was no place for him any longer. Once you've killed a man, especially an innocent like Stuart Endfield, then there's nowhere to hide, least of all from yourself."

He paused briefly, watching Tatiana wipe at her eyes with a faded blue handkerchief. "We didn't want you to see it, but you did, and so suffer through it as you think best, but remember you're now free and that's what we've been doing it all for."

Struggling with her emotions, she asked, "Would it have been different had the policemen not been there?"

"No, not in the slightest," he replied quickly. "They only made for taking a different road. When they appeared on the docks I knew we needed a different purpose, so we played the charade with them, and unfortunately yourself, as the audience. I was forced to act the villain and thankfully Thomas quickly caught on to it, playing his part brilliantly. I'm sorry I let Musters take that swing at you," he said to Tom, "but the quest for realism got the better of me, and did you see the look in the coppers' eyes?"

"I'm afraid I didn't, John," he replied.

"Well if they had any doubt the kind of man Musters was, it ended there. Strangely, it was getting him on board that was the most difficult. I had to convince him of the millions to be made. Then, with him on the freighter I was simply going to knock him on the head and send him to the bottom along with his gun, as was the arrangement with the buyer. It was all so straightforward until the gendarmes appeared. I'm still at a loss as to how they found us."

"But they know everything now," said Tatiana.

"Yes, they know Musters was responsible for most all that was sinister, with Yuri as his dupe, but they'll struggle for anything further."

"But they'll come after you, John," she warned.

Taking a long drag on his cigar, he smiled. "No, I've been prepared for an Inspector Beauviér or someone like him for many years. You're not to worry about me."

Tom Breck said, "The Renoir and the million francs, John. We didn't count on that."

John Clark shook his head. "No, the arrangement was always to split it up amongst ourselves, the eight hundred thousand that is, and nothing more. Liam can get his new ship and Francis Dwyer will be paid handsomely for an evening of idleness. As for myself, there's enough to keep me modestly in a place I've been wanting to visit for some time now."

"And where is that, John?" asked Tatiana.

"You'll forgive me if I keep the last bit to myself, young lady. It'll keep me from lying to you because I never want to do that again."

Squeezing his hand, she smiled respectfully.

John Clark's eyes narrowed, a tone of concern in his voice. "And, Thomas, there's another reason I'd like to distance myself from the Renoir. It came as a surprise, like you said, that it would fall back into our hands so easily. It's the one thing I was truly not prepared for. You know it's the only tangible bit of evidence Beauviér's aware of and I'm afraid he might not let it go. I mean he'll be searching for the painting until he dies, if I understand this man. You've thought about that, have you?"

"I have," Tom said, turning the Mercedes off the main road into the parking area of a train depot. "I believe there's a way to make him forget all about it, and us."

"Is there now, Thomas?" said John Clark as the Mercedes came to a stop. "Well, for that alone we must meet again, since I can't imagine such a solution." He shook Liam Campbell's leg. "Wake up lad. There's a northbound train approaching and you'd best be on it."

Opening his eyes slowly, the captain mumbled, "Are we there?"

"We are, Liam," John answered. "Now there's your train. You have your passport?"

"I do," he said, opening his door.

"And what will you be telling your friends you did this Christmas?"

Liam Campbell climbed out, turning to look at John Clark. "Even in the Irish Republic, there's hardly a man who'd believe this tale," he said somberly. "It all stays on the bottom with *Mary*

343

Celeste and of that, you can be sure. Good-bye everyone. I'll think of you from time to time."

Pushing the door closed, he moved quickly to the far platform, hesitating at the first train car before climbing on board.

"To think they complain about the youth of today," said John Clark. He then indicated the near platform. "And there's my train. I hope there's a sleeper on it." He took Tom's hand. "Thank you, Thomas. Always remember, in Ireland there's a pub called the Rose and Thistle, and if you sit there long enough, I just might appear— but only then if you're accompanied by the young lady."

Tatiana threw her arms about his shoulders, holding him tight.

John Clark whispered to her, "Never forget that when the sadness passes, and it shall, there are very few people who've had love given them so great, as from your friend of all those years. I know no one's ever loved me that much, young lady."

Pulling from Tatiana's embrace with some effort, he exited the car and, offering her a smile, moved away.

Tatiana jumped out of the car and called to him, "I love you that much, John Clark."

He did not turn to acknowledge the words if he heard them, but climbed on board, the doors slapping closed as if they'd been waiting for him alone. There was a shrill whistle from the engine while the train steadily pulled away from the station and soon vanished from sight. Then the depot was empty.

EPILOGUE

Pierre-Charles de Calonne sat at his desk in the top floor office of the Ste. Claire police station, casually studying a police dossier and, occasionally, his fingernails. He wore the uniform of the Director General of the Belgian Gendarmerie, as he had for over ten years. Standing behind him, his adjutant, Captain Valéry François de Grandiér, also wore the dress of his rank. Both men were of noble lineage and had served together during the 1960 Congo uprising, willingly, on the front line. And though each displayed a certain delicacy, possibly from their breeding, neither man would shrug from a pitched battle, regardless of the outcome.

Consequently, the Director General knew the difference between a soldier and a policeman, and he never let one interfere with the other. A good soldier was the most important commodity a country could possess, but for the day to day, a country at peace looked for the policeman to maintain order. And to his eyes, the finest in the Belgian Gendarmerie was the man sitting patiently across the desk from him: Chief Inspector Jules Beauviér.

Sitting dutifully beside Beauviér was Sergeant Henri Martin, his hands folded and his eyes fixed on each movement of the Director General, who remained all but silent, flipping to another page of the dossier.

Beauviér maintained a more relaxed pose, slumped back with his legs crossed at the ankles, his eyes drifting, only infrequently looking to the Director General or his adjutant, Captain de Grandiér. Beauviér's gaze moved to the bank of windows overlooking the courtyard, then to a calendar attached to the nearby wall. The date, accentuated by a movable red square, indicated that it was Monday, December 30, 1984.

Abruptly, the Director General looked up from his reading. Staring over the top of his half-glasses, he cleared his throat, as was

345

his habit before commencing a meeting of any gravity, and said, "You still assert, Inspector, that the ship you and Sergeant Martin boarded on the evening of December 25 was named the *Ondine*?"

"I do," replied Beauviér. "And it was."

"Sergeant?" said the Director General, glancing at Martin.

"Yes, monsieur. The name was *Ondine*."

"I see," said the Director General, nodding. "And the captain of this freighter, you heard him called by the name of Francis Dwyer?"

"Yes," said Beauviér. "The Irishman, John Clark, called him that as we were taken to our car. He said it quite clearly."

Adjusting the glasses to the bridge of his nose, the Director General turned a page of the dossier. "John Clark was the man you interrogated following the death of the British Embassy employee, Stuart Endfield. Is that correct?"

"Yes, monsieur," said Beauviér, uncrossing his legs to sit up slightly straighter in his chair. "That same evening. Although I would not term it an interrogation. I simply questioned the man, as he had been seen with Stuart Endfield only an hour before his death."

"You suspected him?"

"No, monsieur, I was only trying to determine his relationship with the murdered man."

"And what did you determine?"

"Nothing, monsieur. He spoke a great deal, but said little to incriminate himself with that or anything we were investigating."

"The American, Thomas Breck, and the smuggled paintings you mean?"

"At that time, yes."

The Director General turned another page. "So the giant gun came later, Inspector?"

"Yes, monsieur."

"And how many paintings were there?"

"Two, monsieur. The Monet, as was found in Namur at the gallery of Buchon, and the Renoir."

"Did you see the Renoir?"

"No, monsieur. They only spoke of it—that it was currently, at that time I mean, being hidden in the fender of the Mercedes."

"Along with the million francs, correct?"

"Yes, monsieur."

"And the giant gun… Pardon me, Inspector, I don't mean to jump around, however, I am trying to get all this straight in my mind. The chronology will take care of itself, " he said apologetically. "Now, the gun—you did not see it?"

"No, monsieur."

"And, Sergeant? I assume your silence means you concur with Inspector Beauviér and his recollections?"

"Yes, monsieur, absolutely," Martin answered quickly.

"Very good, Sergeant. Now just jump in if you wish to add anything, we are informal here. The civilian-dressed police sometimes mention our uniforms can be intimidating and I hope that is not the case with us," he noted, moving his eyes between the two men opposite him. "Now, what I am going to state is the facts as I have them before me, and I would like either of you, messieurs, to fill any holes as you feel the need.

First—though I am starting, I suppose, at the end of this affair—is the Harbor Master's manifest and subsequent notes from the Port of Zeebrugge on the dates of December 24, 25 and 26 respectively. That reads: 'The freighter at mooring number A-12, in the outer harbor, was in fact the *Mary Celeste* out of Aberdeen, Scotland. The freighter arrived on December 24 at some five minutes before midnight and left the morning of December 26 at sometime before dawn, possibly as early as midnight.' " The Director General looked up. "Its location in the North Sea when it sank required that amount of time out of harbor.

"Now, the Danish fishermen who witnessed the *Mary Celeste* go down said there was no possibility of survivors. After contacting shore they searched the area themselves for over two hours before turning over any rescue attempt to our navy. There was one thing that survived intact, which was a single lifeboat, the name *Mary Celeste* on it."

"It was the *Ondine*, monsieur," protested Beauviér.

"No, Inspector," said the Director General firmly. "The *Ondine* was docked during this time in the inner harbor and would have needed to access the locks, of which the records are impeccable. The *Ondine's* captain, a man named Francis Dwyer, spent all but a few hours in the office of the Harbor Master, playing cards. He is said to have lost some forty thousand francs to various duty officers and passing sailors. There is no doubt in this, Inspector.

"Now, secondly, the gun—this enormous gun that was in the hold of the freighter, supposedly brought by the American truck. There is no record of anything being loaded onto the Mary Celeste or the Ondine, for that matter."

"But, the dock workers—the stevedores. They're all mavericks; they could have been paid in cash and would never admit it," said Beauviér.

"I suppose. However, there is no account at customs for entry of anything resembling such a thing."

"You forget customs was closed. There was no one in the bureau."

"I have not forgotten, Inspector," agreed the Director General, searching the documents. "At customs there is but one duty officer at any given time on Christmas day, and the officer in question admits to leaving his post for just over an hour. When questioned, he admitted he'd had a rendezvous with a young lady in a nearby hotel. An Irish girl, it turns out, who has since disappeared without a trace. All we know is she had red hair and dark green eyes, first name of Kathleen. We thought her at first a convenient fabrication, however, with the customs officer being married it seemed an unlikely alibi. He knows nothing of any giant gun and is in league with no one. We are now certain of this and can charge him with dereliction, but little else."

"She was Irish, monsieur?" asked Beauviér softly.

"Yes, Inspector, which brings us to the third issue... or is it the fourth? At any rate, the man, John Clark—" Turning slightly in his chair to glance at Captain de Grandiér, the Director General asked, "Where are those papers on him?"

"Under those you are reading, monsieur," replied de Grandiér, lifting the top file from the desk to expose another.

"Captain," said the Director General, and again adjusting his half-glasses, opened the file. "These papers are from the Royal Ulster Constabulary in Dublin—"

"That is *Belfast*, monsieur," corrected Captain de Grandiér.

"Yes, of course, Belfast... They are on John Clark and quite complete, to a point." He put his forefinger under the top line of print. " 'John Edward Clark, born 1919 in the village of Shankhill, Northern Ireland.' He was sixty-five. Is that possible, Inspector?"

"It is possible, although I found him to be quite nimble... What do you mean *was*, monsieur?"

"I'll get to that, Inspector. Now, I'm mixing in a bit of what we had on record with this from the RUC as they tend to contradict, but, 'John Edward Clark purchased the bar on La Grand' Place called Le Cerf in the autumn of 1946, for the sum of...' That's not important—oh yes, here we are: 'After discharge from the

Parachute Corps of the British Army, he bought Le Cerf.' Now those are my notes from our records, but the RUC state that: 'John Edward Clark served in no army and was considered to be of questionable loyalty with his move in 1939 to the non-aligned Republic of Ireland. In that country the Second World War was referred to simply as *The Emergency*.' "

The Director General let out a deep breath. "An RUC commander noted that for me, Inspector Beauviér. I suppose he thinks I didn't attend school." Again finding his place on the document with his finger, he continued, "And then there is only random notation of movement, not to exclude a six month prison term in 1965 for unlawful assembly... until the spring of 1972, 'When, during a routine roadblock in Northern Ireland, a man trying to smuggle a bomb attempted to flee and was subsequently killed. That man was John Edward Clark.' "

"You mean he was blown up?" asked Beauviér, sitting up in his chair.

"No, he was shot, according to this," said the Director General, removing a square of paper attached to the file. He handed it to Beauviér. "Is that him?"

Beauviér gripped a black and white photograph of a man approximately forty years old, wearing prison issue clothing and the oppressed semblance of incarceration. Slowly lifting his eyes from the picture, he said, "No, this is not John Clark."

"Unfortunately, it is, Inspector," said the Director General, removing his glasses as he leaned back in his chair. "The fingerprints sent to us by the RUC, and those we maintained when John Clark purchased Le Cerf, are one and the same. There is no doubt of this, so whoever held you and Sergeant Martin at gunpoint is, at this time, a mystery. A man took over the identity of John Edward Clark, I'll grant you that, but nothing more can be assumed."

"But you don't just take over a man's life without someone noticing," complained Beauviér.

"This bar, Le Cerf, did very little business, I am told. It has astronomical prices which limit its clientele to no more than a half-dozen in total on any given evening. It would be a wonderful place to hide, in a business that does no business. Don't you think?"

Beauviér dropped the photograph onto the corner of the desk, but said nothing.

"And miraculously the heirs of the late John Edward Clark, who died some twelve years back, have recently appeared to make their claim of Le Cerf," said the Director General, grinning. "Did they think those little green men they have up in Ireland had been watching things all this time?"

Not seeming to find any humor in the Director General's comment, Beauviér's eyes became hard. "A charade," he whispered.

The Director General did not respond to Beauviér's opinion, as he was uncertain to whom the Inspector referred. Returning the glasses to the end of his nose, he leaned forward and slowly began flipping the pages of a third file.

"In the report you completed the afternoon of December 26, Inspector, you wrote of overhearing the man called Yuri—the assumed bodyguard of Tatiana Gregòsh—confess to the killing of Stuart Endfield."

"I did, monsieur."

"And also the murders of two Hungarian state policemen, somewhere outside of Budapest in an unnamed hotel on the Danube... That is also correct?"

Beauviér ran his hand down his face. "It is."

"Well, we have contacted the Hungarian authorities," he said, turning his head slightly. "Have we not, Captain?"

"Yes, monsieur," replied de Grandiér.

"And?"

"Nothing to this point, monsieur," answered de Grandiér, standing straight with his arms at his sides as if he were speaking into a microphone. "They did not even acknowledge the receipt of the telex."

The Director General smiled. "We will hear something eventually, maybe in four or five years when they require our assistance with a fleeing counter-revolutionary," he mused. "Until then, we have the murder of Stuart Endfield to concern us." The smile dropped from his face. "As you know, the British Embassy has been quite upset with us of late, having inscrutably and violently lost three of its employees in as many weeks. They call it the Belgian Plague, Inspector."

"I am aware of that, monsieur," grumbled Beauviér.

"Yes, of course you are. So we must be patient with them by not pointing our fingers at one of their own, this Ian Musters, and referring to him as the mastermind of a great gun smuggling operation when we have no evidence such a gun existed."

Beauviér mumbled, "No, monsieur."

"And further," he continued, "in your report you mention that Ian Musters, because of a red scarf seen in his possession, is the main suspect in the murder of this fellow Fouchét in Mons, also known as Mégot." He stopped his study of the dossier and chuckled. "Really? He called himself Mégot?"

Reluctantly, Beauviér said, "Yes, monsieur."

"Not a clever man, was he?"

"Not particularly, monsieur."

As the Director General's bureaucratic manner slowly resurfaced, he said, "So we'll have to give them—the British, I mean—a few weeks to digest what we have presented. By that point they and the French should be at each others' throats again; we'll just sneak it all through, I suspect, and this Plague issue will take care of itself."

Pursing his lips, Beauviér developed an uneasy look in his eyes, but said nothing.

The Director General studied the two men opposite him before removing a package of cigarettes from a side drawer of his desk. He offered one to Beauviér, then to Martin, much as a dentist might offer a sweet to a young patient for not squirming excessively. Both men refused the gesture and he returned the package to the drawer. Placing his forearms on the desk, he folded his hands, gazing over the top of his glasses. "Which brings us to the end—or should I say the beginning—of all this. It started with the American and the discovery of his name written on the frame of the Monet discovered in Namur. That, in itself means nothing as he was a dealer of sorts and could have contacted the gallery owner for any number of reasons."

"Have you searched his home in Wolowe St. Pierre?" interrupted Beauviér.

The Director General nodded. "We have, and found only that it is now in the transient possession of a Mademoiselle Chantal de Plaen."

Beauviér's eyes narrowed. "Who?"

"She is, or was, the American's maid."

"His maid?"

"Yes, she is now the executor of his estate. We saw all the pertinent documents; it was all duly registered by a well-respected attorney."

"But Breck had a wife, a French woman."

"He did, Inspector, but there is the conundrum. As you know, we have no corpse to confirm his death and there is a seven year waiting period in Belgium before a spouse can claim or sell off any possessions acquired during marriage; that is, when there is no absolute proof of death. Now Madame Breck—Michelle is her Christian name—is welcome by law to remain in the house until the waiting period has elapsed. However, she would be obliged to maintain the residence, financially that is, and she appears reluctant. A maison de maitre can be quite expensive."

"But the maid has such means?"

"As the executor, yes."

"So anytime during the next seven years the American can return as if... as if nothing happened?" protested Beauviér.

"He can, though we would definitely wish to speak with him at great length, Inspector," offered the Director General. "But we know with a level of certainty that the American will not as he is— unofficially, mind you—quite dead. Especially considering the witnesses we have."

"Witnesses?"

"Yes—you, and Sergeant Martin. According to your report, Inspector Beauviér, no one got off the freighter that evening, be it the *Mary Celeste* or the *Ondine* as you wish, except you and Sergeant Martin and, of course, the man we will call John Clark. Then you stated that you watched the freighter leave harbor and move into the North Sea, where eight hours later it sank some forty kilometers from shore as further witnessed by the Danish fisherman. There were no, I repeat, *no* survivors."

Removing his glasses, he massaged the bridge of his nose with his thumb and forefinger. Blinking repeatedly, he then replaced the glasses and continued, "The American, Thomas Allan Breck, and the Poles, Tatiana Gregòsh and her bodyguard, Yuri; the Englishman, Ian Musters, and of course the captain of the freighter." He read off each person slowly, as if he stood before a war memorial. "They are all dead, Inspector. You have, in your own report, all but confirmed this."

Beauviér said, "And if I were to assume the freighter in mooring number A-12 *was* the *Mary Celeste*, then *who* was her captain?"

Closing one file, the Director General opened another, cautiously turning the pages. After a few seconds, he said, "The captain's name was Liam Campbell, Scot-Irish, and he was also the owner of the freighter, along with the Bank of Caledonia, according to the telex we received from the port authority in Aberdeen. The *Mary Celeste* was a forty-seven-year-old vessel and uninsurable due to its poor condition." He slowly looked up at Beauviér. "So any motive for fraud is dispelled. Also, this Liam Campbell was quite young—as yet, he had no wife or children and subsequently no life insurance, either. In other words, if he were to walk into this office right now there would be no charges brought against him."

"I see," said Beauviér, rolling his hands together in a gradual wringing fashion. "So you won't be contacting the Scottish police?"

With frustration in his voice, the Director General said, "He is dead, Chief Inspector. They are all dead. And the only survivor of this affair, the Irishman, is gone and is nameless. You'd best accept the facts as we have them." He glanced at Captain de Grandiér. "Is there anything else?"

Seemingly prepared for the question, de Grandiér said rapidly, "The car, monsieur."

"The... yes, of course, the Mercedes. We only touched on that, didn't we?" He reshuffled the files before him, searching for a particular one. "It was found yesterday, Inspector."

"It was found? Where?" asked Beauviér excitedly.

The Director General tugged a single sheet of paper from beneath a stack of others. "It was discovered in an underground parking garage in Paris," he said. "On Sunday morning, by the attendant on duty."

Beauviér squinted. "A parking attendant had been notified we were searching for it?"

"No, of course not, Inspector," he said, reading the paper, nodding to confirm what he already knew. "It came to his attention amongst the two hundred other parked cars because its left rear fender was missing—not a common sight. He was concerned that it might be stolen and finding the trunk unlocked, discovered numerous license plates inside: French, Belgian, Hungarian, Austrian, and so on. He then contacted the Paris police and they in turn notified the gendarmes who had received our query for a seven-liter, 1980 Mercedes as you'd described in your report."

"And?"

The Director General shook his head. "And nothing, I'm afraid." He tapped the paper with the side of his thumb as he leaned back in his chair. "The vehicle identification numbers had all been removed so even finding its original point of sale would prove quite impossible. But it does add to the possibility that something had been hidden in the car."

"The possibility?" exclaimed Beauviér

Frowning, the Director General closed the files before him, stacking them neatly on the side of his desk. Looking at Beauviér, he was about to speak when Captain de Grandiér leaned forward and whispered in his ear. The Director General shook his head, then nodded reluctantly as he glanced at Sergeant Martin. Taking a deep breath, he removed his glasses, placing them in the center drawer of his desk. He looked again to Beauviér, and said, "There is one last thing, messieurs, that we should speak about, as you will see it soon enough in the evening papers. We did our best to keep it out, but with the freedom the press enjoys these days..." His voice trailed off. Placing his hands together as if in prayer, he cleared his throat. "In your report you mentioned more than once the armaments factory called Magellan. You stated a gun was supposedly fabricated there and that Ian Musters had requested more to be made. That is correct?"

Beauviér nodded.

"Well, on the morning of December 26, within minutes after the sinking of the *Mary Celeste*, the Magellan armaments factory was destroyed."

"What? How?" demanded Beauviér.

"At this point we are uncertain. The factory was well guarded, as you can imagine. However, simultaneous explosions occurred in the bunkers used for their varied products—white phosphorus, kinetic shells, tank turrets, and the like. It seems to have been targeted by forces unknown. The guards at the front and those patrolling the perimeter saw nothing and only just escaped with their lives as the facility went up. It burned for six hours as the firemen were unable, or unwilling, to do anything about it. We cordoned off the four hectares of the factory, reporting to the press that the explosions were controlled and meant for testing purposes so as not to alarm the local residents. However, since Magellan was completely destroyed, our little story has fallen apart."

"You have no idea who did this?" asked Beauviér.

"This will seem unusual to you both, Inspector… and Sergeant. But this act will not be pursued any further than this conversation, as those responsible are not our concern." He held up his hand to prevent any interruption. "We, that is to say, I, received a telephone call from the foreign minister and he was speaking for the King on this matter. It seems a complaint was filed against Magellan Armaments by an undisclosed Middle Eastern government. The minister and others attempted to close it down in the last few months without success, as the cartel owning it had, well, powers of its own. So this little pyrotechnic display resolves the Magellan Armaments problem and I will now request you never mention this further. Not any gun, not Magellan Armaments, and not your own suspicions… ever again. We have already amended your report, Inspector, deleting all references to it. As subjects of the King, we must all forget this bit of business. May I have your word, messieurs?"

"You have my word," Martin agreed.

The office fell quiet as Beauviér sat motionless in his chair. Cautiously shifting his gaze to the Director General, he said, "You find this to be nothing more than coincidence, monsieur?"

"You have shown me no tangible evidence to support your theories, Inspector. What would you do, if our positions were reversed?"

Beauviér sat up in his chair and squared his shoulders. "I would expect you to find the evidence, monsieur."

And with those words, the Director General stood as Captain de Grandiér came to attention.

The meeting was over.

A moment later, Beauviér and Martin were descending the stairs from the Director General's office to the ground floor. They passed through booking and holding, passed interrogation and sundry desks, walking out onto the street without once speaking. Such silence had become so customary with them that neither took affront, avoiding idle comments about politics or weather to fill the gaps.

Even when saying good-bye.

Reaching the parked Peugeot, Beauviér opened the driver's door. He looked over its roof to Martin, standing on the sidewalk.

"May I give you a lift, Sergeant?"

"No, monsieur, thank you," he replied, smiling awkwardly. "I'm going to stay in Brussels for the day."

"All right, then." With one foot inside the car, he paused. "Is there something you wish to say, Sergeant?"

"No, monsieur," he said. "I mean, yes. Yes, there is. I think the Director General must have forgotten tomorrow is your last day with the gendarmerie."

"No, he did not forget, Sergeant. He knows there is little that will happen in the next twenty-four hours and he is right. I'm going home."

"But—"

"It's over, Sergeant," he advised firmly. "For the gendarmerie, anyway. But not for me."

"Yes, monsieur. You'll call me if I might help?"

"I will, Sergeant."

Martin smiled. "Do you need any assistance removing things from your office?"

"I only brought a pen, and I have it in my pocket."

"Oh, I see."

Beauviér looked down the street, first one way then the other, as if uncertain what to say. "I'll need to return this thing tomorrow," he said finally, tapping the roof of the black Peugeot. "Maybe we can take a coffee?"

"Oh, I'd like that, monsieur."

"I'll see you then, Sergeant," he said, climbing into the car.

Any further words spoken were muffled by the starting engine, though Beauviér nodded, seeming to hear someone say good-bye.

* * *

In the failing afternoon light, Jules Beauviér stood before the waist-high gate of his small house, a grocery bag in each arm. He was staring at the yard, comparing it with those of his neighbors on each side and frowned. Weeds had grown round the concrete threshold, seeming to flourish in spite of the cold, but his small garden showed no signs of life. The wind, having pushed away the topsoil he had layered with great effort, left only sand in its wake. Nothing grew in the meticulously planted rows that were identified by seed packets tacked to weathered sticks which now resembled a small, highly neglected, cemetery.

Moving to the front door, he juggled the two grocery bags, shoving the key into the lock. Creaking on hinges in need of oil, the door immediately jarred and he was forced to open it with his shoulder before stepping inside the small entry.

At his feet laid a scattering of correspondence that had collected in his absence, the majority of it being publicity from nearby businesses, then a bill or two. Flipping the light switch with his elbow, he was pleased to find the electricity still on. In the faint light, he moved through the dining room toward the kitchen.

Jules Beauviér was feeling bothered. There was no cheer, no great relief in being home. The small cottage offered little comfort and he doubted his ability to relax. He was too restless and, though he would not admit it, quite sad.

Dropping the groceries on the kitchen counter, he turned on the small light above the sink. As the florescent tube spread out its yellow-white glow, something strange appeared on the counter tile, just beside the sink. It was a black mark, possibly a scuffmark like that left by a shoe, with another immediately below the window. They were similar not only in appearance, but he was certain he hadn't made or seen them before.

Checking the window, he found it to be secure, as were all the other locks in the house following a through investigation. In his bedroom the pocket watch given him by his father sat atop the dresser and, just beside it, a gold fountain pen. Initially imagining there had been a break-in, Beauviér smiled. Nothing had been taken and nothing had been damaged. The black marks on the counter could have come from anywhere, possibly made by him after all. Three months away seemed a lifetime and were he asked the color of the tiles at his feet, he would have been at a loss. For the moment, it was all somehow foreign, though, looking at a handful of withered stems in a vase, whose water had long since evaporated, he remembered purchasing the flowers at a street fair. He even remembered their price.

At last removing his overcoat and gloves, Beauviér poured himself a glass of Sherry, running it under his nose. He remembered the bouquet, although no fond memories came rushing back. It was just a glass of Sherry, the same as he always drank and always alone. He wandered into the dining room and turned on the radio. There was a station sponsored by the government that played only classical music and tonight they were playing Brahms. Taking a seat at the table, Beauviér was determining the Symphony when

357

something further caught his eye—something that might possibly explain the marks on the kitchen counter.

Sitting on the floor, leaning between the dish cabinet and a chair, was a rectangular cardboard box. Although for the most part hidden in the shadows, he could make out a slip of paper attached to the box, and on it was his name. He hurriedly stood and finding the wall switch, turned on the overhead light. He then stared at the box before taking it from the floor and laying it on the dining table. The box was not heavy, though it was sealed tight with a rather thick tape around all the edges. This same tape held the slip of paper, which Beauvier was now reading, the words written in French:

Monsieur Beauviér,
I hope you will be able to find the rightful home for this. It will certainly cause further unhappiness until it is returned to those from whom it was taken all those years ago.

There was nothing more written, and it was not signed.

Letting the paper drop from his grip, he removed a penknife from his pocket and cut at the tape holding the box lid in place. It took over a minute before the lid loosened and was removed, revealing a layer of excelsior underneath. What was inside? What had been delivered so painstakingly to him? Beauviér gently dug into it, uncertain if something would snap at his fingers or a detonation might occur. But there was no explosion or cached beast; there was something however, just beneath the wood shavings, which made his breathing accelerate. It was a painting, as beautiful a painting as he had ever seen. He brushed the remnants of the excelsior away, lifting it into the light of the room. At first he did not really notice the subject of the work, only the beauty it contained. It seemed so out of place in his home, or in his hands for that matter. He looked to the right hand corner for the artist responsible. It read, Auguste Renoir, 1862.

"Breck," he whispered.

It was the American, he was alive and he'd left the painting just as certainly as the Polish woman had written the note. They were attempting to buy him off, so he would no longer continue the hunt.

Beauviér returned the painting to the box and moving to the kitchen, lifted the receiver from the wall telephone. He dialed a number and while listening to the line ring, glanced again to the painting on his dining table. The evidence that the Director General demanded now sat within reach. Beauviér's final case as a policeman was not closed, with everyone dead and buried, but on again. The line continued to ring as he thought of the evening on the freighter, recalling that his hands were never bound, that he and Sergeant Martin were never hurt. He also remembered the keys to the police car left on the seat, along with the semi-automatic, and the words of the Irishman, laying out each detail of the crime. It had all been done, as the Irishman said, to keep everyone abreast of the changes.

Beauviér's eyes narrowed. He now understood. It was he and Sergeant Martin that were the *changes*—the stumbling gendarmes were the odd lot out. It was all so clear. The Irishman had not stolen the gun from the American, whereas he'd intended to destroy it all along. The theatrics Ian Musters referred to that evening was in fact for him, and the two unsuspecting gendarmes—to make them go away and, just possibly, to keep them both alive.

The freighter's galley that evening had been a makeshift courtroom, with all witnesses and defendants present. A due hearing was given; Beauviér heard the confessions for each murder, for each crime, and the penalties handed down. A dilapidated vessel was sent to the bottom of the North Sea along with the gun and the two killers, Ian Musters and Yuri. He'd seen the Polish woman's bodyguard agree; he'd seen it in the man's eyes. And the Renoir was not in the Irishman's bargain, or it would not be sitting on Beauviér's table.

In this, Beauviér saw the last case of his career coming to an end. Solved by a band of smugglers, with finality by a freighter's crew.

The telephone continued to ring, its sound now irritating. He realized that his presence in this affair was nothing more than a footnote; others cleverer than he had determined the outcome; others who in their desperation took charge.

Consequently, the Director General had been right; the *Mary Celeste* had no survivors. And the American certainly left the Renoir behind, along with the note from the Polish woman, however, they did it well before the freighter set sail, possibly weeks ago.

And to anyone asking, that is what Beauviér would say.

Abruptly, a secretary for the Director General answered the line.

Beauviér said softly, "Wrong number, monsieur," and hung up.

Returning to the dining room, he removed an old print from the wall, setting it on the floor. He then lifted the Renoir from its box and hooking its makeshift frame onto the exposed nail, took a step back. He smiled.

It was all perfect, more perfect than anything he could remember. He wished Sergeant Martin were with him. Tomorrow, Beauviér would tell him all about it.

The End

Artwork and Cover Design by
Ken Small